PENGUIN BOOKS

HOTEL PASTIS

Peter Mayle escaped Madison Avenue in 1975 to write books after fifteen years in the advertising business. He has contributed to a wide range of publications and his work has been translated into seventeen languages. His previous books are *A Year in Provence*, which was made into a successful television series, and *Toujours Provence*. *Hotel Pastis* is his first novel and is also available as a Penguin Audiobook, read by Tim Pigott-Smith.

PETER MAYLE

HOTEL PASTIS

PENGUIN BOOKS

PENGUIN BOOKS

Published by the Penguin Group
Penguin Books Ltd, 27 Wrights Lane, London W8 5TZ, England
Penguin Books USA Inc., 375 Hudson Street, New York, New York 10014, USA
Penguin Books Australia Ltd, Ringwood, Victoria, Australia
Penguin Books Canada Ltd, 10 Alcorn Avenue, Toronto, Ontario, Canada M4V 3B2
Penguin Books (NZ) Ltd, 182–190 Wairau Road, Auckland 10, New Zealand

Penguin Books Ltd, Registered Offices: Harmondsworth, Middlesex, England

First published by Hamish Hamilton 1993
Published in Penguin Books 1994
3 5 7 9 10 8 6 4

Permission to quote from 'Let's Get It On' by Marvin Gaye/Ed Townsend has been
granted © 1973, Cherritown Music Co./Stone Diamond Music Corp./Jobete Music Co.
Inc., USA. Reproduced by permission of Jobete Music (UK) Ltd, London, WC2H 0EA.

Printed in England by Clays Ltd, St Ives plc

For Frank

1

'The trouble with all these divorces,' Ernest said as he put the tea tray on the packing case, 'is the refurnishing. Look at that. We're not going to find another one like that. Wasted on her, of course.'

Simon Shaw looked up and watched one of the removal men packing the Hockney in bubble-wrap. As the man bent over, he displayed the traditional emblem of the British labourer, the buttock cleavage revealed by the separation of T-shirt from grimy, low-slung jeans. Ernest sniffed and went back to the kitchen, picking his way through the piles of expensive relics that were destined for the ex-Mrs Shaw's bijou cottage in Eaton Mews South.

Simon sipped his tea, the mixture of Lapsang Souchong and Earl Grey that Ernest blended with such ceremony, and considered his surroundings.

The best house, everybody had said, in central London – large, elegant, almost secluded at the end of a quiet Kensington square. Caroline had spent three years and God knows how much money decorating it until it had reached that state of mannered perfection which made the disorder of normal daily life unthinkable. Rag-rolled paint in artfully faded colours on ceilings and walls, antique silk curtains that overflowed across the floor, eighteenth-century fireplaces brought over from France, hand-embroidered cushions, tablescapes of meticulously arranged artefacts. A magazine house.

Caroline's friends – those thin, smart friends who lived on salads and the occasional wicked glass of dry white wine – had cooed over the house. Caroline and her team of decorators adored it. Simon had always felt like an untidy intruder, smoking furtively in his panelled study because she didn't like the smell of cigar smoke in the sitting room, or because some vulpine woman was 'styling' the main rooms for a photographic essay on gracious urban living.

Towards the end, Simon had been living in the house like a visitor, spending his days in the office and his evenings with clients while Caroline entertained, joking with a slight sting in her voice that she had become an advertising widow. If he came home before her guests had left, Caroline would introduce him as poor darling, who's been working so hard. But when they were alone, there would be tight-lipped verbal jabs about his absence, his tiredness, his preoccupation with business, his neglect – there was no other word for it, neglect – of her. From there, it was only a short step to the Other Woman in the office, Simon's secretary, who always seemed to be there no matter how late Caroline called. Caroline knew all about secretaries. She'd been one, and she'd been there, all sympathy and short skirts, when Simon had divorced his first wife. There had been no complaints then about working late.

In fact, Caroline must have known that there was no other woman. Simon didn't have the privacy for adultery. His life was run by other people, even down to his bath, which was run by Ernest. The battle of the bath had been one of the few that Caroline had lost, and she had been at war with Ernest ever since. There was something not quite right about the relationship between the two men, she used to say in those late-night recriminations. Something unhealthy.

Ernest had been with Simon for nearly ten years, starting as his chauffeur in the early days when the only company car was an elderly Ford, and gradually becoming indispensable as the manager of Simon's existence: part valet, part personal assistant, part confidant, part friend, the master of detail, tireless in his efficiency. He was a qualified Rolls-Royce mechanic, an inspired flower arranger, and a better cook than Caroline ever wanted to be. He disapproved of her extravagance, her social pretensions and her total lack of domestic skills. She detested him because she couldn't dislodge him. Simon had spent years in the crossfire. At least that was finished. What was it Caroline had said as they were leaving the lawyers' offices after the settlement? Something about him having custody of Ernest.

'Excuse me, squire.' Two removal men were standing over Simon, their arms piled with dust covers. 'We'll have the couch now, if you don't mind. For Eaton Mews, innit, like the rest of the stuff?'

'You want the cup and saucer too?'

'Just doing our job, squire. Just doing our job.'

'I'm not a bloody squire.'

'Please yourself, cock.'

Simon surrendered the couch, and went through the double doors into the naked dining room. Ernest was clattering next door in the kitchen, whistling a few bars of music that Simon recognized as part of a Rossini overture. Caroline had loathed any kind of classical music, enduring Glyndebourne for social reasons and the excuse for a new dress.

The kitchen was Simon's favourite room in the house, partly, he admitted now, because it had been so rarely visited by Caroline. He and Ernest had designed it between them, equipping it to professional standards with a Le Cornu range the size of a small tank, pans of the heaviest cast-iron and copper, knives and cleavers and end-grain chopping blocks, a chilled marble slab for pastry, two mammoth brushed-steel refrigerators, a separate pantry at the end of the long room. In the middle, on the oiled teak table, Ernest had collected bottles and decanters from the bar in the sitting room. He stopped whistling as Simon came in.

'Liz called,' he said. 'There's an Executive Committee meeting at six, and that security analyst at Goodmans wants you to call him about the last quarter's projections.' Ernest looked at the message-pad by the phone. 'And the agents want to know if they can show someone the house tomorrow. A musician, they said – whatever that means nowadays.'

'It's probably the assistant drummer from a rock group.'

'I know, dear. Most unsuitable, but what can you do? They're the ones with the money.'

Simon pulled a chair away from the table and sat down heavily. His back ached, and his shirt felt uncomfortably

3

tight against his stomach. He was carrying too much weight. Too many lunches, too many meetings, not enough exercise. He looked at Ernest, who admitted to forty-eight but could have been ten years younger – slim, with a narrow, unlined face, close-cropped blond hair, immaculate in his dark blue suit and white shirt, no paunch, no jowls. That's what years of self-discipline did for you, Simon thought. There was a rumour in the agency that Ernest had slipped away for a face-lift during one of his exotic holidays, but Simon knew it was the skin cream from the dermatologist in Harley Street – £50 a tube, and put through on expenses as office supplies. It was one of Ernest's perks.

'Shall I get Liz for you?' Ernest picked up the phone, one eyebrow cocked, his mouth slightly pursed.

'Ern, I don't think I can face all that crap this evening. Ask Liz if she can fit it in tomorrow.'

Ernest nodded, and Simon reached among the bottles on the table for the Laphroaig. The glasses had all been packed. He poured the whisky into a tea-cup and half-listened to Ernest.

'. . . well, if Mr Jordan gets upset he'll just have to go into the garden and eat worms. Mr Shaw has had to postpone the meeting. We have had a ghastly day. Our home is being dismantled around our ears, and we are not feeling like a captain of industry.'

Ernest looked at Simon and rolled his eyes upwards as he listened to Liz's reply. He cut her short.

'I know, I know. We'll deal with the little man from Goodmans tomorrow, when we're feeling more like our old self. Do something diplomatic, dear. A tiny white lie. I know you can do it when you want to. I've heard you talking to that boyfriend of yours.'

Ernest winced at her reply, and held the phone away from his ear.

'And to you, dear. See you in the morning.'

He put down the phone, glanced at the tea-cup in front of Simon, and frowned. He opened a packing carton, took out a cut-glass tumbler, polished it with the silk handkerchief from his top pocket and poured a large measure of whisky.

4

'There.' He removed the tea-cup and put it in the sink. 'I know these are trying times, but we mustn't let standards slip. A little water?'

'What did she say?'

'Oh, the usual wailing and gnashing of teeth.' Ernest shrugged. 'Apparently the Executive Committee meeting has already been put off twice, and they'll all be in a snit. Especially Mr Jordan, but then it doesn't take much to put our Mr Jordan in a snit, as we know.'

He was right. Jordan, whose talent for handling dull clients was equalled only by his acute sense of self-importance, would feel slighted. Simon made a mental note to massage him in the morning, and took a mouthful of whisky. He felt the shudder go down to his stomach, and remembered that he hadn't eaten all day.

For once, the evening was free. He could take a book and go to a corner table in the Connaught, but he didn't feel like eating alone. He could call some friends, but dinner with friends would mean edging around the subject of Caroline and the divorce. Dinner with someone from the agency would be all the usual tired gossip about clients and new business prospects and office politics. He looked down the table, narrowing his eyes against the sun as it reflected needles of light from the bottles. He would miss this room.

'Ern, what are you doing tonight?'

Ernest backed out of a cupboard with a pile of plates. He put them down and stood with one hand on his cheek, the other cradling his elbow, graceful and slightly theatrical.

'Well now. I can't quite decide between a masked ball in Wimbledon or a gala curry at the Star of India.'

'How about dinner here, in the kitchen? We've never done it, and the house might be sold by next week.'

'As it happens,' Ernest said, 'I might be able to make myself available.' He smiled. 'Yes, I'd like that. The last supper. What would you like to eat?'

'I took a bottle of the '73 Petrus out of the cellar before they moved the rest of the wine. Something to go with that.'

Ernest looked at his watch. 'I'll be back in an hour. Why don't you call the little man at Goodmans? Get it over with.'

Simon heard the front door close and the sound of the big Mercedes pulling away as he walked through to his study, which the removal men had taken over as their temporary canteen. The handsome room was empty except for a phone on the floor and Simon's briefcase in the corner where the desk used to be, and an upturned packing case cluttered with the remains of numerous tea breaks: stained mugs, an old electric kettle, used tea-bags, an open bottle of milk, a copy of the *Sun* and a crystal ashtray, one of a pair that Simon had bought from Asprey's, piled high with cigarette ends. The air was sickly with the smell of spilt milk and smoke and sweat. Simon opened a window and lit a cigar in self-defence, sat on the floor and picked up the phone.

'Goodman Brothers, Levine, Russell and Fine.' The telephonist sounded bored and irritated, as though she had been interrupted while at work doing her nails and reading *Cosmopolitan*.

'Mr Wilkinson, please. It's Simon Shaw.'

'I'm sorry.' She sounded pleased. 'Mr Wilkinson's in conference. Who did you say it was?'

'Shaw, Simon Shaw. Of the Shaw Group. That makes four times I've told you. I'm returning Mr Wilkinson's call. He said it was important. The name is Shaw. Do you want me to spell it?'

Simon heard her sigh, as he was meant to. 'I'll see if Mr Wilkinson can be disturbed.'

Jesus. An airhead answering the phone, and now he was forced to listen to Ravel's *Bolero* while Wilkinson made up his mind whether or not he could be disturbed. Not for the first time, Simon wondered if it had been such a good idea to go public.

Ravel was cut off in mid-swoop, and Wilkinson's faintly patronizing voice came on the line. 'Mr Shaw?'

Who else was he expecting? 'Good afternoon,' said Simon. 'You wanted to speak to me?'

'Indeed I do, Mr Shaw. We're in conference at the moment, looking at your fourth quarter.' From the tone of his voice, he might have been a doctor discussing a bad case of piles. Simon could hear the rustle of papers. 'These projections of yours – correct me if I'm wrong – represent over 40 per cent of your annual billings.'

'That's right.'

'I see. Don't you think this might be a little optimistic, given the current state of the retail market? You'll forgive my saying so, but the City is a little nervous about the advertising sector these days. The institutions are not happy. Returns haven't been up to expectations. It might be advisable to be a little more considered in your estimates, wouldn't you say?'

Here we go, Simon thought. Lesson number one all over again. 'Mr Wilkinson, the advertising business makes most of its profits in the fourth quarter. Every year, strangely enough, Christmas comes in December. Companies advertise. Consumers buy. Everybody spends money. We are now at the end of September, and all the budgets have been committed. Air time and press space have been booked.'

'Booked doesn't necessarily mean paid for, Mr Shaw. We all know that. Are you confident that your clients are soundly based? No imminent mergers or takeovers? No cash-flow problems?'

'Not to my knowledge, no.'

'Not to your knowledge.' There was a pause while Wilkinson allowed his scepticism to be felt. He was a man who used silence like a bucket of cold water.

Simon tried again. 'Mr Wilkinson, short of nuclear war or an outbreak of bubonic plague we will achieve the figures shown in our projections. In the event of war or bubonic plague, we will go down the tubes, along with the rest of British industry and possibly even Goodman Brothers.'

'Down the tubes, Mr Shaw?'

'Out of business, Mr Wilkinson.'

'I see. There's nothing more you care to add to that rather unhelpful comment?'

'Each year for the past nine years, Mr Wilkinson, as you very well know, the agency has shown increased billings and increased profits. This is our best year ever. It has just over ninety days to run, and there is no reason to assume any shortfall from our projected figures. Do you want a press release? If you people had a proper understanding of the advertising business, we wouldn't have to go through this absurd cross-examination every month.'

Wilkinson's voice became smug, the smugness that professional men use as a refuge from argument. 'I think the City has a very clear understanding of the advertising business. More prudence and less conjecture would do it the world of good.'

'Bollocks.' Simon slammed the phone down, dropping cigar ash on his trousers. He stood up and stared out of the window at the square, dusty gold as the flat evening sun caught the yellowing leaves on the trees. He tried to remember how the square had looked in spring and summer, and realized that he'd never noticed. He didn't look out of windows any more. His life was spent looking at people in rooms, nursing staff, stroking clients, enduring the Wilkinsons and Executive Committees and financial journalists. It wasn't surprising that Caroline had resented them all. At least she'd had the fun of spending the money.

He had succeeded in not thinking too much about his marriage ever since it became obvious that it had been a mistake. The transition from a secretary to a rich man's wife had changed Caroline. Or maybe she'd always been a cow under that decorative exterior. Well, it was all over now bar the alimony, and he was once again, as Ernest had remarked in one of his friskier moments, a bachelor gay.

Simon crossed the hall and finished his cigar in the sitting room. Someone had once told him that the scent of a good Havana in an empty house could add a few thousand to the price. Subliminal advertising. He left the butt still smoking in the fireplace and went back to the kitchen.

He found the bottle of Petrus and put it gently on the table, and enjoyed the careful ritual of opening it, cutting the lead capsule cleanly and drawing the long cork with a slow, even pull. What a wine. A thousand pounds a case if you were lucky enough to get hold of any. Now that would be a job worth having, the proprietor of a great vineyard. No presentations to clients, no idiots from the City, no board meetings – just a few acres of gravel and clay to deal with, and nectar at the end of every year. He held the bottle against the light and poured the dense, rich wine into a decanter until he saw the first traces of sediment reach the neck of the bottle. Even at arm's length, he was aware of the powerful, soft–sweet bouquet.

He had just placed the decanter on the table when he heard the front door, and Ernest's light tenor singing 'The Teddy Bears' Picnic'. Simon smiled. Divorce obviously agreed with Ernest; he had been noticeably happier since Caroline had left the house.

'Well!' said Ernest as he put a shopping bag down. 'The Food Halls at Harrods are not what they used to be. A *zoo*. People in running shoes and track-suits with saggy bottoms, hardly an English voice to be heard, and those poor boys behind the counters rushed off their feet. Where are the days of grace and leisure, I ask myself? Never mind. I escaped with enough for a simple peasant meal.'

He took off his jacket and put on a long chef's apron, and started to unpack the bag. 'A *salade tiède* to begin with, I thought, with slices of *foie gras*, and then your favourite.' He took out a plump leg of lamb. 'With garlic and flageolets. And to finish . . .' he unwrapped two packages and held them out '. . . some Brillat-Savarin and a fierce little Cheddar.'

'Couldn't be better,' Simon said. He opened the fridge and took out a bottle of champagne. 'You'll break the habit of a lifetime, won't you?'

Ernest looked up from the garlic cloves he was peeling. 'Just a glass to encourage the cook.' He put the knife down as Simon twisted the cork out and filled two glasses.

'Cheers, Ern. Thanks for taking care of all this.' He waved a hand at the packing cases stacked against the wall.

'Happy days, dear. You won't be too sorry to go, will you? You never really felt at home here.'

'I suppose not.'

The two men drank.

'If I may say so,' Ernest said, 'the state of our trousers is not what it should be for this evening. Not quite up to the wine.'

9

Simon looked down at the grey smear of cigar ash, and started to rub it.

'No, no, no. You're rubbing it in, not rubbing it off. What would our tailor say? You go up and change while I get on down here. Leave those out and I'll see to them tomorrow.'

Simon took his glass and went up the broad staircase and into what the decorators always referred to as the master suite. The scent that Caroline wore was still there, very faint, as he passed the line of fitted closets that had held her last few dozen dresses, the overflow from the dressing room. He pushed back the folding doors. Hangers had been dropped on the floor in a spiky pile next to discarded shopping bags from Joseph, Max Mara, Saint Laurent – glossy, crumpled souvenirs from half the boutiques in Knightsbridge. A pair of beige and black Chanel shoes, their soles barely scuffed, lay on their sides in the corner. Why had she left them? Simon picked them up and noticed a nick in the leather of one of the heels; £250 tossed away because of an almost invisible scar.

He put the shoes back and undressed, dropping his clothes on the four-poster bed. It was too big for Caroline's new house, and he wondered idly who would be sleeping in it after him. He'd always hated the damned thing. With its pleats and ruffles and billowing curtains, it made him feel like a trespasser in a decorator's boudoir. But then the whole house made him feel like that.

He walked into the bathroom and met his reflection in the full-length mirror, a naked middle-aged man holding a glass. God, he looked older than forty-two. Tired eyes, deep creases either side of his mouth, a streak of grey in one of his eyebrows, silver tips beginning to show in his straight black hair. Another few years and he'd be pear-shaped if he didn't do something more than the occasional snatched game of tennis. He sucked in his belly and pushed out his chest. Right. Hold that for the next ten years, eat less, drink less – a lot less – go to a gym. Boring. He exhaled, finished his champagne and ducked into the shower without looking at the mirror again, and spent fifteen minutes letting the water beat down on the back of his neck.

The bedroom phone rang as he finished drying himself. 'Chez Nous is open,' Ernest said. 'We can eat in half an hour.'

Simon put on old cotton trousers and a frayed silk shirt that Caroline had tried to throw away several times, and walked down to the kitchen barefoot. The tiled floor was cool and smooth, and the feel of it reminded him of holidays long ago in hot places.

Ernest had set the table with candles and a shallow dish of white rose heads. A box of Partagas and a cigar cutter were beside Simon's place, and the sound of a Mozart piano concerto came from the speakers recessed in the wall at the far end of the room. Simon felt clean and relaxed and hungry. He took the champagne from the fridge.

'Ern?' He held up the bottle.

Ernest noticed Simon's bare feet while the glasses were being filled. 'I can see we're in bohemian mood tonight,' he said. 'Quite the beachcomber, aren't we?'

Simon smiled. 'Caroline would have had a fit.'

Ernest wiped his hands on his apron and picked up his glass. 'The trouble is,' he said, 'that your entire life is spent with sensitive flowers who have fits. The sainted Executive Committee, the clients, those pipsqueaks in the City, that frightful old adolescent who's supposed to run the Creative Department – how he thinks nobody notices when he goes to the Gents every half-hour and comes back with a runny nose I don't know I'm sure – all of them are more trouble than they're worth, if you ask me.' He managed to sip his champagne and look disdainful at the same time. 'Which of course you didn't.'

Ernest put down his glass and mixed the salad dressing as though he were punishing it, beating the olive oil and vinegar until it was almost frothing. He dipped his little finger in the bowl and licked it. 'Delicious.'

'It's business, Ern. You can't expect to like everyone you have to work with.'

Ernest cut the block of *foie gras* into thin pink slices and put them in a blackened cast-iron pan that had been warming on the hob.

11

'Well, I'm not going to let them spoil our dinner.' He poured the dressing over the salad and tossed it with quick, deft hands, wiped his oily fingers and moved across to peer into the pan. 'It can all vanish, you know, the *foie gras*, if it gets too hot. It melts away.' He put the salad on two plates, and, as the first tiny bubbles appeared round the edge of the *foie gras*, took the pan off the heat and slid the soft slices on to their lettuce beds.

Simon took his first mouthful, the lettuce crisp and cool, the *foie gras* warm and rich. Across the table, Ernest was conducting an investigation of the wine with long, appreciative sniffs, his eyes half-closed.

'Will it do?' asked Simon. 'According to the books, we should be drinking Sauternes with this.'

Ernest held the wine in his mouth for a moment before answering. 'Absolute heaven,' he said. 'Let's not send it back.'

They ate in silence until they had finished. Simon wiped his plate with a piece of bread and leaned back in his chair. 'I haven't enjoyed anything as much as that for months.' He drank some wine slowly, rolling it around his mouth before swallowing. 'What's the kitchen in the new place like?'

'Horrid,' said Ernest as he started carving the lamb. 'Poky and plastic. Perfect for a dwarf with no taste who loathes cooking. The letting agent was very proud of it. Purpose-built, she said. Purpose-built for what, I said, TV dinners for one?'

Simon had taken a short lease on a flat in Rutland Gate, mainly because it was round the corner from the office. He'd hardly looked at it; the car had been waiting to take him to the airport. What the hell. It was only somewhere to sleep until he found somewhere to live.

'It won't be for long, Ern. We'll look at flats as soon as I've got some time.'

Ernest served the lamb, rosy and running with juice. 'Well, I won't hold my breath. I know you. Off to New York every five minutes, or Paris, or Düsseldorf. Rush rush rush, jet-lag and bad temper, and when you're in London it's one dreary meeting after another.' Ernest finished his wine and poured some more. His cheeks were flushed as he leaned forward into the candlelight. 'They don't care, you know, at the office.'

'What are you talking about?'

'They don't care about you. All they care about is what you can do for them. Their new cars, their bonuses, their silly little status games – I heard Jordan having the vapours for half an hour the other day because a client had parked in his space in the garage. You'd have thought someone had touched up his secretary. "I shall have to take this up with Simon if something isn't done at once." Pathetic. Well, you know better than I do. They're all like children.'

'I thought you weren't going to let them spoil dinner.'

Ernest went on as if he hadn't heard. 'And another thing. Holidays. Three hundred people in that office, and only one of them hasn't had a holiday this year.' He reached for the decanter. 'Another glass of wine if you can guess who that is.'

Simon held out his glass. 'Me.'

'You. No wonder you look so peaky.'

Simon remembered his reflection in the bathroom mirror. When was the last time he'd taken a few days off? It must have been nearly two years ago, when he and Caroline had been pretending they still had a marriage. He'd been delighted to get back to the office.

Ernest cleared the plates and put the cheese on the table. 'Maybe it's the wine talking,' he said, 'and you can call me an old nag if you like, but I don't care. You need a holiday.' He fussed over the cheese board. 'A bit of each?'

'I don't know, Ern. I've got a lot on at the moment.'

'Leave Jordan in charge. He'd be thrilled. He could use your parking space.' Ernest put the cheese in front of Simon. 'There. Have a nibble of the Brillat-Savarin, close your eyes and think of France. You're always saying how much you love it. Take a car and drive down to the south.' He cocked his head and smiled at Simon. 'You know what they say about all work and no play?'

'Yes, Ern. It makes you rich.' And then he took a mouthful of cheese and thought of the south. The warm,

13

seductive south, with its polished light and soft air and lavender evening skies. And no Executive Committee. 'It's tempting, I must say.'

'Well then,' said Ernest, as if he'd just won an argument, 'lie back and enjoy it. That's what temptation's for.'

Simon reached for his glass. 'Maybe you're right.' The wine felt warm and round in his mouth, comforting and relaxing. He grinned at Ernest. 'OK, I give in. Just a few days. Why not?'

2

The wiry little man they called Jojo was there early, leaning against the warm stone wall, watching the huge moss-skinned water-wheel as it turned slowly, shiny green and dripping in the sun. Behind the wheel he could see the ornate gingerbread bulk of the Caisse d'Épargne, a picture postcard building with its elaborate architectural flourishes and fat tubs of geraniums on the entrance steps, more like a melon millionaire's villa than a bank. People said it was the most picturesque bank in Provence, a fitting bank for the picturesque town of Isle-sur-Sorgue. According to Jojo's information, it could be taken. There was a way in. He lit a cigarette, and turned to look for a familiar face among the crowds drifting through the Sunday morning market.

It was getting on for the end of the season, late September, but the fine weather had tempted them out – the sturdy, suspicious housewives with their bulging baskets, the Arabs buying their lunch live from the chicken stalls, the tourists with their reddened skins and bright holiday clothes. They moved slowly, clogging the pavements, spilling out into the road. Cars attempting to drive through the town were reduced to an irate, honking crawl. That might be a problem, Jojo thought. He took a last drag on his cigarette, cupping the butt in the curve of his hand, an old prison habit.

The man he'd been waiting for sauntered across the road, a half-eaten croissant in his hand, his belly bigger than ever. Life must have treated him well since the old days, although he'd never been thin.

'Eh, General!'

The other man waved his croissant. '*Salut*, Jojo. *Ça va?*'

They shook hands and stood back, smiling, as they inspected each other.

'How long has it been? Two years?'

'More.' The big man laughed. 'You haven't grown much.' He took a bite from his croissant and wiped golden flakes of pastry from his moustache with the back of his hand – a hand, Jojo noticed, that hadn't done any manual labour for years, unlike his own scarred fingers and roughened palms.

'Well, are we going to stand here all day?' The General slapped Jojo on the back. 'Come on. I'll buy you a drink.'

'Two seconds,' said Jojo. 'Let me show you something first.' He took the General's arm and led him over to the stone wall. 'Look over there.' He nodded down at the water flowing below. 'On the other side.'

On the opposite bank, the top of a stone arch cleared the surface of the water by three feet. The stone was dry and clean; obviously, the water hadn't risen that high for years.

The General glanced at the arch, then threw the last morsels of croissant into the water and watched two ducks arguing over them. 'So?' he said. 'A hundred years ago, some *con* put the door in the wrong place.'

'You think so?' Jojo winked, and tapped the side of his nose. 'Maybe not. That's why I called you. *Allez*. Let's go and have that drink.'

As they walked into the centre of town, they caught up with each other's lives since their release from Les Baumettes, the jail in Marseille. They had been close then, they and a handful of others, all local petty criminals who had run out of luck at the same time. Jojo's wife had left him while he'd been inside, gone up north somewhere with a Pernod salesman. Now he was living in a couple of rooms in Cavaillon, working like a donkey for a *maçon* who specialized in restoring old houses. It was young man's work and he wasn't young any more, but what could he do except buy his Loto tickets every week and hope to God that his back didn't give out?

The General was sympathetic, the sympathy that comes from relief that there are others worse off than you are. The General had been lucky. Not only had he kept his wife, but he'd lost his mother-in-law, and the money she'd left had been enough to buy a small pizza restaurant in Cheval-Blanc. Nothing fancy, but it was steady, and one ate and

16

drank on the business. The General had laughed when he'd said that, and patted his stomach. Life could be worse. His wife kept a tight hand on the till, but otherwise he couldn't complain.

They found a table under the shade of the plane trees outside the Café de France, opposite the old church.

'What are you drinking?' The General took off his sunglasses and waved them at a waiter.

'*Pastis*. Anything but Pernod.'

Jojo looked around, and edged his chair closer to the General's. 'I'll tell you why I called.' He talked quietly, his eyes watching the crowd as he spoke, dropping his voice when anyone passed close to their table.

'My *patron* has an old friend who used to be a *flic* until he got into trouble and they kicked him out. Now he's set himself up in the security business, selling alarm systems to all those people who buy second homes down here. They're not short of a few *sous*, and they get nervous when they hear about empty houses being broken into every winter. Each house we work on, the *patron* always tells the owner there are more burglars than bakers in the Vaucluse, and then he recommends his *copain*. If the owner installs an alarm system, the *patron* gets an envelope.' Jojo rubbed his thumb and index finger together.

The waiter came with the drinks, and Jojo watched him go back inside the café before he spoke again.

'The other day, this guy – Jean-Louis, he's called – comes to the *chantier* and he's laughing like he's heard the best joke of his life. I was working on the roof and they were talking right underneath me. I heard everything.'

'It wasn't the one about the Parisian and the transvestite and the postman?'

Jojo lit a cigarette, and blew smoke at a dog who was looking for sugar-lumps under the table. 'It was funny, but it wasn't a joke. Listen to this: they've just put in a new security system at the Caisse d'Épargne – electronic eyes, pressure pads on the floor, metal detectors at the door, the works. One of the big companies from Lyon put it in. Millions, it cost.'

The General was puzzled. It was always a pleasure to hear about a bank having to spend millions of francs, but he'd heard things at funerals that had made him laugh more. 'What was so funny? Did the bank's cheque bounce?'

Jojo grinned, and wagged his finger. 'Better than that. What happened was they moved the strong-room — all of the *coffres-forts* — right to the back of the bank for extra security. Five-centimetre steel bars on the door, triple locks . . .' Jojo paused for effect '. . . but no electronic eyes. Not one.'

'*Ah bon?*'

'No. And why? Because clients going through their strong-boxes don't want to be on TV in the manager's office while they're counting their cash.'

The General shrugged. '*C'est normal, non?*'

'But the best of it' — Jojo sipped his *pastis* and looked round the other tables before leaning forward — 'the best of it is that the new strong-room is exactly over the old river drain. But exactly.'

'The old river drain?'

'That arch we just looked at. That's where it comes out. Twenty, twenty-five metres up that, and you're under the floor of the strong-room. A little *plastique* and *boum*! You're through.'

'*Formidable*. And then you can dance on the pressure pads until the *flics* arrive.'

Jojo shook his head, and grinned again. He was enjoying this. 'No, that's the other funny thing. There aren't any pressure pads. The floor isn't wired. They reckoned the door was enough. Jean-Louis couldn't believe it.'

The General pulled unconsciously at his moustache, a habit his wife said made him look lopsided. Isle-sur-Sorgue, he knew, was a rich little town, full of antique dealers who did most of their business in cash. A few hours looking through their strong-boxes wouldn't be wasted. He felt the first stirrings of interest. More than interest, he had to admit. It was the old tickle of excitement he always used to feel when he was planning a job. That was his skill, planning. That was why the others called him the General, because he could use his head.

18

Jojo looked at him like a cuckoo waiting for a worm, his eyes bright and dark in his lean brown face. '*Alors?* What do you think?'

'How do we know it's true? The whole thing stinks.' The General looked round for a waiter. 'But we might as well have another drink.'

Jojo smiled. He was like that, the General. A real pessimist, always looking for problems. But he hadn't said no.

As the crowds thinned and started to make their way home for lunch, the two men talked on and the square became quiet except for the striking of the church clock.

3

Simon was in the office by eight-thirty. The long and tastefully stark corridors were quiet, empty except for the potted palms and ficus trees that were now so numerous an official agency gardener had been hired to look after them, a willowy young man who wore cotton gloves and spent his days polishing leaves. Ernest called him the foliage executive.

Passing an open door, Simon saw a junior account man crouched over his first memo of the day. He looked up, pleased that his diligence had been noticed. Simon nodded good morning, and wondered what his name was. There were so many of them now, and most of them looked the same in their suits of serious colour and fashionable cut. Maybe he should get them to wear identification tags.

He went through Liz's office and into his own. A visiting American had once told him that it was a power office, because it occupied a corner and so had twice the view that less exalted employees could enjoy, and – a great touch, so the American had said – there was nothing as humble as a desk in sight. Deep leather couches, low tables, a wall of TV and computer screens, conspicuously larger and lusher plants than those which decorated the agency's common parts. Tycoon heaven.

Liz had left the previous day's accumulation of paperwork on a side table, neatly divided into four piles: messages, correspondence, contact reports and, the most forbidding pile of all, strategy documents and marketing plans, several hours of intense boredom bound in glossy dark blue covers.

The fax machine chirped next door as Simon looked through the message pile. Ziegler had called from New York. Caroline's lawyers. Four clients. The Creative Director, the Financial Director, two Account Supervisors and the Head of Television. And Jordan. God, what a way to start the day. And then Simon remembered the decision he had taken last night, and his mood lightened. He was going on holiday.

He took Jordan's message – *Must see you ASAP* – and scrawled on the bottom, *Ready when you are. 8 a.m.* The small lie would put Jordan on the defensive. He never got in before nine-thirty. Simon took the message across the hall to deliver it, and to catch up on Jordan's latest hobby, traces of which were always on casual but prominent display in his office. It must be hell for him, Simon thought, trying to keep ahead of the rank and file. Tennis had been abandoned a long time ago, when junior executives had taken it up. There had been a period of shotguns and game bags when Jordan first bought his country seat, and then a nautical phase marked by sea-boots and oilskins. Now, apparently, it was polo.

Three mallets were propped against the wall behind Jordan's desk, and a pristine helmet hung above them, next to the pinboard where the fixture list of the Ham Polo Club partially obscured an invitation to drinks at the Reform. Polo, of course, was the ultimate hobby for the socially ambitious advertising man – ruinously expensive, glamorous upper-class accoutrements and, with any kind of luck, a chance to be on swearing terms with royalty. Simon smiled, and wondered how long it would be before Jordan wanted a parking space for his ponies and a company helicopter to whisk him off to Windsor.

He heard the click of high heels on the tiled floor, and left the message tucked into the frame of a photograph of Jordan's acceptably pretty and, according to gossip, very rich wife.

Liz was sorting through the faxes that had come in overnight from America, her body silhouetted against the window, long dark hair falling forward across her cheek. She was dressed with a businesslike severity that accentuated a spectacular pair of legs. Simon considered himself a connoisseur of legs, and Liz's were as good as he'd seen anywhere, very long from knee to ankle. For all his good intentions to hire plain middle-aged spinsters with halitosis and flat feet, he always ended up with attractive secretaries, and took great pleasure in looking at them. The sight of Liz bending over had sustained him through countless meetings.

'Good morning, Elizabeth.'

'Good morning, Mr Shaw. How are you today?' She smiled at him over her bouquet of faxes. Whenever he called her Elizabeth she knew he was in a good mood.

'I'm fine, and a cup of coffee would make me even better. And then we must look for my bucket and spade and sunhat.'

Liz stopped on her way to the coffee percolator, eyebrows raised.

'I'm going to take a few days off. I thought I'd drive down through France and see if it's true what they say about Saint-Tropez.'

'I think it would do you good. What do they say about Saint-Tropez?'

'Autumn in Saint-Tropez,' said Simon, 'is completely devoid of temptation. It will be just me and the seagulls on the beach, and solitary evenings in my monk-like cell. Could you fax the Byblos and make a reservation?'

Liz bent over her desk to make a note on her pad. 'You'll need a place on the car ferry.'

'And one night in Paris. The Lancaster.'

'When do you want to leave?'

'Tomorrow. Give Philippe Murat a call and see if he's free for dinner. And for God's sake tell him it's business, otherwise he'll bring one of his girlfriends from *Elle* and he'll be blowing in her ear all evening. You know what he's like – beneath that veneer of after-shave lurks a sex maniac.'

Liz looked prim. 'I think Mr Murat is very charming.'

'Well, don't ever get into a lift alone with him, that's all.'

Simon felt almost happy, impatient to get away from the office. Ernest could organize the flat in Rutland Gate, and Jordan would have the time of his life playing Chief Executive for a week. Nothing much could go wrong in a week.

Liz came back with the coffee. 'Shall we do the calls?'

'Just the clients. Jordan can deal with the agency stuff.'

'And Mrs Shaw's lawyers?'

'Ah. Them. You don't think I could send them a postcard from Saint-Tropez?'

'I had the senior partner on yesterday. He said it was urgent.'

Simon sipped his coffee. 'Elizabeth, did you know he has a timer next to his phone? He charges by the minute. If, God forbid, you should ever be desperate enough to call and invite him to dinner, he'd charge you for the call. A postcard would be cheaper.'

'You'll only have to speak to him when you get back.'

'You're right. I know you're right.' Simon sighed. 'OK. Let's get the thieving swine before he issues a writ for contempt of phone calls. But you listen when he comes on the line. You can hear the timer. It ticks. It's one of those things you use for boiling eggs.'

The call was brief and expensive. Caroline wanted a new car. She needed a new car. She was entitled to a new car, under the terms of the settlement. Simon agreed to a BMW, but haggled about the stereophonic equipment until he realized that he could have bought it for the price of a five-minute legal conversation. As he put the phone down, he wondered if killing a lawyer could ever be excused as a *crime passionnel*.

He looked up to see Jordan standing in the doorway, a cup of coffee in his hand, the sartorial antithesis of most people's idea of an advertising man. His appearance was old-fashioned and deeply respectable, which was probably why clients felt safe with him. Ernest swore that he'd once heard Jordan's suit creak, it was so heavy.

Today he was disguised as a successful merchant banker – three-piece pinstriped suit, striped shirt, sober tie, the gold watch-chain in his lapel disappearing into the voluminous silk folds of his breast-pocket handkerchief, highly polished black shoes. His mouse-coloured hair was brushed straight back, and made wings over his ears. Simon noticed that he was cultivating small tufts of hair on his cheekbones in the manner of retired naval officers, embryonic buggers' grips. He could not have been anything but English.

Simon didn't give him a chance to speak.

'Come in, Nigel, come in. Listen, I'm sorry I had to cancel last night, but I'd had a hell of a day. Just wasn't up to it. Have some more coffee. Have a cigar. Tell me I'm forgiven.'

Jordan folded his lanky body on to a couch and put down his coffee so that he could shoot his cuffs and smooth back his hair.

'It's not that I mind, Simon,' he said. He spoke as if his shirt collar were too tight. 'It's the others. They're beginning to wonder if the Executive Committee still exists. Three meetings in a row cancelled. Feathers are ruffled, old boy, I can tell you.'

Simon could guess whose feathers were the most ruffled. 'Anyone in particular? Anyone you think I should pop in and see?'

Jordan produced a gold cigarette case, and took his time selecting a cigarette. He took a gold lighter from his waistcoat pocket. The light caught his heavy gold signet ring, and his gold cufflinks. The man's a walking bloody jewellery store, Simon thought.

'I think I can handle them this time, Simon. A drink at the end of the day should do it, a quiet word over the whisky. Why don't you leave it to me?'

Simon tried to look suitably grateful. 'If you're sure.'

'Don't give it another thought.' Jordan blew a plume of smoke into the air. He had a studied, complacent way of smoking that always made Simon want to give him an exploding cigarette. 'In fact, I'm probably a little more in touch with the troops than you are at the moment. Personal problems and everything. Takes your mind off management.'

Jordan's theories on management were aired at great length whenever he was with anyone he considered his corporate equal, and Simon had heard them a hundred times.

'That's what I wanted to talk to you about.' Jordan, sensing a revelation, leaned forward as Simon's voice became confidential. 'The fact is, I could really do with a break. The last few months have been pretty difficult.'

Jordan nodded sagely. 'Seriously bad news, divorce.'

'Well, I'll get over it, but I could do with a few days out of the firing line, and I was wondering if you could take over for a week or so. I hate to ask you. God knows you must have enough on your plate already, but I wouldn't feel comfortable unless I knew there weren't going to be any disasters.'

Jordan did his best not to preen.

'I'd like to leave tomorrow,' Simon said, 'but obviously that depends on how you're fixed. Bloody short notice, I know, but I think sooner is better than later, the way I'm feeling.'

'Tomorrow?' Jordan frowned as he considered the burdens of high office. 'I'll need to juggle a few meetings around. The diary looks seriously sticky for the next few days.'

Simon had glanced at Jordan's diary earlier. One entire day had a line through it, and the single word 'Cotswolds' written at the top of the page. There were no agency clients in that part of the English countryside. Horses, however, were plentiful.

'Look, if it's too . . .'

Jordan held up his hand. 'I'll manage somehow.' He frowned again. 'Might need to borrow Liz, though. Susan's frightfully good, but she might get snowed under if I'm wearing two hats.'

Simon had a vision of Jordan conducting meetings with two polo helmets balanced on his head.

'Of course.' Simon fed him the plum. 'I think it might make sense if you moved in here. Might be easier.'

Jordan pretended to ponder the massive inconvenience of moving ten yards down the corridor, then gave Simon the sincere look with furrowed brow that always worked so well with clients. 'Might be better, old boy. Might be better. More reassuring for the troops.'

'Let them know there's a firm hand on the reins,' said Simon.

'My point exactly. Never thought of taking up riding, have you? Great fun. Magnificent creature, the horse.'

'You know what Oscar Wilde said about horses, don't

you? "Dangerous at both ends, and uncomfortable in the middle." I rather agree with him.'

'Don't know what you're missing, old boy.' Jordan unfolded himself, stood up, and delivered a left and a right with his cuffs. 'Well, I'd better get on. I'll catch up with you before you go tonight.'

Simon heard him talking to Liz next door. '. . . holding the fort while Simon's away . . . liaise with Susan . . . all meetings in here, I think.'

Now there, thought Simon, is a happy man. He spent the rest of the day on the phone.

He was in Paris late the following afternoon, and found a message waiting for him at the Lancaster: Monsieur Murat would meet him at Chez L'Ami Louis at eight o'clock. A good start to the holiday. It was Simon's favourite restaurant in Paris, and he wouldn't have to wear a tie. He showered and changed and decided to walk over to Saint-Germain for a drink at the Deux Magots.

He'd forgotten what a beautiful city Paris was. It seemed very clean after London, no garbage bags on the pavements, no For Sale signs on the houses. He stopped on the Pont-Neuf and looked back across the river towards the Louvre. The dusk was tinged with blue, dotted with light from windows and street lamps, and he had a moment's regret about dinner. Much as he liked Murat, an evening like this should be spent with a pretty girl.

The Deux Magots was as crowded as ever, the waiters as supercilious as ever, the poses of the clientele as world-weary as ever. The girls were in black yet again this autumn, with carefully tangled long hair and pale faces, oversized leather jackets and the heavy flat shoes that Simon hated – brothel-creepers that made even the best pair of legs look clumsy. Why did they all want to look the same?

Simon lit a cigar and ordered a *kir*. It was good to be in France again, good to hear French spoken. He was surprised how much he could understand. It had been a long time, more than twenty years, since he had spent six months working as a waiter in Nice. He'd been fluent then, or fluent

26

enough to make a living, and he was pleased that some of it had stuck.

He watched a Japanese couple in the corner trying to order from a waiter who was playing the popular Parisian game of blank incomprehension in the face of the foreigner.

'Scosh.' The Japanese man held up two fingers. 'Scosh.'

'*Comment?*'

'Scosh.'

The waiter shrugged. The Japanese picked up the small menu card and held it open, pointing half-way down the page. 'Scosh.'

The waiter condescended to look, and sighed. '*Non,*' he said. 'Whisky.'

'*Hai, hai.* Scosh whisky.'

'*Deux?*'

The Japanese grinned and bobbed his head, and the waiter, satisfied that his superiority had been established, snaked away through the tables to the bar.

The *kir* had made Simon hungry, and he wondered if it was too early in the year for the wild *cèpes* that made a brief annual appearance on the menu at L'Ami Louis. He realized that he hadn't thought about the office all afternoon, hadn't even called Liz to tell her he'd arrived. France was already doing him good. He paid his bill and crossed Boulevard Saint-Germain to the taxi rank.

The taxi dropped him off in the narrow Rue du Vertbois, and he stood for a moment outside the restaurant. Thank God it hadn't been tarted up and sanitized. He pushed open the door and stepped into the bustling warmth of one of the last great bistros in Paris.

The decorative style was early twentieth-century shabby, with cracked paint the colour of a good dark brown stew and floor tiles that had worn through to the bare concrete. Apart from a photograph of the old *patron*, the grey-whiskered Antoine, and one or two mirrors stained with age, the walls were bare beneath the coat-rack that ran the length of the room. Nothing much had changed here for more than half a century, and Simon felt, as he did each time he came, that he was in the ramshackle dining room of an old friend.

27

Murat had reserved a table behind the ancient wood-burning stove, and Simon settled back to wait and to speculate about the people round him. There was usually an interesting mixture of fame, wealth and notoriety – movie stars and directors, politicians hoping to be recognized and statesmen trying to be incognito, young men from rich Parisian families, actresses with their admirers, middle-aged playboys and, almost always, a tentative group on their first visit, not quite sure what to make of the well-worn surroundings.

Two American couples came through the door, the women in premature fur coats and frosted hair, the men still in summer blazers. Simon noticed the expressions of alarm on the women's faces as several thousand dollars' worth of prime chinchilla was casually bundled up by the waiter and tossed on to the rack above their table. 'Clayton,' one of them said to her husband, 'are you sure this is the place?' The husband patted her into her seat. 'It's a bistro, honey. What do you expect, valet parking?'

Simon's waiter came with a bottle of Meursault, and he breathed in the bouquet that made him think of cobwebs and dark cellars. The wine was chilled, not too cold to mask the taste. Simon sipped and nodded.

The waiter filled his glass. '*C'est pas terrible, eh?*'

There was a thump on the door of the restaurant and Murat came skidding through, late and dishevelled in a rumpled black suit and long pink scarf, teeth and glasses gleaming against his tanned face as he turned to Simon, his shoulder-length hair giving him the appearance of a fugitive from the Sixties. How he managed to run the Paris office and keep his suntan and attend to his complicated and energetic love life Simon never knew. They had met when Simon had bought a majority share in Murat's agency, and business had turned into friendship.

'Philippe. Good to see you.'

'Simon! You're early. No? I'm late. *Merde*. The meeting went on and on.'

'Who was she?'

Murat looked at Simon as he sat down and unwrapped the pink cashmere bandage from around his neck. He smiled the innocent and charming smile that Simon was sure he practised in the mirror every morning.

'You have a dirty mind, my friend. But I remember what you once told me: never bullshit a bullshitter.' Murat spoke the phrase with relish. He enjoyed being colloquial in his English, and collected slang wherever he found it. 'OK, I'll tell you. It was the yogurt client, you know? She's a woman of a certain age, and . . .'

'. . . and you gave her one for the sake of the agency,' Simon said.

Murat helped himself to wine. 'She bought the campaign for next year, and then we celebrated with a little drink, and then, well . . .' He shrugged.

'Don't depress me with the details. What are you going to eat?'

As they were looking at the menu, they overheard the conversation from the American table. '. . . and you know what it turned out to be in the end? A hiatus hernia. I'm going for the roast chicken. So he gets out of hospital and sues for malpractice . . .'

Simon grinned at Murat. 'I think I'd rather hear about your sex life than that.' He beckoned to a waiter, and they ordered.

'How long are you in Paris?' asked Murat. 'There's a party on Saturday with guaranteed pretty girls. Nobody from advertising. You should come.' He winked, and tried out his latest phrase. 'Get the dirty water off your chest, you know?'

'You make it sound so romantic,' Simon said. 'But I can't. I'm leaving early tomorrow, driving down to Saint-Tropez for a few days.'

The waiter arrived with scallops, sizzling and pungent with garlic, the *foie gras* that Simon could never resist, and a plate piled with warm slices of toasted *baguette*. A bottle of red Burgundy, dull with dust, was placed at one side of the table to breathe. Simon took off his jacket and looked around the room. All the tables were full now, full and noisy. There was always the sound of laughter here; it was a place for enjoyment. Diets were forbidden, and portions were enormous. Nobody came to L'Ami Louis to sit quietly over a couple of lettuce leaves.

'Saint-Tropez?' Murat made a small, dismissive grimace. 'It's finished now. The whole coast is finished, unless you want to play golf with a bunch of tight-asses from Paris. The BCBG have taken over – *Bon Chic Bon Genre* – and you get fined if you're not wearing a Lacoste shirt.'

'Suppose you haven't got a Lacoste shirt? Where do you go?'

Murat chased some sauce around the plate with his last scallop. 'Have you ever been to the Lubéron? Between Avignon and Aix. It's getting a little chi-chi, specially in August, but it's beautiful – old villages, mountains, no crowds, fantastic light – I was there for a week in June with Nathalie. It was *très romantique*, until her husband arrived.'

The waiter cleared the table. Simon had never been to the Lubéron. Like hundreds of thousands of others, he had gone straight to the Côte d'Azur, fried on the beach, and gone straight home again. The back country of Provence was unknown territory, a blur of names on the *autoroute* signs.

'Where do you drive to?'

'Leave the *autoroute* at Cavaillon, and go towards Apt. It's nothing, twenty minutes. I can tell you where Nathalie and I stayed, a little place, *beaucoup de charme*, a private terrace where the two of you can sunbathe naked . . .'

'Philippe, I'm on my own.'

'So? Sunbathe naked on your own. You might get lucky.' Murat leaned forward. 'The maid comes in one morning to make your bed – one of those ripe little Provençale girls of seventeen with the olive skin and the big brown eyes – and she discovers the English *milord*. He is on the terrace *tout nu*. She cannot resist him. *Voilà*! It is a legover.'

Murat's version of a quiet and uncomplicated holiday was interrupted by the arrival of the gigantic roast pheasant that they were sharing, and a pyramid of crisp, finely cut *pommes frites*. There was audible consternation from the American table at the size of the chicken that one of the women had ordered. 'All for *moi*? My God.'

Murat poured the red wine and raised his glass. '*Bonnes vacances*, my friend. I'm serious about the Lubéron; it's a little special. You should try it.'

4

Chez Mathilde, the pizzeria grill on the road leading into Cheval-Blanc, was closed on Sundays. The General's wife liked to spend the day with her sister in Orange, and the General was happy to be left to play *boules*. This Sunday, however, his *boules* stayed in their case in the garage. The General was expecting visitors.

He had done his homework and made his plans and passed the word around. The old bunch from Baumettes – or most of them, the ones who had managed to stay out of jail – were coming to listen to a proposition.

The General took the chairs off the big round table where they'd been left after cleaning up on Saturday night, and brought out *pastis* and wine and glasses, a bowl of olives and a couple of the large pizzas. They were cold, but still good. Anyway, nobody was coming for the food. He counted the chairs. Eight. He'd hoped they would be ten, but Raoul and Jacques had been careless one night and the police had caught them, during a routine check for drunk drivers, with guns and a vanload of stolen carpets. They wouldn't be going anywhere for a few years. The thought of it made the General shake his head. He'd always told them to avoid guns. Guns doubled the sentence.

He heard the sputter of a Mobylette, and went to the back door. Jojo, in a clean T-shirt and a Sunday shave, came across the dusty parking area, nodding his head and grinning.

'*Salut*!' They shook hands. Jojo peered over the General's shoulder. 'Mathilde?'

'It's OK,' said the General, 'she's in Orange until this evening.'

'*Bon.* A big day, eh? What do you think? Is it going to work?'

The General clapped Jojo on the back, and felt the solid pad of muscle developed by ten-hour days shifting stones and sacks of cement. 'If they're all as fit as you, it can work.'

Jojo knew the General well enough not to ask any more questions. The General liked his moment of drama, and a full audience. They went through the narrow passage stacked with beer kegs and into the restaurant. Jojo looked around at the rough-cast plaster walls and the wrought-iron wall lamps in the shape of gondolas, the posters of Venice and Pisa, the small tiled bar with the parchment scroll hanging behind it – 'The house does not extend credit' – and the framed photograph of Mathilde and the General posing stiffly with a man in a tie.

'Nice place, very *sympa*.' Jojo pointed at the photograph. 'Who's he?'

'That's the Mayor. He loves pizza. His father came from Italy.' There was the sound of cars outside, and the General squeezed his bulk past Jojo. 'Help yourself to a drink.'

A Renault van and a dirty white Peugeot had parked in the shade, and the passengers were standing in a noisy group as one of them relieved himself against a tree. The General counted them. All here.

'*Salut les copains*!' He walked out to meet them, men he hadn't seen for years. As he shook their hands, he looked them over. They all seemed to be in good health, and he led them into the restaurant with a sense of anticipation. This was just like the old days. It was all very well, the respectable life, but after a while a man needed a little excitement.

'*Allez*! Sit down, sit down.' They pulled up chairs, Jojo as second-in-command being careful to stay next to the General. Bottles were passed, glasses filled, cigarettes lighted. The General looked round the table, smiling and tugging on his moustache. 'Well, it's been a long time. Tell me how you've all become *milliardaires*.' Nobody was anxious to be first. '*Alors*? Do you think there's a cop hiding behind the bar? Tell me.'

It was not a series of success stories. Fernand the *plasti-queur*, two fingers missing and a cheek puckered with scar tissue from a mistimed explosion, worked in a garage.

33

Bachir, with his narrow Arab face and his fondness for flick-knives, had found less dangerous work as a waiter in an Avignon café. Claude, as big as ever, was using his broad back and massive arms as a *maçon*, working with Jojo. The Borel brothers, two short, square men with weathered skin, had given up stealing cars to work for a landscape gardener near Carpentras. Of them all, the only one still practising his trade was Jean, the silent one with the deft hands who made a borderline living picking pockets at railway stations and country markets.

The General listened closely to each of them. It was as he had hoped. They could all use a windfall. The glasses were refilled and he started to talk.

At first, he said, when Jojo had come to him with the idea, he hadn't taken it too seriously. But for old times' sake, and out of curiosity, he had made a few calls, done some research – all very casual, all very discreet – and, little by little, he had started to believe that it could be done. It would take time, many months, but it could be done.

The faces round the table reflected cautious interest. Claude looked up from rolling a cigarette and asked the question they all wanted to ask. 'So? What is it?'

'A bank, my friend. A nice, rich little bank.'

'*Merde.*' Bachir shook his head. 'You're the one who always told us to stay away from guns.'

'No guns,' said the General. 'You won't even need that nail file of yours.'

'*Ah bon?* We just go in and tell them we're broke, is that it?'

'They won't be there. We'll have the bank to ourselves for six, maybe eight hours.'

The General leaned back, smiling. This was the part he always liked, when they were hooked and waiting. He took a drink, and wiped his moustache carefully with the back of his hand. 'Now,' he said, 'imagine that it is Saturday night in Isle-sur-Sorgue, the weekend of the *foire des antiquaires.*' He wagged a finger at the attentive faces. 'It happens next year to fall on the 14th of July – the town *en fête*, hundreds of antique dealers, their cash tucked up for the night in the

Caisse d'Épargne.' He paused for an instant. 'A shitload of *fric*, my friends. All for us.'

There was the carrot, out on the table. The men were quiet as the General told them how they could take it.

Some time before midnight on the Saturday, while the town was celebrating, they would slip into the river and up the drain tunnel. The July weather would be perfect for a quick paddle. Fernand would use his *plastique* to blow through the floor of the strong-room. Among the fireworks of the *fête*, nobody would think twice about another muffled thump. Blowing the strong-boxes was nothing, a few pops. And then they would have an entertaining night among the contents.

Fernand rubbed the scar on his cheek, the scar that still itched after all these years. 'What about the alarm system? *Normalement*, it would be linked to the *gendarmerie*.'

The General was enjoying himself, letting out the details one by one. '*Beh oui*.' He shrugged. 'It is. But they haven't wired the strong-room floor. Only the two doors. One leads into the bank, and the other out to the back, into a little park.'

The men smoked and thought about money, and the General cut himself a slice of pizza. Next to him, Jojo fidgeted with impatience. Getting into the bank was the part he knew about; getting out and getting away, that was the big problem.

'*Alors*,' the General went on, 'we have amused ourselves in the strong-room, cleaned out all the boxes. It is now Sunday morning, and there is the market. The town is packed, the cars are stuck like nuts in nougat. But, as agreeable as it is in the strong-room, we must leave.' The General eased his stomach away from the table, belched, and picked a shred of anchovy from his teeth with a matchstick.

'There are two little inconveniences.' He held up a stubby finger. 'The first is that some time between noon and one o'clock every Sunday there is a security check. I've watched it four Sundays in a row. Two cops, just routine, but they always come as the market is finishing, count the flower-pots on the bank steps and go home to lunch. Anyway, we

35

need to be out well before noon. And *évidemment*, we can't leave the way we came in. Even in July, it would look odd to see men coming out of the river waving bundles of 500-franc notes.' He paused for a drink. 'No, the way out is through the back, into the park.'

Jojo's glass stopped half-way to his mouth. 'Through the door?'

'Of course through the door.' The General raised two fingers. '*Voilà le deuxième problème*. Because, as we know, the door is wired.'

'And the alarm will go off,' Bachir said. 'And we'll be back in the *pissoir* for ten years. No thanks.'

The General smiled. 'You haven't changed, *mon vieux*. Still the happy optimist. But you're forgetting something. We have time to get away. Not much, two or three minutes – maybe more if the traffic's as bad as it usually is on market day.'

Claude's moon face crumpled with the effort of thought. 'But if the traffic's that bad . . .'

'It will be bad,' said the General, 'bad for a car. But we won't be using a car. Who wants some pizza? It's good.'

Jean the pickpocket made his longest speech of the morning. '*Merde* to the pizza. How do we get away?'

'Simple. By *vélo*.' The General brought up his left hand and smacked it with his right. 'In two minutes we'll be through the traffic and out of town while the cops are still sitting on their *klaxons*.' He gave his moustache a satisfied tug. 'It works.'

He held up his hands to stop the babble of questions, and did some more explaining. Each of them would take into the strong-room their *tenues de vélo* – the shoes and shorts and caps and brightly coloured, multi-pocketed jerseys that all serious cyclists wear. Their pockets would be bulging, but a cyclist's pockets are often bulging. Who would suspect that the bulges were banknotes? Who would even bother to look? With thousands of cyclists out on the road every Sunday, they would be anonymous. They would disappear. It was the perfect disguise, one of the most common sights of summer. And it was fast.

36

'*Mais attention.*' The General wagged a warning finger. 'There is one detail: you must be *en forme* – fit enough to ride twenty or thirty kilometres at top speed without puking over the handlebars. But that's nothing, just training.' He waved a hand airily. 'We have months for that. A hundred kilometres every Sunday and you'll be ready for the Tour de France.'

The *pastis* was finished, and the General went behind the bar for another bottle while the men round the table looked at each other, then started to talk. He'd let them chew it over, commit themselves before he suggested the split he'd worked out.

'General?' One of the Borel brothers was grinning. 'When was the last time you did a hundred kilometres?'

'The other day. The way I always do, in a car. God made some arses for saddles, but not mine. Let me ask you a question.' The General unscrewed the cap and pushed the bottle across the table. 'When was the last time you had some money in your pocket? Some real money?'

'A shitload of *fric*,' said Jojo.

Borel said nothing. The General reached over and patted his cheek.

'Drink up,' he said. 'One day it'll be champagne.'

5

Simon left the hotel early to do battle with the Parisian rush-hour traffic, the kamikaze pilots in their Renault 5s, wired on caffeine and determined to assert French superiority over anyone foolish enough to be driving a car with foreign plates. He had chosen the most relaxed of his three cars for the trip, the Congo-black Porsche convertible with a top speed of 160. It was, as he knew, a ridiculous machine to have in London, where it rarely got out of second gear, an advertising man's toy. But out on the *autoroute* he could let it go, and with luck and a heavy foot on the accelerator he should be down in the south in six hours.

The cars gave way to trucks as he cleared Paris and left the jam of the *périphérique* behind him, and he nudged the speed up to 120. The phone, which in London would be almost continuously beeping to announce news of a client crisis or a changed meeting, was silent. He pressed the call button to see if he could reach Liz. NO SERVICE. There was nothing to do except drive and think.

Unattached, healthy and paper-rich with agency shares, he was in a position that many people would envy. As long as the business prospered he would never be short of a few hundred thousand pounds, despite Caroline's unlimited enthusiasm for spending money. He remembered the time when her American Express card had been stolen. He hadn't reported the loss for weeks; the thief had been spending less than she normally did. Although she was going to be a continuing source of trouble and expense, she could always be paid off.

His business life was less straightforward. The challenge of building an agency was over. It was built, and now it had to be maintained and fed constantly with new clients. A £5,000,000 account, which in the early days would have been the excuse for euphoric celebration, was now just another bone to toss to the City. The excitement had gone, to be replaced by well-rewarded drudgery.

And then there was New York, and Ziegler. When Simon had been forced to follow the Saatchis and Lowe into America, he had done a share-swap deal with Global Resources, one of the most aggressive of the advertising conglomerates, run by one of the most unpleasant of men. Nobody admitted to liking Ziegler. But nobody could deny that he was effective. He seemed to be able to bully clients into the agency, to overpower them with promises of more sales and bigger profits. Simon had seen him in operation dozens of times, brutal to his subordinates and almost manic in his pursuit of clients. Fear was the club he used within the agency, overpaying and then terrorizing his staff. Fear of a different kind – the fear of losing market share – was always the basis of his presentations. He could deliver a sixty-minute tirade on his favourite topic, 'Selling is war, and those bastards are out to get you', which was usually successful in making even the most sophisticated clients look nervously over their shoulders before increasing their budgets.

Simon's relationship with Ziegler had been described (not within either man's hearing, of course) as two dogs sharing a kennel that was too small. Each was jealous of his own territory. Each wanted the whole kennel – which in this case was the world – to himself. Their mutual dislike was camouflaged with the corporate politeness that fools nobody, carefully phrased memos bristling with needles and a stilted camaraderie whenever they were on public view together. The moment wasn't right yet for a decisive fight, but it would come. Simon knew it, and the thought of it, which once would have stimulated him, just made him weary.

Like many advertising men, he thought often and vaguely about leaving the business. But to do what? He had no desire to go into politics or to become a gentleman farmer or to jump over the fence and become a client, running a company that made beer or soap powder. Besides, what else paid like advertising? He might be in a rut, but it was a rut of considerable luxury, hard to give up without an over-whelmingly attractive alternative. And so he dealt with these moments of discontent as many of his colleagues dealt with them, by finding a new distraction – a faster car, a bigger house, another expensive hobby. Living well is not only the best revenge, but the easiest.

He had reached the long, rolling hills of the Burgundy countryside, and thought about stopping at Chagny to have lunch at Lameloise. Dangerous. He stopped instead at a service station, had a cup of bitter coffee and looked at the map. He could be in Avignon by mid-afternoon, sitting in the shade of a plane tree with a *pastis*, the back of the journey broken. He filled up the Porsche and continued south.

As the names flicked by – Vonnas, Vienne, Valence – the light became brighter and the sky seemed to expand, blue and endless, the countryside harsher with rock and stunted scrub oak. In the vineyards cut out of the hills, small, scattered groups of figures, their backs bent under the sun, were gathering the first grapes of the harvest. This was Côtes du Rhône country, producing solid wine for people with outdoor thirsts and appetites. Simon looked forward to his first bottle.

The sign for Avignon came up and flashed by while he was trying to decide whether to go down to the coast as he'd planned or to take Murat's advice. *Prochaine sortie Cavaillon.* Why not? He could always move on tomorrow if he didn't like it.

He turned off at the Cavaillon exit and crossed the bridge over the Durance, more of a trickle than a river after the summer drought. As he came into town, he saw the café tables under the trees, brown faces, cool golden glasses of beer. He parked the Porsche, eased his back, and went through the minor acrobatics necessary to get out. After the tinted glass and the air-conditioning of the car, the glare and the heat came like a sudden shock. He felt the sun hit his head with a force that made him wince. In Paris, it had been autumn; here it was still like August.

He could have closed his eyes and known from the smell

of the café that he was in France – black tobacco, strong coffee, and the sharp tang of aniseed from the glasses of *pastis* on the bar. The men playing cards at the table, most of them in sleeveless vests and faded, shapeless caps, looked up at him through the smoke of their cigarettes, and he was aware of his clean, out-of-place clothes.

'*Bière, s'il vous plaît.*'

'*Bouteille ou pressiong?*' The barman's voice was throaty, his accent thick. It sounded like French, but not the French of Paris, or even the coast..It twanged.

Simon took his Kronenbourg and sat by the window. Every other vehicle passing by seemed to be a huge truck, grunting and hissing its way through the traffic, loaded with the fruit and vegetables that Provence grew in such abundance. Simon listened to the voices around him, and wondered how his French was going to cope with the swirling verbal syrup. He realized that, for the first time in years, nobody knew exactly where he was. He himself didn't know where he was going to be spending the night, and it pleased him to think that he was just another anonymous stranger.

A boy came into the café selling newspapers, and Simon bought a copy of *Le Provençal*. The main story on the front page was a *boules* tournament, and the rest of the paper was filled with news of the local villages – a *fête* in Lourmarin, a wine-tasting in Rognes, more *boules* tournaments. Despite its modern layout and excitable headlines, it had an old-fashioned, almost sleepy air about it after the British press.

Simon finished his beer. Where had Murat told him to head for? Apt? He left the coolness of the café, watched again by the card-players, and went back to the Porsche. It was being inspected by three boys, and he saw one of them stroke the fat curve of the wheel arch tentatively, as if the car might bite. The boys stepped back as they saw Simon, and watched him open the door.

'*Ça gaze, monsieur?*' The bravest boy craned his head to look inside the cockpit.

'*Oui.*' Simon pointed to the speedometer. '*Deux cent quarante. Même plus.*'

41

The little boy shook his hand as though he'd burnt his fingers. '*Ça boum, alors.*'

As Simon drove off, all of them shook their hands at him, three brown grinning monkeys. He eased into the traffic and followed the road under the railway bridge towards Apt. On his right, behind the forest of placards that sprout on the fringes of most provincial French towns, he could see a low, grey-green shape that rose away into the distance, the lower slopes of the Lubéron mountains. He turned off the air-conditioning and pulled over to take the top down. It was four-thirty, the sun warm on his shoulders, the breeze in his hair. He'd have dinner on a quiet terrace somewhere. Life was getting better.

He turned off the N100 road to escape from local Grand Prix drivers determined to overtake a Porsche, and followed a narrow road that twisted up into the hills. Far above him, he could see the bleached stone and old tiled roofs of a village, and he dropped down a gear to accelerate. Maybe there would be a little *auberge* with a fat cook and a terrace overlooking the mountains.

As he rounded a blind, steep bend, he had to stamp on the brake to avoid running into the tractor that was taking up the centre of the road. The tractor's driver looked down at Simon, his brick-red face impassive beneath his cap. He jerked his thumb at the large container he was towing, filled with a pile of purple grapes. He shrugged his heavy shoulders. He wasn't going to reverse.

Simon backed off the road into a field, and heard something grate under the back of the car, a noise that any Porsche owner knows and dreads, an expensive noise. Shit. The tractor driver raised his hand and drove off while Simon was getting out of the car.

He looked at the remains of his exhaust pipe, mangled and hanging by a strut, jammed against a rock half-concealed in the grass. He continued up the hill gingerly, in bottom gear, the dangling exhaust scraping noisily against the road.

The village of Brassière-les-Deux-Églises (winter population 702, summer population approximately 2000) is balanced precariously on the crest of a foothill below the southern slope of Mont Ventoux. It has two churches, one café, a butcher, a baker, a *mairie* that is open for two hours on Tuesday afternoons, an *épicerie*, a two-pump Citroën garage and a magnificent view of the Lubéron to the south. Apart from plans (which have been under discussion for four years) to install a public WC, there is no provision for the tourist trade. The regular summer visitors have their own highly restored houses in the village, but these stay shuttered and empty for ten months of the year.

The Porsche limped up to the garage and stopped. Simon could hear the sound of a radio coming from the small workshop. He stepped over a large greasy Alsatian sleeping in the sun and looked into the dark shambles of Garage Duclos. The proprietor's oily canvas boots were visible, tapping together in time to the music from the radio. The rest of him was under a Citroën van. Simon knocked on the van's door, and Duclos rolled into view on a low trolley.

He lay there, looking up, a spanner in one blackened hand, a rag in the other. '*Oui?*'

'*Monsieur, bonjour. J'ai un petit problème.*'

'*Comme tout le monde.*' Duclos sat up and wiped his hands. '*Alors, qu'est-ce que c'est?*'

'*Ma voiture . . .*'

Duclos levered himself off his trolley and took out a packet of Bastos as they went out to the Porsche. Simon realized that his vocabulary didn't include exhaust pipes, so he crouched down and pointed. Duclos crouched beside him, dragging on his cigarette. The dog got up and joined them, pushing his way between them to sniff the back wheel of the Porsche thoughtfully before lifting his leg against it.

'Filou! *Va t'en!*' Duclos cuffed the dog away and bent forward for a closer look at the hanging, bent pipe. '*Putain.*' He reached out and tapped the twisted metal, and shook his head. '*Il faut le remplacer.*' Another reflective drag on his cigarette. '*Beh oui. C'est foutu.*'

But, as he explained to Simon, a spare part for such a car – a German car, not at all common in these parts – would take time. A new exhaust assembly would have to be ordered from Avignon, maybe even from Paris. Two days, three days. And then there was the fitting. Could Monsieur come back at the end of the week? By then, *normalement*, it would be done.

Simon's first reaction was to make a phone call. All problems in life could be solved with a phone call. But whom could he call, and what good would it do? It was late afternoon, and the village didn't look the kind of place to have a resident taxi. He was stranded. Duclos looked at him and shrugged. Simon smiled at him and shrugged back. He was, after all, on holiday.

He took his bags from the Porsche and walked up to the tiny village square. Four sun-wizened old men were playing *boules* in front of the café – *Le Sporting*, it said in washed-out blue letters above the door – and Simon dumped his bags by a tin table and went into the bar.

It was empty except for the flies buzzing over the dented ice-cream cabinet in one corner. Plastic-topped tables and an assortment of old chairs were arranged haphazardly around the room, and behind the long zinc bar a fly curtain made from what looked like dead caterpillars hung in a doorway, turning slowly in the warm, quiet air. Well, Simon thought, it's not the Ritz. He strolled over to the wide plate-glass window at the end of the room and whistled softly at the view.

It was full south, overlooking a long flat plain that ended at the foot of the Lubéron, perhaps five miles away. The evening sunlight, slanting in from the west, made shadows of deep black in the folds of the mountain, contrasting with the lighter haze, somewhere between purple and grey, of the rock face, and the green of pine and oak trees. Down on the plain, the orderly lines of vines were broken up by scattered farm buildings that might have been painted on to the landscape, flat and sharp and glowing. A toy tractor, bright yellow, moved silently along the black ribbon of road. Everything else was motionless.

'*Monsieur?*'

Simon looked round and saw a girl behind the bar. He ordered a *pastis*, and smiled at the memory of what Murat had said; here she was, just as he'd described her – the ripe young Provençale with the dark eyes and olive skin. She reached up to fill his glass from one of the bottles fixed behind the bar, and Simon watched the flicker of muscles on her bare arms. Murat would have been over the bar with a rose between his teeth by now.

'*Merci, mademoiselle.*' Simon topped up his glass with water and went outside. It was curious how much he enjoyed *pastis* in the heat of southern France, and how he never drank it anywhere else. He remembered ordering it once in the Connaught, and it hadn't tasted the same at all. But here it was perfect – sweet and sharp and heady. He took a mouthful and thought about the unusual position he found himself in.

He had no car, no hotel reservation – and, from the look of the village, no hotel – no Liz, no Ernest. He was on his own, cut off from the human support system that normally took care of the daily details of his life. But, rather to his surprise, he found that he was enjoying the novelty of it all. Alone in a foreign wilderness, with nothing between him and starvation except a wallet stuffed to bursting with 500-franc notes. It was hardly a major catastrophe. In any case, it was impossible to feel depressed here, watching the old men laugh and argue over their *boules*.

The girl came out of the café and saw his empty glass. She came over to the table, walking in the loose, indolent way of people who live in the sun.

'*Un autre?*'

'*Merci.*' She smiled at him, and he watched her walk away, hips rolling lazily under her short cotton skirt, her down-at-heel espadrilles slapping softly against her feet. Simon wondered what she'd look like in twenty years' time, if the peach would turn into a prune.

When she came back, he asked her if there was anywhere nearby he could stay for the night.

She made the classic French grimace, eyebrows up, lips pushed forward and turned down. '*Beh non.*' There was the *gîte* of Madame Dufour, but that was closed now until Easter. Or there were hotels in Gordes. She waved a brown arm over towards the west, as though Gordes were on the very rim of civilization, a thousand miles away.

The problem, said Simon, was that he had no way of getting to Gordes.

'*Ah bon.*' The girl thought for a moment, biting her lower lip with small white teeth. '*Attends. Je vais chercher Maman.*'

Simon heard the girl calling her mother, and then a loud, rapid exchange that he couldn't follow. Maman appeared, a vast billow of a woman in a floral dress and carpet slippers, the girl following behind.

Maman beamed at Simon, gold teeth glinting beneath the faint shadow of a moustache. '*Ah, ce pauvre monsieur.*' She lowered herself until she had engulfed the chair next to Simon and leaned towards him, emanating garlic and good-will. All was not lost, she said. Monsieur would not be obliged to pass the night under the tree in the village square. There was a room over the café, *pas grand' chose*, but clean. Monsieur could stay there, and since there was no restaurant in the village he could eat with them *en famille*. Three hundred francs, including the use of the family shower. *Voilà*. It was settled.

Simon took his bags and followed the girl up two flights of narrow stairs, trying unsuccessfully not to be mesmerized by the hips swaying a few inches from his face. Close your eyes and think of Mum's moustache. They reached a tiny landing, and the girl opened a door and led him into a room that was very little bigger, an attic with a low, steeply pitched ceiling, twilight-dark and as hot as an oven. '*Ça chauffe, eh?*' The girl opened the window and then the shutters, letting in the view that Simon had admired earlier. He looked at the room – a single bed, a bare bulb hanging above it, worn linoleum on the floor. It reminded him of the junior dormitory when he had been at boarding school. Except for the view.

'*Formidable,*' he said. He put down his bags and stretched.

'*C'est pas un grand lit, mais vous êtes seul.*' The girl smiled.

'*Malheureusement, oui.*' Simon found himself shrugging, the contagious tic of France.

The girl became businesslike. Dinner was in an hour, in

the kitchen. The bathroom was on the floor below, through the blue door. If there was anything else Monsieur needed, she and Maman would be downstairs.

Simon thought about the phone, and decided not to bother until tomorrow. He unpacked, and went to look for the blue door and a shower.

The plumbing arrangements of the French, a nation of great ingenuity and style, often come as a shock to foreigners who are used to concealed pipes, discreetly muted lavatory flushes and firmly anchored taps, and Simon spent a few minutes working out how the flimsy but complicated arrangement of pipes and nozzles worked. He finally succeeded in showering by sections with a hand-held rubber contraption that alternated between scalding and freezing water, to the accompaniment of gurgling echoes from the pipes. A sign on the back of the bathroom door, stolen from a hotel on Lake Annecy, caught his eye as he was leaving the bathroom: *The Management welcomes dogs. They do not clean their shoes on the curtains, or make pipi in the bidet. We ask our amiable clientele to follow their example.*

He went downstairs, and followed the sound of conversation coming from the kitchen. A long table, covered in checked oilcloth, was set for four, with litre bottles of wine and water, a giant *baguette*, a basin-sized plastic bowl filled with salad and, at one end, a television with the sound turned down. Maman and the girl were rubbing steaks with olive oil and cloves of garlic, and washing his hands at the sink was the man with the brick-red face Simon had last seen driving a tractor. Papa.

He turned from the sink, his hands still wet, and offered Simon his elbow to shake.

'Bonetto.'

'Shaw. Simon Shaw.'

'*Bieng. Un verre?*'

He filled two thick glass tumblers with wine, and motioned Simon to sit down at the table. Maman put a dish of sliced sausage and *cornichons* between them, and Simon's first long and exhausting experience of Provençal hospitality began.

47

Sausage was followed by pizza, then by steak and roast peppers, salad, cheese, a home-made *tarte au citron*. Three litres of the young, fruity red wine, the wine from Bonetto's own vines. And in between mouthfuls, a lecture in that accent – part French, part soup, with bellows of laughter from Maman and giggles from the girl at Simon's desperate attempts to follow the rumbles and twangs of Bonetto's increasingly rapid speech.

Some glimmers of comprehension came like flashes in the fog: Bonetto was not only the owner of the café and several *hectares* of vines, but also the Mayor of Brassière, a socialist, a hunter, a true *paysan du coin*. He had never been further from the village than Marseille, a hundred kilometres away, and then he'd taken his gun, as it was well known that Marseille was inhabited entirely by criminals. In Brassière, he said proudly, there was no crime.

Simon nodded and smiled and said '*Ah bon*' whenever it seemed appropriate. Drink and concentration were making him drowsy, and when Bonetto produced a bottle of *marc*, yellowy-white and viscous, he tried to refuse. But it was no good. A guest in the Bonetto house was not allowed to go to bed thirsty. And so, while the women cleared away and washed the dishes, the level in the bottle went down and Simon reached a state of comfortable numbness where it didn't seem to matter whether they understood each other or not. He was finally allowed upstairs, with a parting slap on the back from Bonetto that almost knocked him over, and slept like a stone.

It was strange to be woken by the sun on his face, and for a few seconds Simon wasn't sure where he was. He looked out of the window. The plain was white with morning mist under a spotless blue sky, and to his surprise he didn't have a hangover.

He declined Maman's offer of a sausage sandwich for breakfast, and took his bowl of coffee outside. It was not yet hot, and the air – the purest air in France, so Bonetto had said, as though it were something that he personally had arranged – smelt fresh. In the village square, two women had put down their shopping baskets to leave both hands free for conversation, and a dog came out of an alley looking guilty, the remains of a *baguette* in its mouth. Simon decided to explore before going down to the garage. There would be time enough to call the office later on.

He walked down the widest street leading off the square, past the *épicerie* on the corner and the narrow house that served as the *mairie*, and stopped in front of a gutted building. No windows, no shutters, no doors. A weather-stained notice, propped against the wall, said *L'ancienne gendarmerie*, and listed names and permit numbers and an announcement that the dossier could be inspected on request. Simon looked through the arched stone doorway and saw the Lubéron, framed like a picture in an opening on the far side of the building. He stepped over a pile of rubble into a high, long space littered with old beams, sacks of plaster, empty beer bottles and piles of flagstones. Worms of electrical wiring twisted from the walls, and a cement-mixer stood next to a waist-high drum of dusty water in one corner, at the end of a wide flight of stone steps. Openings had been made at regular intervals along the length of one wall, and the sun poured through to light the room with an intense halogen glow.

He walked over to look through one of the openings. Below him, the land fell away in steep terraces. He could see steps leading down to the deep rectangular hole of a raw swimming pool, still at the concrete and bare pipe stage, and beyond that the view. Simon thought he'd never seen a more spectacular setting for a swim, and felt a moment of envy for the owner. But what was it going to be? The place was enormous, far too big for a house. He took one last look at the mountains, now turning a faded purple as the sun rose higher, and left to check on the progress of the injured Porsche.

He found Duclos performing the jerky aerobics that accompany any heated conversation in Provence – shoulders twitching, arms waving, hands waggling in emphasis, eyebrows threatening to disappear upwards into his cap. The woman he was talking to seemed unimpressed. She sniffed in disbelief at the piece of paper she was holding, and Simon heard her cut across Duclos' protestations of diligent labour and honest charges. '*Non, non et non. C'est pas possible. C'est trop.*'

'*Mais madame . . .*' Duclos noticed Simon standing by the pumps, and took the opportunity to escape. '*Ah, monsieur, j'arrive, j'arrive. Excusez-moi, madame.*'

Madame lit a cigarette and puffed angrily, pacing across the forecourt. From the look of her, Simon thought, she was not a native of the village. Blonde and slim, in her mid-thirties, she might have been an elegant refugee from the Armani boutique in the Place Vendôme -- but country Armani, with a casual shirt of heavy silk, pale gaberdine trousers, soft leather shoes and bag. Not the kind of woman one would expect to see haggling over a garage bill of a few hundred francs.

Duclos and Simon went over to the Porsche, and the woman stopped her pacing to watch them. As her clothes suggested, she was originally from Paris and, until the new girlfriend of her ex-husband had started dipping into the alimony, comfortably off. But now, now that the cheques arrived erratically or not at all, there were problems. Nicole Bouvier spent her life either feeling the pinch or anticipating it. How she was going to keep her house in Brassière and her tiny apartment in the Place des Vosges was becoming an increasingly difficult exercise in stretching money, and it wasn't helped by a *garageiste* who padded his bills so shamelessly. She thought of driving off and paying him next time, but curiosity prevented her. Porsches were rare in Brassière, and the owner was not an unattractive man; a little rumpled, certainly, and he hadn't shaved, but he had an interesting face. She moved closer to the two men so she could hear what they were saying.

It was as Duclos had thought. He had telephoned – he held his oily left hand, thumb and little finger cocked, to his ear – to order the new exhaust assembly. *Malheureusement*, it would not arrive for at least three days, possibly a week. But that is always how it is with exotic cars. Had Monsieur been driving a more reasonable car, a French car, this unfortunate matter could have arranged itself within twenty-four hours.

Simon thought for a few moments. Was it possible that Duclos could rent him a car?

A deeply apologetic shrug, and a clicking of the tongue against the teeth. '*Beh non. Il faut aller à Cavaillon.*'

A taxi?

Duclos rubbed his forehead with the back of his wrist, leaving a skid-mark of oil on his skin. There was always Pierrot, with his ambulance, but he'd be out in the vines. '*Non.*'

Madame Bouvier looked at Simon, his hands thrust in his trouser-pockets, biting his lip thoughtfully. A pleasant face, she thought, and perhaps a pleasant man. She took pity on him.

'*Monsieur?*' Simon turned to look at her. '*Je peux vous amener à Cavaillon. C'est pas loin.*'

'*Mais, madame, c'est . . .*'

'*C'est rien.*' She walked to her car. '*Allons-y.*'

Before Simon could argue or Duclos could return to the dispute over her bill, Madame Bouvier got into her car and leaned across to open the passenger door, exposing a hint of perfectly tanned cleavage beneath her silk shirt. Simon's hasty farewell and Duclos' reply hung in the air as the car accelerated away.

How kind people were down here, Simon thought, as he turned to his rescuer. '*Madame, c'est vraiment très gentil.*'

She changed gear with a jerk as she drove down the hill, and changed languages. 'You're English, *non*? The plates on your car.'

'That's right.'

'I was in England three years, in London, close to 'Arrods.' She spoke with a pronounced accent, and Simon hoped his French had the same charm as her English.

'I have an office there, in Knightsbridge.'

'*Ah bon*? And where do you stay in Provence?'

'The penthouse suite in the café in Brassière.'

Madame Bouvier took both hands off the wheel in dramatic astonishment, and the car veered towards the ditch. '*Mais c'est pas vrai*! You cannot continue there.'

Simon clutched at the dashboard as Madame Bouvier

resumed control of the car and took up her position in the middle of the road. 'I thought I'd find somewhere else this afternoon,' he said, 'after I've picked up a car.'

'*Bon*.' She tapped her fingers on the wheel, and then accelerated decisively. 'I know a little place – the Domaine de l'Enclos, just above Gordes. Very *tranquille*, and the restaurant is good. I take you there, and then we go to Cavaillon.'

Simon looked away from the road, which seemed to become narrower as the car's speed increased, and turned towards Madame Bouvier's fine-boned profile under the mane of blonde hair. He could hardly have hoped for a better-looking chauffeur.

'Look, I'm already taking up too much of your time. But if you're not too busy, let me buy you lunch. If it weren't for you, I'd be waiting for Duclos' friend to pick me up in his ambulance.'

'*Ouf*. That little robber. The most expensive garage in Provence. They all smile here, you know, and then you find their hand in your pocket. Not everyone is honest.'

'Not everyone is honest anywhere. But at least they smile here.'

Madame Bouvier slowed down as they came to a crossroads. GORDES 4 kilometres. She turned right, on to a wider tarmac road, and looked at the wafer of gold on her wrist. 'I would like lunch. Thank you.'

They drove up the hill towards Gordes and turned left just before the village, on the road that was signposted to the Abbaye de Sénanque. There were signposts everywhere here, and the village looked as if it were posing for a postcard – beautiful, but almost too perfect. Simon preferred the less manicured appearance of Brassière-les-Deux-Églises.

They drove through the gate in the high drystone wall that protected the Domaine de l'Enclos from the rest of the world, and Simon suddenly felt scruffy. This was not quite the simple little country hotel he'd expected; the grounds were immaculate, the trees carefully barbered, the small stone cottages widely separated from each other and the main building of the hotel. He could have been in Bel Air instead of rural France.

Madame Bouvier pulled into the shaded parking area and found a space between a Mercedes with Swiss plates and a British-registered Jaguar. '*Voilà*. I think you will be more comfortable here than the café.'

'I'm amazed a place like this exists.' They walked down through the trees to the hotel entrance. 'Does it do well? Where do they find the customers?'

'You'd be surprised. People come from the north, from all over Europe, sometimes from America. And the season is long, from Easter to Christmas. Next time you must bring your helicopter.' She pointed through a gap in the trees. 'There's a *piste* over there.'

Next time, Simon thought, I should shave before I come, and bring a token suitcase. This was a hell of a way to arrive at a smart hotel.

But the girl at the desk smiled and said yes, there was a cottage he could have for a week and yes, there was a table on the terrace for lunch.

Simon relaxed, and began to feel hungry. 'A good hotel always gives you the benefit of the doubt,' he said.

Madame Bouvier frowned. 'Doubt? What do you mean?'

'Well, look at me.' He rubbed his chin. 'No shave, no luggage, arriving with you . . .'

'What would they do in England?'

'Oh, look down their noses, probably make me wear a jacket and tie, generally make me feel uncomfortable.'

Madame Bouvier gave a little snort of disapproval. 'Here is not so formal. Nobody wears a tie.' She looked at Simon and smiled. 'But sometimes they shave. Come.' She led the way out on to the terrace.

As they ate, overlooking the long view south towards the Lubéron, the formalities dropped away. By the main course they were Nicole and Simon, and with the arrival of the second bottle of crisp pink wine they began to compare divorces. Simon found her easy and amusing company, and when he lit her cigarette and she touched his hand, he felt a brief twinge of lust. That would have to stop; he was still paying for the last twinge. He ordered coffee and moved the conversation to safe ground.

53

'That place in Brassière, the big place they're restoring. What's that going to be?'

Nicole dipped a sugar-lump in her coffee and bit into it. 'The old *gendarmerie*? It was empty since five years, when they built a new *gendarmerie* down on the N100. Brassière is not a criminal place, except for that little *voleur* in the garage.' She took a sip of her coffee. 'Anyway, there was a man from Avignon, a building entrepreneur, who bought the *gendarmerie* for a handful of *poussière* . . .'

'*Poussière*?'

'Dust. Nothing. I think less than a million francs, and it is a big *barraque*, two levels – and *en plus* you have the cells underneath. *Bon*. So he buys also some land at the back, and he has the plan to make apartments with a pool and of course the view.'

'It's a good idea. When's it going to be finished?'

Nicole shook her head. 'Never. It ate his money. It's always like this with the old buildings, the little *inconnus* that you cannot imagine. You break a wall and *plok!* the ceiling falls down.' She took out another cigarette and leaned forward to the match Simon held for her. Another button of her shirt had somehow come undone.

'*Merci*.' She sat back and tilted her head up to blow smoke into the air, and Simon found himself staring at her neck, slender and smooth. He busied himself with a cigar as Nicole continued. 'So more money is borrowed, and then more. And he needs to have on a new roof. And the *piscine* costs double because there is no access by truck, and all the cement, all the stones, everything must be carried down by hand. *Bref*, he runs out of money.' She pulled a finger across her throat. 'He goes bankrupt. It happens often here – people are too much optimists, and they believe the *maçon* when he tells them a price. And once the work is started . . .' Nicole made climbing motions in the air with two fingers, and shrugged.

'It's the same in England,' Simon said. He remembered the bills for the house in Kensington, bills that had made his eyes water. 'And decorators are even worse.'

Nicole laughed. 'When I was in London, I had a little

garden, no bigger than a bed. I wanted to make it grass – you know, *la pelouse anglaise* – so I look in the dictionary and find turf. *Bon*. Then I go to a little shop in Chelsea, full of men, and I ask for six metres of turf, and they look at me like I am a crazy woman.'

'Why?'

'I was in the shop of a turf accountant.' She laughed again, and made a face at her own ignorance. One of the pleasures of life, Simon thought, is the way women become progressively prettier and more amusing the longer lunch lasts.

Nicole dropped him in Cavaillon, and he drove slowly back to Brassière in his rented car, collected his bags and returned to the hotel. He walked round the grounds, putting off the duty call to London. He'd been out of touch for two days, and he'd enjoyed every second of it. Back in his cottage, he looked at the phone, squat, plastic, accusing. He picked it up and pressed the digits that would connect him to reality.

'Where are you?' Liz sounded like a worried mother. 'We've been calling the Byblos all the time, then we tried Mr Murat in Paris but . . .'

'What did he say?'

'Oh, he was awful. He said you'd run off with a girl from the Crazy Horse. He seemed to think it was very funny. Are you all right?'

'I'm fine. I just changed my mind on the way down, and then I had a shunt with the car – nothing serious, but I've been sorting that out. Anyway, I'll be here in Gordes until it's repaired.'

He gave Liz the number of the hotel, and heard her talking to someone in the office.

'Liz?'

'Just a minute. Ernest wants to speak to you. But don't go away. There's an urgent message from Mr Ziegler.'

'Hello, hello, wherever you are,' said Ernest. 'I can't tell you what a fuss there's been – panic stations, man overboard, Liz turning grey overnight, we seek him here, we seek him there . . .'

'I've only been gone two days.'

'That's what I said. Give the poor man a chance to unpack his toothbrush, I said, but you know what they're like, can't leave you alone for five minutes. Now, would you like a bit of good news?'

'Always.'

'The musician who came to see the house – dreadful little person, absolutely *swathed* in leather – well, he's made a very good offer as long as he can move in next month.'

'He can move in tomorrow if his cheque doesn't bounce. What's the offer?'

'A hundred thousand under the asking price.'

'Two point four million?'

'Including the bed. He adored the bed. I think he had visions of himself . . .'

'I can imagine. OK. Tell the agents to get on with it.'

'I'll do that now. I'd better pass you back to Liz. She's making faces at me. Have fun. Don't do anything I wouldn't do.'

'You're not going to like this, I'm afraid,' said Liz, 'but Mr Ziegler's asking you to come back to London at once. The President of Morgan's is coming through tomorrow on his way back to New York, and Mr Ziegler thinks . . .'

'I know what Mr Ziegler thinks,' said Simon. 'Mr Ziegler thinks that the Presidential hand should be held.'

'Exactly. I'm sorry, but he was rather agitated when he found out you were away.'

Simon looked out of the window. The sun was catching the top of a group of olive trees, turning the leaves silver-green. Behind them, the Lubéron was softened by the heat haze, and the sound of someone diving into the pool hung for a second in the still evening air.

'Liz, at the risk of giving Mr Ziegler a heart attack, I'm going to stay here.'

'Do you want me to tell him?'

Simon sighed. 'No, I'd better call him. Don't worry. I'll talk to you soon.'

He put the phone down and looked at his watch for the first time that day. Bloody Ziegler. He kicked off his shoes and called New York.

Ziegler's voice had a faint echo to it, and Simon could tell that he had switched his phone to the loudspeaker. He loved to pace up and down as he bellowed, a habit that Simon found intensely irritating.

'Bob, tell me something. Is your secretary with you?'

'Sure. She's right here. Why?'

'Are you still trying to screw her?'

'Jesus.' There was a pause, and then a click as Ziegler turned off the loudspeaker and picked up the handset. His voice sounded much closer. 'Is that your idea of a goddamn joke?'

'Now I can hear you better. What's the panic?'

'A thirty-million-dollar client is coming to London tomorrow, and you're goofing off in France. Is that what you call running a business?'

'I call it a holiday, Bob. Remember holidays?'

'Fuck holidays. You better pack your bags.'

'I'm not going anywhere. All he wants is dinner and a little stroking. Jordan can stroke him.'

'I don't believe what I'm hearing. Thirty million dollars, and you can't spare one day off from sitting on your butt. Jesus.'

'You know as well as I do that the business is solid. There's no need for a bloody circus every time a client stops off in London. I'm running an advertising agency, not an escort service.'

'Let me tell you something. You're not running shit from where you are.'

'I'm not going, Bob.'

'Then I am.'

The line went dead, and Simon felt a sense of satisfaction. For years, he had followed the advertising man's reflex to jump to attention whenever a client appeared, to go through the process that was so inaccurately described as 'entertaining'. There was nothing entertaining about it. It was hard graft with a knife and fork and a pretence of interest. With one or two exceptions, the men Simon spent most of his life with bored him. Some of them, the corporate bullies who used their advertising budgets like offensive weapons, he

57

despised. And they paid him. He was beginning to despise that too. Was he getting soft and tired, or was he growing up?

He had dinner alone on the terrace with the ten-mile view, and enjoyed the idea of Ziegler stuck in the traffic on the way to JFK. Concorde to London, hold the man's hand, Concorde back to New York. Another gallant victory for the agency–client relationship, another defeat for the digestion. Simon took his cigar and strolled back to his cottage. The air was still warm, the sky was clear and pricked with stars, the insistent, rustling chirrup of *cigales* came from the bushes. His last thought before falling asleep was looking forward to tomorrow.

The days were long, but passed too quickly. Simon explored the villages, drove up to the bare white crest of Mont Ventoux, walked through the ruins of the Marquis de Sade's château at Lacoste, dawdled in cafés. Every evening when he got back to the hotel there were messages from London, messages that seemed curiously unreal when he looked through them sitting barefoot on his terrace. The contrast between the peace of his surroundings and the reports of trivial events in the agency, exaggerated into crises, was something he thought about more and more. Living versus business.

It was time to be thinking about getting back. Duclos should have repaired the Porsche by now, although it was strange that he hadn't called. Simon decided to go to Brassière the next morning, and maybe have lunch with the perfectly tanned cleavage after he'd picked up the car. He found the number that Nicole had written on a book of matches.

'Nicole? It's Simon Shaw.'

'Ah, the disappearing Englishman. Where have you been?'

'I'm sorry. I meant to call, but . . .'

Nicole laughed. 'That's the Provençal disease . . . to do it *demain*. Maybe.'

'I wondered if I could take you to lunch tomorrow. The

garage has had the car for nearly a week. It should be ready.'

'A week here is nothing, Simon. But yes to lunch, *volontiers*.'

They arranged to meet at the café, and Simon spent a pleasant half-hour looking through the Gault Millau guide for a restaurant. He should have called Nicole before, but perhaps he needed to get London out of his system first. He caught himself shrugging again, and smiled.

He arrived in Brassière the next morning to find Duclos in the position he had first seen him in, under a car. It looked suspiciously like the same car. Simon said good morning to the oily boots, and the body slid out on its trolley.

'*Ah, monsieur. C'est vous.*'

Duclos had some good news. The spare parts would be arriving next week – *certain, garanti, pas de problème*. He had meant to call, but . . .

In London, Simon would have been furious, but here it didn't seem to matter. It was a glorious day. He was having lunch with a pretty woman. He could send Ernest down for the car when it was ready. He was surprised at his philosophical attitude, that he was beginning to shrug mentally as well as physically. He thanked Duclos, and walked up towards the café.

The sun made a divided tunnel of the street that led off the square, half blinding light, half deep shade, and Simon was drawn again to the old *gendarmerie*. He went up the stairs. The second storey looked even bigger than the ground floor, a huge space, cleared and ready for the next stage of building. If anything, the extra height made the view even better – the vines, now turning scarlet and brown, a pine-covered hill with stone buildings visible among the trees, flat backlit silhouettes against the sun, and, behind it all, the mountain. The air was so clear that Simon could see the outlines of the trees on the highest ridge, tiny but distinct. He heard laughter coming up from the terraces below him, and the sound of a tractor starting up. It was noon, the time when every good Provençal leaves the fields to go home to lunch.

Nicole was sitting at an outside table when Simon got back to the café. She offered both cheeks to be kissed, and he was aware of her scent, fresh and spicy.

'How does it go with your car? I hope you didn't pay what he asked.'

'He's still waiting for the spare parts. It doesn't matter. I'll send someone down from London to pick it up.'

Nicole rummaged in her bag for cigarettes. She was wearing a sleeveless linen dress the colour of putty that set off the even tan of her arms and bare legs. Simon regretted not having called her before.

'So,' she said, 'you have to go back?'

'That's what they tell me at the office.' Simon ordered drinks from the girl, who was studying Nicole's clothes with undisguised interest. She smiled at Simon, and swayed back into the café.

'Pretty girl,' said Simon.

'You've met the mother?' Nicole puffed out her cheeks and laughed.

'You're an evil, jealous woman. Just because you haven't got a moustache and can't drive a tractor.'

'Is that what you like?' Nicole looked at him through the smoke of her cigarette, and Simon felt the tug of attraction between them. No, he thought, what I like is opposite me.

'I love women with moustaches,' he said. 'I think it's the way they tickle.'

Nicole pulled a thick strand of hair across her face and held it under her nose. '*C'est bon*?'

Simon nodded. 'Fantastic. Can you eat like that?'

He had chosen a restaurant outside Gordes, a converted farmhouse with tables set out in the courtyard and a chef whom the Gault Millau guide described as one of the stars of the future. Their lunch was long and easy and they laughed often and drank a little too much wine. And then, over coffee, Nicole asked him how he felt about returning to London.

Simon watched the smoke of his cigar curl up into the leaves of the plane tree that shaded them from the sun, and wondered what he'd be doing at lunchtime tomorrow.

Perrier water, probably, and a client agonizing over his market share.

'I can't say I'm looking forward to it,' he said. 'The trouble is, I've seen it all before – the clients have the same old problems, the people I work with bore me . . .' He stopped, and blew on the tip of his cigar until it glowed under its blue-grey layer of ash. 'I suppose that's it; I'm bored. I used to love it, and now I don't.'

'But still you do it.'

'It's this character defect I have. I like the money.' With a rueful smile, he looked at his watch, and signalled for the bill. 'I'm sorry. I'd better get going.'

They sat in silence while he paid, and then he took a card from his wallet and passed it across the table. 'Here's my number in London. If you ever come over, let me know. Maybe we could have dinner.'

Nicole paused as she was putting on her sunglasses, leaving them perched on the end of her nose while she looked at him. 'I thought you always had dinner with clients.'

'You could be a new business prospect.' Her eyebrows went up, and Simon grinned. 'It's what you say in advertising when you're fishing.'

He drove back to the hotel to collect his bags, and Nicole went home. They were both quite sure they would meet again.

6

Simon suddenly hated London. The flat, despite Ernest's efforts with flowers and some paintings rescued from the house, was as cheerless and impersonal as a suite in a hotel. The long, dull prelude to the British winter had begun. The sky was a low grey ceiling, and people on the streets huddled against the drizzle and jousted with their umbrellas. There was not enough light. Provence was a bright, distant memory.

The first day back in the office did nothing to lift Simon's mood. Jordan had clearly loved his week as the lord of all he surveyed, and was reluctant to let go, drifting in and out of Simon's office to offer advice on what he called matters of state. He was particularly concerned over an incident that had taken place the previous Friday evening, which he reported to Simon in between slow and significant puffs of his cigarette.

David Fry, the agency's Creative Director and a source of constant irritation to Jordan because of his evident disdain for executives, had been seen in a fashionable restaurant behaving extremely badly.

'What was he doing?' Simon asked.

'Hog-whimpering drunk, for a start,' said Jordan. 'And then he apparently got out some cocaine and started powdering his nose at the table. Didn't even bother to go to the bog.' He pursed his lips in disapproval. 'Chum of mine who was there called me in Wiltshire on Saturday morning, so I got on to David straight away, asked him what the hell he thought he was doing. That sort of thing gets into *Private Eye*, upsets clients, gives the whole agency a bad name.'

Simon sighed. Jordan was right. 'What did David say?'

'I read him the riot act. Told him that directors of public companies couldn't go around behaving like oiks.' Jordan shot his cuffs vigorously, as if they were attempting to escape up the sleeves of his jacket.

'Well? What did he say?'

'Told me to piss off. I had half a mind to drive up and give him a hiding. Insufferable little shit.'

'I'll talk to him once we've got the presentation out of the way. How's it looking?'

'Usual panic in the Creative Department while they keep the whole agency waiting. I am unreliably informed by David's secretary that they'll be ready to show us the ideas tomorrow. They need a firmer hand, those people. No idea about sticking to deadlines.'

Simon sensed that this might be the start of a lecture on management techniques, and picked up a pile of documents. 'I'd better start catching up on all this,' he said. 'I'm supposed to have an intimate understanding of the contraceptive market by Thursday.'

Jordan smiled, exposing long, slightly yellow teeth. He's beginning to look like one of his bloody horses, Simon thought. 'Rather you than me, old boy. Always hated the wretched things. Like drinking claret through a straw.' He whinnied with laughter, and strolled back to his office.

The Condom Marketing Board, or the Rubber Barons, as they were unofficially known in the agency, had asked to see presentations for their £5,000,000 account. Simon knew that two other agencies were pitching, and he wanted the business. Although the billing wasn't enormous, it would be worth having for the creative opportunities it offered. Sex and social responsibility, a copywriter's dream assignment, could be the basis for some showy, noticeable work that would be in dramatic contrast to the package-goods advertising the agency produced for its major clients. And the City would be pleased to see another few million on the turnover. It would be, as Jordan had been heard to say, a rubber feather in the agency's cap.

Simon looked through the documents that would be incorporated into a single glossy volume for Thursday's presentation: Attitude Research, Marketing Statistics and Strategy, Creative Strategy, Media Plan – reams of figures and careful assumptions, the proof that the agency had done its homework. Simon had learned many years before that any advertising idea had to be sold within the framework of logical argument, and the more unusual the idea was, the more comprehensive the supporting material needed to be. Clients had long ago given up the dangerous habit of trusting their agency's creative judgement, and insisted on paper crutches to help them make their decisions. And the Condom Marketing Board, made up of a group of independent manufacturers, was likely to behave in classic committee fashion – dithering, backbiting, compromising and sitting as firmly as possible on the fence. Simon forced himself to concentrate.

The days leading up to the presentation passed in a series of skirmishes between the various departments of the agency. The research people accused the creative people of ignoring their findings. The creative people sulked, and complained about lack of time. The media people complained about lack of sufficient money for a national campaign. The executives complained about everybody else's unreasonable and childish behaviour. The agency bitched and snarled its way towards Thursday, working late and muttering about pressure and brutal hours. It was always the same, Simon thought. Give them three days or six months, it didn't matter. Panic was part of the game.

The Rubber Barons were late. The presentation had been set for two-thirty. The receptionist had hidden her copy of *Hello!* magazine, the charts in the conference room had been checked for the twentieth time, secretaries briefed to look busy, the dart-board taken down from the Art Department bull-pen, fresh rolls of paper installed in the conference room lavatory – the Shaw Group was ready, poised for another triumph, and the members of the presentation team gathered in Simon's office, trying to look relaxed and quietly confident.

And now it was nearly three. The bastards were late, and jittery speculation was rife. They'd been out to lunch with one of the other agencies. They'd given them the business, and been celebrating. Bastards. All that work for nothing. The least they could do was call. Probably too pissed, too busy getting stuck into the third bottle of port. Simon's office was thick with smoke and pessimism, and Liz wrinkled her nose as she put her head round the door.

'They're here. Seven of them. They brought one extra.'

Shit. There were only six in the agency team, and it would never do to be one man short, to leave a client dangling at the end of the conference table all on his own. Clients got very touchy about little things like that, felt they weren't getting enough respect.

Simon looked around. 'We need another body. Who'd be most useful?'

A young man in a dark suit – a Planner, solemn and safe – was suggested, elected and summoned while Simon went out to the reception area. It resembled a small convention of attaché case salesmen: seven black, leather-look cases, seven sober suits, seven earnest faces. Simon adopted his most welcoming manner as he identified the senior Rubber Baron and shook him by the hand.

'I'm so sorry to keep you. One of those interminable phone calls. How are you?'

'I think we should be making the apologies, Mr Shaw. One of those interminable lunches.' The Rubber Baron bared his teeth. His cheeks had a three-gin flush, and Simon wondered whether he'd last the course without falling asleep.

He shepherded the group down the corridor, past secretaries bowed diligently over their keyboards, and into the sombre luxury of the main conference room, windowless, thickly carpeted, silent except for the ruffle of air-conditioning. The agency team rose from their chairs around the large oval table as the herd of clients filed in. Names and titles were exchanged and promptly forgotten in a flurry of introductions, attaché cases snapped open in a brisk fusillade, notepads adjusted, orders taken for coffee and tea and mineral water. The senior Rubber Baron accepted a cigar, and Simon stood up to deliver the preliminary patter that he had delivered a thousand times before.

'Let me start by saying how delighted we are to have the opportunity to make this presentation.' The senior Rubber Baron studied his cigar while his colleagues avoided any chance of eye-contact by gazing intently at their blank notepads. 'I think you already know, from the material we've sent you, that the agency has a consistent record of producing highly visible and effective work across a broad range of products and services. I must say, however, that your business has a special interest for all of us.'

Simon paused, and smiled at seven impassive faces. 'After all,' he said, 'it's not often we get the chance to work on a product that is so close to every man's heart.'

Not a flicker from the impassive faces. This was going to be like digging a ditch with a teaspoon. The senior Rubber Baron seemed to be fascinated by the conference room ceiling, and the rest of them continued their communion with their notepads.

While Simon resumed his efforts to inject some enthusiasm into his recitation of the agency's specialized and perceptive methods of problem analysis, he was making an assessment of the degree of attention that was being paid to what he was saying. Years of experience had taught him to gauge the mood of his audience, and this one could have had anaesthetic for lunch. If they had to sit through an hour of research findings and media planning, they'd be so deeply tranquillized that someone would have to set fire to their trousers to wake them up. He decided to alter the pre-arranged order of the presentation.

'Normally,' he said, 'we'd take you through the research and the thinking that led us to our creative recommendations. But today we're not going to do that.' The Research Director, a man who relished his spot in the limelight on these occasions, looked up from his notes with a frown. Simon saw his mouth begin to open, and hurried on. 'Today, we're going to go straight into the campaign.' The Creative Director stopped doodling on his pad and sent agitated signals to Simon with his eyebrows.

'We're doing this for two reasons. First, so that you can see the campaign as the consumer will see it – no demographic breakdowns, no statistical analysis, no marketing forecasts. Just the advertising. And the second reason . . .' Simon directed a look of enthusiastic sincerity at the senior Rubber Baron, who inclined his head graciously '. . . well, the second reason is that we believe this is one of the most appropriate and exciting campaigns this agency has ever produced. And frankly, we can't wait to get your reaction to it.' Simon glanced round the table, and two or three heads rose briefly from their notepads. Thank God they hadn't dropped off yet.

'There'll be plenty of time for questions after you've seen the work, and of course we've summarized the presentation in a document for you to take away.' Simon tapped the pile of bulky, spiral-bound tomes on the table in front of him, and hoped that the Creative Director had had time to recover from his surprise. 'So now, I'd like to ask David Fry, our Creative Director, to show you what we believe to be an extraordinarily powerful idea. David?'

Bottoms were adjusted on chairs, and the attention of the meeting turned to focus on the slight figure in the baggy but clearly expensive suit at the other end of the conference table.

David Fry, a little too old to be wearing his hair in a ponytail, hunched his shoulders as he leaned forward, raising the upholstery in his jacket to just below ear level, his eyes bright with enthusiasm and the residual effects of an earlier hurried snort in the executive washroom. The product of an ordinary middle-class upbringing and a private education, he had spent many years trying to eradicate all traces of his comfortable background and cultivate what he liked to call 'street edge'. He had a fondness for vernacular that was often obsolete by the time he overheard it in the Groucho Club, but nevertheless he managed to give the impression that he was a deprived South London boy made good. His idols were the Cockney photographers and actors, and Nigel Kennedy was his main man in classical music.

He adjusted his round, wire-rimmed glasses and addressed the Rubber Barons. 'I've got to tell you,' he said, 'this wasn't an easy one. What you've got here is two problems.

You've got your product image – slot machines in toilets, packet of three for the weekend, that sort of thing – and then you've got the practical side. Product use.' He paused, and shrugged his suit. 'It's all systems go, and then it's hang about for a minute while you do the business. Know what I mean?'

Simon looked down the table. The Rubber Barons were keeping their eyes glued to their notepads.

Fry stood up and eased his thin shoulders under their pillows. 'But it's not all bad news, because we've got a couple of things going for us.' He picked up a chart from the table, and displayed it to his audience. The Rubber Barons started to pay attention. Charts they liked. Charts were serious.

'Now then,' said Fry, and pointed to the first item, printed in bright red block capitals: RECOMMENDED BY THE MEDICAL PROFESSION. 'Doctors love us, right?'

His finger moved to item two: SOCIALLY RESPONS-IBLE. 'What does that mean? It means that we're doing our bit to stop sixteen-year-olds getting in the club.

'And – very important nowadays – the health bit.' The third item read: PROTECTION AGAINST SEXU-ALLY TRANSMITTED DISEASES. 'We all know it's a nasty old world. Say no more on that one.'

He put down the chart, and the clients resumed their study of the notepads.

Fry went on, talking quickly, fidgeting inside his suit. 'That's all well and good, but it's not enough. And you know why?' Nobody volunteered an answer. Fry nodded, as though their reaction was exactly what he had anticipated. 'It's boring. B-o-r-i-n-g. It's safety, it's do what the doctor tells you, it's got about as much sex appeal as a laxative.' He paused for emphasis, and spread his words. 'A. Total. Turnoff.' He shook his head, and his ponytail wagged agreement with him. 'It's got nothing to do with what you should be selling. Nothing.'

There was a brief silence to allow the Rubber Barons a chance to reflect on this criticism of their contribution to society.

'What you should be selling,' said Fry, 'is the most popular commodity in the history of the world.'

Another silence. Simon could imagine the thoughts going through the collective client brain. Is this maniac suggesting that we re-equip our factories, cancel our latex orders, abandon our impressive quality-control systems, 99.9 per cent effective except for Friday afternoons?

'But don't panic. We're not suggesting you should change this.' Fry produced a foil-wrapped condom from his pocket and placed it, with suitable reverence, on the table. 'What we are suggesting is this: Change. The Way. You Sell It.'

The Rubber Barons gazed intently at the condom on the table, as if waiting for it to do something. Fry leaned forward and placed his hands either side of it. 'The most popular commodity in the history of the world,' he repeated. 'Know what it is? It's love! The irresistible desire to be irresistibly desired! The cosmic tickle! And this . . .' he picked up the condom, and gave it a fond nod of his head '. . . this is part of it.'

He mopped his nose with a silk handkerchief. Either the emotion of the moment or cocaine was causing a plumbing problem in his nasal passages.

'What we're going to do,' he went on, 'is to change the condom's positioning in terms of product usage. We're not going to rabbit on about health and safety and doctor's orders – all the kids know about that already, and they're not buying it. No, we're going to make the condom an integral, essential, very, very romantic – yes, *romantic* – part of the old warm-up.'

He noticed a puzzled expression on the face of one of the older clients.

'You know. Foreplay.'

'Ah,' said the client.

'And this, gentlemen, is how we're going to do it. But before I show you, try to imagine this scenario.' Fry lowered his voice. 'You're at the movies, right? By your side is a Very Tasty young lady you've had your eye on for weeks. Tonight's your big chance. You've got your arm round her, within striking distance of her Bristols. This. Could. Be. It.'

69

Simon glanced sideways at the senior Rubber Baron, and wondered when he'd last been in the circumstances which Fry was describing with such breathy excitement.

With a wave of his arm, Fry commanded the room lights to be dimmed. 'You're all set,' he said in the darkness, 'and then – wallop! – this comes on the screen.'

The projection screen, four times TV size, turned bright white, and Fry's silhouette, ponytail bobbing in anticipation, hovered at one side. There was a subdued hiss of static, and an image appeared on the screen – a young couple, apparently naked, artfully lit, copiously oiled, glistened together on a bed. From the speakers hidden in the walls around the room came a low thump of bass and the howl of a guitar. And then, as Fry's silhouette jerked in time to the beat and the oily couple slithered on the sheets, came a moan of youthful concupiscence.

'LET'S ... GET IT ON ... OOOOOOH, LET'S GET IT ON ...'

The young couple on the screen did their best, within the limits of media propriety, to simulate spontaneous passion. The director had been careful with his sliding pans and cuts, avoiding full exposure of the female bosom – nipples, in Fry's words, were a total no-no – or any hint, however shady, of pubic hair.

'... IF THE SPIRIT MOVES YOU, LET ME GROOVE YOU, AIN'T NOTHIN' WRONG. IF YOU BELIEVE IN LOVE ...'

The film cut to a close-up of a female hand delicately extracting a condom from its wrapper, which had been decorated by the agency Art Department with the Condom Marketing Board's graphically friendly logo.

'... COME ON COME ON COME ON ...' cut to closed eyes, moist lips, shining flesh '... STOP BEATIN' ROUND THE ... BOOOOOWOOOSH ... OOOOOOH ...'

Fry's shadow capered by the side of the screen, knees jerking, ponytail in a frenzy of agitation, as the singer sighed and ooooohed and the young couple continued their precisely choreographed writhing. With a final, long-drawn-out gasp of passion spent, the screen went black, and a tasteful title, reversed out in white, beseeched the audience to Get It On, compliments of the Condom Marketing Board.

The lights went up, and the agency team inspected the client team's face for reactions – a hint of approval, a nod, an expression of shock, anything. As one, the seven Rubber Barons lowered their heads and made notes on their pads. Apart from that, nothing.

Fry plunged into the vacuum of silence. 'Killer track, isn't it? Brilliant. It's an old classic, of course. But, I mean, so fantastically right for today, and in the cinema, with Dolby, well, it's going to knock their socks off. That's your market, cinema and MTV. And everything else ties in – posters, point of sale, radio, T-shirts – can we have the slides please, Terry?'

For ten minutes, Fry took his mute audience through the supporting material, from radio commercials to redesigned dispensing machines for pubs and service stations and T-shirts – 'You've each got one to take away' – and then, with the volume up a couple of notches, there was a second screening of the commercial.

Fry blew his nose and sat down, and silence descended again on the conference room. Simon leaned over to the senior Rubber Baron.

'First impressions?'

The senior Rubber Baron took a considered puff of his cigar, and looked down the table towards the most junior member of the Condom Marketing Board, a young man who had taken over the mantle of Hygienic Supplies (Basingstoke) Ltd. from his father. In the time-honoured way of these things, comments were delivered in reverse order of eminence, so that the top man could assess the mood of his minions before committing himself to anything approaching an opinion.

'Brian, would you like to kick off?'

Brian cleared his throat and shuffled his notes. 'Yes. Well. I must say that the agency has come up with a very, ah, striking approach. Very striking. Obviously, I have one or two questions – indeed, a couple of reservations – and it

71

might be premature to express a final judgement without seeing the detailed background which I understand is contained in the presentation document.' He paused for breath.

Here we go again, thought Simon. Why don't the bastards ever say what they really think? He kept his voice bright and sympathetic. 'I'm sure you'll find we've covered just about everything, but it would be most interesting to hear your reactions to the advertising.'

'Yes. Quite.' Brian searched in his notes for an exit line that would maintain his position on the fence. It wouldn't do to be the odd man out when the committee's decision was made. Balance, that was the thing, balance and a line of escape in case the majority vote went against the agency. Committees, like boats, shouldn't be rocked. Consensus was the key. Hygienic Supplies (Basingstoke) should be a team player. 'Well, as I said, a striking approach, and I shall be fascinated to see from the document how the agency arrived at it.' Brian took off his glasses and polished them with brisk, decisive movements.

And so it went on up the ladder of corporate importance, more than two hours of tap-dancing, faint praise laced with cautious qualifications. Simon had to make a conscious effort not to yawn. Why was it always the same? An immediate 'no' would almost be better than this interminable cud-chewing; at least the meetings would be shorter. But he smiled and nodded and appeared attentive and said of course when the senior Rubber Baron told him that the committee would have to go away and consider the agency's proposals in detail – and what interesting proposals they were too, deserving of many another meeting back at Rubber House – before making a decision of this importance and, well . . . yes. The same old vapid and inconclusive waffle.

And the same old post-mortem in the conference room after the clients had been bowed out of the agency. Recriminations from the Research Director who had been denied his moment of glory, David Fry in a post-coke depression at the lack of response to the creative work, anti-climax spread thick among the rest of them. It was a relief when Liz came in and handed Simon a note, but a relief that was short-lived: *Mrs Shaw is in reception. She says she has to see you.*

Simon arrived in reception to find his ex-wife fluttering her eyelashes at Jordan, who was pawing the ground and smoothing his hair flirtatiously. He was known for his roving hand under the table at dinner parties, a habit that Caroline and Simon used to joke about in the days when they made jokes. The thigh-creeper, they called him, and always tried to avoid seating him next to a client's wife.

'Hello, Caroline. How are you?'

The eyelashes stopped fluttering and the smile faded. 'Hello, Simon.'

Jordan suddenly remembered a pressing engagement. 'Nice to see you again, old thing,' he said. 'I'd better run.' He shot his cuffs in farewell and sauntered off towards the lift.

'Shall we go into my office?' Simon followed the long legs and short skirt out of reception and past Liz's discreetly averted head. He shut the door.

'Would you like a drink?'

A superior shake of the head. 'It's a little early for me.'

Simon shrugged, and went over to the small bar in the corner. He hesitated over whisky, sighed, and poured a glass of Perrier. Caroline arranged herself at the far end of the leather couch and puffed on a cigarette – short, cross little puffs with a toss of the head when she exhaled.

'When did you start smoking?'

'I've had a terribly upsetting time. Those bloody builders every day.' She tapped ash from her cigarette with a red-tipped finger. Her nail varnish was an exact match for her lipstick. Her crocodile shoes matched her crocodile bag. The dark tan suit of fine wool set off her lighter brown hair, and the silk shirt picked up the distinctive pale blue of her eyes. Simon thought she'd probably spent a hard morning getting dressed for a three-hour lunch at San Lorenzo before an exhausting session with her hairdresser. He was surprised and rather pleased that he no longer found her at all attractive.

He sat down at the other end of the couch. 'Well?'

'I thought it was more civilized to come and see you instead of going through the lawyers.'

'We've already been through the lawyers.' Simon sipped his drink. 'Remember? Or do you want to see the bills?'

Caroline sighed. 'I'm trying to be reasonable, Simon. There's no need to jump down my throat.' She looked at him, and pulled at her skirt until it almost covered her knees. Don't think you're going to jump anywhere else, either.

'OK, let's be reasonable.'

'It's the house. They just haven't stuck to their estimates, none of them. The curtains, painting, the kitchen – God, the kitchen – it's been an absolute nightmare. You've no idea.'

'Sounds just like last time.'

Caroline stubbed out her cigarette. 'It's not funny. Every tiny thing has been more than they said it was going to be. I mean, lots more.' She widened her eyes as she looked at Simon, a sure sign, he remembered, that news of extravagance was about to follow. 'And now they're all wanting to be paid.'

'Well,' said Simon, 'it's one of those irritating little habits they have.' He wondered how long it would be before she mentioned a figure, before the veneer of strained politeness would wear off to be replaced by threats or tears or hysterics. He felt oddly detached, and bored. It had all happened dozens of times since they'd been separated.

Caroline mistook his calm for acceptance, and smiled. She did have nice teeth, Simon thought, even and beautifully capped by some bandit in New York for twenty-five thousand dollars. 'I knew it would be best to come and see you,' she said. 'I knew you'd understand.'

'What are we talking about?'

'Well, it's difficult to say exactly, because there are still one or two . . .'

'Roughly.'

'Well. Thirty thousand. Thirty-five at the most.'

Simon went back to the bar and refilled his glass. He looked at Caroline, who was lighting another cigarette.

'Thirty-five at the most,' he said. 'Let me just get this clear. I bought you the house. You and your lawyers suggested a budget for doing it up. I agreed to the budget. You agreed to the budget. Am I right so far?'

'It was only supposed to be . . .'

'It was supposed to be a budget. You know what a budget is, don't you? It's a finite amount of money.'

Caroline mangled her cigarette in the ashtray. 'There's no need to talk to me like one of your dreary little executives.'

'Why not? You talk to me as if I was a cash dispenser.'

'Thirty-five thousand is nothing to you. You're rich. My lawyers said you got off lightly. They could have . . .'

'Your lawyers are a bunch of greedy, dishonest bastards who pad their bills and expect me to pay for their bloody children to go through Eton.'

They stared at each other in silence. Caroline's face was tight with animosity. Later on, if Simon allowed the conversation to continue, animosity would dissolve into sobbing, and if that didn't work there would be abuse. He looked at his watch.

'Look, I'm sorry, but I've got a meeting going on.'

Caroline mimicked him. 'I've got a meeting.' She pushed back her hair as if it exasperated her. 'God, you've always got a meeting. Our marriage was fitted in between meetings. I wasn't married to you; I was married to an advertising agency.' She sniffed. 'If you could call it a marriage. Too busy to take a holiday, too tired to go out, too tired to . . .'

'Caroline, we've been through all this before.'

'And now, when all I want is a home, you resent it.'

'I resent thirty-five thousand pounds being thrown away on bloody cushions.'

Caroline stood up. With quick, angry movements she put her cigarettes into her bag and smoothed her skirt. 'Well, I tried. I'm not staying here to be shouted at. Go back to your precious meeting.' She walked over to the door and opened it so that Liz could hear her exit line. 'You'll be hearing from my lawyers.'

Simon thought about going back to the wake being conducted in the conference room, but decided against it. What was the point? Either they'd get the business or they wouldn't, and the way he was feeling he didn't particularly care. He put on his jacket, said goodnight to Liz and walked through the early evening bustle of the streets to the flat in Rutland Gate.

Ernest came out of the kitchen, wiping his hands on his apron, his eyebrows raised in exaggerated surprise.

'Fancy seeing you before eight o'clock. What happened? Has the factory burned down, or did those little rubber people have a puncture and not turn up?'

'No, Ern. They came and went. So did Caroline.'

'Oh dear. I thought you looked a tiny bit ruffled. I expect you'd like a drink.' He continued talking as he put ice and whisky in a tumbler. 'What was it this time? Danger money for living in Belgravia? Say what one may about that young lady, she's never short of ideas.'

Simon slumped in a chair and Ernest passed him his drink, then bent down to undo the button of Simon's jacket. 'If we sit like that with our jacket done up, we're going to look like a concertina.'

'Yes, Ern. Cheers.'

'Oh, I nearly forgot. There was a message from foreign parts, a French person who says she has some good news.' Ernest sucked in his cheeks and looked down his nose at Simon. 'She wasn't prepared to tell me, so I assume it's frightfully personal.' He hovered above Simon, a human question mark.

Simon laughed for the first time that day. It must be Nicole. 'I expect it's about my exhaust pipe.'

'Well, far be it from me to pry, dear. You call it what you like. Anyway, she left a number for you.' Ernest disappeared into the kitchen and, with a sniff and an ostentatious display of tact, closed the door behind him. Simon lit a cigar and thought about his few days in Provence – the warmth, the light, the perfectly tanned cleavage – and went over to the phone.

'*Oui?*'

'Nicole, it's Simon. How are you?'

'I'm well, thank you. And so is your car. At last the little monster has repaired it. Let's hope he hasn't stolen the radio.' She laughed, husky and intimate, and Simon wished he could see her.

'I'd love to come down and get it, but I don't think it's possible. There's too much going on at the office. I'll have to send someone down to pick it up.'

'Your gentleman's gentleman?'

'Who?'

'The one who answered your phone. He sounds very correct.'

'Ah, that's Ernest. Yes, I'll send him. You'll like him.'

There was a pause, and Simon could hear the scratch of a match as Nicole lit a cigarette.

'I have a better idea,' she said. 'I have a *copine* – a girl friend in London from the old days. She is always telling me to stay with her. Why don't I bring your car? It would be fun, no?'

'It would be wonderful, but I don't . . .'

'You don't trust me with your expensive car?'

'I'd trust you with my auntie's best bicycle.'

She laughed again. 'So it's a deal?'

'It's a deal.'

Simon put down the phone and went into the kitchen whistling. Ernest looked up from the bowl of mussels that he was cleaning, and took a sip from a glass of white wine. 'Do I detect a certain improvement in our mood? I must say she has a very cultured voice for a garage mechanic.'

'She's doing me a favour, bringing the Porsche back. Sweet of her.'

Ernest gave Simon a sceptical, sideways glance. 'How rare it is to find a good fairy in this cruel world.'

'You should know, Ern.'

'I do, dear. I do.'

Nicole put a coat on against the chill of the evening, and walked through the centre of the village, empty except for a dog sitting patiently outside the butcher's, to the old *gendarmerie*. Simon had sounded pleased to hear from her. It was a pity he couldn't come down. There was an idea forming in her mind, but it all depended: did he mean what he said about being tired of the advertising business? You could never tell with the English. They laughed and complained at the same time.

She stood looking through the doorway of the *gendarmerie*, and then picked her way across the concrete floor to one of the openings in the far wall. The moon above the Lubéron cast a milky light on the terrace below, pale piles of stones around the inky pit of the unfinished swimming pool. Nicole tried to imagine how it could be, landscaped and floodlit, with music and laughter around her instead of the moan of the wind and the flapping of plastic that covered the sacks of cement against the wall.

She decided to do some research, maybe go and see the *notaire* before she went to London. Businessmen always wanted figures and details. It was an interesting idea, if he was as bored as he said. Or was he just looking for a little sympathy at lunchtime? They were so difficult to believe sometimes, the English, so foreign with their odd, dismissive sense of humour and their infuriating *sang-froid*. She found it slightly strange that she was looking forward so much to seeing him again.

She flinched as she felt something touch her ankle, and looked down to see a scrawny village cat winding its way through her feet, its tail erect and twitching, its mouth open in a soundless greeting.

'So? What do you think? Is this something that would amuse him?'

7

It had been a stroke of luck for the General, finding the barn. It was out in the wild country north of Joucas, big enough to hide everything that had to be hidden, screened from the road by a high, ragged row of cypress trees. The owner had given up farming years ago and moved to Apt. He'd been happy to take 500 francs a month and believe the story about using the space to keep a couple of tractors. All the General had needed to do was buy a new padlock for the massive wooden doors.

The dim interior echoed with the sound of early morning coughs as the first cigarettes of the day were lit while the men inspected the bicycles that were propped against the wall. Claude, his bulk straining against a threadbare track-suit, lumbered over and picked one up by the crossbar. He grunted.

'Don't tell me it's heavy,' said the General. 'These are the lightest bikes in Provence, pro bikes – ten-speed gears, racing tyres, water-bottles, moulded saddles, everything.'

Claude grunted again. 'No cigar lighter?'

Fernand hoisted a leg over the crossbar of his bike and tried the saddle. He winced through the smoke of his cigarette. '*Ouf*. This is like having an operation.'

The others stopped laughing when they tried their own saddles. 'The pros – they sit on these razor-blades all through the Tour de France?'

The General tried to be patient with them. 'Listen. I got you the best bikes. They don't come with armchairs. After a week or two, the saddles will soften up. *Bon*, so you have sore backsides until they do.' He looked at them perching gingerly on their bikes. 'But, my friends, when this is over, you'll be sitting on a cushion. Nice, comfortable money.'

There was a silence while each man thought about his

share. Jojo remembered his role as the faithful lieutenant. 'He's right. What's a sore arse, anyway? Eh?'

The General nodded. 'What we're going to do this morning is a little warm-up, just to get you used to riding – twenty, thirty kilometres. Every Sunday we'll increase the distance until you can do a hundred kilometres without passing out, and then we'll do a bit of hill work. You'll have steel legs by the spring. *Allez*!'

They wheeled their bikes out of the barn and into the autumn sunlight, dressed in an assortment of outfits that ranged from Claude's track-suit to the Borels' brightly coloured boxer shorts and Fernand's oily blue mechanic's overalls. The General made a mental note to buy them something more suitable for winter cycling, those thick black tights that kept the wind out and the muscles warm.

'Turn left at the end of the track,' he said. 'I'll catch you up.' He closed and padlocked the doors, feeling good now that it had started, alert and optimistic, and glad that he'd taken for himself the job of team driver. Those saddles really were bastards.

Nobody could have mistaken the group for practised cyclists. They wobbled, they wove, they cursed as they fumbled with the gears. Two or three of them had been unable to get into the toe-clips, and were pedalling flat-footed, like old women going to the market. Bachir's saddle was too low, and he had adopted an ungainly, splay-legged style, his knees sticking out either side of the bike. Jojo was smoking. The General realized that they needed a little elementary instruction. He overtook them and waved them to stop.

'How much further?' Jean rubbed his buttocks, coughed and spat.

The General got out of the car. 'A long way,' he said, 'and it'll seem twice as long the way you're riding. Haven't you ever been on bikes before?' He went over to Jojo. 'Watch this.' He adjusted the height of the saddle. 'You should just be able to touch the ground either side on tiptoe, OK? Like that, your legs will be straight on the downstroke. Otherwise, you'll be riding as if you've wet your pants, like our friend here.' He grinned at Bachir.

'Next, you should always pedal with the ball of your foot, and that means using the toe-clips. They're to stop your feet from slipping. If your foot slips, you'll have sore balls from the saddle, take my word for it. And keep pedalling when you change gear. If you don't, the chain will jump off the cogs.' The General pulled at his moustache. What else? 'Ah yes.' He wagged a finger at Jojo. 'No smoking.'

'*Merde*. I can't give up smoking. I tried.'

'I'm not asking you to give it up. Just don't smoke while you're riding. It doesn't look right. You don't see Lemond with a *clop* hanging out of his mouth, do you? By the time we do the job, you've got to look like you're part of your bike. You understand? You've got to look like all those other keen bastards. That's what will make you invisible.'

Jojo nodded. '*Tout à fait*,' he said. 'Invisible.'

'And rich,' said the General.

They set off again, this time looking less like a drunken circus act, and the General drove slowly behind them. The first few rides were going to be the worst, he thought, when the legs were like blancmange and the lungs were on fire. That was when the weaker ones would think of giving up. Jojo was fine, determined and fit. Jean the pickpocket hadn't said much so far, but then he never did. Claude would growl and keep going. The Borel brothers, who were now riding shoulder to shoulder, would probably encourage each other, and Fernand was a tough little brute. Bachir – well, Bachir would need coaxing along. He'd been used to quick jobs, two minutes with a knife and off down an alley. Did he have the stamina, did he have the patience? Nine months of training and waiting and planning wasn't his style. Yes, a little special treatment for Bachir, maybe a good *cous-cous* dinner one night and a quiet chat.

The General pulled out to overtake, and studied the faces as he passed. They were all showing signs of effort, but nobody had puked yet, and Jojo actually winked as the car drew level with him. Ten kilometres to go. The General led them off on to a side road with a gentle downhill gradient, and watched them in the mirror as they freewheeled behind him, straightening up from the handlebars to ease their

81

backs. They were good boys. It was going to work. He was sure it was going to work.

He had drifted out into the middle of the road, and had to squeeze into the verge to avoid the black Porsche coming the other way, a flash of blonde hair behind the wheel, the deep rumble of the exhaust. *Putain*, he thought, what a car. Half a million francs minimum, and a few million more for the optional extra with the blonde hair. Some men had all the luck.

Nicole hardly noticed the oddly dressed group of cyclists as she went up the hill and joined the road that led to Cavaillon and the *autoroute*. She was still irritated after her exchange with Duclos at the garage, who had refused to let her take the car unless she paid there and then for the repairs. And what a bill! A bill suitable for framing, she'd said to him as she wrote out a cheque that would undoubtedly bounce unless she called Monsieur Gilles at the Crédit Agricole when she reached London on Monday. It was true that Monsieur Gilles was *sympathique*, and terribly understanding about her frequent financial problems, but even so, it was a bad way to start the journey.

The Sunday morning traffic was light going through Cavaillon and over the bridge, and there were no trucks on the *autoroute*. Nicole kept the Porsche down to a comfortable cruising speed and enjoyed the snug fit of the bucket seat around her hips, the smell of leather and the way the car took a long bend. What a pleasure it was after driving her little heap which, according to Duclos, needed new tyres and God knows what else if it was going to get through another year. Then there was the work that had to be done on the house in Brassière – just odds and ends of mainten-ance, but it always ended up costing thousands of francs – and the *taxe d'habitation* that was due in November. Her life was spent stretching the alimony, and even that was at risk since her ex-husband had moved to New York. Ex-husbands had a habit of vanishing in America. It had happened to two of her friends.

She'd tried to make some extra money. There had been the job in a boutique in Avignon, and when that had gone bankrupt she'd worked for a man in real estate until he'd made one pass too many. She'd managed to let the house once or twice in the season, and done some public relations work for a property developer, but it was all hand to mouth, and she was tired of it. Tired, and beginning to feel, as her thirties passed by, a little apprehensive. The tiny apartment in Paris was over-mortgaged, and either that or the house would have to go next year. Maybe it would be best to move back to Paris. She didn't want to, but at least she might meet someone there. Unattached men were thin on the ground in Provence.

She stamped on the accelerator to pass a big Renault. The jolt of speed was exhilarating, and her mood changed. She was being morbid, imagining herself as an old crone living with a poodle in Paris. Something would turn up. She was, after all, going to meet an unattached man in London. Quite a promising unattached man.

She had looked for traces of him in the car – a pair of sunglasses, a sweater, a box of cigars, a book – but there was nothing. It was perfectly maintained, hardly used, impersonal. A rich man's occasional toy. When she had spoken to him, it was almost as if he'd forgotten he had it. He'd sounded pleased to talk to her, though, warm and ready to laugh, the way he'd been when they had lunch together. A Frenchman would have been either very formal or over-intimate, but he'd been – what was that word the English used so much? – nice. Very nice. She decided not to stop in Paris for the night, but to drive all the way to Calais so she could be in London by midday.

The weather at Dover was doing its best to rain. Nicole drove off the car ferry and joined the queue waiting to go through Customs and Immigration. She got out her passport and lit a cigarette as the cars moved up to pass through the green channel.

The two Customs officers standing in the lee of the building looked at the Porsche, black and sleek among the travel-stained family saloons, and studied the blonde driver. It had been a slow morning, and a pretty woman travelling alone in an expensive car – well, could be a mule, couldn't it? Classic. A few kilos hidden in the door panels. Worth a look. Definitely worth a look. One of the officers strolled down the line of cars and tapped on Nicole's window.

'Morning, madam. Mind if I see your passport?'

Nicole handed it through the window.

French. Might have known it from the perfume. This early in the morning, too. 'Where did you start your journey, madam?'

'From Provence.'

'Provence?'

'In the south of France.'

'Now where exactly would that be? Nice? Marseille? Round there?'

'Yes. About an hour from Marseille.'

'I see. About an hour from Marseille.'

The Customs officer returned the passport and walked to the front of the car, looked at the number plate and walked back. 'Your car, is it, madam?'

'No. I bring it back for a friend in London.'

'A friend. I see.' He leaned down until his face, with its official, polite half-smile, was level with Nicole's. 'Mind taking the car over there, madam?' He pointed to the empty red channel. Nicole was aware of passengers in the other cars turning to look at her.

'But I . . .'

'Thank you, madam.' He straightened up and followed the Porsche over to the red channel. Couldn't be too careful these days, the things people got up to. Anyway, he had a couple of hours to kill before his shift was over, and he never did like the French. Toffee-nosed buggers. Why would anyone in their right mind want a bloody Channel Tunnel? He watched Nicole get out of the car, high heels, silk legs, expensive-looking piece of work. Classic mule, if ever he'd seen one.

They took the car away and put Nicole in a small, drab room that smelled of a thousand stale cigarettes. She stared at the rabies poster on the wall and looked through the window as the last cars from the ferry drove away through

84

the drizzle. Welcome to England. She shivered, and felt irrationally guilty. In France, she would have argued, demanded some kind of explanation; but here, a foreigner, she wasn't sure enough of herself or her English to complain to the man with the raw red face and the hostile eyes. She longed for a cup of coffee.

An hour went by, and then the door opened.

'Everything seems to be in order, madam. Here are your keys. Sorry to have kept you.'

'What were you looking for?'

'Illegal substances, madam, illegal substances.' He watched as she got up, stood aside to let her pass through the door, stayed watching from the doorway as she started the car, stalled it, and started again. Pity about that. He could have sworn she was a live one.

Nicole had to make an effort to drive away slowly. Silly to get nervous about nothing. She was grateful for the sign reminding her to drive on the left, and joined the traffic going towards London. It was nearly eleven-fifteen, and she'd be lucky to get there in time for lunch. Her friend Emma would be wondering what had happened to her. *Merde.*

It wasn't until she glanced down for her cigarettes that she noticed the car phone. Emma's well-bred, slightly strangulated voice cut through the static.

'Darling, how are you? Where are you?'

'I just left Dover. The Customs stopped me.'

'What jolly bad luck, darling. Did they find anything? Horrid little men. They just adore going through one's underwear. I hope you made them wear gloves.'

'No, I had nothing. They looked at the car, that's all.'

'Well, don't you worry. Get to the flat when you can, and we'll have something here. Julian's away, as usual, so we can rummage through his Burgundy. I'll put some Montrachet in the fridge and we'll have a lovely chat. Don't stick your tongue out at any policemen. *A tout à l'heure,* darling. Bye.'

Nicole smiled as she put the phone back in its cradle. Emma was good for her, always had been ever since the divorce – permanently cheerful, addicted to gossip, kind, and happily married to an older man who did something important in Brussels. It had been too long since they'd seen each other.

Emma's flat was in a crescent of ruddy brick buildings behind Harrods, solid and self-important like the Victorians who had built them. Nicole found a space between two Range Rovers, and wondered why anyone living in central London would need a car that was designed to conquer the wilderness. She took her bags up the marble steps and pressed the button beside the mahogany door, flinching at the shriek of welcome that came from the entryphone.

Emma was waiting at the door of the flat, a small, glossy woman with formidable earrings. Her hair, which changed colour with the discovery of each new treasure of a hairdresser, was tawny today, with blonde highlights. The two women pecked cheeks enthusiastically.

'Lovely to see you darling, and still *bronzée*. My God, I feel like a slug.'

They held each other at arm's length for the mutual assessment that was necessary after three years.

'You look wonderful, Emma. I love your hair.'

'I've been going to Bruno in Beauchamp Place – an absolute poppet, and frightfully indiscreet. They see all the face-lift marks, you know, hairdressers. You'd be amazed who's had them. Come on in.'

The flat was light and high-ceilinged, prosperously decorated and furnished. Whatever Julian did in Brussels, Nicole thought, it certainly paid well. 'How is he, Julian?' she asked.

Emma was pouring two glasses of wine. 'Desperately bored with the EC, and rather peeved with the French, actually, who seem to spend the entire time either being difficult or having lunch. I'd love him to give it up, but of course we need the pennies. Very dreary. Here you are, darling.'

They sat opposite each other in plump armchairs covered in faded chintz. 'Now then,' said Emma, 'I want to hear all about the new man. Has he got a twinkle in his eye?'

Nicole smiled and shrugged. 'Oh, maybe. I don't know. I only saw him twice. It just seemed like good luck with the car – a chance to come over and see you.'

Emma cocked her head. 'Sweet of you, darling, but I don't believe a word of it. When are you seeing him?'

'I have to call him at his office.' She looked in her bag for the card Simon had given her. 'Somewhere in Knightsbridge.'

'You go over there and call him, darling, and I'll pretend not to listen.'

Nicole got through to Liz, who told her that Mr Shaw, unfortunately, was at a client lunch. But he had left a message. Would Nicole be free to join him for a drink at Rutland Gate, and then dinner? Yes? Good, he will be pleased. He's terribly grateful about the car. About six-thirty, then?

Emma looked at Nicole's face as she came back and sat down. 'I have a feeling I shall be left to nibble my fish fingers all by myself this evening.'

Nicole tried to look apologetic. 'I hate to leave you on the first night.'

'Nonsense, darling. You're quivering with anticipation already, I can tell. Now, what are you going to wear? Do you want to borrow some earrings?'

It took Nicole five minutes to drive to Rutland Gate and twenty minutes to find a parking space. She looked at her watch as she walked along the pavement, which was slippery with fallen leaves and booby-trapped with offerings left by the neighbourhood dogs. God, the English and their dogs. She wondered if Simon had one. It was just after seven as she rang the doorbell and pushed back her hair, feeling pleasantly nervous.

The door was opened by Ernest, trim in a dark grey suit and pink shirt, eyebrows raised as if surprised to find anyone on the doorstep. 'Good evening,' he said. 'You must be Madame Bouvier.'

Nicole smiled and nodded.

'Please.' Ernest stood back to let her in, and followed her

down the hall. She could feel that she was being studied from behind as Ernest continued talking. 'Mr Shaw only got back himself a few minutes ago, but he won't be a moment. If you'd like to make yourself comfortable on that hideous couch – practically impossible, I know – I'll get you a glass of champagne.' He looked back over his shoulder as he went into the kitchen. 'We're renting, you see, while we look for something more suitable.'

Nicole heard him sniff loudly, and then the muffled pop of a champagne cork. Ernest's head suddenly appeared round the kitchen door. 'I've quite forgotten my manners. Perhaps you'd prefer Scotch? Sherry?'

'Champagne is very nice. Thank you.'

Ernest brought out a small silver tray with a flute of champagne, a bowl of Macadamia nuts and a small linen napkin, and arranged them carefully on the low table in front of Nicole. '*Voilà*.'

'You speak French?'

'Like a terribly backward schoolboy. But I do have the most expressive shrug, although I say it myself.' He twitched his shoulders at her, and put one hand on his hip. 'Very Gallic, don't you think?'

Nicole laughed, and raised her glass to him. '*Santé*.'

There were hurried footsteps on the parquet floor, and Simon came into the room, his hair still damp from the shower, spotted tie slightly crooked. 'I'm sorry.' He looked at Nicole apologetically, and grinned. 'Still speaking to me?' He bent down to kiss her. As his lips touched the scented skin of her cheek he wished he'd shaved again. Their eyes met for two seconds longer than was socially necessary. 'Hello, Simon.'

'A glass of champagne for you, Mr Shaw?'

'Thank you, Ernest.' Simon stepped back and took the glass, and held it up to Nicole. 'To the chauffeur. It was very kind of you. I hope it wasn't too much of a bore.'

Nicole wanted to straighten his tie. 'No, really . . .'

Ernest delivered a small but emphatic cough. 'Well, I shall take myself off to the leafy glades of Wimbledon.' He looked at Simon. 'Unless you need me for anything.'

'I don't think so, Ern, thank you. I'll see you tomorrow.'

Ernest inclined his head towards Nicole. *'Bon appétit, madame.'*

'Merci, Airnest.'

'Ah, Airnest,' he repeated. 'It does have a ring to it, doesn't it? *So* much nicer than Ern. Good night.'

The front door closed behind him, and Nicole laughed. 'He's an original, isn't he? I like him. How long has he been with you?'

Simon told her about Ernest and the early days of the agency, when it had been fun – the time when Ernest had pretended to be a client to impress a visiting bank manager, his feuds with ex-wives and secretaries, his disdain for office politicians, his persistent and undemanding loyalty.

'You're very close with him, aren't you?'

Simon nodded. 'I trust him. He's about the only person I do.' He looked at his watch. 'We should be going. I've made a reservation at an Italian restaurant – I hope that's OK. I thought you'd like a change from French cooking.'

As Simon stood aside to let Nicole through the door, she stopped. 'Sorry. Impossible to resist.'

He looked down at her and felt a tightness in his throat as she straightened his tie. 'I suppose Ernest usually does that, *non*?'

'I think he gave me up as a slob a long time ago.'

'Slob? What's a slob?'

While they walked to the car, Simon explained about slobs, and as they drove through Hyde Park towards Kensington he was conscious of her closeness, and realized that he hadn't been out with a woman in London for months. Nicole watched his profile as he talked, the straight nose and determined jaw, the dark hair that needed cutting, the formality of his tie and suit. He had looked more comfortable in Provence, she thought.

The restaurant that Simon had chosen was still enjoying the patronage of that small, apparently recession-proof nucleus of Londoners who treat dinner as a spectator sport. For six months, maybe a year, they fight for tables, cultivate the head waiter and wave to each other across barely noticed food. The restaurant becomes hysterically fashionable. The owner dreams of early retirement in Tuscany or Ischia while the waiters flourish their pepper mills, their Parmesan cheese and their olive oil – '*Extra virgine, signorina*' – with increasing familiarity. And then, quite suddenly, the nucleus moves on, to be replaced by sensible couples from the Home Counties who are prepared to put up with the noise and the prices because they have heard that this is the new temple of glamour, garnished with white truffles, sun-dried tomatoes and one or two minor members of the media aristocracy.

Simon had known Gino, the manager, since they were both struggling, many years and many restaurants ago. He greeted Nicole and Simon with a genuine smile and showed them to a table in the corner, arranging Nicole's napkin on her lap with obvious enjoyment.

'Don't make a beast of yourself, Gino.'

'Eh.' Gino beamed. 'It's natural. I'm Italian. *Signorina*, a drink?'

Nicole looked at Simon. 'I don't know. Some white wine?'

Gino snapped his fingers at a waiter. 'A bottle of Pino Grigio for the *signorina*.' He handed out the menus, kissed his fingertips and trotted off to the front of the restaurant, smile at the ready, to welcome a group of young men and women in black clothes and sunglasses.

'So.' Nicole glanced round the crowded room, mirrored and marbled in pink and black. 'This is where the chic people eat in London. Do you come often?'

'No, not really. I'm usually with clients in the evening, and they like the more formal places – the Gavroche, or the Connaught. Here they wouldn't feel important enough.' He shrugged. 'They're not the most amusing people in the world, most of them.' He tried the wine, and nodded at the waiter. 'But then I'm not much better myself at the moment. I haven't finished a book for months, haven't been to the movies, if I'm not in the agency I'm on a plane . . .' He stopped abruptly, and smiled. 'I'm sorry. It's very boring. What would you like to eat?'

They looked at the menu, unaware that they were the

subject of considerable speculation at a table on the other side of the restaurant, where a group of Caroline's friends were studying Nicole.

'Simon seems to be getting over the divorce, I see.'

'Who is she? One of his clients?'

'Don't be ridiculous, Rupert. Clients don't dress like that. I'm going to the Ladies.'

The woman got up and zig-zagged through the tables, feigning interest in the contents of her handbag until she was close enough to pounce.

'Simon, darling! What a nice surprise. How lovely to see you!'

Simon looked up from the menu and got to his feet, dutifully kissing the air two inches away from the proffered cheek. 'Hello, Sophie. How are you?'

'Fine, darling.' She looked past Simon at Nicole. 'It's been ages.' She showed no sign of moving.

Simon gave in with minimal politeness. 'Nicole, this is Sophie Lawson.' The two women exchanged nods and bright, insincere smiles.

'Nicole . . .?'

'Bouvier,' said Nicole. 'How do you do?'

'What a charming accent. Well, I mustn't keep you. Do call, Simon, and we'll have dinner. We never see you these days. I don't know where you've been hiding yourself.'

'Have you tried looking in the office?'

'Ah yes. The office.' With a twitch of a smile and a final sideways glance at Nicole, she continued on her way, mission accomplished.

Nicole laughed. 'You were not nice with her.'

'I can't stand the bloody woman. One of Caroline's poisonous friends. She'll spend the whole evening keeping an eye on us, and she'll be on the phone first thing tomorrow morning to tell Caroline all about it.'

They ordered, and Simon tried to ignore the sensation that they were being watched. 'Tell me about Provence,' he said. 'What's it like in the winter?'

'Very quiet, sometimes very cold. We make big fires and drink too much red wine and read, and there's skiing. I sometimes think I like it better than summer.' She picked up her glass, and Simon noticed that she was still wearing her wedding ring.

'We?'

'The people who live in the Lubéron all year round.'

'I loved it down there. It's very beautiful.'

'You should come again. But next time, don't drive your car in the fields.' They both laughed, and the group at the table on the other side of the restaurant thought that they were beginning to look very cosy. Poor Caroline. Sophie could hardly wait to tell her.

Nicole ate with a good appetite, pasta and osso bucco and plenty of bread. It was a pleasant change, Simon thought, from watching Caroline pushing salad round her plate. He realized how much he liked to watch a woman enjoying food – the slight frown of concentration as meat was cut away from bone, the occasional flick of a pink tongue at the corner of the mouth, the small sounds of appreciation.

'You eat like a cat,' he said.

'No, I think more like a *routier*.' Nicole patted her lips with her napkin, drank some wine and reached for her cigarettes. Simon held a match for her and she touched his hand as she leaned towards the flame. Sophie Lawson looked at her watch and wondered if it was too late to call Caroline.

The restaurant was becoming quieter now. Simon ordered coffee and lit a cigar. 'What are you going to do while you're in London?'

'Nothing special. I'll spend some time with Emma, but I have to be back for the weekend. A friend from Paris is coming down. Besides, I don't like to be too long in a city now. The country is better for me.'

Simon thought about his weekend – Saturday in the office, Sunday collapsed over the newspapers or in front of the television, waiting for Monday morning when it would start all over again. Like most advertising men, he thought often about getting out, and like most advertising men he found reasons to do nothing about it. What else would he do?

'You're lucky,' he said. 'You enjoy where you're living. A lot of people don't.'

'You?'

Simon shook his head. 'I live in an office.'

'Do you have to?'

'I think I'd better have a drink before I answer that. Would you like a glass of champagne?' Nicole smiled and nodded. Simon beckoned to a waiter, who called over to the barman.

'Well!' said Sophie Lawson as she was getting up to leave. 'Did you hear that? Champagne, my dear. Do you think he's going to drink it out of her shoe?' She fluttered her fingers at Simon from across the room. 'Do call, darling.'

Simon nodded goodbye with a sense of relief, and leaned back as he considered Nicole's question. She remained silent, her chin resting on one hand, looking at his face – a tired face, she thought, with a lined forehead and that grey streak in one eyebrow, and sad.

'So tell me,' she said, 'why do you have to live in an office if you don't want to?'

'I suppose I don't have to, really. It's a habit, the way I've been living for years.'

'And now you don't enjoy it.'

'I stopped enjoying it a long time ago.' Simon stared into his champagne, and shrugged. 'I don't know. It pays the alimony. I've often thought about doing something else – I nearly bought a share in a vineyard once – but there's always some crisis at the agency, so you deal with that, and the next one, and then you suddenly realize that six months have gone by and you've done nothing except . . .'

'Except make money?'

'Exactly. And so you buy a new car or a new house and tell yourself that living well is the best revenge – it's like a consolation prize for being bored and having to work during weekends and not liking what you do very much.' Simon drew on his cigar, and frowned. 'I don't make it sound very attractive, do I? The poor old advertising man, suffering in luxury, dragging himself from the Concorde to the Mercedes to the restaurant.' He smiled. 'Breaks your heart, doesn't it?'

They were both quiet while they considered the problem

of affluent dissatisfaction, a problem which Nicole found some difficulty taking seriously. She wondered if this was the moment to tell Simon about the idea she'd had, but decided against it. She didn't know enough yet, didn't even know if it would be possible. She should have found out from the *notaire* if the place was still for sale before she left Brassière.

She caught him looking at her, and her mouth turned down in mock sympathy. 'Poor little rich man,' she said. 'It's a terrible life, with the cigars and the champagne and the Ernest to take care of you. *Quelle tristesse!*' She rolled her eyes upwards, and laughed.

Simon shook his head. 'You're quite right. It's pathetic. I should do something about it.' He finished his champagne and called for the bill. 'But what?'

Nicole decided to call the *notaire* tomorrow. 'Think of something you enjoy to do.'

'Let's have dinner tomorrow. That would be a start.'

They left the restaurant in a state of tentative excitement, reluctant for the evening to end, each wondering if the other felt the same way. Nicole slipped her arm through Simon's, and he enjoyed it like a caress.

As he unlocked the car and opened the passenger door for Nicole, the phone was beeping. Instinctively, he picked it up and immediately wished he hadn't. It was Liz.

'I'm sorry to call you so late, but I didn't want to give Mr Ziegler the restaurant's number.'

'Thank God for that.' Simon looked over at Nicole and smiled an apology. 'What does he want that can't wait until tomorrow?'

'Well, I'm afraid he'd like you to be in New York tomorrow. He says it's absolutely vital.' Simon could hear the rustle of paper as Liz looked through her notes. 'Parker Foods Worldwide, three hundred million dollars. Mr Parker's coming to the agency tomorrow afternoon. Apparently he wants to make a quick decision.'

Simon stared through the windscreen. Here we go again, jumping through the hoop like a well-paid seal. Bloody Ziegler. He certainly picked his moments.

'Mr Shaw?'

'Yes, Liz. Sorry.'

'I've booked you on Concorde. You should be there in plenty of time. Mr Ziegler would like you to call him tonight. He'll be in the office until eight, and then at Lutèce. Do you want the number there?'

'No, it's OK. I'll get him before he leaves. See you in the morning.'

'Good night, Mr Shaw. Don't forget your passport, will you?'

Simon put the phone down, the mood of the past few hours gone. He felt angry at himself. Why hadn't he just said no? Why didn't he call Ziegler and tell him to get on with it? He was as bad as all the rest of them, full of talk about getting out until someone waved an account under his nose, and then he was off like a rat up a drainpipe. And for what? Money. And what would he do with it? Buy another house, which he'd visit to sleep in? Another car? Polo ponies, football teams, art collections, first-growth claret, ocean-going yachts? Toys and distractions.

'You look sad. Is it bad news?' Nicole's face was half in shadow. Simon wanted to touch the cheekbone that was thrown into relief by the slanting red glow of a traffic light.

'It's not bad. It's just boring. I've got to go to New York tomorrow.'

'You say boring a lot.'

'Do I? Yes, I suppose I do. Sorry.'

'You say sorry a lot too.'

A taxi behind them sounded its horn as the lights changed. Simon pulled away and turned into Knightsbridge, past Harrods and into the crescent where Nicole was staying. She looked up at the lighted windows of the flat. Emma would be waiting, wanting to hear about the evening.

Simon switched off the engine. 'God, I almost forgot. The garage bill, and the tickets – just call Liz. I'll tell her tomorrow morning before I go. If you'd like to use the car while you're in London, keep the keys. I'll walk home.'

'Emma has a car if I need one. But thank you.' She leaned across and kissed Simon on the cheek. 'It was fun. Enjoy New York.'

Simon watched her walk to the door and let herself in without looking back, and promised himself another trip to Provence once the panic was over. Just get New York out of the way, and then he'd start to make some sense out of his life. He'd think about it on the plane. Bloody Ziegler. He'd better get back and call him.

Nicole heard the engine of the Porsche start as she was walking up the stairs, and tried to look bright for Emma.

The two women, their shoes kicked off, legs tucked comfortably beneath them, shared the deep cushions of the couch and sipped at the absent Julian's oldest cognac.

Emma took off her earrings and massaged her ears. 'Now then, darling. Tell me all. Is he Mr Right, or just another dreary old businessman?'

Nicole laughed. 'I like him. He's sweet, not at all *pompeux*, you know? I kept wanting to tidy him up. We had a nice time, except there was a woman he knew, very curious about us. Sophie something, one of his ex-wife's friends. Sophie Lawson.'

'Oh, God.' Emma rolled her eyes. 'I met her at Queen's last summer. An absolute cow, and she shouldn't wear those silly little skirts. Legs like Boris Becker's, my dear. I mean, *Wagnerian*.' Emma studied her own fashionably bony knees with satisfaction. 'Anyway, what did you talk about?'

'Oh, him mostly. He's tired with his business, but he doesn't know what else to do. I feel sorry for him, somehow. I don't think he has fun in his life.'

Emma hesitated over her cognac, and then looked at Nicole with bright, inquisitive eyes. 'You're showing all the signs, darling – wanting to tidy him up, feeling sorry for him. Do you want to go to bed with him?'

'Emma!'

'Well, men and women have been known to do it.'

Nicole felt a warmth come over her face as she realized that tidying him up was just an excuse. She wanted to touch him, and see him smile. She wanted him to touch her. 'Oh, Emma,' she said, 'I don't know.'

'You've gone quite pink, darling. I expect it's the brandy.'

8

Jojo was taking his role as the General's second-in-command seriously, and enjoying the experience – unusual for him – of using his brain while his body went through the arduous motions of work on the *chantier*. It was practically finished, another old wreck of a farmhouse rebuilt, and his *patron* was casting around for the next job. He'd find something, Fonzi, he always did. He knew all the local architects, and they trusted him. After all, he was one of the few *maçons* in Provence who had never gone bust half-way through a job, never cheated on insurance payments, never took black money. Too honest for his own good, Jojo thought, but that was his problem.

Jojo's concern, as the trusty lieutenant, was the physical condition of two members of his team. Claude and the Borel brothers, and even Fernand at the garage where he did demolition and panel-beating, were kept reasonably fit by the demands of their work. But Bachir spent his days having surreptitious cigarettes behind the bar and ferrying cups of coffee around. And Jean – well, Jean was a walking catastrophe. Lifting anything heavier than someone else's wallet brought him out in a sweat. Jojo had watched them both on the training spins. They invariably finished last, and with evident difficulty. One ride a week wasn't enough. If they were going to keep up with the others, they'd have to be toughened up. Jojo decided to talk it over with Claude.

They went off one evening after work to a bar in Bonnieux that Jojo liked because of its refusal to comply with the anti-smoking laws, and the good rump steak and *frites* that Madame served up for 50 francs. They settled at a corner table and killed the first *pastis* without speaking. Jojo sighed with relief, and nodded for two more.

'Mother's milk, eh?'

97

Claude swirled the ice cubes round in his empty glass. 'You know something? I'd rather have this than champagne.'

'I'll get you a crate when we've done the job. You can stick it in the back of your Mercedes in case you get thirsty going to the hairdresser.'

The big man pushed back his hair, disturbing the fine dust that had gathered there while he'd been cutting stone that afternoon. His hands, like Jojo's, were scarred and rough, the fingers thickened by years of labour, the nails blunt and split. 'Might have a manicure, too,' he said.

Madame came to their table with the second round of *pastis*. 'You eating, boys?' Jojo nodded, and she went into her recitation. 'Double *frites*, steak *à point*, don't forget the mustard and a litre of red, is that right?'

'You're a princess,' Jojo said.

'Tell my husband.' The woman went back to the bar, yelling the order through to the kitchen.

Jojo lit a cigarette, and leaned towards Claude. 'Listen, we've got to do some thinking.'

Claude's face looked grave over his *pastis*, the uneasy expression that Jojo knew signalled the anticipation of mental effort.

'It's Bachir and Jean. I've seen them after training, and they're completely *crevé*.' Jojo dragged on his cigarette and blew smoke at a fly that was threatening his glass. 'The rest of us are going to be fine. We work, you know? We're strong. But those two, they're standing around all day. They've got no condition, no endurance.'

Claude nodded. 'Bachir chucked it last Sunday, remember? All over his front wheel. And Jean looked like a piece of veal, he was so white.'

'*Voilà*.' Jojo leaned back, satisfied that Claude had appreciated the nature of the problem. 'We've got to find some way to get them fit, or we're going to have to tow them back.'

The two men were silent, staring into their drinks for inspiration. 'I don't know,' said Claude, 'maybe they could work with us on the next *chantier*. Digging, humping sacks, Fonzi always needs a couple of donkeys. Eh?' He shrugged. 'Just an idea.'

A smile spread over Jojo's face as he looked at Claude's anxious expression. '*C'est pas con*,' he said. '*C'est pas con du tout.*' He slapped Claude's shoulder, raising a small cloud of masonry dust. 'My friend, there are times I could kiss you.'

'Do you boys want to be left alone, or are you ready to eat?' Madame unloaded her tray on to their table, the steaks still spitting with heat, a plate piled high with *pommes frites*, an unlabelled litre bottle of red wine, a basket of bread, a pot of Amora. 'There's cheese or *crème caramel* afterwards. You want water? Silly question.' She pushed a strand of hair from her perspiring forehead, and cleared away the empty *pastis* glasses. '*Allez. Bon appétit.*'

The following Sunday, Jojo took the General aside and talked to him, lieutenant to commanding officer. The General applied traction to his moustache, and looked at Jojo approvingly. He liked it when someone else used his head. 'Do you think Fonzi will hire them?'

'If the next *chantier*'s big enough, why not? He can always use cheap backs. I could talk to him.'

'*Bon.*' The General nodded. 'I'll break the bad news. We'd better get Jean a truss. Oh, and Jojo?' He winked and tapped his head. 'Well done.' The little man swaggered as he went off to get his bicycle.

At the end of the morning's ride, the General called them together. The noisy reluctance of Jean and Bachir to give up sedentary work was shouted down by the others. Democracy, the General called it, and pretended not to hear Bachir's suggestion about what he could do with it.

'There's one more thing,' said the General, 'very important.' He held up an authoritarian finger. 'Don't start talking among yourselves about what you're going to do with the money, *d'accord*? Not even when there's nobody else around.'

Jojo shook his head sagely. You had to spell it out to some people.

'I'll tell you why,' said the General. 'It becomes a habit — you start making little jokes about it, you don't even realize you're talking about it, and one day some *petit merdeux* with

99

long ears will overhear something, and then . . .' the General pulled his finger across his throat '. . . *foutu*. So keep it behind the teeth.'

The offices of Global Communications Resources, Inc. occupied the top five floors of a steel and glass and polished granite monument on Sixth Avenue in midtown Manhattan. The employees, according to advertising gossip, were the most highly paid and most paranoid men and women in the business. Five years at Global were enough to drive any normal person crazy, so they said, but at least you'd have enough money to buy your own asylum. It was a reputation that the Chief Executive Officer, Bob ($3.5 million a year, plus options and bonuses) Ziegler enjoyed and encouraged. The biggest goddamn carrot and the biggest goddamn stick in town was the way he liked to put it to his staff. Get rich or get out.

Simon took the express elevator that went non-stop to the forty-second floor, and was escorted past the matched pair of executive secretaries into the corner office that was exactly twice the size of any other office in the building. Ziegler was tilted back in his leather chair, the phone growing out of his ear, an elderly shoeshine boy at his feet. Behind him, on the oiled teak wall, hung a large black and white photograph which showed him shaking hands with ex-President Bush. Ziegler had many such photographs, starring himself and eminent politicians of both parties, and they were changed according to the client of the day. Parker, of Parker Foods, was obviously a Republican.

The shoeshine boy gave a final snap of his cloth and tapped the side of Ziegler's gleaming black foot to indicate that he'd finished. He got up stiffly, nodded thanks for the five-dollar bill that Ziegler flicked at him, and looked inquiringly at Simon, who shook his head. The old man shuffled out of the office to attend to the footwear of other Global directors, and Simon wondered what he must think about the multi-million dollar conversations that he overheard every day.

Ziegler, by now satisfied that he had made Simon wait

long enough, finished his call and stood up, smoothing the lapels of his grey silk suit over the wide red braces that he'd recently taken to wearing. Four inches taller and twenty pounds lighter, he might have looked well-dressed. Simon noticed that he had abandoned his attempts to grow side-burns, and his sparse, sandy hair was trimmed close to his head. His cold grey eyes were fixed on Simon as the rest of his face went through the motions of a smile.

'So you made it. How was the flight?'

'Not bad. Quick, at any rate.'

'It needs to be. Goddamn sardine can. OK, enough socializing. Parker's going to be here in a couple of hours, and I need to fill you in.' Ziegler started to pace up and down in front of his desk. 'He's 99 per cent in the bag. As long as he's happy about Europe, my information is we've got it – three hundred mil, maybe more if we can get him to really stick it to Heinz. That's the league we're in.'

'What's he like, Parker?'

'I've never met him. We've talked on the phone, but I've been dealing with his marketing guys. The word is that he doesn't like spending too much time with agency people. I'll get to that in a minute.' Ziegler paused to pick up a thick file, then tossed it back on the desk. 'You've read the briefing document, right? So you know he started in some hole in the wall in Texas forty years ago and now he's in *Fortune*'s top five hundred, and going up every year. He's smart. Over the phone, he comes across like a good old boy from the boondocks, probably wears a string tie and one of those dumb hats, but he's been in some rough takeovers and never lost. Now here's a psychology lesson, OK?'

Simon lit a cigar and saw Ziegler's expression of distaste. Ziegler got up at six every morning to work out in his weight-room, the only thing that saved him from being portly. He liked to get you to feel his biceps, and he was a firm believer in the theory that lung cancer could be contracted second-hand at a distance of six feet.

'Jesus, I don't know how you can smoke that shit. Do you know what it does to you? Just don't die this afternoon, that's all.'

'I'm touched, Bob. What about the psychology?'

'Right. This is important. From what I hear, Parker likes to think of himself as a simple guy, nothing fancy. Plus the fact that he's not only American, he's Texan. Are you hearing what I'm saying?'

'What do you mean?'

Ziegler sighed. 'I'll spell it out for you. My reading of him is that he thinks most people in advertising are goddamn ballet dancers in disguise, and that Europe is a little village full of flakes.'

Simon had a vision of Ziegler in tights, and coughed on a mouthful of smoke.

Ziegler shook his head. 'Well, they're your fucking lungs. Anyway, you get the idea. No smartass European crap about different cultural values, OK? The line to take is the McDonald's line – American quality, American value, American efficiency, American . . .' Ziegler searched for another word that would do justice to this catalogue of virtues.

'Money?'

'You bet your grandmother's ass, money. Do you realize what this will do to billings? To the share price? To your own personal net worth? You could buy fucking Havana and smoke yourself to death.'

'You know, Bob? There's a sweet, generous side to your personality sometimes.'

Ziegler looked at Simon through narrow, unfriendly eyes. 'Don't kid around, Simon. I've been working on this one for months, and I don't want it screwed up by any wisecracks from you. Save your jokes for next time you have tea with the Queen.'

Ziegler strutted back and forth as he delivered his opinions on the conduct of the meeting, his bulky, pugnacious figure silhouetted against the floor-to-ceiling plate glass and the view down Sixth Avenue to Lower Manhattan. Simon looked at his watch. It was 7 p.m. English time, and he felt like a drink. If he'd been in London, he'd be getting ready to have dinner with Nicole, somewhere quiet, preferably somewhere like the flat where he could take her clothes off

102

afterwards. He shook himself, and tried to pay attention as Ziegler came to the end of his performance.

'. . . so just remember that, OK? We give him one big fucking hammer of a campaign worldwide – no chintzy little special market shit. The world is hungry, and we're going to feed it.' Ziegler stopped pacing, and jabbed a finger at Simon. 'Hey, that's not a bad line, you know? Who needs fucking copywriters?'

Simon had declined the microwaved, gourmet-in-the-sky meal on the plane, and hadn't eaten all day. 'It worked on me, Bob. I'm starving.'

Ziegler cocked his head suspiciously. He was never quite sure when Simon was serious and when he was making one of those snotty remarks that passed for the British sense of humour. In the interests of corporate harmony, he gave him the benefit of the doubt. 'Sure. We'll order in. Parker could be early.'

But he was punctual to the minute, shadowed by a trio of large, smiling executives with booming voices and force-ten handshakes. After Ziegler's remarks about Parker, Simon had been half-expecting bandy legs and a stetson, and was a little surprised to see a dapper man in what looked very much like a Savile Row suit. A loosely knotted bow-tie, a lean face, dark and wrinkled from the sun, heavy-lidded eyes. Simon thought of a lizard.

'Hampton Parker. Good to meet you, Mr Shaw.' He had a dry smoker's voice softened by the pleasant trace of a drawl. 'They tell me you came over from London for our little meeting.'

'That's right. Flew in this morning.'

They sat down, and Simon noticed that Texans really did wear boots with their business suits.

'Tell me, Mr Shaw,' said Parker, 'do you get to see much opera over there? That's one thing I miss back home.'

Simon saw Ziegler's smile become a little more fixed. 'Not as much as I'd like. I try to go whenever Pavarotti's in London.'

Parker nodded. 'Hell of a voice.' He took out a pack of unfiltered Chesterfields, and leaned back. 'All right, boys. Let's get to it.'

The little meeting, as Parker had called it, turned into a two-day inquisition of such thoroughness that both Simon and Ziegler were exhausted by the time it was over. On the morning of the third day they were sitting over coffee speculating on their chances, Ziegler's cockiness tempered by fatigue, and Simon, adrenalin gone, anxious to get back to London. The faxes he'd been getting from the office had been the usual litany of problems.

One of the secretaries put her head round the door. 'Package for you, Mr Ziegler.' A messenger appeared pushing a trolley, his head barely visible behind an enormous carton which he lowered carefully to the floor.

Ziegler called out to his secretary, 'Get that out of here, will you? This isn't a goddamn warehouse. Jesus.'

'I'm sorry, Mr Ziegler. It was for you personally.'

'Shit.' Ziegler got up and hacked at the heavy tape sealing the carton with a letter opener before ripping the top open. The carton was packed with cans and tubes and boxes, all with the red star Parker Foods logo. Tucked in the middle was an envelope.

Ziegler opened it and took out a single sheet of paper.

'Son of a bitch!' He slapped the paper on the table in front of Simon, punched him on the arm, and grinned. 'Son of a bitch!'

Simon looked at the letter. It was headed: 'From the Office of the President'. It read: *'Congratulations. Hampton Parker.'*

By the time Simon looked up, Ziegler was on the phone to Public Relations on the floor below, telling them to arrange a press conference, all signs of tiredness gone, arrogant, swollen with triumph. There was a time when Simon would have felt that same charge of excitement instead of a weary sense of satisfaction mixed with anti-climax. In the end, it was just another hand to hold, even if the hand was stuffed with money.

Ziegler banged the phone down and looked at Simon across the polished acreage of his desk. 'Three fucking hundred fucking million. Minimum!'

'That should keep the wolf from the door.' Simon stretched. 'Congratulations, Bob.'

'There'll be some dead bodies thrown out of the windows over at M & R when this gets out.' Ziegler seemed to relish the thought of the massive and instant redundancies that inevitably followed the loss of a giant account. 'They'll be vulnerable. Better take a look at their list and see what else we can knock off.' He made a note on his pad.

Simon stood up. 'Well, I can't hang around having fun with you all day. I'm going to see if I can get on the one forty-five.'

Ziegler was delighted, as Simon knew he would be. He'd have the press conference all to himself. 'Sure. I'll talk to you in a couple of days.' Simon hadn't reached the door before Ziegler was on the phone again. 'News? You bet I have fucking news. Listen to this . . .'

Simon was the last to board British Airways 004. The other passengers looked up as he made his way down the aisle and then, seeing just another tired man in a dark suit and not a celebrity or even an ex-President, went back to the contents of their briefcases. Concorde and its cargo of business gypsies took off and pointed its snout across the Atlantic.

Simon made a half-hearted attempt to concentrate on his bundle of faxes, and then gave up in favour of a glass of champagne. He stared out at the stratosphere. It had been an incredibly successful trip, one of the biggest account gains for many years. It would keep the City sweet, keep the share price up, keep him rich. He yawned, and accepted another glass of champagne from the stewardess. He thought of the empty, impersonal flat in Rutland Gate. He thought of working with Ziegler for the next few years until one of them got rid of the other. He thought of the problems waiting for him in London, and he thought about the business of advertising.

For years, he had been happy to defend his occupation in the face of condescending comments from his contemporaries – acquaintances in banking or law or publishing or journalism – who wondered, with superior smiles, how he could possibly be interested in making commercials for lavatory paper or beer. Their barely concealed resentment used to surprise him. An 'adman', they called him, always with a patronizing curl of the lip. The curl disappeared, of course, when they wanted favours like Centre Court tickets.

Well, to hell with them. They were irritating, but unimportant, and Simon no longer cared what they thought. More and more, he no longer cared about the business either, not enough to put up with the squabbles in the office or the tedium of the meetings or, most of all, the incessant stroking of clients. From the Chairman to the most lowly Brand Manager, they wanted constant attention, reassurance, endless discussions, frequent meals – the whole wearisome ritual dance that was officially described as 'servicing' an account. And it was never, ever over.

Simon dozed. When he woke, the sky was black, the plane angling down on its landing approach. The pilot's professionally cheerful voice informed passengers that it was raining in London.

It was nearly eleven by the time Simon cleared Customs, and the Arrivals lounge had been taken over by cleaners, moving with the deliberate slowness that characterizes workers on overtime. A tall figure in a black hat and a long black raincoat was watching the passengers as they came out, and walked briskly towards Simon.

'Welcome to Heathrow, dear. Isn't it glamorous at this time of night?'

Simon laughed. 'I didn't recognize you in the hat, Ern. How are you?'

'Breasting the waves like a dolphin at play. You'll see when we get outside. The monsoon season has started.'

As Ernest drove the big Mercedes through the downpour towards central London, he gave Simon his personal summary of events that had taken place in the agency over the past few days. Jordan and the Creative Director, David Fry, weren't speaking to each other. The Rubber Barons still hadn't made a decision about their account. There had been a piece in the trade press about a rumoured breakaway, and Liz had started going out with an undesirable young man who wore an earring and drove racing cars. Apart from that, there were several flats to see when Simon had a moment, and a stew waiting in the kitchen at Rutland Gate that just needed heating up.

'And how was New York? Is our Mr Ziegler as modest and charming as ever?'

'We got the business,' Simon said, 'so he's very pleased with himself. You'll be fascinated to hear that he's started wearing red braces.'

Ernest sniffed disdainfully. He and Ziegler had loathed each other at first sight. 'A belt as well, I hope. The thought of how that man would look if he lost his trousers is enough to shrivel the imagination.'

The car turned into Rutland Gate and pulled up outside the flat.

'Home sweet home,' said Ernest. 'Such as it is. Never mind. The place I saw in Wilton Crescent has distinct possibilities.'

They said goodnight, and Simon let himself in. He dropped his bags in the hall and went through to the sitting room, wrinkling his nose at the stuffy, sterile smell of central heating and warm carpet. A hotel-room smell. He went through a pile of compact discs until he came to Errol Garner's *Concert by the Sea*, poured a glass of whisky, lit a cigar, putting off the moment of going through the folder of papers that Liz had left for him on the table. He sometimes felt that he'd be buried one day beneath a mountain of memos, contact reports, strategy documents, financial projections, staff assessments, the great mass of corporate chewing gum. He sighed, and opened the folder.

There was a clipping from *Campaign*, the advertising magazine. It was an item in the Hotline section, the magazine's repository for the least plausible rumours of the week, and it hinted that a group of key executives planned to leave the agency, taking 'significant' accounts with them. No names were mentioned, and there was no substance to the report. It ended with the old standby, calculated to add credibility to the rumour, that 'top management were unavailable for comment'. Simon wondered how hard the reporter had tried to reach top management.

He worked his way through the papers, scribbling notes

to remind himself of the duty calls he'd have to make in the morning, and then came to an envelope that appeared to have been stamped on by an agitated spider with inky feet. He recognized the scrawl, and winced. Uncle William was obviously broke again.

Dearest boy,

Forgive me for disturbing your Olympian delibera-
tions, but I find myself, through no fault of my own,
struggling to survive in desperate circumstances . . .

Simon shook his head and sighed. Uncle William, artist and elderly philanderer, came into Simon's life infrequently and expensively, pinching bottoms and bouncing cheques with the vigour of a man half his age, a walking embarrass-ment. With some difficulty, Simon had managed to keep him away from London, fending him off with bribes. Even Ernest had never met him, and Caroline had never known of his existence. Any feelings of guilt that Simon experienced were cancelled out by thinking of the social carnage that would ensue if ever Uncle William were allowed to escape from Norfolk. Simon looked in his attaché case for his chequebook.

Another envelope, this time in neat, unfamiliar handwriting.

Dear Simon,
Un grand merci for dinner. I hope New York was not as
terrible as you imagined.

I leave London tomorrow for Provence and maybe
some sun after three days like a wet rat in the rain.
How do you support this weather?

I have a little idea for you, but my writing English
is not good. It's better if we talk.
Bisous,

Nicole

Simon looked at his watch. One in London, two in France. He'd call first thing in the morning. That, at least, would be a pleasant conversation before dealing with the office. He got up and gave himself another tot of whisky.

Bisous. He liked that. Kisses. He looked through the rest of the papers – a letter from Caroline's lawyers, a status report on new business prospects, a request for his presence at a client's think-tank on increasing the market for frozen chicken. Now there was a challenge to stir the imagination. He yawned, and went to bed.

9

Simon's conversation with Nicole had been brief and irresistible. She had refused to answer his questions about her idea. It's something you must see, she'd said. Why don't you come down? Through the fog of early morning and jet-lag, he'd suddenly realized that it was Saturday, and two hours later he was in a taxi on the way to Heathrow.

He picked up his ticket at the desk and went through to the duty-free area, dodging past small, determined Japanese women as they stripped the shelves of malt whisky. What brand of cigarettes did Nicole smoke? What scent did she wear? As the final call for his flight was announced, he settled for two bottles of Dom Perignon. She was certainly a champagne girl, he thought, as all the best girls are, and he wondered what she'd found that couldn't be explained over the phone. Whatever it was, it would be more interesting than his usual Saturday of working in an empty office. He had the pleasant feeling of playing truant, of taking a secret holiday.

The plane rose above the cushion of cloud positioned almost permanently over Heathrow, and his mood became even better at the sight of blue skies. French voices in the seats behind him discussed the glories of Harrods and Marks and Spencer, and compared cashmere prices and London restaurants. He looked forward to dinner, a long, quiet dinner a million miles away from anyone who knew him. Escape felt very good.

Simon had never landed at Marseille before. It could almost have been North Africa – rail-thin dark men with their plump wives and fat plastic suitcases, the guttural cough of Arabic, the smell of black tobacco and sweat mixed with pungent, sweet cologne, flight announcements for Oran and Djibouti. Hard to believe it was less than two hours from London.

Nicole's blonde head stood out in a sea of swarthy faces. She was dressed for the Mediterranean winter in pale grey flannel trousers and a dark blue sweater, her skin still the colour of honey from the sun.

'*Bonjour*, Mr Shaw.' She held up her face for two kisses.

Simon smiled. 'How are you, Madame Bouvier?'

She put her arm through his as they walked across the concourse to the baggage-claim area. 'You forgive me for taking you from the office?'

Simon looked down at her. 'I have a nasty feeling it'll still be there on Monday.'

They found Nicole's little white car, and she was silent with concentration until they had filtered on to the *autoroute*. '*Bon*,' she said, and shook a cigarette from the packet on the dashboard. 'It's easy to miss the turn, and then you find yourself in Aix.'

'There are worse places to end up.' Simon settled back and watched Nicole jab the cigar lighter with an impatient finger. He was pleased she didn't wear nail varnish.

'*Merde*,' she said. 'This car. Nothing works.'

Simon found some matches, reached over and took the cigarette from her mouth and lit it, enjoying the faint taste of lipstick.

'*Merci*.' She blew smoke out of the open window. 'You don't ask any questions, so I think you like to be surprised.' She glanced over at him.

'I'm on holiday, and I never ask questions on holiday. I turn into a giant vegetable. All I want is to be driven up and down the *autoroute* at dangerously high speed by a blonde who's not looking at the road. That's my idea of a nice relaxed time.'

Nicole laughed. Tiny lines appeared at the corners of her eyes, and one slightly irregular tooth stood out from the rest. She looked as good as he remembered.

They talked, easily and of nothing important, and, as they left the *autoroute*, Simon noticed that autumn had settled on the landscape. The sky was summer-blue, but there were splashes of red leaves on the cherry trees now, some of the vines brown as rust, others yellow, dense pockets of shadow

111

in the folds of the Lubéron, smoke rising from faraway bonfires.

They turned off the main road and began the climb up the long hill leading towards Gordes. 'I made you a reservation at the same hotel,' Nicole said. 'It's OK?'

'Best view in Provence,' said Simon.

Nicole smiled and said nothing. She waited in the car while Simon checked in and left his suitcase. He came back carrying a bright yellow plastic bag.

'I almost forgot,' he said. 'This is for you. Take it twice a day before meals, and you'll never have indigestion.'

Nicole looked inside the bag, and laughed. 'A Frenchman would say more elegant things about champagne.'

'A Frenchman would only have bought one bottle. Where are we going?'

'To my house first, and then we walk.'

Nicole's house, the highest in Brassière-les-Deux-Églises, was at the end of a cul-de-sac, a narrow, three-storey building of weathered stone with wooden shutters painted in a colour somewhere between grey and faded green. Steps led up to a carved wooden front door with a knocker in the form of a hand holding a ball, and the leaves of an old wild-grape vine flared autumn-red against the wall.

'This is lovely,' said Simon. 'How long have you had it?'

'Ten, eleven years.' Nicole turned the key in the door and nudged it open with her hip. 'One day it will be finished. The top floor is still to do. Be careful with your head.'

Simon ducked inside. At the far end of the long, low room, through a glass door, he could see a small terrace with blue hills beyond. Comfortable, slightly shabby armchairs were arranged in front of a cut-stone fireplace that had been laid with vine clippings. On the other side of the room, the wall had been knocked away to waist-height to make a bar, with a gap at one end leading through to the kitchen. Books were everywhere, books and flowers. The air smelled faintly of lavender.

Nicole unpacked the champagne and put it in the refrigerator, looking up at Simon as she closed the door. 'Twice a day?'

'Absolutely, doctor's orders.' He ran his hand over the stone top of the bar. 'I like your house. I love places that aren't fussy.'

'Fussy? What is that?'

Simon thought of the house in Kensington where he and Caroline used to live. 'Well, it's when every square foot is decorated to death – when you have so much going on in a room that people spoil it. I had a house like that once, and I hated it. I was always sitting on the wrong cushion or putting cigar ash into the antique porcelain. It was like a bloody obstacle course. All that space and nowhere to live.'

Nicole nodded, and laughed. 'That's good you don't like fussy places. You'll see when I show you.'

They left the house and walked down to the centre of the village, the afternoon sun already beginning to drop in the west. Fallen leaves the size of hands made a yellow carpet outside the café where Simon had spent his first night in Brassière, and he could see an old woman watching them from a window of the house next door, her face partly hidden by the folds of a lace curtain.

They turned to go down the street leading from the main *place*, and Simon saw the façade of the old *gendarmerie*, still without doors or windows, still abandoned.

Nicole touched his arm. 'Have you guessed?'

They stopped, and looked through the empty building towards the Lubéron, a series of spectacular pictures framed by the openings in the far wall.

'Give me a clue.'

'You say you want to change how you live, change what you do, *non*?'

Simon nodded, half-smiling at the serious expression on Nicole's face.

She led him through the doorway of the *gendarmerie*, picking her way through the rubble to one of the window openings. 'Look. *There* is the best view in Provence, and this . . .' she waved her arm at the dusty, cavernous room '. . . this, well, imagine how this could be. And then on top you have bedrooms, and below, the restaurant . . .'

'The restaurant?'

'Of course a restaurant, not too big, but with the *terrasse* in the summer, space for maybe forty people, a little bar by the *piscine* . . .'

'Nicole?'

'*Oui*?'

'What are you talking about?'

She laughed. 'You didn't guess already? This is your hotel. It's perfect. Small, but with a charm – I can see it in my head – and the view, and so much work already done . . .' Her voice tailed off. She perched on a stone window-ledge and looked up at Simon. '*Voilà*. That's my idea for you.'

He took out a cigar and lit it, feeling like a client who had just been shown a campaign he wasn't expecting. It was ridiculous, of course. He knew nothing about running hotels, and it would be a full-time job just getting the place restored. Then finding staff, building up the business – although with his contacts that shouldn't be a problem. All the same, it was a big undertaking, not something he could do sitting in an advertising agency in London. It would be a leap, a gamble, a complete change. But wasn't that what he said he wanted? And Nicole was right; it could be spectacular. He looked at her. She was backlit by the last slanting rays of the sun, an image straight out of a shampoo commercial. Once an advertising man, always an advertising man. Or was he?

'You're very quiet, Simon.'

'I'm very surprised. It's not every day I get offered a little hotel.'

'Do you see how it could be?' Nicole stood up and shivered. The chill in the air was having a distracting effect on her nipples under the thin sweater.

'It could be a lot warmer. Come on. Let me buy you a drink.'

'You already did. We have champagne at home. Doctor's orders.'

If I had a doctor like you, Simon thought, I'd be an Olympic-standard hypochondriac. 'Nicole, it's a fascinating idea.' He winced at his own words. 'God, I'm sorry. I sound

114

exactly like one of my clients. It's just that I need to think about it, and I need to know a lot more. Let's get back, and you can tell me about it.'

By the time they reached the house the sun was gone, leaving a pink afterglow in the sky. Nicole lit the fire and asked Simon to choose some music from the compact discs stacked between piles of books on the shelf, Tina Turner next to Mozart (he would have enjoyed that, Simon thought), Couperin, Fauré, Piaf, Brahms, Montserrat Caballé, Jeff Beck. He hesitated between Pavarotti and Chopin before picking Keith Jarrett. The first few quiet notes of the Köln Concert were accompanied by the sound of a champagne cork. The room was warm, and aromatic with the scent of burning wood. Rutland Gate seemed a long way away.

Nicole handed him a glass. '*Santé*.'

'Here's to small and charming hotels.'

They sat in front of the fire, and Simon started with the obvious questions. Nicole had done her homework – she knew the square metres on each floor, the details of the work that had already been completed, the asking price. As she'd told him before, the original plan had been to turn the *gendarmerie* into small apartments. Basic electrical and plumbing work had been finished. The pool had been dug and lined. The property was now ready for *les finitions* – plaster and glass and flagstones and fittings, lighting and landscaping, the exciting part of restoration that follows months and millions of francs devoted to essential but often invisible preparatory work.

'Let me ask you an impossible question,' Simon said. 'What do you think it would cost to finish?'

Nicole leaned forward in her chair, elbows on her knees, her glass cradled in both hands. She wrinkled her nose in concentration. With her hair pushed back behind her ears, she looked about twenty. Simon felt himself slipping gently down the slope that leads from simple attraction to something more complicated.

'The *main d'œuvre* of the workers, that can always be calculated,' she said. 'For the rest, it depends on your materials. There is one price for marble and another for stone from the local quarry. For me, the way to do this is with materials from the region, very clean, not fussy. Like that, and with good furniture, maybe one or two antiques . . .' she looked up at the ceiling, and Simon admired the line of her throat '. . . I make a big guess: seven, eight million francs.'

'How long would it take?'

'This is Provence, remember. Five years?' Nicole laughed. 'No, I'm not serious, but to be impatient here is expensive.'

'Could it be done in six months?'

Nicole held up one hand and rubbed fingers and thumb together. 'With enough money, enough men, yes. Even here.'

Simon went on with his questions – architects, building permissions, a licence to serve alcohol, staff, a chef. A chef. He glanced at his watch. 'I think we should do some research on chefs. Where would you like to eat?'

Nicole pretended to think. What she wanted was to stay here with this smiling, untidy man who still needed a hair-cut, and talk without the distractions of menus and waiters. He brought a warmth to the room that she liked very much.

'There are three or four places not too far away. But it's Saturday. Without a reservation . . . I could try.' She hesitated, and shrugged. 'Or I have pasta, with a fresh tomato sauce. Very simple.'

Simon closed his eyes in mock ecstasy, then opened one to look at her. 'Fresh tomato sauce? With basil?'

'Of course with basil.'

'I'll help. I'm good in kitchens. I wash dishes, I keep the cook's glass filled, I don't bump into things.'

Nicole laughed, and stood up. 'Bon. Do you open wine too?'

'No cork can resist me. It's something I learned in the Boy Scouts.' He followed her into the kitchen and watched as she slipped a long chef's apron over her head, pushed up the sleeves of her sweater and took a bottle of red wine from the rack.

'Voilà, monsieur. Château Val-Joanis. It comes from just

116

the other side of the Lubéron.' She held out the bottle, and he noticed the delicate blue veins on the inside of her forearm. He liked a woman who rolled up her sleeves to cook, something that Caroline had never done. 'Corkscrew and glasses on the bar.'

It was a fine kitchen, he thought, a proper cook's kitchen, with copper pans hanging where you could get at them, knives with blades worn thin by years of sharpening, a stove with a cast-iron top, a shelf of battered cookbooks, a round table of scarred, thick wood. Everything well-used, well-cared for. He poured the wine, and took a glass to Nicole, who was ladling tomato sauce into a pan. He bent his head over the pan to inhale the wonderful summery smell, and then, with a quick, guilty dab, dipped a finger into the sauce and licked it clean.

Nicole tapped the back of his hand with the ladle. 'No more. You help me better if you sit and talk.'

Simon retired to the table, sucking sauce from his knuckles. He enjoyed watching Nicole as she moved, reaching for knives, chopping and stirring, wiping her hands on her thighs before picking up her glass, the unhurried, sensual rhythm of a confident cook. She looked almost elegant in her apron, tied tightly so that it accentuated her slim waist.

'Tell me about hotels down here,' he said. 'What happens in the winter? Do they all close, like they do on the coast?'

Nicole put a pan of water on the stove, added salt and a bay leaf, and picked up her glass. 'For one month, maybe two. It's changed since the years when the season was just July and August. From Easter it's busy until October. Then you have the holidays like Toussaint in November, then you have Christmas and the New Year. Spring begins in March.' She sipped her wine. 'The season is nine months, and the clientele is not just French, not just Parisians – Germans, Dutch, Belgians, Swiss, English – they all come, more and more each year. A good hotel will always work, and here round Brassière it is a corner without hotels. The nearest is Gordes.' She put down her glass and started to mix a dressing for the salad, beating the oil and vinegar with a little mustard and brown sugar, adding a few drops of fresh lemon juice. 'I tell you, it's not a crazy idea.'

117

'No,' Simon said, 'it's not.' He thought about it, thought about the kind of hotel that he would like to stay in, small, friendly, simple, perfectly run. Could he run it? Probably not. He didn't have the patience, or the eye for detail. But Ernest – meticulous, efficient, reliable, knowledgeable about food and drink, a prince among flower arrangers and a good man with people – now there was a born hotel manager. If he wanted to do it.

'I wonder what Ern would think about it?'

Nicole tore off a small piece of bread, dipped it in the salad dressing and offered it to Simon. 'Why don't you ask him?'

He bit into the bread, and the sharp–sweet dressing dripped on to his chin. Nicole bent over to wipe it with the corner of her apron. Their faces were very close.

'I hope you're better with tomato sauce,' she said.

Simon swallowed. Nicole had moved back to the stove. She put the pasta into boiling water, took cutlery and napkins from a drawer, poured the dressing over the salad and passed him the wooden bowl. 'Mix that, and then we can eat.'

Anyone watching this domestic scene might have taken them for an established couple, except that they glanced at each other a little too often, and when they happened to touch it was not in the casual, familiar way of a man and a woman who are used to being together. Simon felt his chin where Nicole had wiped it. He would have kissed her if he hadn't had his mouth full.

Nicole drained the pasta, added olive oil, and slipped the loop of the apron over her head. There was a flush in her cheeks from the heat of the stove, and she made a face as she pushed back her hair. 'I think I must look terrible.'

Simon grinned, and stood up to pull out her chair. 'Completely hideous,' he said. 'Let's hope you're a decent cook.'

Pasta and conversation don't mix, and there was a contented silence while they ate. Simon mopped up the last of his sauce with a scrap of bread, and wiped his mouth with exaggerated care. 'There you are,' he said. 'A clean chin. A spotless chin.'

Nicole smiled at him, and shook her head. 'I think you wiped it on your shirt.' She got up and fetched a cloth and a bowl of water. Simon looked down at the oily, dark blotches that had made a rash on the blue poplin of his shirt front.

'Stand up.'

'I'm sorry. I told you I was a slob.'

'Yes,' Nicole said. 'A big slob.' She put the bowl down, dipped the cloth in the water and undid a button of his shirt, slipping her hand inside. He felt her fingers against his heart, and this time he didn't have his mouth full.

It was midday before they got up, showered, started to dress and went back to bed, and mid-afternoon before they left the house to pick up Simon's case from the hotel.

'God knows what they think of me at this place,' he said. 'The first time I arrived without a suitcase, and this time I didn't even use the room.'

Simon went into the reception area, conscious of his unshaven face and the faint traces of acne on his shirt. The girl at the desk was charming, and he found himself thinking of her as someone to remember if he went ahead with the hotel.

'I hope you enjoyed your stay, Mr Shaw.'

He signed the bill, and smiled. 'Yes,' he said. 'Yes, I did, very much. The scenery's lovely at this time of year.'

They had an hour to kill before going to the airport, and went back to the *gendarmerie*. The idea was taking hold of Simon's imagination; he could see it finished in his mind, stone and glass and sunlight. He wondered how much of this enthusiasm came from a detached business perspective, and how much from the woman who was standing beside him. There had been a shock of happiness when he had woken up to see Nicole's face on the pillow. He put his arm round her waist and pulled her towards him.

'I want to do it,' he said. 'But on two conditions. The first is Ernest. He could make it work if he wanted to come.'

'And?'

119

'You have to make pasta for me again.' He looked down at Nicole, and noticed the burn that his stubble had made on her throat. 'I'll bring a spare shirt.'

10

By two o'clock, the lunch-time customers at Chez Mathilde
were gone, the tables had been reset for dinner, and the girl
who helped in the kitchen was making her customary clatter
as she scoured pans and stacked plates. Mathilde was bent
suspiciously over the till, glasses on the end of her nose,
smoothing wrinkled banknotes into neat piles and frowning
at the occasional cheque which would have to pass through
the bank and therefore be liable to tax. She looked up as the
General put on his jacket and patted his pockets.

'*Merde*,' he said. 'I won't have time to stop. You'd better
let me have some cash.'

Mathilde licked her thumb and counted out five 100-franc
notes. 'Make sure he gives you a discount.' She put the
money on top of the till. 'When will you be back?'

'Not late, unless he finds something serious.' The General
took the money and ducked under Mathilde's glasses to kiss
her cheek. 'Have a little nap, eh?'

Mathilde nodded. 'Yes, *chéri*. I'll take a nap, and nothing
will be ready for tonight. Off you go. Don't forget – a
discount for cash.'

The General was still smiling as he got into the car. A
good woman, Mathilde, careful with the centimes. She'd
probably be the same if they had millions, and if this job
came off, they would. He turned right at the sign for Isle-
sur-Sorgue and felt a slight emptiness in his stomach, a
ripple of excitement. Mathilde thought he was going to the
dentist. In fact, he was going to do some research at the
scene of the crime.

He parked a hundred yards from the Caisse d'Épargne,
and looked at his watch. Plenty of time to buy what he
needed before the appointment. He picked up two copies of
Le Provençal, and then found a stationery shop. He chose a

small notebook and two large manila envelopes which bulged in a satisfactory way when he put the folded newspapers inside them.

Ten minutes to kill. He went into the bar at the end of the narrow bridge across the river and ordered a Calva to settle the nerves. The town was quiet, almost deserted, just another slow autumn afternoon. The General felt the Calvados go down, a warm and comforting jolt, and imagined how different the view from the bar would be on that Sunday next July. There would be market stalls all along the river, the *bric-à-brac* dealers lining the main road, tourists everywhere, traffic at a standstill and the cops nowhere to be seen, keeping out of the heat and letting the motorists argue among themselves. Perfect.

The General wiped his moustache, tucked his envelopes under his arm and crossed the bridge, walking briskly, as a man would who had important and confidential business to transact. He passed the old water-wheel at the side of the bank with no more than a quick glance at the top of the opening that showed above the green flow of the river, and climbed the flight of steps to the entrance.

The clerk behind the counter ignored him for the statutory two minutes, as laid down in bank regulations, before looking up from his computer sheets.

'I have a rendezvous,' said the General, 'with Monsieur Millet.'

The clerk sighed, and left his vital work to lead the General over to a cubicle in the corner. He tapped on the glass door before pushing it open, and murmured at the top of a dark head that was bent over a desk. Monsieur Millet removed his glasses, placed them carefully in the exact centre of the document he had been studying, rose to his feet and extended a small, pale hand. He was slight and neat in his white shirt and precisely knotted tie. His desk was uncluttered, his pencils sharp. A framed photograph of a neat woman and a neat child stood next to his empty in-tray. The General was wondering why he had no telephone when one of the drawers rang.

'Excuse me,' said Monsieur Millet. 'Please sit down.' He

opened the drawer and picked up the phone. The General decided not to disturb the symmetry of the desk with his manila envelopes, and kept them on his lap.

Monsieur Millet finished his conversation and hid the phone. He placed his elbows on the desk and clasped his hands, leaning forward to give the General his full attention. '*Alors* . . .'

The General tapped the envelopes in his lap. 'I have some papers – deeds and contracts – the kind of papers that one would not wish to lose.'

'Deeds and contracts,' said Monsieur Millet. 'I understand. Documents of value and importance.'

'Exactly. That is why I feel they should be kept in a place of great security.'

'Maximum security, my dear *monsieur*. Maximum security.' The fingers of the small, pale hands fidgeted with concern. 'Without correct documentation, as I keep telling my staff, the world would cease to function. Documents should be treated like gold.'

The General nodded, and once again tapped his two folded copies of *Le Provençal*. 'These particularly.' He leaned forward. 'I would like to keep them here, in one of your strong-boxes. Safer than at home.'

'Ah, if only everyone were as prudent as you. Here in the Vaucluse, we have the highest rate of burglary in France – except for Paris, of course.' Millet shrugged his skinny shoulders, and then permitted himself a smile. 'Fortunately, people are learning.' He reached into his pocket and took out a bunch of keys that was attached to his belt by a chain, unlocked the deep drawer below the home of his telephone and produced a thick dossier.

'In here,' he said, putting on his glasses, 'I have the details of our strong-box rentals. Three hundred boxes were installed last year – on my recommendation, I may say – and today, let me see . . . we have just thirty-eight boxes un-rented.' He pursed his lips and rearranged an errant sheet of paper that was protruding slightly from the pile. 'Two hundred and sixty-two boxes rented in less than a year.' He looked at the General. 'Yes, people are learning.'

The General tugged his moustache. 'How very encouraging. Local people, I suppose, like myself?'

'That, *monsieur*, I cannot tell you.' Millet took off his glasses, and his hands resumed their embrace. 'Discretion is guaranteed to all our clients. Discretion and security.'

'Excellent,' said the General. 'That's the way it should be, like it is in Switzerland.'

Millet sniffed. 'We have nothing to learn from the Swiss. You will see when I take you through to the strong-room. Now then. Shall we deal with the formalities?'

The General had considered using a false name, but had decided that it was an unnecessary complication. He was doing nothing wrong. His box would be robbed like everyone else's. What was the point of taking the risk, however slight, of bumping into Millet one day on the street and being greeted with a name that wasn't his? So he filled in the form and made out a cheque for a year's rental, using the chequebook that Mathilde didn't know about, the account he'd built up over the years that was now funding the operation.

Millet excused himself for a few minutes, returning with the keys of the strong-room and the General's personal box. Together, they went to an unmarked door at the back of the bank.

'Now,' said Millet, 'let us imagine that you are a bank robber.' He smiled at the General. 'An amusing hypothesis, no?' He didn't wait for a reply. '*Bon*. You have arrived here. What do you see?'

The General looked, and shrugged. 'A door.'

Millet's index finger came up and wagged like a metronome. 'Your first mistake. It is a shield of solid steel. Watch.'

He selected two keys, unlocked the door and pulled it open. Six or seven centimetres thick, the General estimated. Definitely not a sardine can. He nodded, and tried to look impressed.

Millet gestured proudly at the next obstacle, a second door, this time of square steel bars, each bar the thickness of his wrist. The General inspected it dutifully.

'Tell me, Monsieur Millet,' he said, 'why is this second door made of bars?'

Millet chose two more keys from his collection. 'We have, of course, electronic surveillance throughout the bank – video cameras, alarms, the latest, most sensitive technology. But we must not forget one thing.' He turned towards the General and brandished a key under his nose. 'Discretion, my dear *monsieur*, discretion. For that reason, there is no surveillance within the strong-room itself. Our clients have complete privacy while they are inside this room. And complete security, because they are locked in.'

He tapped the solid steel door with a key. 'This, as you can imagine, is soundproof. Let us suppose it is locked. A client is inside. He has a *crise cardiaque*' – Millet clutched his breast dramatically – 'he collapses, he cries out, but he cannot be heard. There is also, for some, the problem of claustrophobia. We have to think of these possibilities. That is why the first door remains open, and the second door is locked. *Voilà.*'

Millet led the General into the strong-room. It was in the shape of an L, lined with numbered, grey steel boxes, a small table and two chairs placed in the corner, out of sight to anyone standing at the doorway.

'The boxes can only be opened by the master-key used in conjunction with the client's personal key,' said Millet. 'Security, always security.' He turned the master-lock on box 263, and handed the General two stubby inches of chromed steel. 'Your personal key, made by Fichet, imposs- ible to duplicate.'

He stood back, waiting for the opening ceremony to be performed.

'If I could have a few minutes,' said the General, 'I'd like to go through the papers just once more before I put them away.'

'But of course. Take as long as you wish, *monsieur*.' He cocked his head and smiled. 'Obviously, I will lock you up. A novel experience, no, to be behind bars?'

The General smiled back. 'How does one escape?'

'Press this red button by the door, and we will come to release you. We treat our prisoners very well here.'

'I can see,' said the General. 'Thank you.'

He sat down at the table and took out his notebook and a pocket tape-measure. Fernand needed to know steel thicknesses to calculate the amount of explosive. Then there was the back door and the floor. The General busied himself guiltily for ten minutes, measuring and sketching in between frequent glances through the bars until he had a rough plan of the room, dimensions of the door, and confirmation, after peeling back a small patch of carpet in the corner, that the floor was reinforced concrete. That was going to be the loudest explosion, he thought. The rest would be muffled by the steel doors. But it would be a noisy night. He looked at the rows of boxes, and sucked at the end of his moustache. How much? Hundreds of thousands? Millions? Gold coins? Jewels?

He had as much as he needed for the time being. He could always come back. He slid the manila envelopes into box 263 and locked up. Yes, it would be a noisy night.

11

Liz put a cup of coffee and a stack of correspondence on the table in front of Simon.

'You poor thing,' she said. 'You look exhausted. Was it awful in New York?'

'Ziegler was his old charming self. He's like a gorilla on steroids, that man. Still, we got the business.' He handed her a draft press release.

'Well, I think you're overdoing it. You should try to take the weekends off, at least. I suppose you were in here again all day Saturday and Sunday catching up.'

Simon sighed dramatically. 'A tycoon's work is never done, Elizabeth.'

'You joke about it, but I'm serious.'

'I know you are.' He sipped his coffee. 'Now then. Could you type up the release and then ask Mr Jordan to canter in here when he has a moment?'

Liz smiled. 'I've just seen him. You're going to love his outfit.'

Jordan had, as usual, spent the weekend in his country house, and to make sure that the rest of the agency knew it, he was wearing his squire's tweeds – a whiskery suit the colour of dead moss, the jacket deep-vented and multi-flapped, the trousers looking rigid enough to stand up without the benefit of internal support. A Tattersall check shirt, a bright yellow tie, ginger suede brogues. Simon wondered if the suit was biodegradable, if it would ever wear out. Probably not. It looked bullet-proof.

'Morning, Nigel. I keep meaning to ask you for the name of your tailor.'

Jordan sat down, hitching up his trousers to reveal thick, heather-mixture socks. 'Chap in Cork Street. Been going to him for years. He gets his tweed specially woven by a little man in Scotland.' He looked with satisfaction at his furry legs. 'You won't find stuff like this easily nowadays.'

Simon nodded. 'I'm sure.' He passed a sheet of paper across the table. 'Well, we got it. Three hundred million dollars worldwide, possibly more. That's a draft press release. We'd better send it out today before Ziegler starts calling every editor in London.'

Jordan's hand stopped in mid-air above the press release. 'Good God, that was quick. Congratulations are in order, old boy. Well done. Couldn't have happened at a better time.' He read through the release, nodded, and put it down. 'Spot on. Our friends in the City will be pleased. So will the troops.'

'Some of the troops,' said Simon. He pulled out the cutting from *Campaign* magazine. 'I gather from this that one or two of the others are restless. A breakaway, it says here, top executives, big pieces of business. What do you think? Is there anything in it, or is it just the usual shit they make up when they don't have enough news?'

Simon had never seen Jordan blush before. Patches of red mottled his cheeks, and his neck swelled visibly. He studied the contents of his cigarette case with exaggerated interest before choosing one and lighting it.

'Ah,' he said, 'that. I was going to speak to you about that, actually. It could possibly have been a slip of the tongue. Very unfortunate.'

'Whose tongue?'

'Well, mine. Actually.'

'Go on.'

'I was in Annabel's last week with Jeremy Scott – you know, the Chairman of Anglo . . .'

'The name rings a bell,' said Simon. Anglo Holdings was one of the agency's three biggest accounts.

'Well, we'd had a bite to eat together, and then went on for a nightcap, and we were joking at the bar about the size of the account – they put the budget up again, as you know – and Jeremy said something about Anglo being big enough to support an entire agency.' Jordan stopped to inspect the end of his cigarette. 'And then the old whisky started talking, I suppose, and I may have said something silly.'

'About starting your own agency?'

'That sort of thing – but just joking, old boy, just joking.'

'Of course,' said Simon. 'But how did it get into *Campaign*?'

'Well, I didn't notice until we were leaving, but there were a couple of chaps from JWT at the other end of the bar who might have heard us and got hold of the wrong end of the stick. A quick phone call to *Campaign* . . .' Jordan shook his head. 'Bloody disgraceful, really. If you can't have a quiet chat in Annabel's without the press picking it up, I don't know what the world's coming to.'

Simon sighed. If you wanted gossip to turn into fact overnight, the bar at Annabel's was a good place to start. He leaned forward. 'Nigel, do you realize what the Parker business is going to do to our share price? To your personal net worth?' God, he thought, I'm beginning to sound like Ziegler's little echo. 'I'm working on some developments here which could be very interesting. I need to know I can count on you.'

Relief, curiosity and greed chased across Jordan's face, to be replaced by solemn sincerity. 'Absolutely, old boy. To the grave.'

'Let's hope that won't be necessary.' Simon stood up, and clapped Jordan on the shoulder. His suit felt like undergrowth. 'Good. I'm glad that's been cleared up.'

Jordan left, and Simon realized how fortunate the timing had been. Shifty bastard, of course he'd been planning to take the business and run. But now, with the new account, Simon could wave enough money under his nose to make him stay, and that was essential. Simon's departure from the agency depended on the continuity that Jordan could provide. All the big clients felt comfortable with him, God only knew why. They probably all went to the same bloody tailor.

Simon took the press release through to Liz's office. 'Could you send that out, Liz? The usual list, please. And I need to see Ernest. Do you know where he is?'

'Ernest is with Leonard, Mr Shaw. They're having a review of the agency's plants.'

'I see. Well, when he pokes his little green fingers round the door, perhaps you could ask him to come in.'

Simon returned to his office and stared out of the window at Hyde Park. The leaves had gone from the trees, and the joggers – where did they find the time to jog? – were muffled up against the damp, their breath grey in the air. He thought about exercise, and he thought about Nicole's slender, almost muscular body. She ate like a horse, too. He was smiling as he heard a tap on the door and turned away from the window to see Ernest poised in the doorway.

'Morning, Ern. How are the plants?'

'Verdant, I'm happy to say, despite young Leonard's rather heavy hand with the plant food. I think he longs for a jungle. Before we know it, he'll be putting in a requisition for parrots. You called?'

'Yes, come in. Better shut the door.'

Ernest allowed his eyebrows a fractional twitch of surprise. Closed doors meant secrets.

'Sit down, Ern. I've got a surprise for you.' Simon hesitated, searching for the right words. He should have worked this out, not been so impatient. 'Ern, I'm thinking of leaving the agency. I've seen a place in Provence I'd like to buy.'

Ernest said nothing, his expression suddenly very serious.

'It would make a fantastic little hotel, absolutely fantastic, and it could be put together by next summer – restaurant, pool, a dozen rooms, the most extraordinary view. Everything's there. It just needs finishing. I'd really like to do it.'

Ernest stared down at his hands, which were clasped tightly round one knee. 'It sounds very nice.' He sighed, and suddenly looked older. 'Oh well. It had to happen, I suppose, something like this. The agency doesn't make you happy any more, does it?' He looked at Simon and tried to smile. 'Yes, you're probably ready for a change. Well . . . good luck, dear. Good luck.'

'No, Ern, I'm putting this very badly.' Simon felt clumsy and stupid. 'Look, I wouldn't dream of doing it unless you wanted to come in with me. Not just for old times' sake, either. I couldn't run a hotel to save my life – I've got money, I've got contacts, I've got enthusiasm, but that's not enough. Good hotels – the best hotels – are good because every detail is right. You know what I'm like with detail, completely hopeless. But you ... I don't know. I can just see you there, running the place. I couldn't do it on my own.' Simon shrugged and grinned. 'Besides, I'd probably miss you, even though you are a bloody old nag.'

It was almost embarrassing to watch the joy come back to Ernest's face. It lit up as he took a long, deep sigh. The slump went from his shoulders. And then he blinked very quickly several times and blew his nose loudly.

'Well!' he said at last. 'I think I'll have a sherry, if I may.' He got up and went to the bar in the corner. 'A hotel! You are the sly one, aren't you?'

'I'm not asking you to make an instant decision, Ern. Think about it for a day or two. It's not like just changing your job.'

Ernest swivelled around from the bar on his toes, beamed, and held up his glass. 'Farewell, Wimbledon!' He took a large mouthful, and shuddered.

'We'll talk about it this evening, at the flat.' Simon felt exhilarated and impatient, the way he used to feel when the agency had just started. 'There's a lot to sort out, and until we're ready ...' he put a finger to his lips '... not a word, OK?'

Ernest took another swig of sherry. He seemed unable to stop smiling. 'I shall be as silent as the oyster.'

There was a knock on the door, and Liz looked in. 'I'm sorry to disturb you, Mr Shaw, but your eleven o'clock is here.' She noticed the glass in Ernest's hand. 'Celebrating, Ernest?'

'Medicinal, dear.' He patted his chest. 'For the hiccups. I'd better be off, before young Leonard drapes the reception-ist in variegated ivy.'

Liz stood aside to let him through the door, and frowned at Simon. 'Is he all right?'

Simon smiled. 'Yes,' he said. 'Yes, I think he is. Let's have the next victim. Wheel him in, would you?'

*

131

Ernest was having great difficulty concentrating on the agency's plant problems. A hotel in Provence! He felt giddy with excitement. He would have followed Simon anywhere, of course, with the possible exception, he had to admit, of Milton Keynes. But this – the chance to decorate and run a little jewel in the sun, away from all those dreary people and the impossible climate – this was the opportunity of a lifetime, something to stretch his creative talents. He would bloom, he was sure of it, and in his private euphoria he was unusually receptive to young Leonard's requests for Kentia palms in the Media Department. Have a grotto in the underground car park while you're at it, dear, he thought. I won't be here to see it. I shall be in Provence. He decided to spend his lunch-hour finding out about French courses at Berlitz.

Simon plodded through the day, resisting the impulse to call Nicole until he was satisfied that Ernest's initial reaction had survived any second thoughts. Farewell Wimbledon, farewell Ziegler, farewell Jordan, farewell afternoons spent in artificial light. He looked at his watch, willing time to hurry.

Six o'clock, and the Research Director was just getting into his stride. A breakthrough in demographic analysis, invaluable marketing tool, charts and documents, hot air, hot air. Simon looked at the group assembled in his office and swallowed a yawn. He had been waiting for a pause in the monologue for ten minutes, but the Research Director didn't seem to need as much breath as normal human beings.

Simon stood up abruptly, feigning a sudden realization of the time. 'God, I'm sorry, Andrew. This is fascinating, but I had no idea it was so late. I'm supposed to be in the City by six-thirty.' He rescued his jacket from the back of the couch. 'Listen, help yourselves to a drink and carry on. I'll catch up tomorrow. I think you've really got something there.' He was out of the office before the Research Director's mouth had time to recover from its gape of surprise.

As Simon let himself into the flat, he heard the sound of

Beethoven's 'Pastoral', and found Ernest in the sitting room. A map of southern France was spread out on the table next to a Michelin Guide and a handful of language course brochures. Ernest was still wearing the broad smile that had been more or less permanently on his face all day.

'You haven't changed your mind, then, Ern?'

'*Moi*? Certainly not. I can hardly wait to slip into my espadrilles and scamper through the thyme.' He leaned over the map. 'But where are we, exactly?'

'Brassière-les-Deux Églises.' Simon found the dot on the map. 'There. It's about forty minutes from Avignon. Very pretty countryside, not too far from the *autoroute* and the airport, and there isn't another hotel within ten or fifteen miles. It's a good position. It could do very well.' He tossed his jacket on a chair and went into the kitchen. 'What are you having?'

Ernest looked up from the map. 'I put something appropriate in the fridge. My little treat.'

Simon took the bottle out and smiled. Mumm Grand Cordon Rosé. 'What an old tart you are, Ern.'

'There's nothing like pink champagne to bring a becoming blush to the cheek, I always say. And it is a festive occasion.'

Simon brought the glasses through, and handed one to Ernest. 'You're sure you want to do it? Really sure?'

'What would I do if you left the agency? Dogsbody-in-chief to his lordship Mr Jordan? Can you imagine anything more ghastly? Besides, this is going to be fun, like the old days. Starting something new. You feel the same way, I can tell.' He sniffed. 'So let's not have any more nonsense. I am positively rigid with resolve.'

They sat at the table, and Simon started to describe the old *gendarmerie* and go through a timetable that he'd worked out. During the next few days an offer would be made for the property. Unless there were any snags, they could go over at the weekend to sign the act of sale and brief an architect. Give him a month to prepare plans and estimates, start work before Christmas, finish by the end of May. In the meantime, Simon would extricate himself as discreetly as possible from the agency, and Ernest would take himself off to Berlitz.

Ernest had been making notes while Simon was talking, and was looking increasingly puzzled.

'What I'm just a tiny bit concerned about,' he said, 'is how all this can be done from London, even if we pop over two or three times a month. You remember what the builders were like in Kensington – the moment one left them, they either did nothing, or something completely hideous.' He looked down at his notepad. 'And then there's staff, furniture, the chef, the wine cellar, endless things that have to be done on the spot. I'd be thrilled to go there tomorrow, but I don't know a soul. It would take me months to find the right people. Or am I being an old wet blanket?'

Simon grinned. 'I should have told you, Ern. I've got a secret weapon over there. You remember Nicole Bouvier?'

Ernest raised his head and looked at Simon through speculative, half-closed eyes. 'Ah. Our lady of the exhaust pipe.'

'That's the one. Well, I went over to see her last weekend, and I think she could be the answer. In fact, it was her idea. She knows everybody down there, and, well . . . she could be our man on the spot.'

'So to speak.'

'So to speak, Ern. Yes.'

Ernest went into the kitchen and refilled their glasses. He wasn't surprised. Simon was susceptible. It was one of the reasons Ernest was so fond of him. And he had to admit that she was an attractive woman, a very suitable woman for Simon. A very useful woman, as it happened, and she seemed to like him. Airnést, she called him. In every way, she was a great improvement over Caroline.

'Do I take it that you and Madame Bouvier are slightly more than acquaintances?'

'Ern, if you keep waggling your eyebrows like that, they'll drop off. We're what they call good friends.'

'Ah. Quite.' Ernest consulted his notepad again. 'Well, I have a little confession to make too, since this seems to be

134

the moment for revelations. I don't think I've ever told you about Mrs Gibbons.'

Simon knew very little about Ernest's private life. He made occasional references to 'a companion', whom Simon always assumed was a man. Mrs Gibbons had never been mentioned.

'I'd be heartbroken if she couldn't come,' Ernest added. 'She'd be no trouble, I promise.'

Simon shrugged. 'What's one more? If you like her, Ern, I'm sure I will.'

'Past her youth now, poor old thing, but you'll adore her, I know. One black eye, and a completely hairless pink tummy. Walks like a drunken sailor, and very good with mice.'

'Oh,' said Simon. 'A cat.'

'Heavens, no. She eats cats, if she can catch them. No, she's a bull terrier. I inherited her from a friend in the merchant marine – he was always away, the rascal – and she took to me just like that. I've had her for three years now.'

'Anyone else up your sleeve, Ern? A marmoset? A tame python?'

Ernest shuddered, and shook his head.

'Good. Well, now we've got the hotel dog, we'd better buy the hotel. I'll call Nicole, and see if she can get everything organized for next weekend.' He looked at Ernest. 'No second thoughts?'

Ernest shook his head again, and the smile returned to his face. He was already planning his new wardrobe. Pastel colours, he thought, with maybe just a dash of turquoise here and there. Something sunny, to go with the weather.

12

The three of them stood in the *gendarmerie*, shivering and damp. It had been raining when Simon and Ernest landed the night before, and it hadn't stopped — grey sluices of water, blown by the wind, dropping in sheets from the overhang of the tiled roofs to gurgle noisily down the gutters of the narrow streets, a true Provençal shower. Nothing moved in Brassière, no cats, no dogs, no people. The village was enveloped in cloud, shrouded in the depressing gloom that descends on normally sunny places when there is no sun.

They had spent the morning in the *notaire*'s office, going through the act of sale line by interminable line, as required by custom. Finally, the pages had been initialled and signed, the bank draft for nearly half a million pounds had been inspected and found acceptable, and the *gendarmerie* had passed into Simon's hands. Now they had an appointment with the architect recommended by Nicole. He was late.

Simon felt personally responsible for the weather. 'I'm sorry about this, Ern,' he said. 'Not much of a view today.'

Ernest peered out at the cloud that hid the Lubéron. 'It reminds me of Brighton on August Bank Holiday,' he said. 'But it's a stunning place, I must say. Endless possibilities. I'm going to have a peek downstairs while we're waiting.' He disappeared, humming happily.

Nicole smiled at Simon. 'Congratulations, *monsieur le patron*.' She kissed him, cold lips, warm tongue. 'No regrets?'

There was a cough behind them, and they turned to see a tall, dripping figure in the doorway, shaking water from a diminutive telescopic umbrella. '*M'sieu dame, bonjour. Quel temps!*'

François Blanc had discovered the Lubéron a few crucial

years before other Parisian architects had realized that sunshine and picturesque ruins and rich clients offered a profitable and pleasant alternative to working on office blocks and apartments in Neuilly. He had moved down, endured some lean times when Mitterand first got into power and nobody was spending any money, and was now in considerable demand – some said rather too considerable – because of his good taste and the charm that got him out of trouble when the bills exceeded the estimates. His excuse was that he was never late finishing a job, and it was for this reason that Nicole had chosen him.

His long, bony face under a shock of brown hair was animated as they exchanged handshakes. An immediately likeable man, Simon thought, the kind of man who would be good with clients in an agency. As they walked through the building, he kept up a stream of comments about the space, the views, the possibilities. A professional enthusiast. Simon recognized the type, and warmed to the man. A salesman himself, he responded to salesmanship in others.

They went downstairs, and found Ernest pacing out measurements and tracing lines with his foot on the gravelled floor. He paused as he saw Simon. 'Have you seen those vaulted ceilings? What a dining room this could be! I can see it now. Such charm, and with the view . . .'

'Ern, this is the architect, Monsieur Blanc.'

The two men shook hands, nodding at each other like two angular storks.

'*Enchanté. C'est monsieur . . .?*'

'Airnest,' said Ernest.

Simon smiled. Airnest. He'd be flitting around in a beret before long. It was good to see him so excited.

They spent the rest of the afternoon going slowly through the rooms, Blanc making notes, Nicole translating, Ernest cooing at each suggestion, Simon happy that they appeared to be getting on so well. Long may it last, he thought, and allowed himself to be optimistic. Why shouldn't it? They were all going to benefit, one way or another, without having to compete. As long as Ernest and Nicole could work together – that was vital. He looked at the two of them, both blonde, both elegant, laughing as Ernest tried to describe something complicated to the architect in pidgin French and sign language. So far, so good.

The meeting finished with a flurry of smiles and reassurances and handshakes. Monsieur Blanc was, he said, ravished to have the opportunity to work on such a fascinating project, and with such delightful clients. He would return to the *gendarmerie* tomorrow, even though it was Sunday, to take detailed measurements. Not a second should be wasted. One must advance with all possible speed. He erected his miniature umbrella with a flourish and disappeared into the mist.

They followed him out and ducked into the empty café, sitting at a table with the cloud three feet away on the other side of the window. The young girl pushed through the curtain of dead caterpillars behind the bar and speculated about the cost of Nicole's clothes as they ordered coffee.

Ernest patted his face with a handkerchief, and ran a finger along each eyebrow to collect any stray drips. 'I must say that, despite the weather, I see a vision of enchantment. I am not downhearted. *Pas du tout.*'

'Wait till you see the view, Ern.' Simon turned to Nicole, and pushed a damp strand of hair from her forehead. 'Well, *madame*? Do you think our architect's going to be able to get it done by next summer?'

'Blanc is well known for finishing on time,' she said. 'And he is famous for being expensive. But when you have ten, twenty men working on a *chantier*, often at weekends too, it costs.'

The girl brought their coffee, smiled at Simon and swayed back to the bar. He made a mental note to invite her father for a drink on his next visit. It would be important to have him on their side, to make sure he didn't feel left out. The mayor of a tiny village was not a man to upset.

Ernest dipped a sugar-lump in his coffee and nibbled at it thoughtfully. 'Now, I know these are early days, but it's something we shouldn't leave till the last minute.' He looked up at Simon and Nicole. 'What are we going to call this little haven of *luxe* and *volupté*? Mon Repos? The Brassière Hilton? We need a name.'

He was right, Simon thought. If they wanted to get some publicity for the hotel in the early summer, the magazines would need details – or a name, at least – months in advance. He tried to remember the names of local hotels that he'd seen in the guides. There were one or two Domaines, several Mas, a Bastide. Better to avoid adding to an already long list.

'La Gendarmerie?' said Nicole.

'Mmmm,' said Ernest. 'We could put all the young waiters in policemen's uniforms. Very severe, with a red stripe down the trousers.'

'Steady on, Ern. Don't get carried away.' Simon shook his head. 'No, it should be something that says Provence, not just France. Something distinctive, easy to remember . . .'

'Easy for foreigners to pronounce,' said Nicole.

'Exactly. Short, if possible, and something you could make into a good strong logo.'

Nicole didn't understand. Simon squeezed her hand. 'Sorry,' he said, 'that's advertising language. All it means is a sort of trade-mark, and some names adapt better than others. It's only a detail, but we'll be spending a lot of money on it – writing paper, napkins, towels, brochures, ashtrays, book-matches, postcards, on the building itself. Most hotels go for a fancy script, because they think it's elegant. I think we should try for something more original.'

Ernest mused aloud. 'Let's see – lavender, thyme, rosemary, the light, the sun – not the best day to bring that up, I know, but hope springs eternal, Cézanne, Mistral, van Gogh . . .'

Nicole shrugged. '*Pastis?*'

Ernest leaned towards her. 'What?'

'*Pastis*. It comes from Provence, nowhere else.'

'*Pastis*,' Simon said, and repeated it with emphasis, hitting the final 's'. '*Pastis*.'

The girl called over from the bar. '*Trois pastis?*'

'Do you know,' said Ernest, 'I've never tried it.'

'Today's the day, Ern.' Simon nodded at the girl. '*Oui, merci*.' He looked at the bottles lined up behind the bar. As in most cafés in southern France, *pastis* was well represented. He counted five: Ricard, Pernod and Casanis he knew; the other two, Granier and Henri Bardouin, presumably local, he'd never seen before. 'It's not exactly ideal weather for *pastis*,' he said. 'It should be hot. That's how I always think of it, a sunshine drink.'

The girl placed three tumblers on the table, a saucer of olives, and a flat-sided glass carafe. Simon added water, and watched the liquid turn cloudy. The carafe was old and scratched, decorated with the Ricard name in bright yellow letters against a background of vivid blue. 'Look at those colours,' he said. 'Sun and sky. That says Provence, doesn't it?' He slid the carafe across the table towards Nicole. 'There. That's what I meant by a logo.'

She studied it for a moment, her head to one side. 'So there's your name. Hotel Pastis. With the yellow and the blue.'

Simon sat back. It wasn't such a bad idea; short, simple, easy to remember, and any good art director could do something very striking with the graphics. And it had direct associations with Provence. Not bad at all. 'What do you think, Ern?'

Ernest removed an olive pit from his mouth and placed it next to the row of others in front of him. 'Mmmm. Well, even a determined non-linguist like our friend Jordan could say that without tripping over his teeth. And I adore yellow and blue. Yes, I think it will do very nicely. Bravo, *madame*. Have an olive.'

Simon smiled at them. A decision like that in the advertising business would have taken several weeks, a dozen meetings and a research document. He raised his glass to Nicole. 'Hotel Pastis it is,' he said. 'Here's to it.'

That evening, when they had eaten and dropped Ernest off at his hotel, Nicole and Simon sat at the kitchen table over a last glass of wine and the sheaf of notes that he'd made during the day. The list was long, expensive and suddenly very daunting, and Simon's initial excitement was tempered by a more realistic mood. There was a lot that could go wrong. The restoration was going to take all the money he had, and he'd have to borrow against his shares. Ernest was sacrificing his job. Getting out of the agency would be complicated, and if the hotel didn't work, getting back in would be impossible. Ziegler, no doubt supported by Jordan, would make sure of that.

Nicole had been watching Simon as he frowned over his notes, his wine untouched, his cigar dead in the ashtray.

'You look like an advertising man again,' she said. 'Tired and worried.'

Simon pushed his notes aside and relit his cigar. 'It's a mild attack of common sense,' he said. 'It'll pass. But there's a hell of a lot to be done. And it's a new job, a new country, a new life.' He watched a plume of smoke as it turned into a wreath around the light hanging over the table. 'I'm entitled to be nervous.' He reached out and stroked the side of her neck, and smiled. 'It's my mid-life crisis. All the best middle-aged executives have one.'

'You weren't so middle-aged last night.' Nicole took his hand and bit the pad of flesh at the base of his thumb.

'You're a shameless and insatiable woman.'

Nicole stuck out her tongue. 'Yes please.'

Ernest and Simon made their way past the two stewardesses and the deeply bronzed purser – 'Far too much makeup,' Ernest whispered disapprovingly – and settled into their seats in front of the limp curtain that is the only visible benefit of flying Club Class between Marseille and London. It had been a better day, a beautiful day, in fact, and Ernest had been able to see the views from the *gendarmerie* for the first time. He had been speechless with delight for three minutes, and hadn't stopped talking since, planning the landscaping over lunch and becoming slightly tipsy with pink wine and excitement. His enthusiasm was contagious, and Simon was feeling more optimistic. It had been harder this time to say goodbye to Nicole. At her suggestion, he had left some clothes at her house. He already missed her.

Simon listened as Ernest delivered his thoughts on garden statuary: one good piece, maybe something quite saucy, among the cypress trees, with discreet floodlighting to pick up the contrast between weathered stone and vegetation. And what about a fountain?

'Fountains are nice, Ern,' said Simon. 'Very nice. But we've got quite a way to go before we get to the fountains.' He shook his head at the stewardess who was offering plastic-shrouded dinners to those in the terminal stages of hunger. 'Fountains and trees and statues are easy. It's finding the people.'

'Ah,' said Ernest. 'I've been thinking about them.' He bent forward and fished in the bag under his seat for his Filofax. Everyone in the Shaw Group above the rank of messenger had a Filofax, but only Ernest had the ostrich-skin model, the gift of a grateful supplier of plants and flowers to the agency.

'Let's see.' Ernest unfolded his year-at-a-glance planners, one for the current year, one for the next. 'Here we are in early November. Two months intensive at Berlitz brings us to mid-January, and what a frightful time in London that is, as we know. It would be no hardship to leave. Mrs Gibbons, I can tell you, would be thrilled. She loathes the winter. Arthritis.'

'Well, we don't want Mrs Gibbons to suffer. So what you're saying is that you'll move over in January.'

'I shall closet myself with Nicole and that charming Mr Blanc and make sure everything gets done.' He pursed his lips, and peered at Simon over the top of the half-glasses he wore for reading. 'Properly done. You know me. I can be a martinet when I have to be.'

Simon smiled, remembering the last time Ernest had displayed his talents for organization, during the move of three hundred staff into new offices. He had been merciless with everyone from the architect downwards. The office manager had resigned because of what he called inhuman hours, and it was the only time Simon had ever seen a building contractor in genuine hysterics. And the move had been accomplished on schedule. If Ernest was on the spot, the hotel would open in the summer.

'That takes care of one of us,' said Simon. 'Getting me out is going to be a bit more difficult.'

Ernest patted him on the knee. 'Don't worry, dear. You'll think of something. You always have before.'

'I've never left before.'

'Something tells me it will be easier than you think. You know what most of them are like, particularly our friend in the self-supporting suits.' Simon nodded. Jordan would be delighted. 'They'll all move up one. Isn't that what they want? There may be a few crocodile tears, and then they'll start arguing about who gets your cars. You mark my words.'

Ernest sniffed, and returned to his Filofax, and Simon spent the rest of the flight considering the strategy for his departure from the agency. He was under no illusions; once he'd gone, every penny due to him would be resented and disputed. He'd be a non-productive drain on resources, and he'd heard a dozen stories about the legal acrobatics performed by agencies in order to minimize payments to departed directors. Also, he was committing the cardinal sin in advertising of willingly leaving the business, which was something you were supposed to talk about rather than do.

For all Ernest's optimism, it wasn't going to be that easy. And for the sake of the business, it couldn't be done with any public disagreement that might make clients nervous. The whole thing would somehow have to be presented as a positive step in the planned development of one of Europe's largest advertising networks. Good. He was already thinking like a press release. Simon made a list of the people he'd have to take to lunch. It was time to start up the bullshit machine.

13

'It's Simon Shaw. Put me through to Mr Ziegler, would you?'

Simon looked out of his office window. The sky was turning dark at the end of a brief grey afternoon. London was already showing signs of Christmas, even though it was a month away, and the corner of Harrods he could see through the rain-streaked window was festooned with lights. It wouldn't be long before the Creative Department embarked on its annual marathon of four-hour lunches and office parties, and the agency would slip gradually into hibernation until early January. In the past, Simon had taken advantage of the dead period to get some work done. This year, like everyone else, he was going to take a holiday – maybe quite an extended holiday, he thought, as he heard a click at the other end of the line.

'OK. What is it?' Ziegler's voice was like a slap in the ear.

'How are you, Bob?'

'Busy.'

'Glad to hear you're keeping out of mischief. Tell me, how are you fixed between Christmas and the beginning of January? Skiing in Vail? A cruise in the Caribbean? Pottery classes in New Mexico?'

'What the fuck is this about?'

'I'd like to have a meeting with you when there aren't a thousand other things going on, and that's a quiet time of year.'

'A meeting? What's wrong with the goddamn phone?'

'It's not the same as face to face, Bob. You know that. And what I have to say is personal.'

There was a pause. Ziegler's curiosity was almost audible. Personal in his vocabulary meant only two things: a career move, or a terminal illness.

'How are you feeling, Simon? OK?'

'Afraid so, Bob. But we need to talk. How about December 27th? That'll give you time to get out of your Santa Claus outfit.'

So it was a career move, Ziegler thought as he looked at his diary. 'Sure. I can do the 27th. Where?'

'We'll need to see someone else. Here would be best. I'll book you into Claridge's.'

'Tell them to turn the goddamn heating up.'

For the second time in a few days, Simon felt a sense of nervous exhilaration at having gone further down the road to a new life. He'd committed himself to the hotel, and now to Ziegler. Jordan, the third member of the meeting, had better be kept in the dark for the time being. His capacity for discretion was limited, particularly in the bar at Annabel's. Where would he be over Christmas? Killing small animals in Wiltshire, probably, unless he'd managed to get himself invited to Mustique. Simon made a note to find out, and returned to the press release he was drafting which would announce his departure from London.

There are certain traditions that have to be observed in the advertising business whenever a senior executive in a public agency does anything so dramatic as changing his job. The boat must not be rocked, otherwise the share price will go to hell and competitive agencies will increase their efforts to poach business. On the other hand, the departing executive will want his departure to be seen as a personally positive move. And so, even in amicable separations, there is a conflict of interest. The agency needs to diminish the importance of the loss of a top man, while the top man himself does not want to be publicly positioned as a superfluous nonentity.

This often leads to marvels of highly implausible puffery, and frozen-smile photographs in the trade press to show how simply delighted everyone is with everything. It was a nonsense, Simon had always thought, but it was surprising how it seemed to work on clients and the experts in the City. He jotted down a couple of essential clichés – highly effective management team, continuing close ties with the agency – and looked for somewhere to put them in his release.

He had decided to use Europe as his excuse. He could disappear in Europe, as many advertising men before him had done, under the guise of a roving trouble-shooter and acquisition hunter, constantly on the move for the greater glory of the Group. That would explain the absence of an official fixed base. He would have to play down his association with the hotel, but that was a comfortable six months away. By then, the business would be talking about someone else. Advertising is not noted for the length of its attention span.

There was a tap on the door, and Simon slipped the draft release into a folder and looked up.

'*Bonjour, jeune homme*,' said Ernest. 'May I intrude?'

'Come in, Ern. How's it going?' Ernest was in the first days of his Berlitz course, and was taking the role of student to heart, wearing a long scarf and carrying a superior kind of school satchel made from chocolate-brown suede.

'My dear, I'm limp with exhaustion. Four hours alone with Miss Dunlap – or Mademoiselle Dunlap, as she prefers to be called – is completely draining. But my studies are making progress. I'm told that my musical ear helps.' Ernest unwrapped his neck, and let his scarf hang down to his knees. 'Apparently, my vowels are particularly good.'

'I've always admired your vowels, Ern.'

'According to Miss Dunlap, very few of us can pronounce the French "u" correctly.' Ernest perched on the arm of the couch. 'Anyway, I didn't come to bore you with tales of my schooldays. I've had an idea.'

Simon took a cigar from the box on the table and leaned back.

'You remember saying how important it was to have the Mayor on our side when the hotel opens? Well, it occurred to me – just a *pensée*, but rather a good one, I thought – that we might give a Christmas party. The Mayor and his lady wife, of course, that nice Monsieur Blanc, one or two of the locals. Nicole could advise us on the guest list. It would be a

146

friendly gesture, a little *entente cordiale*, just to let them know what we're up to. I suppose one could call it public relations.'

Simon nodded. It was sensible. It might even be fun. 'Have you thought about where we could do it?'

'Where else, dear? The hotel itself. Our very first *soirée*.'

Simon thought of the bare stones, the holes in the wall, the Mistral. 'Ern, it's going to be cold. It may be freezing. It's a construction site, not a hotel.'

'Ah,' said Ernest, 'you're being a tiny bit unimaginative. And, if I may say so, terribly unromantic.'

'I can't be romantic when I'm cold. I remember one of my honeymoons – Zermatt? Yes, Zermatt – what a bloody disaster that was.'

Ernest looked disapproving. 'It was the temperature of the wife, I suspect, rather than the weather.' He dismissed her with a sniff. 'Anyway, you won't be cold, I promise you. We'll have shutters up at the windows by then. The festive log will be roaring in the chimney, there'll be braziers of glowing coals *partout*, the flicker of candlelight on stone, plenty to eat and far too much to drink – it will all be tremendously cosy. And another thing . . .'

Simon held up both hands in surrender. 'Ernest?'

'Yes?'

'It's a wonderful idea.'

Later that evening, when the last meeting of the day had ended and the whistling of the office cleaners had replaced the sound of ringing phones, Simon called Nicole. Ernest had already spoken to her.

'What do you think?' Simon asked.

'Well, the village is talking already. The *notaire*'s secretary told the baker, the baker told the Mayor's wife, everybody knows there is a new *propriétaire*. It would be good for you to meet them and tell them what you're doing. Ernest is right.'

'Who should we invite? Everybody? There's always a problem with these things – you miss a couple of people out, and they get upset.'

Nicole laughed. '*Chéri*, some will be against you whatever you do.'

'The villagers?'

'No, I think not them. You're bringing work into the village, work and money. No, it's the others – the ones who think they discovered Provence, you know? Parisians, British . some of them want nothing to change.'

Simon thought for a moment. It was probably true. He didn't know much about Parisians, but he could remember, from the time he'd worked as a waiter in Nice, the attitude of some of the long-established British expatriates who would come to the restaurant from time to time. Patronizing, often arrogant, complaining about the prices and the tourists, conveniently forgetting that they had once been tourists themselves. And, he also remembered, distinguished by the smallness of their tips. The French waiters had competed to avoid serving them.

'Well,' he said, 'let's invite them anyway. All we can do is try. Do you know these people?'

'Of course. In a village of this size, one knows everybody. I'll tell you about them when you come next week.'

'What can I bring you?'

'More old shirts. I wear your shirts to sleep in.'

Simon smiled. That was a vision to sustain him through the days of tedium laid out in segments in his diary like an obstacle course between London and Provence.

Nicole put down the phone and went back to the pile of plans and estimates that Blanc the architect had delivered that afternoon. He had suggested starting with the completion of the swimming pool before moving into the building, so that landscaping could be done in the early spring. It was logical, although Simon would be disappointed that the interior would be as unfinished as ever by Christmas. Still, Ernest had been full of ideas to dress it up for the party. What a close couple they were, she thought. It would be easy to feel jealous. Yes, easy and stupid. Look what had happened to the other women in Simon's life.

She shrugged, and lit a cigarette. There was no point in trying to guess about the future of their relationship, no sense in trying to push it. Things were good at the moment, and that would have to do. Meanwhile, there was the exercise in village diplomacy to deal with. Nicole brought the phone directory and a notepad to the kitchen table, and started to make a guest list.

The Mayor and the year-round inhabitants, Blanc and some of his senior workmen, one or two of the local real estate agents – all of these, for their own reasons, could be expected to welcome the hotel. But then there were the part-time residents, many of whom would be coming down to Brassière for the Christmas holidays. Harmless and pleasant, most of them, they tended to shuttle between each other's houses for drinks and dinner and limit their contact with villagers to a few minutes each day in the *boulangerie* or the butcher's shop. Their reactions would be mixed. Nicole remembered the outcry that had been raised by a small group of Parisians when the *gendarmerie* had first been sold for development. They would complain like last time, she was sure. And like last time, the Mayor would nod politely and wait for them to go back home and leave him in peace.

But the shrillest squeals of protest would come not from any Parisian, nor indeed from any Frenchman. After a moment's hesitation, Nicole added a final name to the list: Ambrose Crouch, the village's longest-serving Englishman, who existed on the retainer paid to him by a London newspaper for his weekly Sunday column on Provence. He was a contentious, self-appointed guardian of the purity of peasant life (for peasants, it should be said, rather than for himself), a snob and a scrounger. Nicole detested him for his malice and his clammy, undisciplined hands. The people of Brassière tolerated him. The summer residents gave him food and drink in return for gossip. When sufficiently drunk, which was quite often, he would deliver a tirade on the vulgarity of modern times and the horrors of what he called 'human interference' with the fabric of rural society. He could be counted on to be violently and loudly opposed to the hotel. Nicole put a question mark next to his name. She would call Simon tomorrow and warn him about Ambrose Crouch.

*

The weather had settled into its winter pattern of bright days and clear, hard nights, and when the General went out to his car there was frost on the windscreen. Not the best weather for cycling, he thought. The air would be bitter on the face and like ice in the lungs. He left the car running while he went back for a bottle of *marc*. The boys would need some encouragement today.

They were waiting for him when he arrived at the barn, and he was pleased to see that they were beginning to look like authentic cyclists in their black tights and close-fitting wool hats.

'*Salut, l'équipe!*' He held up the bottle of *marc*. 'This is for later. Today will be short and steep, up to Murs, along to Gordes and back. And then I have some good news for you. *Allez!*'

They mounted up, flinching at the coldness of the saddles, and rode off while the General locked the barn. He checked them one by one as he overtook. Not bad. They were all using their toe-clips, riding straight, looking comfortable. Not bad at all.

After fifteen minutes of fairly flat, easy riding, the road began to curl upwards into the hills. The General stopped and got out of the car. As the cyclists passed him, he cupped his hands round his mouth. 'Don't stop. Go as slow as you like, use the width of the road to zig-zag, but don't stop. *Courage, mes enfants, courage!*'

Rather you than me, he thought as he got back in the car. The Murs hill was seven steep, twisting kilometres. Nothing like the Ventoux climb, of course, but more than enough to make a man sweat, even in this weather. If none of them threw up today, it would be a miracle. He gave them a five-minute start, and then followed them up the hill.

They were strung out over fifty yards, some bent over with their noses almost touching the handlebars, others standing on their pedals, faces livid with effort. Those with breath to spare spat. The General passed them slowly, shouting encouragement, and drove on until he reached the half-way mark, where he pulled into the verge and got out.

'Only three kilometres to go,' he shouted at them as they

crept past him. 'Downhill all the way from Murs. France salutes you!'

Bachir had just enough breath to respond. 'Up your ass with France.'

'Anything you like,' said the General, 'but don't stop. *Courage, toujours courage!*' He lit a cigarette and leaned back against the car, enjoying the sun. Nobody had stopped. They were all taking it seriously.

The road down from Murs came as a visible, audible relief to the seven men. Freewheeling after the climb, they unkinked their backs, caught their breath, felt the fluttering subside in their thigh muscles, cursed and grinned at each other with a sense of shared achievement, shouted obscenities at the General as he drove past, and swept through Gordes feeling like pros. It made a change from feeling sick, and they loved it.

Back at the barn, still glowing with the elation that often follows extraordinarily hard physical effort, they compared souvenirs of bursting lungs and tortured legs as they passed the bottle of *marc* round.

'You rode like champions, all of you.' The General took a swig from the bottle and wiped his moustache. 'And I promise you, next time will be easier.'

Fernand coughed over his cigarette. 'That's the good news, is it?'

'No. The good news is that I paid a little visit to the Caisse d'Épargne, rented a strong-box, had a look around.' He looked at their faces, and smiled at the sight of the bottle of *marc* frozen just below big Claude's open mouth. '*C'est normal, non?* I wouldn't want you to find any nasty surprises.'

'That's right,' said Jojo as though he'd known about it all along. '*C'est normal. Tout à fait.*'

The General took out the sketches and notes he'd made. 'Now then . . .'

Half an hour later, when they locked up the barn and went their different ways, they hardly noticed the beginnings of stiffness in their legs. It had been a good morning for morale. Sunday lunch would go down well.

*

London was sinking deeper into the festive spirit. Pre-Christmas traffic clogged the streets and taxi drivers performed their monologues of complaint. Responding to the large numbers of shoppers coming in from the suburbs by train, British Rail cut their services. A shoplifter was stopped as he tried to walk out of Harrods wearing two suits, and a man was arrested for assault while trying to prevent his car from being clamped. The season of goodwill had got off to a promising start.

In the headquarters of the Shaw Group, executives fought manfully against indigestion as they worked their way through the list of mandatory Christmas lunches with their clients. It had been an excellent year for the agency, and thoughts of substantial salary increases and larger cars brought an atmosphere of cheerful expectancy to the offices. Jordan, more expectant than most after the hint dropped by Simon about future developments, had decided to test the water, and sauntered along the corridor towards Simon's office, holding details of what he hoped would be his Christmas bonus.

'Got a minute, old boy?'

Simon beckoned him in. 'Let me just get rid of these and I'll be with you.' He signed half a dozen letters and pushed them aside. 'Right.' He sat back and tried not to wince at the broad chalk stripes that seemed to vibrate against the dark blue of Jordan's suit.

'Bumped into a chap the other day,' Jordan said, 'who put me on to rather a good thing.' He tossed a brochure on to the table and went through the selection process with his cigarettes while Simon turned the glossy pages.

Jordan tapped the end of the winning cigarette before lighting it. 'Magnificent beast, isn't it? Bentley Mulsanne Turbo, with all the bells and whistles.'

'Nice car, Nigel.' Simon nodded. 'Very practical for the country. What do these go for?'

'About the same as a decent little flat in Fulham – that's if you can get hold of one. The waiting list on that model is as long as your arm. Seriously good investment. They appreciate, you know.' He blew a smoke ring into the air-conditioning.

Simon smiled. How straightforward it was keeping people like Jordan happy. 'Do I take it we're thinking of investing?'

'Well, I was coming to that. This chap I bumped into has just been let down. Customer ordered the car eighteen months ago – one of the names at Lloyds, actually – and now he's feeling the pinch.'

'And he can't pay for the car?'

'Poor bugger will be lucky to keep his cufflinks.' Jordan paused, and looked solemn. 'Dicey business, unlimited liability.' The moment of grief passed. 'Anyway, my chap's prepared to knock ten thousand off the price for a quick sale.'

Simon turned to the back page of the brochure, found the dealer's number and picked up the phone.

'Good morning. You have a Bentley Mulsanne in the showroom, I think?' He smiled at Jordan. 'Yes, that's the one. Mr Jordan will be round with a cheque this afternoon. Put some petrol in it for him, would you? Thanks.'

Jordan's face was still recovering from the surprise. 'Well, old boy, I must say this is . . .'

Simon waved him to silence. 'What's the point of having a good year if we don't allow ourselves a few simple pleasures?' He stood up and looked at his watch as Jordan retrieved the brochure. 'I meant to ask you – what are you doing over Christmas?'

'Tour of duty, I'm afraid. The in-laws are descending on Wiltshire. He'll bang on about the stock market and his gout, and she'll want to play bridge all day. If I'm lucky, I might fit in a bit of shooting.'

'Nobody in the family, I hope.'

'Tempting, old boy, tempting. Specially the old trout.'

Jordan's back view as he left Simon's office was jaunty and brisk, and Simon wondered if he'd have the patience to wait until the afternoon before picking up the Bentley. God, the money the agency spent on cars.

The phone buzzed. 'Mr Shaw? I have Mr Ashby's secretary on the line.'

It took Simon a few seconds to remember that Mr Ashby

was the senior Rubber Baron, a man who clearly liked to observe telephone protocol by making Simon – the supplier, and therefore the subordinate – hold on until he – the client, and therefore the master – was ready to speak. 'OK, Liz. Put her through.'

'Mr Shaw? I have Mr Ashby for you.' Simon looked at the second hand on his watch, timing the wait and feeling hopeful. Prospective clients rarely called to tell you bad news; they preferred to write.

'How are you today, Mr Shaw? Beginning to feel festive, I hope?'

'Not too bad, thanks. And yourself?'

'Busy time of year for us, you know.' Simon vaguely recalled that the condom market peaked just before Christmas, presumably to cater to a surge in the nation's libido brought on by office parties and invigorating amounts of alcohol. 'Yes, the industry's at full capacity, I'm happy to say. And I'm also pleased to tell you that the CMB has decided to appoint your agency with effect from January 1st.'

'That's marvellous news, Mr Ashby. I couldn't be happier, and I know my colleagues will be delighted. They were particularly excited about the advertising they produced for you.'

'Ah yes.' Mr Ashby paused. 'Well, we shall need to have a little chat about that as soon as the holidays are out of the way. Some of our chaps feel that . . . well, it's a little near the knuckle.'

Simon smiled to himself. The knuckle was one of the few parts of the anatomy that hadn't appeared in the commercial.

Ashby hurried on. 'Anyway, that's something our chaps can discuss with your chaps. The main thing is, we were all most impressed by your document. Very sound. And, of course, the agency's track record.'

Simon had heard the death knell sounded for advertising campaigns many times before, and he was hearing it again now. But he didn't care. He'd be a long way away by the time the chaps got together. 'I'm sure we'll be able to iron out any creative problems, Mr Ashby. Very few campaigns are born perfect.'

'Splendid, splendid.' Ashby sounded relieved. 'I knew the two of us would see eye to eye. Let the young Turks lock horns, eh? Well, I must fly. I take it we can count on your discretion until the letters have gone out to the other agencies?'

'Of course.'

'Good, good, good. Must have lunch in the New Year. A great deal to discuss. The market's expanding, you know. The sales curve is going up very satisfactorily.'

Simon restrained himself from making the obvious comment. 'I'm very pleased to hear it. And thank you for the news. The agency will have a very happy Christmas. I hope you do too.'

'Jolly good,' said Ashby. 'We'll be in touch after the holidays.'

Simon went through to Liz's office. 'Elizabeth, we are now one of the very few agencies that will be able to purchase condoms at cost price, direct from the factory. Aren't you thrilled?'

Liz looked up from some letters and gave him her sweetest smile. 'Real men have vasectomies, Mr Shaw,' she said. 'And you're late for your lunch appointment.'

The business year was over. Simon had fed and watered his most important clients, circulated dutifully at the office party, dispensed bonuses and raises and reduced Liz to tears with his present of a Cartier watch. Now it was his turn.

He had decided to give himself for Christmas ninety minutes of total luxury and privilege, one last glorious rip of extravagance before leaving the agency. He had always hated Heathrow, hated the seething scrum at the check-in desk, hated being herded through the airport, told to hurry up, told to wait. It was unreasonable, he knew, but he hated it just the same. And so, this time, he was taking the billionaire's alternative. He had chartered a jet – a modest seven-seater – to fly him from London to the little airport outside Avignon.

The car pulled up outside the private aircraft terminal, and Simon followed the porter who had taken his luggage into the building. A girl was waiting just inside the door.

'Good afternoon, sir. Mr Shaw for Avignon, is that right?'

'It certainly is.'

'If you'd like to follow me, we'll just go through Passport Control. Your luggage is being taken to the plane, and your pilot's waiting for you.'

My pilot, thought Simon. This is the life for the weary executive. The immigration officer handed back his passport, and Simon looked around for someone in a uniform.

A tall man in a well-cut dark suit smiled at him and came forward. 'Mr Shaw? Tim Fletcher. I'm your pilot. We've got our slot, and everything seems to be taking off on schedule today, so we should be in Avignon by 1800 local time. We'll just get you settled in the aircraft and I'll get on with the driving.'

Simon went up the steps and ducked into the sleek white plane. The interior smelt faintly of leather, like a new car. The girl who had met him was already on board. She came out of the tiny galley in the back.

'Let me take your jacket and hang it up. Do you need anything from the pockets – cigarettes, cigars?'

'Are cigars allowed?'

'Oh, yes. A lot of our clients are cigar smokers.' She took his jacket. 'May I offer you a glass of champagne while we're waiting for take-off? Or we have single malt Scotch, vodka . . .'

'Champagne would be lovely. Thank you.' Simon chose a seat, loosened his tie and stretched his legs as the girl served the champagne. By the side of the glass she placed a box of Upmann extra-long cigar matches. It was the kind of detail Ernest would have approved of, he thought. A pity he'd had to go on ahead last week. He'd have enjoyed this.

The plane started taxiing to its take-off position, and Simon opened the folder that Liz had given him just before he left – cuttings of articles, a short CV and a black and white head shot. The material had been compiled at Simon's request as the result of a conversation with Nicole. It was a brief introduction to the life and works of Ambrose Crouch.

Simon glanced through the CV. A minor public school, an undistinguished performance at university, a list of jobs in publishing and journalism, two novels, now out of print. Success had eluded Mr Crouch, and this was reflected in his face – middle-aged and slightly puffy, with a thin-lipped mouth and unfriendly eyes; a dissatisfied, belligerent face.

The articles, a recent selection of his columns from the *Sunday Globe*, were bile disguised as environmental concern. Crouch, it appeared, was opposed to anything more modern than a donkey. From his medieval refuge in Provence, he looked with horror at supermarkets, high-speed trains, *autoroutes* and property development. Progress appalled him, and tourism infuriated him. With impartial xenophobia, he sneered at everyone – Dutch, Swiss, German or British – who dared to visit what he constantly referred to as his village, driving their ostentatious cars, dressed in their vulgar bright clothes. Vulgar was a word that cropped up frequently.

Simon looked through the final sheet in the folder, statistics about the *Globe*'s readership and advertising revenue, and wondered what kind of following Crouch had. Full of malice and snobbery though his work was, the man could certainly write. It was also certain that he would see the hotel as an irresistible target. Curiosity would make him turn up at the party, and a venomous column would follow very shortly afterwards. It was a problem that Simon hadn't anticipated. How could he have known that a rogue journalist was going to be living on his doorstep? He looked again at the circulation statistics, and an idea began to form in his mind.

'Some more champagne, Mr Shaw?' The girl filled his glass. 'Another twenty minutes and we'll be there.'

Simon smiled his thanks, closed the folder and tried to forget about Crouch. He was going to spend Christmas in Provence, Christmas with Nicole. He felt the champagne prickle his tongue, and looked out of the window at the pink and mauve glow left by the setting sun.

The plane touched down, turned off the runway and rolled to a stop a hundred yards from the terminal. The flight had been a pleasure; not quite a bargain, at a little over £4000 more than the regular economy fare, but a fitting way to end a career largely subsidized by expenses, Simon thought.

He looked for someone to show his passport to, but the immigration desk was empty, the Arrivals area deserted. He shrugged, and walked through to meet Nicole – a momentary flutter in his pulse as she came towards him with her coat swinging away from her legs, her face lit up by a smile that he felt in his stomach. He bent down and kissed her neck, and stood back to take a look at her.

'You're far too chic to be hanging around an airport meeting an out-of-work executive.' He grinned, and touched her cheek. 'You've been having lunch in Avignon with that elderly lover of yours. I can tell.'

Nicole straightened his tie, and winked. 'Of course. He buys me diamonds and silk lingerie.'

'I've brought some smoked salmon,' Simon said. 'Will that do?'

They walked over to the baggage-claim area, Simon's arm round her shoulder, the movement of her hip smooth against his thigh. 'I'm afraid there's quite a lot of stuff,' he said. 'Ern gave me an enormous shopping list. How is he?'

'Happy. Very excited. He's cooking for us tonight. I took him to buy truffles at Richerenches.'

As they drove back into the hills, Nicole gave Simon a progress report. He would see a lot of changes: the pool was almost finished, the terraces cleared, preparations made for the party. Ernest had found a tiny house to rent in the village. Blanc was optimistic, the villagers curious but friendly.

'How about Crouch?'

Nicole's expression, in the half-light, looked as though she had smelt something unpleasant. 'I sent him an invitation. He came to the *gendarmerie*, asking questions, but Blanc told him nothing. He's *vaseux*, you know? What did Ernest say? Slimy. Is that right?'

'Probably. We'll find out tomorrow.' Simon put his hand on Nicole's thigh, and squeezed. 'I missed you.'

They drove up the hill, and Simon saw that the village was dressed for the holidays. Both churches were floodlit, and coloured lights on a frame slung between two plane trees wished everyone *Joyeuses Fêtes*. The butcher and the baker displayed bottles of champagne in their windows, and a poster on the café door announced a grand Christmas Loto, first prize a microwave oven, second prize a leg of lamb from Sisteron, *nombreuses bouteilles* for the runners-up.

Simon got out of the car, and looked up at the vast, cold sky. He took a deep breath, clean air and wood-smoke. Very soon, this would be home. Nicole was watching him as he looked around.

'Happy?'

'It's wonderful.' He leaned his elbows on the roof of the car. The mist of his breath floated upwards, transparent against the lights from the café, and as a man came out he heard a gust of laughter through the open door. 'I can't think of anywhere I'd rather be, specially at Christmas.' He straightened up, and shivered. 'You go on. I'll bring the bags.'

The house, now familiar to Simon, was warm and full of music. Ernest was going through a Puccini phase, and the voice of Mirella Freni poured through the room, pure and sweet. Simon piled the bags in the hall and went through to the kitchen, sniffing the air to catch the gamy scent of truffles, smiling as Ernest, dapper in dark blue sweater and slacks, handed him a glass.

'How are you, Ern? Surviving?'

'Full of the joys, dear. What a busy time we've had these last few days. I think you'll be pleased. How about you? I want to hear all about the office party. Drunkenness and licence everywhere as usual, I suppose. I hope several people disgraced themselves.' He raised his glass. 'Welcome back.'

Nicole came down the stairs and joined them as they laughed and talked, trying to follow the gossip about the agency. She wondered if Simon would miss all that when he finally left it for the quiet, closed life of the village.

'. . . and then,' Simon was saying, 'Jordan's wife arrived to pick him up while he was in the conference room with Valerie from the Art Department . . .'

'The tall creature with the bottom?'

'That's the one. So I had to park the wife in my office with a copy of *Horse and Hound* while I went to find him.' Simon stopped to take a drink. 'Do you know, it's the first time I've ever seen him with his waistcoat undone.'

Ernest shuddered dramatically. 'Don't go on, dear. I can just imagine the whole squalid spectacle.'

Simon turned to Nicole. 'I'm sorry – it's not very interesting when you don't know the people. No more social news from London, I promise.'

Nicole was looking puzzled. 'Why didn't they go to an hotel?'

'Ah,' said Simon, 'a Frenchman would have done that, but there's this tradition at British office parties – love among the filing cabinets. It's cheaper.'

Nicole wrinkled her nose. 'It's not at all elegant.'

'No, you can't often accuse us of elegance, I suppose. But we can be very lovable.' He leaned over and kissed her.

'Don't spoil your appetite,' Ernest said. 'We have *omelette aux truffes* and a simply enormous rabbit in mustard sauce. And after the cheese, I am poised to make a chocolate soufflé, unless we feel that would be too many eggs.' He looked at them enquiringly. 'How is our cholesterol?'

During dinner, they discussed the work that had been done so far on the hotel and the details of the following night's party. Ernest was in his element, rhapsodizing over the food and the flowers that were being delivered in the morning, confident that the evening would be the social event of the Brassière year.

'There's only one thing that bothers me,' Simon said. 'It's that journalist.'

Ernest raised his eyebrows. 'Why should you worry about him?'

'Normally, I wouldn't. But the timing's awkward. I've got a meeting set up in London for the 27th to tell Ziegler and Jordan what I'm doing. Then the clients have to be told. By us, the way we want them to hear it. If anything gets out before then, particularly in the press, we'll have a lot of explaining to do. You know what the business is like, Ern.' Simon sighed, and reached for a cigar. 'I should have thought of it before.'

The other two were silent while Simon clipped his cigar and lit it, frowning as he watched the blue smoke rising above the table. 'I've got an idea that might work, but he's not going to like it.'

'Disembowelment?' said Ernest.

Simon laughed, and felt better. He'd dealt with journalists before. Why should Crouch be any different? 'That's one way of putting it, Ern.'

14

Simon was woken by the sun slanting through the bedroom window. Beside him, the sheets were still warm from Nicole's body, and he heard the hiss of the coffee machine coming from the kitchen. He rubbed his eyes, and looked at the clothes that had been tossed hurriedly over the back of a chair the night before. Lust comes to the middle-aged man, he thought, and very nice too.

Now he could smell the coffee, and it dragged him out of bed, through the bathroom to pick up a towelling robe, and down the stairs. Nicole was waiting for the coffee jug to fill, dressed in one of Simon's shirts, the hand on her hip pulling the shirt-tail up to the top of her thighs.

'Good morning, Madame Bouvier. I've got a message for you.'

She turned her head and smiled at him over her shoulder. '*Oui*?'

'You're wanted in the bedroom.'

She poured the coffee and brought it over to the table, pushed Simon down into a chair, and sat on his lap. 'Ernest is coming in five minutes.' She kissed him. 'And you have a very busy morning.'

'That's what I was hoping for.'

They were only half-way through the big bowls of coffee when there was a knock on the door. Simon watched Nicole run up the stairs, and was thinking about a siesta as he let Ernest in.

'We couldn't have hoped for a more glorious day, dear.' He tilted his head and looked down his nose at Simon's bathrobe. 'But I dare say you haven't noticed the weather.'

'Jet-lag, Ern. Otherwise I'd have been up hours ago. Help yourself to coffee while I get organized.'

There were still white smudges of frost in the shadows as

the two men left the house and walked down to the square, past the steamed-up windows of the café and the old plane trees, now bare of leaves and pruned back to their mottled grey knuckles. The light was piercing, the sky a hard blue. Except for the lack of green among the vines below the village and the bite in the air, it could have been a day in early summer.

The parking area opposite the *gendarmerie* was crowded with vans and trucks. Monsieur Blanc's BMW, the successful architect's trade-mark, was the only vehicle that wasn't scarred and dusty.

'He comes every day, Monsieur Blanc,' said Ernest, 'and he's quite strict with those poor boys working all day in the cold. Why they don't wear gloves and mufflers, I don't know.' They stopped in front of the entrance. Wooden shutters had been put up at the windows, and there was a temporary but solid door of thick planks. Ernest pushed it open. 'Now then,' he said, 'don't expect the Connaught, but it's coming along.'

The huge room shone with sunlight. A fire was already blazing, with stacks of oak logs arranged either side of the hearth. On a long trestle-table, covered with a cloth of red, white and blue, a forest of bottles and glasses stretched from one end to the other, with a fifty-litre cask of red wine in the centre. Smaller tables and chairs were placed in groups around black braziers, and a second long table was piled with plates. The middle of the room was dominated by a Christmas tree that touched the high ceiling, its branches looped with scarlet ribbon. At intervals around the walls, fat candles were set on antique iron candlesticks six feet high.

'Well?' said Ernest. 'Do we approve? There'll be flowers arriving later, of course, and food and ice. And the electricity's laid on, for music, although I must say I'm dithering a little between Christmas carols and that very loud man they all seem to like – Johnny something. What do you think?'

Simon smiled and shook his head. 'It looks fantastic, Ern. You were right about having it here. It's going to be fun, isn't it?'

'Glittering, dear, glittering.' Ernest glowed with pleasure, and almost skipped across to one of the windows. 'Now, this *is* exciting. Come and see.'

Simon joined him at the window. In the clear winter light, the mountains in the distance looked like a stage-set painted against a blue background, sharp and almost flat. Immediately below him, Simon saw that the terraces had been cleared and paved, and the pool finished. A cement-mixer grumbled and turned, and men were working in a low, open-fronted stone building, set back from the pool and facing west to catch the sunset.

'The poolhouse looks fine,' Simon said. 'As if it's been there for ever.'

'It's all old stones and old tiles. Heaven knows where Monsieur Blanc gets them. When I asked him, he just tapped his nose.'

They went down the stairs and through the vaulted room, now used as a storage area for beams and sacks of cement, that would eventually be the restaurant. Once they finished the poolhouse, the men would move in here and then up through the building. Simon felt a surge of impatience and excitement. It was going to work. He clapped Ernest on the back. 'How do you feel about it?'

'Need you ask, dear? Do you know, I think it's what I've always wanted to do, something special like this.' He looked out at the mountains, screwing up his eyes against the sun. 'Yes, this will do very nicely. It won't be a wrench to give up Wimbledon.'

They walked across the flagstones, which had been set with spaces between them to plant with herbs, and over to the empty pool. The long side facing south had been cut back so that when the pool was filled, the surface of the water would appear to flow into the horizon.

'There can't be many pools with a view like that,' Simon said. 'It must be eight or ten miles, and you can hardly see a house.'

Ernest pointed over to the west. 'And there, righ over that rather dear little peak, is where the sun goes down. You can sit in the poolhouse and watch it. I did the other evening, and it was quite extraordinary. Almost too gaudy to be true, actually.'

They went over to the poolhouse. Blanc was hovering anxiously over the team of masons as they braced themselves to lift a ten-foot slab of stone that was to be the counter of the bar.

'*C'est bon? Attention aux doigts. Allez . . . hop!*'

With a silent scream of muscles, the masons lifted the slab to chest-height and lowered it, with excruciating slowness and delicacy, on to the wet cement that coated the bar. Blanc darted in and laid a spirit level on the slab, studied it, and frowned. '*Non. Il faut le monter un tout petit peu.*' He bent down and picked up two small, wedge-shaped pieces of stone, and motioned to the biggest of the masons.

Claude stooped to get one shoulder under the end of the slab, and with a surge of effort that made the veins of his neck pop with strain, raised the slab while Blanc inserted the wedges and tried again with the spirit level. '*Oui, c'est bon.*' The masons blew with exertion and rubbed cold, sore fingers.

Blanc wiped a dusty hand on the seat of his trousers before greeting Simon and Ernest. It was going well, he said. The weather had been kind; soon the exterior work would be finished, and the masons could spend the rest of the winter indoors. He called one of them over to introduce him to Simon – a young, thick-set man with bulky shoulders that started just below the ears, a light beard and a cheerful, intelligent face.

'Monsieur Fonzi,' Blanc said, '*le chef d'équipe.*'

Fonzi grinned, looked at his cement-coated hands, and extended a forearm for Simon to shake. It felt like a steel hawser.

'You're coming tonight, I hope?' said Simon.

'*Beh oui, volontiers.*' He grinned again, nodded, and turned back to the other masons, who were smoking and watching from the bar – Claude and Jojo breathing easily, Jean and Bachir still massaging frayed hands. '*On prend les vacances? Allez!*'

Blanc excused himself and went back to work. Ernest looked at his watch. 'I'd better go in. They promised to be here with the flowers before lunch.'

165

Simon walked slowly round the pool and sat on a pile of flagstones. He imagined how it would be in full summer – guests in the pool, the scent of thyme and lavender on the terrace, tables laid outside for lunch under those off-white canvas umbrellas that transformed the glare of the sun into a soft, diffused fall of light. He wondered who the first guests would be. Maybe he should invite Philippe down from Paris with one of his decorative friends from *Vogue*. What would Nicole think of him?

The screech of a cutting wheel biting into stone came from the poolhouse, and Simon winced. What a brutal job it was, being a mason; cold, dirty, noisy and dangerous. If any one of them had let that slab slip, it would have been a broken leg or a crushed foot. The cutting wheel skidding off a fossil in the stone would go through flesh and bone in half a second. They certainly earned their money. Simon felt the chill from the flagstones coming through his clothes. With a guilty sense of his own privileged situation, he went inside and put up no resistance at all to Ernest's offer of a glass of red wine.

The three of them had spent a busy afternoon, and it was dusk by the time Ernest pronounced himself satisfied with the arrangements. Braziers glowed, candlelight shadows trembled on the walls, vases of pink tulips decorated every table and there was enough food, Simon thought, for a prolonged siege – *terrines, charcuterie*, salads, cheeses, a vast *daube* keeping warm over a bed of charcoal, *gâteaux* and tarts and a gigantic bowl of Ernest's dangerously alcoholic trifle. Nobody would leave hungry.

Simon opened the door and looked up and down the empty street. The village was silent. He felt the doubt that hosts experience in that empty, waiting period when everything is ready and nobody is there.

'They're not exactly lining up to get in,' he said. 'Perhaps I'd better go into Cavaillon and rent a few bodies.'

Nicole laughed. 'They'll come, don't worry. Didn't you see this afternoon? Half the village was trying to look inside.'

Simon remembered seeing a couple through the open door while a delivery was being made. They were tall, in their mid-thirties, pallid and dressed in dingy colours. The man wore the kind of narrow, faintly sinister sunglasses affected by out-of-work actors hoping to be recognized. The two of them had stared at Simon, expressionless and un-friendly. He described them to Nicole.

'Ah yes,' she said. 'Those.' She shook her head. 'Those you are not going to like. They're English, *très snob*, and they are great friends with Ambrose Crouch.'

'What does he do for a living?'

'He married her. She bought him an antique shop.'

'Do they live here all the time?'

'Oh, sometimes here, sometimes in Paris. In the village they are called Les Valium.'

Ernest snorted with laughter. 'How marvellous. Are they artificially assisted, or just naturally boring?'

Nicole shrugged. 'Who knows? They're very slow, very cold – no, not cold, very . . . *blasé*, you know? Very cool.'

'God help us,' Simon said. 'I should have known from the look they gave me. If they'd had their noses any further up in the air they'd have dislocated their necks. Posers. I wonder if he sleeps in his sunglasses.'

Nicole didn't understand.

'Posers think they're sophisticated. They watch, but they never get involved. They're socially vicious, and extremely dull. You're right. I'm not going to like the Valiums.'

'Really!' said Ernest. 'This is hardly the festive spirit. I think we should have a quiet drink while we can, before the rush starts. And if the Valiums should honour us with a visit, we'll put them in a corner where nobody will fall over them, and wake them up when it's time to go home. What are you going to have?'

They sat at one of the small tables, sipping red wine that was still slightly chilled. Simon felt edgy, a little apprehen-sive, the way he felt before a meeting that he knew was going to be difficult. Supposing Nicole was wrong, and the village hated the idea of an hotel? Supposing Crouch dug his heels in, and wrote a smear piece? Supposing . . .

'*Bon soir, mes amis, bon soir.*' Blanc came through the door, towering above a small, dark woman whom he introduced as his wife. They were followed almost immediately by a group of ruddy, fair-haired young men and girls with an older couple.

'The village Swedes,' Nicole whispered to Simon, 'very *sympa*, and there are always many of them.' She made the introductions – Ebba and Lars, Anna and Carl and Birgitta and Arne and Harald – all tall and smiling and speaking perfect English. Who said Swedes were cold? Simon began to relax, and explained his plans for the hotel. The older couple nodded. It would be good for them. There was never enough room in their house for everyone who wanted to come down. Sometimes it seemed as if they had half of Sweden sleeping on the floor, and last summer, when the *fosse septique* had blocked up – they shuddered and laughed and took another drink.

Nicole touched Simon's arm and nodded towards the door, where Mayor Bonetto and his wife stood as if rooted to the threshold. Simon went over to welcome them, and Madame pretended to scold him. 'You don't stay with us now,' she said, and looked at Nicole. 'You've found a softer bed, eh?'

Bonetto crushed Simon's hand. '*Ça va?*' He moved his grip up to the shoulder. 'So we're going to have our own hotel?' His eyes, bright and inquisitive in his weather-cracked face, studied Simon.

'I hope you approve.'

'I did approve. The whole *Conseil Municipal* approved. Why should everybody stay in Gordes? *C'est bieng, c'est bieng.*' He patted Simon hard enough to leave a bruise. With a sense of relief, Simon took them over to the bar, and Ernest poured *pastis*.

'Tell me,' asked Simon, 'where's your daughter? Isn't she going to come?'

'She stays at the café. She's not pleased, but it's necessary for someone to be there. *Santé.*' Bonetto attacked his *pastis*.

'I'll take her a glass of champagne,' Simon said. 'Cheer her up.'

The room was becoming crowded, and Nicole steered Simon round the guests, feeding names into his ear that he forgot almost instantly – a quartet of Parisians, tactile in soft leather *blousons*, the butcher and the baker, the *notaire* and his wife, an amiable Dutch couple, Madame who ran the tiny post office, Duclos and his oily dog from the garage, Fonzi with his suede-covered, scented girlfriend, Jojo and Claude, shaved and scrubbed, elderly, wrinkled villagers standing quietly against the wall, two real estate agents who slipped their cards into Simon's top pocket, a sharply dressed man who wanted to discuss burglar alarm systems, and the proprietor of the best local vineyard. In the course of a bewildering but encouraging hour of working the room, Simon had found no negative reactions. The atmosphere was warm, and the initial separation between villagers and foreigners was starting to disappear. They'd probably never been thrown together like this before. It was turning into a good party.

Simon made his way to the bar. 'How are you getting on, Ern?'

'Keeping up, dear, but only just.' He drew a hand across his brow. 'The champagne seems to be frightfully popular.'

Simon remembered the girl in the café. 'I thought I might take a glass next door for Bonetto's daughter.' He watched Ernest pour the champagne. 'I think it's going well, don't you?'

'Well, if dead bottles are anything to go by . . .' Ernest was distracted by the sight of Madame Bonetto's empty glass. '*Un petit pastis, madame?*'

Madame Bonetto allowed her glass to be refilled. '*Merci, jeune homme.*' Ernest bridled.

Simon took the champagne and picked his way through the crowd to the door, out into the shock of the night air.

The girl was alone in the café, watching the television at the end of the bar and eating peanuts from a small plastic saucer. She ran her tongue over her teeth before smiling at Simon.

'I'm sorry you have to stay here,' he said. 'I've brought you some champagne.'

'*C'est gentil.*' She looked at him over the top of the glass, her eyes wide and dark. A pretty girl like her would make a good receptionist for the hotel, Simon thought. He'd have a word with her father.

'I've never asked your name,' he said.

'Françoise.'

'Simon.'

'Papa says you're going to make an hotel.'

'That's right. We're hoping to be open next summer.'

She took a sip of champagne and looked down into the glass, black eyelashes against olive skin. 'You will need people to work there.'

'We're going to start looking after Christmas.'

'It would be very interesting for me.' She leaned forward, and Simon found himself staring at the tiny gold crucifix hanging in the opening of her blouse. 'I like to do something new.'

'What would your parents think if you left the café? I can't steal you.'

She stuck out her lower lip and twitched a shoulder. 'There's a cousin. She could come here.'

'I'll talk to your father, OK? Listen, I'd better go.' He backed away from the bar. '*Au revoir*, Françoise.'

'Bye-bye, Simon.'

He walked down towards the *gendarmerie*, smiling in the dark. She'd cause a few heart murmurs among the male guests if she was on the reception desk.

As he approached the open door, he saw three figures standing outside. 'Well,' one of them said, 'I suppose we should go and mingle. He's an adman, didn't you say, Ambrose? Some ghastly little person with a bow-tie.' They went through the door, and Simon recognized the Valiums, followed by a short, slight man with an oversized head. The *beau monde* of Brassière had arrived.

Simon waited outside for a few moments before going back into the convivial warmth of the room. The Valiums and Crouch had found a small table in one corner, and had appropriated a bottle of champagne. They were leaning back, languid and detached from the laughter and conversation around them. Simon steeled himself to be pleasant and went over to their table.

'Glad you could come. I'm Simon Shaw.'

It was like shaking hands with three exhausted fish. Mrs Valium, her blank, almost pretty face framed by long straight hair, offered a half-smile. Mr Valium's expression didn't change beneath the sunglasses he was wearing to shield his eyes from the candlelight. Crouch stared. Simon thought he had rarely seen three more unhealthy-looking faces, pallid and waxy.

'So,' said Crouch, 'you're the famous adman. Well, well. We are honoured.' His voice seemed to be coming through his nose, in a peevish baritone that reminded Simon of a sarcastic master he'd detested at school.

'How did you know I was in advertising?'

'I'm a journalist, Mr Shaw. It's my business to be informed about our gallant captains of industry.' The Valiums smiled faintly and toyed with their champagne glasses.

'I gather,' Crouch went on, 'that this is to become a boutique hotel.' He made it sound as though it were something unpleasant he'd just stepped in.

'A small hotel, yes.'

'Just what the village needs.'

'The villagers seem quite happy about it.'

'Not all the villagers, Mr Shaw. You've read my column, I imagine, so you know my feelings about Provence being ruined by what we so misguidedly call progress.' Crouch took a deep swallow of champagne, and nodded at the Valiums. 'No, not all the villagers want to see the streets crawling with Mercedes and overdressed trippers.'

'I think you're exaggerating.'

Crouch continued as if he hadn't heard. 'But I suppose we must let the public judge. What do they say in your, ah, occupation? Any publicity is good publicity?' He laughed, and the Valiums smiled. 'We shall see.'

Simon reached for the bottle of champagne, filled Crouch's glass and picked it up. 'Funnily enough, I wanted to talk to you about publicity. Perhaps we could go over there. I don't want to bore your friends.'

Crouch looked up at him, and got to his feet. 'Well, this will be amusing.'

Simon led him across the room to a quiet corner behind the bar. The firelight shone on Crouch's face, and Simon noticed the gleam of a light sweat on his forehead and above his top lip. He'd been drinking before he arrived, and Simon caught a gust of his sour white wine breath.

'Now then, Mr Crouch. Publicity.' Simon smiled brightly, and made an effort to keep his voice pleasant and reasonable. 'I'd much prefer it if there were nothing in the press until the hotel is ready to open. You know what a short memory the public has.'

Crouch looked at him without replying, the beginnings of a sneer curling at one side of his mouth. So that was it. This overpaid yob was going to ask him for a favour.

'And so I'd be grateful if you could save any comments you might have for the time being.' Simon reached over to the bar and took a bottle from its nest of ice. 'More champagne?'

'It would take more than champagne to stop me writing about this, Mr Shaw. You're being very naive.' He held out his empty glass. 'But then, you're in a naive business.'

Simon nodded, refusing to be drawn. 'Tell me, what would it take?'

Crouch's sneer came into full bloom. 'I think I can see where this conversation is leading, but I'm going to have to disappoint you.' He took a long pull at his glass, relishing the moment, the power of the press, the glow of satisfaction at the delightful thought of making a rich man squirm. 'No, Mr Shaw, you can look forward to seeing a great deal of publicity in the *Globe*. Plenty of coverage – isn't that the term you people use? I have 750,000 readers, you know.' He muffled a belch, and finished his champagne. He helped himself from the bottle.

A hardness came into Simon's voice. 'You used to have 750,000 readers. You don't now. Circulation has been slipping for three years – or haven't they told you?'

Crouch licked the sweat from his top lip. 'It's still the most influential newspaper in Britain.'

172

'That's one of the reasons my agency spends over four million pounds a year buying space in it.' Simon sighed, as if he were reluctant to dilute this happy statistic with bad news. 'Of course, that's always subject to review.'

Crouch's eyes narrowed above the puffy folds of his cheeks.

'Some of that four million pounds goes towards paying your retainer, Mr Crouch. Have you ever thought of that? Probably not. Anyway, it's not important.'

'No, Mr Shaw, it's not.' Crouch started to move away, but Simon held his arm.

'I haven't quite finished. Let me put it as plainly as I can. If there is any mention of the hotel during the next six months, either in your column or through a plant in another paper, I'll pull the advertising from the *Globe*. All of it.'

Crouch's glass stopped half-way to his mouth. 'You wouldn't dare. You're not dealing with one of your tinpot little printers. You're dealing with the British press. My editor wouldn't tolerate it.'

'I don't deal with your editor. I deal with your owner. Your proprietor' – Simon repeated Crouch's earlier condescending phrase – 'isn't that the term you people use? I have lunch with him two or three times a year. He's a very practical man.'

Simon saw that Crouch's hand was shaking. 'Careful. You're going to spill your champagne.'

'This is outrageous.' Crouch sucked at the contents of his glass, and it seemed to give him inspiration. The sneer returned. 'You know that I could put this – this whole sordid little attempt at blackmail – on the front page, don't you? It would make a nice story, a very nice story.'

Simon nodded. 'Yes, I expect it would. And if it ever ran, three things would happen. I'd deny it. I'd pull the advertising. And I'd sue the shit out of you. Not the paper. You.'

The two men stared at each other for a few moments before Simon broke the hostile silence. 'Another glass?'

'Fuck you.' Crouch lurched past Simon and went back, fast and slightly unsteadily, to the table where the Valiums were sitting. Crouch spoke to them, they looked across at Simon, and got up to leave.

173

Jojo and Claude, leaning over *pastis* at the bar, watched as Crouch and the Valiums pushed their way to the door, lips tight and faces set in expressions of irritated disdain. Jojo nudged his companion. '*Ils sont en colère, les rosbifs.*'

Claude shrugged. '*C'est normal.*' In his limited experience, the English he had come across were usually upset about something – the heat of the sun, the plumbing, slow progress on the *chantier* – they missed no opportunity for restrained despair. But at least most of them were polite, not arrogant like the Parisians. Jesus, the Parisians. He drained his glass and yawned. There was another training session with the General tomorrow, more torture. His backside was still sore from the last time. Bicycle saddles weren't built for big men. '*Alors, on y va?*'

They went over to say goodnight to Simon. He wasn't too bad, they thought, for an Englishman. They shook his hand hard. He was going to keep them in work all through the winter, comfortable indoor work.

Simon felt himself relax. Crouch would behave himself, he was sure. The poisonous little bastard had believed him, and he didn't seem the kind of man with sufficient confidence and guts to take a risk. Nor did he have the journalist's usual advantage of being able to hit and run, to escape from the repercussions of his writing and hide behind his editor, hundreds of miles away. An enemy in the village, Simon thought, would be easier to deal with than an enemy in London.

It was well past midnight by the time the last guest, a flushed and boozily affectionate Mayor Bonetto, hugged the three of them goodbye and staggered home to the café. Ernest cut off the Gypsy Kings in mid-wail and replaced them with Chopin. The room became calm. The wreckage – bottles, glasses, plates and ashtrays everywhere, the food table picked clean – was gratifying to see, the chaotic evidence of a successful evening. Simon had to tilt the cask of red wine to fill three glasses.

Tired, but not yet ready for bed, they compared social notes. Nicole's bottom had been pinched by the Mayor. The burglar alarm salesman had attempted to horrify Simon with local crime statistics. The real estate agents had hinted at a commission for every client they recommended to stay at the hotel. Duclos from the garage had proposed that the dilapidated Citroën ambulance he'd been unable to sell for eighteen months be used as a taxi for the guests. They could lie in the stretcher beds in the back, he said, and sleep all the way from the airport to Brassière. Or, for couples on their honeymoon . . .

'And what about that little man with the perspiration problem?' asked Ernest. 'I saw you having a cosy chat in the corner, and then he slunk away with his friends – who, I must say, would be perfect if one ever wanted to hold a completely silent dinner party.'

Simon repeated his conversation with Crouch.

Nicole shook her head. 'How complicated,' she said. 'In France, it's more simple. You give journalists money.' She shrugged. '*C'est tout.*'

'What do you do when they come back for more?' Simon yawned and stretched. 'I think he'll keep quiet until I've sorted everything out with the agency. After that, it doesn't matter. What's more important is that the villagers seemed happy.'

They sat for another half-hour as Nicole told them what she'd overheard. As she'd predicted, the people of Brassière saw the hotel as a source of diversion and possible profit. Their properties would increase in value, there would be more jobs, perhaps their children wouldn't have to leave the village to find work – for them, tourism was attractive. The postcard version of the peasant's life, picturesque and sunlit, was a long way from the grinding reality of disappointing crops, aching backs and bank loans. A chance to earn a living in clean clothes would be welcome.

And so it was with some satisfaction that they blew out the candles and locked the door on the debris. It had been a good party, and in two days it would be Christmas.

Simon made the call about the time when he thought that Jordan would be two gins into Christmas Eve and beginning to feel a deepening gloom at the prospect of humouring his parents-in-law for the next few days.

'Helleau?' It was Jordan's wife, competing with a dog barking in the background. 'Percy, do shut up. Helleau?'

'Louise, I hope I'm not disturbing you. It's Simon Shaw.'

'Simon, how are you? Happy Christmas. Percy, go and find your slipper, for God's sake. Sorry, Simon.'

'Happy Christmas to you. I wonder if I could have a very quick word with Nigel.'

Simon heard Percy being scolded, and the sound of footsteps on a wooden floor.

'Simon?'

'Nigel, I'm sorry to bother you, but it's important. Could you drag yourself up to London for a meeting on the 27th? I hate to ask you, but . . .'

'My dear fellow . . .' Jordan's voice dropped to just above a whisper '. . . just between you and me, there's nothing I'd like more. What's it about?'

'Good news. Why don't you pick me up at Rutland Gate in the morning and we'll go on from there? How's the car going?'

'Like a bird, old boy, like a bird.'

'See you on the 27th, then. Oh, and Happy Christmas.'

There was a snort from Jordan. 'Very little chance of that unless I lace the port.'

'They say cyanide does the trick. Have fun.'

Simon put down the phone and shook his head. The family Christmas always made him think of Bernard Shaw's comment about marriage. What was it? The triumph of optimism over experience. Everyone he knew approached Christmas with the same dutiful trepidation, as he had done when his parents had been alive. Enforced jollity and alcohol, sooner or later, led inevitably to bad temper and argument, followed by remorse, followed by New Year's Eve and the opportunity to go through it all over again. No wonder January was an evil month.

But he had to admit, by the time the short French Christmas was over, that he'd enjoyed it. They had eaten lunch outside on the sheltered terrace, wrapped in scarves and sweaters, walked for hours in the rough country behind the village and gone to bed early, stunned by fresh air and heavy red wine. The next day had been spent in the *gendarmerie* going over the plans until it was time to leave for the airport to catch the evening flight back to Heathrow. As he and Ernest drove out of the village and down into the valley, Simon thought it had been a long time since he'd looked forward to a new year with such anticipation.

London was dead, sunk in its Boxing Day stupor in front of the television. Rutland Gate felt like a stranger's flat, and Simon passed a restless evening, missing Nicole, unable to concentrate on his notes for tomorrow's meeting, wishing it were over and he was back in the warm little house on the top of the hill. Ziegler was going to be even more of a shock to the system than usual.

He woke early, inspected the empty fridge, and went out looking for somewhere he could get some breakfast. Sloane Street was quiet and grey, with some of the more desperate shops already festooned with Sale notices. As he walked past the Armani boutique, Simon wondered where Caroline had spent her Christmas. St Moritz, probably, where she could change her outfit four times a day and mingle with the Eurotrash.

He went into the Carlton Tower Hotel and found the dining room, normally filled with men in suits having their first meeting of the morning, but now thinly populated with Americans and Japanese studying their guide-books as they struggled with the delights of the traditional English breakfast. Simon ordered coffee, and took out the draft press release he'd prepared. It was, he thought, a model of superficially significant nonsense, and he had managed to fit in several of his favourite clichés: the consulting sabbatical was there, cheek by jowl with the detached global overview and the continuing close ties with the agency. A masterpiece of woolliness. Jordan would probably want a paragraph in it about himself and his management team, but that was easily done. And Ziegler? He'd call it horseshit, and he'd be right. But he knew, as Simon did, that horseshit in advertising is the corporate cement that holds everything together.

Simon made his way along empty streets back to the flat, and settled down with a cigar to wait for Jordan. In a couple of hours it would be done.

Jordan's arrival was announced by a throaty burble from the Bentley as it swept into Rutland Gate, and Simon went out to meet him. He was encased in another of his bullet-proof tweed suits, brown and bristly as a doormat, with a knitted tie the colour of catarrh. He smiled and shot his cuffs in greeting.

'Morning, old boy. Survived the festivities?'

Simon got into the car, and looked appreciatively at the dark brown leather and polished walnut. 'Just about. And you?'

'No casualties so far, but this little break has come at the right moment, I can tell you. Non-stop bridge is seriously boring.' He looked at Simon, his fingers tapping on the steering-wheel. 'This is all frightfully mysterious. What's going on?'

'We're meeting Ziegler at Claridge's, and I'm going to resign.'

Jordan grinned as he turned out of Rutland Gate. 'Pull the other one, old boy.' He stamped on the accelerator, and the big car was doing seventy as it reached Hyde Park Corner, causing a taxi to give way with an angry blast of its horn. 'What do you think of the motor?'

'I'd like it better if it slowed down. You take the next on the right for Claridge's.'

Jordan cut across two lanes of traffic. 'You're not serious? About resigning?'

'If I live that long.'

Jordan said nothing, and Simon smiled to himself. The loudest noise in the car was the ticking of Jordan's brain as he drew up outside the hotel.

Ziegler received them in his suite, dressed for jogging in a grey track-suit and pneumatic running shoes. He frowned at the unexpected sight of Jordan. 'What is this, a goddamn delegation?'

'Compliments of the season, Bob,' said Simon. 'I hope you're well?'

Ziegler looked at them suspiciously. Men in pairs usually meant collusion and trouble, in his experience He decided to start off being pleasant. 'Sure. What are you guys going to have? Juice? Coffee?'

Jordan consulted his watch. 'Wouldn't mind a glass of fizz, actually.' Ziegler looked puzzled. 'Champagne.'

Ziegler called Room Service, and Simon shuffled the papers he'd brought as Jordan went through his cigarette selection routine.

'OK.' Ziegler sat as far away from the smoking area as possible. 'What's the story?'

Simon took them through his plans slowly and unemotionally, emphasizing his desire to make his departure appear to be a positive development for the agency, promising his cooperation and a gradual release of his shares to other directors. He had just given them copies of the press release when the champagne arrived. He got up to tip the waiter, and stood by the door watching the two men frowning over the release as they absorbed the news and calculated its effect on them.

Ziegler would be delighted to see Simon go, and leave him as undisputed master of the world. Jordan would get a bigger office and a bigger title to go with his big new car. Neither of them would miss him personally any more than he would miss them. It was just business, business and self-interest.

Jordan stood up and came over to Simon, his face doing its best to look solemn. He patted Simon's shoulder. 'You'll be sorely missed, old boy. Sorely missed. Valued our friendship enormously.' He sighed gustily at the thought of losing his dear comrade, and reached for the champagne. 'Ah,' he said, 'Perrier-Jouet '85. Splendid.'

Ziegler began pacing up and down. Simon was distracted by his jogging shoes. They looked as if they were inflatable, and gave Ziegler the appearance of bouncing. 'I don't get it. You want to go run some rinky fucking dink hotel out in the boonies?' He stopped, and swivelled to look at Simon, his head thrust forward like a dog examining an unexpected and possibly doctored bone. 'You're blowing smoke up my ass. There's another agency.'

The room was silent except for the sound of Jordan's unlit cigarette – tap, tap, tap on the gold case.

'No, Bob. Nothing like that, cross my heart. I've had enough, that's all. I'm ready for a change.' Simon grinned. 'Wish me luck and tell me you'll miss me.'

Ziegler scowled. 'What do you want, a chicken dinner and a goddamn medal? You give me a problem like this and I'm supposed to be pleased? Jesus.'

But underneath the bluster, Simon could tell that he was, and so was Jordan, and as they talked on into the late afternoon it became clear that neither of them wanted him to stay any longer than was absolutely necessary. In a matter of hours, his position had changed from being indispensable to being a potential embarrassment, an executive who had taken his eye off the corporate ball, a believer who had renounced his faith. People like that were disruptive, even dangerous, because they threatened to undermine the agency's carefully cultivated aura of dedication.

Simon listened as Ziegler and Jordan went through the client list assessing possible damage and discussing adjustments in top management. Not once did they ask his opinion, and he realized that he was already, in Ziegler's terminology, history. The lawyers would take care of the details. He was out.

15

Ernest parked his old Armstrong Siddeley, dignified and gleaming, outside the flat in Rutland Gate. Today they were leaving for good, emigrating, driving down to a new life.

He let himself into the flat and found Simon kneeling on a swollen suitcase, cursing as he tried to close the locks. 'Sorry about this, Ern. I never was a great packer. How much room is there in the car?'

Ernest joined him on the suitcase. 'It might be just a tiny bit cramped, but we'll manage. Is it just this one and the other two?' He snapped the locks shut. 'There. Off we go.'

They carried the cases out to the car, and Ernest opened the boot. 'The big one we can squeeze in here, and the others can go on top of Mrs Gibbons' basket.'

Simon had forgotten about Mrs Gibbons. 'Where's she going to sit?'

'Well, she does have this rather tiresome little habit. She'll only travel in the passenger seat. If you put her behind, she gets terribly upset and eats the upholstery.'

'What about me?'

'You can be the English *milord* and sit in the back.'

Simon peered through the passenger window. Two pink eyes looked back at him, and Mrs Gibbons sat up and yawned. She had, like all bull terriers, a pair of jaws that looked capable of cracking rocks. She cocked her head at Simon. One ragged white ear pricked up, and he heard a low, bubbling growl.

Ernest came round and opened the door. 'We don't want to hear any more of that nastiness. Now you come out and say hello to Mr Shaw.' He turned to Simon. 'Hold out your hand, dear, so she can have a sniff.'

Simon extended a tentative hand, which the dog examined carefully before hopping back into the car and curling up on the seat, one eye open and alert, the other closed.

'That's not a dog, Ern. That's more like a Japanese wrestler.'

'Appearances aren't everything, dear. She has a very sweet disposition. Usually.' Ernest opened the back door of the car and ushered Simon with a flourish into the seat next to the dog basket. 'To France!'

They stopped for the night south of Paris at Fontainebleau, and set off early the next morning, the old car keeping up a steady, silent sixty-five miles an hour, the sky becoming higher and brighter as they entered the Midi.

'We shall be in Brassière for the cocktail hour,' said Ernest, 'and I happen to know that Nicole is making us a *cassoulet*.'

Simon leaned forward, his elbows on the back of the passenger seat. Mrs Gibbons opened a warning eye. 'I'm glad that you and Nicole get on so well.'

'My dear, I can't tell you what a relief she is after our last little venture. Incidentally, did you tell her that you were leaving?'

Simon had decided not to say anything to Caroline until he was safely in France. If she'd known he was leaving the jurisdiction of the English court, the lawyers would have been on him like flies. 'No. I thought I'd drop her a note, tell her not to worry about the alimony. She's got nothing to complain about.'

Ernest sniffed loudly. 'That never stopped her making a pest of herself. An extremely spoilt young woman, in my opinion.' He pulled out to overtake a truck filled with sheep. 'She'll be curious, you know, when she finds out. She'll come down to have a look, nosy little madam.'

'I'm sure.' Simon looked at the rocky, grey-green landscape, and felt suddenly tired. The past few weeks hadn't been easy, and now that they were over he wanted to collapse, to be with Nicole. He was starting to think of her as home. 'Can't you get this old tub to go any faster?'

They reached Brassière just after six, and Nicole came out to greet them, hugging herself against the cold. She was wearing tights and sweater of fine black wool, with a small and totally impractical white apron. Simon picked her up and nuzzled her neck. Her skin was warm from the kitchen. 'You could get arrested wearing an outfit like that. How are you?'

'Welcome home, *chéri*.' She leaned back in his arms to look at his face, and then her eyes widened as she saw something over his shoulder. 'My God, what's that?'

Mrs Gibbons was celebrating her arrival with an investigation of local aromas, moving from lamp-post to dustbin with a rolling, bandy-legged, nautical walk, her tail stiff and quizzical. Nicole watched her with disbelief as she chose a suitable spot to relieve herself, her great blunt snout lifted to take the evening air.

'That,' said Simon, 'is Mrs Gibbons. Unusual, isn't she?'

Nicole laughed and shook her head. A truly ugly dog, she thought, one of God's jokes. She kissed Simon on the nose. 'You don't get a drink until you put me down.'

They unloaded the car and sat round the fire with a bottle of red wine as Nicole brought them up to date. News of the hotel had spread well beyond the village through the *téléphone arabe* – café talk and shop gossip. Every day now, she said, someone would approach her to suggest an arrangement of one kind or another: a job, a discount on meat, an exceptional opportunity to buy antiques, pool maintenance service, fully grown olive trees at a *prix d'ami* – the whole world, it seemed, had something or someone to sell, and nobody was more persistent than the burglar's dedicated foe, Jean-Louis the alarm system salesman.

At least once a day, he would call or drop in with the latest reports of criminal activity in the Vaucluse. Robbery was rampant, according to him, and nothing was safe. Cars disappeared in seconds, houses were violated, garden furniture and statues took flight, even the very knives and forks of the hotel would be at risk. It would be, he told Nicole, his personal pleasure and responsibility to supervise a security system that would rival the Banque de France for impregnability. Not even a rat from the fields would be able to slip through the net.

'He sounds like a con artist to me,' said Simon. 'What do

we need all that for? There'll always be someone in the hotel. Anyway we can train Mrs Gibbons to kill on command.'

Nicole shrugged. 'I think he looks for a job – you know, *chef de sécurité*. He's quite charming, but a little *louche*. You met him at the party.'

'What about the real chef?'

'Two possibilities so far. A young man who is sous-chef at one of the big hotels on the coast. He wants his own kitchen. They say he is good, and ambitious to do something famous. The other . . .' Nicole lit a cigarette, and laughed through the smoke '. . . is Madame Pons. She's from the region, a wonderful cook, but with a temperament. Her last job was in Avignon, but she had a fracas with a client who said the duck was undercooked. She came out of the kitchen and *paf*! It was very dramatic.'

'How do you feel about a dramatic chef, Ern?'

'Artists are never easy, dear. We all know that.'

'I had her *soufflé aux truffes* one night,' said Nicole, 'and chicken with tarragon. *Superbe*.' She looked at her watch and stood up. 'And now all I have for you is my poor little *cassoulet*.'

The poor little *cassoulet*, a heavy, rich stew of sausage and lamb and goose and beans with a light crust of breadcrumbs, was placed in its deep earthenware bowl on the table, next to the wine from Rasteau that they were testing for the hotel cellar. The long, fat loaf was cut into thick slices which felt soft and springy between the fingers. The salad was tossed, the wine poured, and as Nicole broke the crust of the *cassoulet*, a savoury steam came from the bowl. Simon grinned at her as he tucked his napkin into his collar. 'I'm taking care of your shirts.'

'*Bon*. Now eat while it's hot.'

The hiring of the chef, they all agreed, needed to be settled quickly, before the kitchen was built and equipped. A good chef could make an hotel's reputation in a single season, and attract local customers throughout the year. But finding the right chef, being sure, that was the problem. Did you go and try the restaurant, in the anonymous fashion of the Michelin inspector? And if you did, could you be certain that it was the chef, rather than some talented slave, who did the cooking?

Ernest dabbed his mouth with his napkin and took a mouthful of wine, chewing at it for a moment before swallowing. 'Mmmm. Very promising. Shall we try the Cairanne? It's wonderful that all the vineyards are so close.' He got up to fetch clean glasses, and poured the wine. 'Now, are you ready for an answer to the problem?'

'Another *pensée*, is this, Ern?'

'Exactly, dear. What I suggest is that we ask each chef to come to Brassière – which they'd want to do anyway – and cook for us. A test lunch. Why not?'

Nicole and Simon looked at each other. Why not?

They were not prepared, however, for the delicate and highly important matter of gastronomic self-esteem, the ego of a chef who knows he's good, and who sees himself among the masters like Bocuse and Senderens – revered, courted, treated like national treasures by the President, fawned over by movie stars. When Nicole called the young man on the coast, he declined the invitation to lower himself by cooking in a private kitchen. He would come to Brassière, providing a chauffeur-driven car was sent to Nice to pick him up, but there would be a *déplacement* charge of 5000 francs, and he would not cook.

Nicole put the phone down and grimaced. '*Il pète plus haut que son cul.*'

'I beg your pardon?' said Ernest.

Simon laughed. 'They don't teach that one at Berlitz, Ern. It means that he has an exaggerated idea of his own importance – he farts higher than his own arse.'

'An anal ventriloquist. How very distasteful.'

After some difficulty, Nicole managed to track down the second candidate, Madame Pons, and put the same proposition to her. It was agreed that she would come to look at the hotel and Nicole's kitchen. If she liked what she saw, she would cook. If not, they could buy her lunch at the Mas Tourteron outside Gordes, which she had heard was excellent, and that would be her fee for the day. But she was, she said, an optimist. She told Nicole to meet her in Les Halles in Avignon at six the next morning to buy the ingredients for lunch.

The three of them arrived at Les Halles just before six. In the pre-dawn gloom of the Place Pie, the only indications that anyone else was up were the cars jammed into every parking space and the faint glow of light coming from the entrance to the market. It was well below zero, with a wind that chased empty cigarette packets along the gutter and sliced into exposed skin. Simon rubbed his unshaven face, and it felt like frozen sandpaper.

'How are we going to find her?'

'She said she'll be having breakfast at Kiki's bar.'

Darkness and silence became noise and bustle and glaring light as soon as they were inside. The aisles were crowded, the stallholders shouting to make themselves heard as they filled orders and bellowed encouragement at indecisive shoppers. Ernest stood in astonishment as he looked at the stalls, every inch filled with vegetables, with meat, with cheeses and olives and fruit and fish, abundance piled on abundance.

'Well! I can see we'll be spending many happy hours here. Look at the size of those aubergines – they're enough to give a ballet dancer an inferiority complex.'

They made their way through the crowd towards the bar. Men in old work-clothes stood shoulder to shoulder over small *ballons* of red wine and sausage sandwiches. In the corner, a solitary woman was making notes on the back of an envelope, a half-empty flute of champagne in front of her.

Madame Pons had passed the stage of being merely ripe, and was now, in early middle age, voluminous. Below her dark red curly hair and fleshy, handsome face, chins cascaded into a white lace blouse. Her makeup was emphatic, as was her bosom, which rested on the bar like two sleeping puppies. Around her shoulders was slung a cloak of bottle-green, and two surprisingly dainty feet balanced on a pair of elegant high heels.

186

Nicole made the introductions, and Madame Pons looked at them with lively brown eyes as she finished her champagne. Simon put a 100-franc note on the bar. 'Permit me,' he said. Madame Pons nodded graciously, picked up her envelope and tapped it with a plump finger.

'I have the menu for lunch,' she said. 'A little *bouffe* – nothing complicated. Follow me.'

She moved regally along the stalls, prodding, sniffing, rejecting. Most of the stallholders knew her, and were loud in praising their produce, offering lettuces and cheeses for her inspection as though they were works of art. She said little, either shaking her head with disapproving clicks of her tongue, or nodding before moving on, leaving Simon and Ernest to pick up her choices. After nearly two hours, they were both weighed down with plastic shopping bags, and Madame Pons was satisfied. She drove off with Nicole, and the two men followed.

'What do you think of her, Ern?'

Ernest was silent as he swerved to avoid a dog that had stopped in the middle of the road for a scratch. 'If she cooks as well as she shops . . . did you see the look she gave that first man with the fish? Withering. I rather took to her, I must say. Rubens would have adored her.'

'There's certainly a lot to adore. You saw she was dipping into the champagne?'

'Oh, I never trust a chef who doesn't like a tipple. It shows up in the cooking, you know.'

They were out of central Avignon, and Ernest slowed down as they saw a girl in high boots and a micro-skirt bent over the bonnet of a BMW, her bottom presented to the oncoming traffic. 'Do you think we ought to give her a hand?'

Simon laughed. 'Ern, she's a working girl, a hooker. She's there every day. Nicole told me.'

The sun had come up, and the fields and orchards that had once been the private property of the Popes of Avignon glittered with frost. It was going to be a postcard day, clear and blue and bright, the kind of weather that promises good luck.

They gathered in the vaulted rooms that were to be the hotel kitchen and restaurant, now the temporary headquarters of Fonzi and his men, who were knocking through the thick stone walls to make high arched windows. A fog of dust hung in the air, and the jackhammer was in full song. Madame Pons gathered her cloak around her, and tiptoed through the rubble towards the kitchen area.

She stood in the middle of the space, turning slowly as she mentally arranged her ovens and burners and preparation tables, her refrigerators and dishwashers and pot racks. She paced out distances, gauged the height of the ceiling, studied the access to the dining room. The others watched her in silence as she moved back and forth in majestic slow motion. Eventually, she looked at them and nodded.

'It will do,' she said. 'A little small, but it will do.'

With smiles of relief, they escorted Madame Pons through the dining room and up the stairs, unaware of the admiring glances she had attracted from the smallest of the masons. He waited until they were out of earshot, and turned to Fonzi.

'*Elle est magnifique, non?*' He shook one hand vigorously from the wrist. '*Un bon paquet.*'

Fonzi grinned. 'Always the big ones, Jojo, eh? You'd get lost.'

The little mason sighed. One of these days, if the affair of the bank raid worked, he'd be able to buy a suit and take a woman like that out, smother her with money. One of these days. He resumed his assault on the wall and thought about vast expanses of milky flesh.

Madame Pons slipped off her cloak and examined Nicole's kitchen, testing the edge of a knife on her thumb, feeling the weight of a copper pot while Ernest unpacked the bags from the market. She demanded an apron and a glass of white wine, selected Ernest as her assistant, and told Nicole and Simon to come back at noon. As they were going out of the front door, they heard the first of her instructions and a brisk '*D'accord*, dear' from Ernest.

Simon smiled. 'How do you like being thrown out of your own house? She's a tough one, isn't she?'

'All good chefs are dictators.' Nicole looked at her watch. 'It's good, because there's something I want to show you, a surprise for Ernest. We have time.'

'I think he's having a surprise at the moment.'

They drove along the N100, and then up into the hills. Nicole parked by the side of a high fence, and they walked through a pair of sagging gates. In front of them was a plot of land that stretched for three or four acres, still frosty and, despite the sunlight, slightly macabre. It looked as though a violent and untidy giant had demolished a village and tossed the remnants over his shoulder – piles of old beams, blocks of cut stone the size of small cars, pillars, fireplaces, roof tiles, millstones, colossal ornamental tubs, an entire staircase leaning against the side of a barn, terracotta urns as tall as a man, everything chipped and pock-marked with age among the weeds and brambles. Nicole led Simon past a battered nymph with no nose, lying on her back, her hands crossed modestly over lichen-speckled breasts.

'What is this place?' Simon asked.

'A *casse*. Isn't it marvellous? With these things, you can make a new house look two hundred years old.' Nicole stopped to look around. '*Merde*, I'm lost. Where is it?'

'What are we looking for?'

'Ah, *voilà*. Over there, past the beams.'

It was a statue, a large, weather-stained replica of the Manneken-Pis in Brussels, a corpulent cherub micturating pensively into a circular stone basin, blind-eyed and content, one chubby stone fist clutching a penis made from ancient copper piping.

Nicole tapped the copper. 'This, I think, may be a little too evident, but Fonzi can adjust it.' She stood back and looked at Simon, her face a smiling question mark. 'Well?'

Simon laughed as he walked round the statue and patted its bottom. 'I love it. Ern will be thrilled. I know exactly where he'll put the spotlight.' He put an arm round her shoulders. 'You're a clever girl. I can't wait to see his face.'

They spent half an hour wandering through the rest of the domestic graveyard, chose some troughs and pots for the hotel terrace, and found the owner's makeshift office in a corner of the barn. Simon watched with interest as Nicole haggled, asking the prices of several pieces she had no intention of buying, wincing as she heard them, shaking her head.

'If only one was rich,' she said to the owner. 'And the old fountain? How much is that?'

'Ah, that.' His expression was soulful beneath his knitted wool cap. 'My grandmother's fountain. I grew up with it. I have a great sentiment for that fountain.'

'I understand, *monsieur*. Some things are beyond price.' She shrugged. 'Well, that's a pity.'

'Eight thousand francs, *madame*.'

'Cash?'

'Six thousand.'

They got back to the house at noon to find Ernest putting the finishing touches to the table while Madame Pons, glass in hand, supervised.

'Remember, Airnest, flowers are for the eyes, not for the nose. If they are too strong, they fight with the scent of the food.'

'You're so right, dear. Specially freesias.' Ernest stepped back, frowned at the table, decided that it was satisfactory, and reached into the fridge for a bottle of white wine. 'On the menu today,' he said, 'we have a *terrine* of aubergine with a *coulis* of fresh peppers, roast turbot with a sauce of butter and *fines herbes*, *les fromages maison*, and hot *crêpes* wrapped around a filling of chilled whipped cream and vodka.' He poured wine for Nicole and Simon, and then a glass for himself, which he raised to Madame Pons. 'Madame is a jewel.' She looked puzzled. '*Un bijou*.' She beamed.

They sat down at twelve-thirty, and were still at the table, drinking a final cup of coffee, three hours later. Madame Pons had triumphed, and in an unfamiliar kitchen. Warmed by compliments and wine, she became expansive, leaning over to cuff Ernest from time to time at some of his more outrageous flatteries, shuddering with laughter, the flush extending down all her chins to the apron she was still wearing. Simon knew he wanted to hire her when she refused to discuss business over food.

'Eating,' she said, 'is too important to spoil with talk of work. The table is for pleasure. I might take a little Calvados, Airnest, and then I must go.' She held a hand up to her ear, thumb and little finger extended, the gesture that always accompanies the promise of a phone call in Provence. 'We will talk tomorrow.'

They went down with Madame Pons to see her off. On the way back, Ernest stopped at his car to let Mrs Gibbons out. She yawned, and looked at him reproachfully.

'She doesn't like dogs, Ern?'

'Quite the contrary, dear. She kept tossing little bits and pieces at Mrs Gibbons while she was cooking, and it's not good for her. Gives her wind.'

When they got back to the house they were unanimous over the washing-up. The hotel had a chef.

16

There were times during the next few weeks when Simon felt that his only function, the beginning and end of his usefulness, was to sign cheques. Everyone else had a job.

Madame Pons, always in the steepest of heels and usually with a glass in her hand, was supervising the design and equipping of the kitchen, interviewing sous-chefs and constructing the hotel wine list. Two or three times a week, she would hold court at an old tin table in her unfinished kitchen as burly wine-growers or smart young *négociants* came in with their best bottles. These visits were always followed by an invitation to a return tasting at the property, accompanied by a light, three-hour lunch. It was *l'enfer*, Madame Pons kept saying, but how else would one discover the little treasures of the region?

Ernest was spending his life among brochures and swatches of fabric, samples of stone and wood, encyclopaedias of trees and plants, sketches and plans. He had taken to wearing a black, wide-brimmed Provençal hat, and with his bulging portfolio, covered in Venetian marbled paper and tied at each end with ribbons of moiré silk, he was beginning to resemble an artist looking for somewhere to paint his next fresco.

Nicole, when she wasn't inspecting the fingernails and general suitability of potential waiters and chambermaids, worked with Ernest, taking him off for trips to the antique dealers of Isle-sur-Sorgue, the *ateliers* of metal-workers and carpenters, the garden nurseries where one could find anything from a sprig of thyme to a fifty-foot cypress. They would come back in the evening, flushed with the joys of discovery and acquisition, telling Simon how right his decision had been to avoid getting bogged down with all the details. 'Cushions and sanitary fittings, dear,' Ernest had said. 'Frightfully dreary.' It was odd, Simon thought, how both they and Madame Pons seemed to enjoy grumbling about what they obviously found fascinating.

Even the dog had a job. Mrs Gibbons had appointed herself the assistant to Blanc the architect, waiting outside the hotel every morning for him to arrive, and greeting him with circular motions of her tail. For the rest of the day she would be at his heels, gradually accumulating dust and blotches of plaster as she waddled through the rubble, occasionally dragging a plank or a discarded chunk of roof beam to place at his feet. The masons called her '*l'architecte*', and trained her, with the help of scraps left over from their lunch, to fetch twenty-kilo sacks of plaster, making bets on how far she could pull a sack up the flight of stone stairs. (This was done in reverse, to the sound of hideous growls.) Mrs Gibbons was occupied, and content.

Simon, on the other hand, found himself becoming restless. It was exciting, despite the torrent of money going out each week, to see the hotel starting to take shape, to wander through the bare but elegant stone rooms and picture them finished. And yet, for the first time in years, he had nothing to do, no meetings to go to, no phone calls to make. The only time he'd called the agency, Jordan had been pleasant but brisk. Everything was going well, the old clients had settled down with the new management, and there were a couple of interesting prospects in the works. 'Tickety-boo, old boy,' was how Jordan had described it, and as Simon put down the phone he had felt a twinge. He wasn't important any more.

There were consolations. He and Nicole were happy together. He missed her when she was off with Ernest, and had once or twice caught himself feeling jealous of the days she spent with him – unreasonably, since he had chosen to stay away from what he called their shopping expeditions. He'd tried going with them the first time, and had become so impatient and bad-tempered that they'd parked him in a bar after two hours.

But the shopping would soon be over, he told himself. Meanwhile, the days were getting longer, there was a softness in the spring air and a perceptible heat to the midday sun. The almond blossom had come out on the terraces below the hotel, sharp and bright against the drabness of brown earth and grey bark, and the stone bench Simon sat on was warm. He looked over towards the empty pool, where Mrs Gibbons was taking a siesta on the flagstones, her back legs twitching as she dreamed of rabbits and postmen. He tilted his face up and half-closed his eyes, feeling the sun go through to his bones.

'*Monsieur le patron, bonjour*!'

Simon blinked, and squinted at the figure that was bending towards him, hand held out in greeting, sunglasses and teeth agleam. Jean-Louis, the one-man crime prevention squad, had arrived for his daily ambush.

He was short, modish in his oversized trousers and suede *blouson*, well-groomed and slightly over-scented. His sharp features made Simon think of one of those nimble dogs that are sent down rabbit-holes – a fox terrier, with quick, neat movements and an alert slant to his head. He had a terrier's tenacity, too.

'Have you thought about my proposals?' He didn't give Simon a chance to reply, but took from his handbag a newspaper clipping. 'Look at this – the bank in Montfavet was held up last week, Tuesday morning. And then, when the *flics* were gone, what do you think happened? Eh?'

'I don't know, Jean-Louis. Everyone went out to lunch?'

'*Bof*! You joke, but this is a serious matter.' He removed his sunglasses for emphasis, and brandished them at Simon. 'In the afternoon, the robbers returned! *Beh oui*. Twice in one day! That is the Vaucluse for you. Nothing is safe, my friend, nothing. These guys, they come up from Marseille with their *pistolets* and fast cars . . .'

'How do you know they come from Marseille?'

'Ah.' Jean-Louis replaced his sunglasses and looked around to make sure they couldn't be overheard. 'I have connections.' He nodded at Simon. 'Connections in the *milieu*, from the old days.'

Simon raised his eyebrows. The old days of Jean-Louis hadn't been mentioned in previous conversations. 'Were you . . .?'

194

Jean-Louis put a finger to his lips. Simon felt sure there was a wink going on behind the sunglasses. 'Corsica. Undercover work. You've heard of the Union Corse?'

'Whose side were you on?'

'The police.' Jean-Louis shrugged, and smiled. 'Most of the time.'

'Tell me something. Why would you want to come and look after a little hotel like this? It's not very exciting, making sure nobody steals the ashtrays.'

'Contacts, my friend. The guests – Parisians, English, Germans, they come down, they buy a *résidence secondaire*, they need security. The alarm business is getting tough, you know? Too many electricians setting themselves up as security experts at low prices. Well, they can have the cheap clients, the villa people. I want the cream, nice German millionaires with art collections and wives who go shopping in Bulgari for a few holiday jewels to wear in Gordes. Where am I going to meet them? Not in some *bordel* of a bar in Cavaillon.' He waved his arm at the building behind them. 'Here I can meet them. *En plus*, you will have top protection, guaranteed. *Voilà* – something for both of us.' He cocked his head at Simon and fiddled with the gold medallion round his neck. 'Think about it, my friend. I'll make you a special deal.'

Jean-Louis pumped Simon's hand and rushed off to pursue his war against crime elsewhere, leaving a faint souvenir of his after-shave in the air. Not the kind of man you'd buy a second-hand car from, Simon thought, or even a brand-new safe. But he might come in useful, and Nicole seemed to like him.

Ten kilometres away, Nicole and Ernest were admiring an olive tree which, so they were assured, was no less than 250 years old, with a good 750 years of life ahead of it. These impressive statistics were sworn on the head of the proprietor's grandmother. The proprietor himself, a deeply wrinkled man who looked almost as old as the olive, had set up in business forty years ago with a field of lavender and a hard-working wife, and now owned several acres of plants and shrubs and trees, two houses, a small Mercedes and four television sets.

'*Comme il est beau*,' he said, and patted the gnarls and contortions of the twisted trunk. A light breeze sent a ripple through the leaves, changing their colour from green to silver-grey. The tree had been correctly pruned over the centuries, the central branches cut away to allow the sun in and to encourage a wide, graceful spread of foliage. It should be possible, so the old man said, for a small bird to fly through the top branches without catching its wings.

'Magnificent, isn't it?' said Ernest. 'Can you really move them when they're this old?'

Nicole put the question to the old man, who smiled and bent down to scrape away the sandy soil round the base of the trunk until he exposed the wooden rim of a giant tub. The tree, he said, had been brought over from Beaumes-de-Venise two years before, then potted and planted. It could, of course, make another short voyage. In fact, he would personally guarantee its continued health, providing – he wagged a crooked brown finger at them – it was properly oriented. He pointed to a daub of green paint on the bark. That must face south, as the tree had been facing since it was no higher than a thistle. If that were done, it would settle into a new home at once. If not, there would be two or three years of very little growth while the tree became accustomed to its changed position. The old man nodded. One should know these things before making an investment in such a tree.

How much of an investment? Nicole wondered.

'Three thousand francs, *madame*.'

'And for cash?'

The old man smiled. 'Three thousand francs.'

But it was a bargain, they told themselves as they drove back to Brassière – one of nature's antiques, handsome and leafy throughout the year, with that wonderful spread of branches which was wide enough to provide shade for a table and a group of chairs, a true symbol of Provence.

They arrived back at the hotel to find a dishevelled Simon sucking at skinned·and bleeding knuckles. His clothes were dusty and moss-stained, and there was a gash on his cheek. He held up a hand as he saw the expression on Nicole's face.

'It's OK. I won.'

'What happened?'

'Ern's surprise arrived. I was helping them take it down to the terrace, and I slipped on the stairs, squashed my hand against the wall and got poked in the cheek. You're right. We should get the little brute circumcised. He's dangerous.'

Nicole started to laugh. 'You mean . . . I don't believe it. I'm sorry to laugh.'

Simon grinned, and put his hand up to the gash. 'Wounded in action by a tumescent cherub. Do I get a medal?'

Ernest had been listening in puzzled silence. 'Disinfectant first, dear, and then we'll see about medals. I won't be a minute.'

While they were waiting, Nicole dusted Simon down and winced over his raw hand. 'I'm sorry,' she said again. 'It's not funny.'

'Nursing,' he said, 'that's what I need. You'll have to put me to bed and take my temperature. Come here. I'll show you how to do it without a thermometer.'

'Mmmm,' said Nicole a few moments later. 'I think you're going to live.'

They pulled apart as Ernest appeared with cotton-wool and a bottle of Synthol, and Nicole started to dab the disinfectant on.

Simon flinched. 'I hope you're ready for this, Ern. Nicole found it for you. Once you get it house-trained you'll love it.'

They went downstairs and through the restaurant. On the terrace outside, the cherub, temporarily detached from his pedestal and his water supply, was standing next to the stone basin, staring across the valley towards the mountains. Mrs Gibbons was testing the edibility of his copper pipe.

'Oh, my dears,' said Ernest, 'what a splendid little man. Gibbons! Leave him alone.' He walked around the cherub, his face alight with pleasure.

'You said you wanted a fountain.'

'He's divine. Does he actually work?'

'Like someone who's just had eighteen pints of lager, Ern. You don't think he's too rude?'

'Certainly not. He's a study in careless rapture. I can't tell you how thrilled I am.' He came over to hug Nicole. 'It's very sweet of you. I can see him over there, tinkling away. I know exactly where to put him, under the tree.' He stopped, and clapped a hand to his mouth as he looked at Simon. 'Why don't I get you a glass of wine, and we'll tell you about the tree.'

Madame Pons spat delicately into the tin bucket, and made a note in the exercise book that contained her thoughts on the hotel wine list. She was sitting in a small, mud-floored *cave* outside Gigondas, unlabelled bottles ranged along the table in front of her, the cold coming up through the thin soles of her shoes, the feeble light of a forty-watt bulb casting deep shadows on the attentive face of the man opposite her.

'*Eh, alors?*' Monsieur Constant was one of the dozens of *vignerons* in the area who had taken the risk of making and bottling their own wines instead of selling grapes to the co-operative. If the wine is good, the profit is higher. And if a hotel *de luxe*, such as Madame described, were to take a few dozen cases, the reputation of the wine would spread, the price could be raised accordingly, and Monsieur Constant would be able to buy the two hectares next door that his imbecile of a neighbour was exploiting so badly. It was important to impress this large woman.

'*Un petit vin. Pas mal.*' Madame Pons looked at him, polite but impassive. '*Ensuite?*'

'*Un trésor, madame. Un vrai trésor.*' Constant smiled. It was a pity that she'd refused to eat the cheese that he'd offered her, a cheese strong enough to make vinegar taste good, but then she was a professional. He poured the rich, dark wine into two glasses, swirled it around. '*Quelle robe, eh?*' He picked up his glass, closed his eyes, inhaled and shook his head in admiration of his own efforts. He took a sip, chewed and swallowed, shook his head again. '*Cong! Il a du slip, ce vin. Cong!*'

Madame Pons, who had seen similar performances in at least a dozen *caves*, smiled and picked up her own glass, and went through her own unhurried, thorough ritual. There

198

was silence except for a muted gurgle as the wine made its progress from Madame Pons' lips to her back teeth, drawn through by a steady intake of breath. She swallowed. '*Oui*.' She nodded twice, very deliberately. '*Il est bon, très bon*.' As she reached for a piece of cheese, Constant filled her glass and wondered if he could get away with another franc on the price.

The gang celebrated the official arrival of spring by discarding their tights. The General inspected them in their new shorts, black and snug-fitting. He'd paid extra for the Tour de France model with the double seat and the autograph of a past champion scrawled on the front. Even the boys' legs were beginning to look professional, with a good meaty bulge to the thighs, and definition in the calves. Still white, of course, but a few weeks would take care of that. Also, he noticed with satisfaction, they had remembered to shave. Hairy legs were hell if you took a tumble and got badly grazed.

All of them, rather to the General's surprise, had taken well to the discipline and pain of getting fit, and took a collective pride in now being able to climb hills that would have been impossible a few weeks ago. A sense of achievement worked wonders, he thought, particularly when it was linked to the promise of money. That's what he found so satisfying about crime.

'*Bon*.' He unfolded a map, and spread it out on the bonnet of his car. 'Seventy-five kilometres this morning, and we'll finish by coming back through Isle-sur-Sorgue, the way we'll come on the day. Don't look too hard at the bank when you go past.'

While they studied the route he had marked on the map, the General took a bag from the car and unpacked the contents: seven pairs of sunglasses, and seven brightly coloured cotton caps with small peaks.

'*Voilà*. The final touch.' He handed them out. 'This is camouflage. Put these on, and you'll look exactly like the other five thousand cyclists on the road today. Nobody will be able to describe the colour of your hair or the colour of your eyes. You'll vanish.'

'*C'est pas con, eh?*' Jojo put on his glasses, and pulled his cap down low on his forehead. 'What do you think?'

Jean looked him up and down. '*Ravissant.* Specially the legs.'

'*Allez!*' said the General. 'This isn't a fashion show. You know the road to take out of town? I'll be stuck in the traffic.' Seven little cotton caps nodded, and the General nodded back. It worked, the simple disguise. He would hardly recognize them himself if they passed him at speed.

Simon and Ernest stood outside the hotel, looking up through the scaffolding at the façade. Next to them, Bert the painter, who had driven down specially from London for the job, was rolling a cigarette. 'Take a couple of weeks to settle in,' he said. 'Still a touch bright, but what with the sun and the wind you'll get more of that old look. You know, the desired effect, as we call it.'

Bert was an artist in prematurely aged painting – dragging, rag-rolling, sponging, distressing – anything from artificially crazed lacquer to a fake nicotine-stained ceiling could be conjured up with the help of the contents of his van. It stood in the car park behind them, an Old Master on wheels. Painted on each side panel was a detail from the Sistine Chapel which showed the finger of God pointing to a legend that appeared to have been cut in stone: ALBERT WALDIE: THE DESIRED EFFECT. It attracted a lot of attention, did the van.

Bert's latest triumph was the hotel sign. The letters, two feet high with a dropped shadow, were in faded yellow against a background of faded blue, framed by a thin red line. It looked as though, after fifty years of resisting the elements, it was about to peel, an impression that was helped by the chips and cracks Bert had applied so painstakingly over the last two days.

'It's wonderful, Bert. Just what we were after, Ern, isn't it?'

Ernest nodded enthusiastically. 'Quite superb, Bert dear. Do you know, I'm toying with the idea of something on the back wall of the restaurant.'

'A muriel, sort of thing?'

'That sort of thing, yes. When do the others get down?'
Bert's three assistants were coming to join him for the
interior work, now that the masons were getting close to
finishing.

Bert pulled thoughtfully on his cigarette. 'It's your walls,
of course. All very well for those jokers to say they've
finished, but your walls have to dry out. Painting on damp
walls, oh dear me no. Not if you want to get the desired
effect.'

'Why don't we go and have a look?' Simon said. 'We've
had all the windows open and the heating up to maximum,
so downstairs should be dry.'

They went inside, and Bert paused in front of one of the
windows. 'Pity about those mountains, really.'

'Why's that, Bert?'

'Get in the way of the view, don't they?'

Françoise made her way slowly up the steps to Nicole's
front door, hampered by the tightness of her skirt and the
unaccustomed high heels. She'd bought the shoes in Cavaillon when she'd gone in to have her hair done for the
interview. If it went well today, she could leave the café,
leave the endless washing-up of glasses and the slaps on the
bottom from her father's old card-playing friends. She'd
wear high heels every day and meet people from Paris and
London, and maybe a young man with a red Ferrari would
come to the hotel and fall in love with her. She looked
down at the blouse she had ironed with such care last night,
and decided to do up another button, as it was Madame
Bouvier. *Bon.* She knocked at the door.

Nicole let her in and sat her down in an armchair by the
fireplace. It was the first time she had ever seen Françoise
dressed in anything except jeans or old cotton skirts and
espadrilles, and the transformation was almost startling,
from a little country girl to a striking young woman. There
was too much makeup, Nicole thought, and the skirt was
too tight, but those details could be arranged.

'You're looking very pretty, Françoise. I like your hair.'

'*Merci, madame.*' Françoise thought about crossing her legs in that elegant way Madame Bouvier did, but realized that her skirt was already short enough. She crossed her ankles.

Nicole lit a cigarette. 'Tell me about your parents. If you came to the hotel, would they be happy? What about the work at the café? We don't want to upset them.'

There was a shrug from Françoise, and a pout from her full lower lip. 'My cousin would come. My parents – well, they know I don't want to spend my life in the café.' She sat forward in her chair. 'I can type, you know. I took a course after I left school. I could do the hotel correspondence, confirmations, bills, anything.'

Nicole looked at her face, wide-eyed and eager, and smiled. If that was the first face the hotel guests saw, they couldn't complain. Certainly not the men. She stood up. 'Come into the kitchen. I'll make some coffee while we talk.'

Françoise followed her, looking at the silk of her shirt, the cut of her trousers, the way they fitted so smoothly at the back, with none of those little wrinkles. Madame Bouvier was the most chic woman she had ever seen. She smoothed her skirt – last year's skirt, and it must have shrunk – down over her hips and felt awkward. Her mother could never understand why clothes shouldn't be worn until they fell apart. Madame Bouvier would understand. Françoise decided to ask her advice about clothes. If she got the job.

'I could start before the hotel opens. You know, helping.'

Ambrose Crouch sat staring at the screen of his word-processor, a bottle of red wine by his side, getting slowly drunk and increasingly courageous.

The hotel had become something of an obsession. It symbolized all that he publicly sneered at and privately envied – comfort, luxury, money – and it was a daily reminder of his own very different circumstances. His house was small, and smelt of damp all through the winter. His retainer from the *Globe* had not been increased for two years; times were hard in England, so his editor kept telling him. Five publishers had now rejected his proposal for a book, and the American magazines had stopped buying his articles after he had criticized a prominent and well-liked American resident of Lacoste.

He sucked at his wine and brooded. On top of everything else, to be blackmailed into silence by that millionaire thug, with his bloody cigars and his smart little French mistress – that stuck in his throat. He had done some research on Simon Shaw, and had made notes for a long and savage piece about him, which in the more cautious sobriety of the following morning had been put in a drawer. But now he thought he might have found a way to do it.

An old drinking-companion from the Fleet Street days had agreed to print Crouch's piece in his paper, under his own byline. It would have to be carefully written, now that judges were hammering the press for damages in libel suits, but it was better than nothing, and Crouch would be protected.

He filled his glass and smiled to himself as he looked at the headline on the screen: THE RAPE OF A VILLAGE. Maybe he'd slip in a quote from himself, as if he'd been interviewed by the writer. Nothing personal, nothing litigious, just a gentle sigh of disapproval at vanishing traditions and the pollution of village life. He started tapping at the keyboard, and let himself enjoy the feeling of dispensing malice in safety.

Simon looked at the week's bills, from carpenters and plumbers and plasterers and electricians, and shook his head. It was like signing cheques for the Italian football team – Roggiero, Biagini, Ziarelli, Coppa – and probably just as expensive. It was good work they did, though, beautiful work. He signed off the final string of zeros, and went out to the terrace at the back of the house, where Nicole had already started to do some early sunbathing during the middle of the day. It was evening now, and the sky above the mountains was fading from blue to a blush of the palest, lavender-tinted pink, the colour that Ernest described as implausible.

Before long, the lines in the vineyards would become

blurred with green, the cherry blossom would be out, and the Easter tourists would be arriving. Our future clients, Simon thought. Let's hope the plumbing works. He took a last look at the sky, and went indoors to get a drink.

17

'Is that Simon Shaw, the environmental rapist?'

Simon smiled as he recognized the voice on the phone. It was Johnny Harris, once a copywriter with the agency, and now one of London's most diligent gossip columnists. Unlike some of his colleagues in the rumour business, he could be trusted not to stab his targets in the back – at least, not without giving them a chance to defend themselves first. He and Simon had kept in touch over the years and through the marriages, and apart from his habit of describing Simon as 'the susceptible agency chief' in his column, he had always treated him gently.

'Hello, Johnny. What have I done now?'

'Well, apparently you're in the process of ruining the fabric of daily life in one of Provence's most unspoiled villages. It's in the paper, so it must be true, you bloody scoundrel.' Harris laughed. 'It's one of those pieces where everything is implied without confusing the reader with too much in the way of facts. Quite cleverly done, actually. I would have suspected your delightful neighbour, the poison dwarf.'

'So it wasn't Crouch?' It didn't matter now, anyway. It was too late to do much damage.

'Not his paper, and it's not his byline. He's quoted – his usual routine about another nail in the coffin of the Lubéron, the uncaring march of what we mistakenly call progress, all the same old shit – but of course he could have stuck that in himself. It's an old trick; I've done it plenty of times. Anyway, it's been carefully written. Nothing to take to court.'

'How bad is it?'

'Unpleasant – you know, the long-drawn-out sneer – but not terminal. It'll all be forgotten when the next politician gets caught with his trousers down, which seems to happen every week. I'll fax it to you. But you'd better expect some calls, and maybe the odd journalist.' Harris paused, and Simon heard the sound of his lighter and the ringing of phones in the background. 'I'll tell you something, though. A bit of good press wouldn't hurt, and you know me, I'm always ready for a freebie. What about it?'

Simon laughed. 'The subtlety of your approach is quite irresistible.' He thought for a moment. 'Why don't you come down for the opening? It should be early June, and we might be able to round up a few characters for you to write about.'

'I can bring my own, if you like. Do you want some Eurotrash? A couple of Italian princes? Starlets and harlots? Let's see. I could do you a lovely lesbian actress, or a racing driver with a drink problem. Or there's the keyboard player from Stark Naked and the Car Thieves . . .'

'Johnny, I'm hoping this is going to be a nice quiet little hotel. Just bring one of your girls, and leave that lot in the Groucho Club, all right?'

Harris sighed noisily. 'You're turning into an old fart, but I'll humour you. Let me know the date, and I'll be down to uphold the traditions of the British press.'

'I was afraid of that,' Simon said. 'Don't forget to fax the piece.'

'It's on the way. Hold your nose. It's a stinker. I'll talk to you soon.'

Simon was still smiling as he put down the phone. Johnny Harris, shameless and cheerfully cynical, always put him in a good mood. It even survived the arrival of the fax, which lived down to its description. Simon read it through a second time and tore it up. What a way to earn a living.

The hotel, according to Monsieur Blanc, was within days of being finished, a week at most. The masons had gone, the *carreleurs* had finished laying the stone floors, the kitchen was a gleaming vista of stainless steel and copper, the pool was filled, the olive tree – Ernest had nearly wept when they pruned it – had been planted. Albert Waldie and his team of painters disputed wall space with the electricians who were having second thoughts about the wiring, and a symphony of flushing lavatories and running taps testified to the plumber's diligence as he conducted his final checks on optimum water flow and prompt evacuation, darting from bidet to bath and nodding to himself. The carpenters were fitting doors and closets, shaving and sanding, filling the rooms with a fine haze of sawdust which drifted down to settle on Waldie's fresh paintwork and provoke another crisis in Anglo-French relations.

Monsieur Blanc moved purposefully through the bedlam, Mrs Gibbons rolling along behind him with a length of grey PVC piping clamped between her teeth. They joined Nicole and Simon and Ernest in the kitchen, where a *tapenade* soufflé that Madame Pons had suggested should be one of the regular dishes on the menu was being put through its paces.

Blanc allowed his nostrils to flutter with appreciation before he spoke. There was, he said, a little problem, nothing grave. The next-door neighbours, an elderly couple, were concerned about the swimming pool. Not the swimming pool itself, of course, which was a marvel of good taste and completely beyond reproach, but what might happen *around* the swimming pool. The neighbours had read in the newspaper of the unnatural practices occasionally committed in Saint-Tropez, where people had been known to sunbathe *tout nu*. To see such behaviour in Brassière, a village with two churches, would be intensely disturbing to Madame, with her heart as delicate as it was. Monsieur had apparently not expressed any fears. Nevertheless, some form of reassurance would be greatly appreciated.

Simon wiped up the last of his soufflé with a piece of bread. 'That's ridiculous. There's a wall three metres high between their garden and the pool. They'd have to be on stilts to see anything.'

'*Beh oui*.' Blanc smiled apologetically. 'But Madame is the aunt of someone in the Administration in Avignon. *Un gros bonnet*.'

Nicole put her hand on Simon's arm. 'Go on, *chéri*. Be a diplomat for five minutes.'

Simon stood up and inclined his head towards Madame Pons. 'That was delicious.' He practised a diplomatic smile on the others. 'Will that do?'

'A little *tapenade* on one of your teeth, dear,' said Ernest. 'But otherwise, very nice. Auntie won't be able to resist.'

Simon walked fifty yards down the street and knocked twice at the heavy oak door. He heard footsteps, and the small grille fitted into the door slid to one side. Suspicious, bespectacled eyes peered up at him. He had to stoop so that they could see his face.

'*Oui?*'

'*Bonjour, madame.* I am your neighbour, from the hotel.'

'*Oui.*'

'The proprietor of the hotel.'

'*Ah bon.*'

'Yes.' Simon was starting to feel like a door-to-door salesman with halitosis. '*Madame*, would it be possible for us to talk? Just for a few minutes?'

The spectacles studied him, and then the grille slid shut. There was the sound of bolts being drawn. A lock was turned. The door finally opened, and Madame nodded Simon inside.

The house was dark, all the shutters closed against the sun. Simon followed Madame's short, erect figure into the kitchen, and sat opposite her at a long table with a television set at one end. A central light hung from the ceiling. It could have been midnight. Madame folded her hands tightly, and did the same with her lips.

Simon cleared his throat. 'I'm told that you and your husband are worried about, ah, the swimming pool.'

Madame nodded. 'Certain activities.'

'Oh, those.' Simon tried a reassuring smile. The lips opposite remained pursed. 'Well, I can promise you that we will demand our guests to be discreet.'

'Not like Saint-Tropez.'

Simon threw up his hands in horror. 'Certainly not like Saint-Tropez! More like . . .' Oh God, what was the French equivalent of Bognor Regis? '. . . well, more like a quiet family hotel. You know, respectable.' He leaned forward. 'And, of course, there is the wall.'

Madame sniffed at the wall. 'My husband has a ladder.'

And probably a telescope for the girls as well, Simon thought. 'I think I can guarantee that the guests will be completely proper.' He had a mental picture of one of Philippe Murat's popsies parading around in a string, tanned buttocks exposed to the breeze. 'In fact, I will personally pay close attention to this matter.'

The lips unpursed fractionally. '*Bon.*'

The audience was over. Simon was shown out of the gloom and into the sunlight, and Madame stood and watched as he walked back to the hotel. His parting wave was acknowledged by a slight movement of the head, which was, he supposed, a minor triumph for diplomacy.

With the departure of the painters the following week, it was possible to plan an opening date. Staff had been hired, the *cave* was stocked, the repertoire of Madame Pons decided. Trucks arrived daily with beds and crockery, *matelas* for the pool, hundreds of glasses and towels and sheets, telephones, ashtrays and toothpicks, brochures and postcards – enough, it sometimes seemed, to equip the Ritz.

The three of them worked a fourteen-hour day before falling into the kitchen for a late supper, tired, grubby, but satisfied. The hotel was taking shape – a surprisingly warm, comfortable shape considering the amount of stone and the absence of soft surfaces. All the angularities had been smoothed and rounded away, and there were no hard edges to jar the eye. Going from room to room was like walking through sculpture, a blend of honey-coloured floors and pale walls and flowing corners. Blanc had done well, and when the paintings were hung and the rugs from Cotignac laid, they would have achieved what Mr Waldie would have described as the desired effect. Now it was time to think about adding guests.

'Well-connected chatterboxes,' said Ernest. 'That's what we need for the opening. People who like to be everywhere first, and tell their friends. Word of mouth is going to launch us, so we need some big mouths.' He looked at Simon, and raised his eyebrows. 'And we certainly know a few of those, I'm sure.'

'I think Johnny Harris will come down, and Philippe from

Paris.' Simon took a pear to eat with his cheese. 'We can always get the girls from the glossies. And I was wondering about fitting it in with the Cannes festival. It's only a three-hour drive.'

Nicole looked at him in disbelief. 'You think movie stars will come? *Non*. Be reasonable, *chéri*.'

'I wasn't thinking of the real festival. There's another one, in June. Everybody in advertising with a good enough excuse and a pair of sunglasses comes down – directors, producers, agency people – and the last thing they want to do is sit in the dark and watch the commercials.'

'So what is it they do?'

'Oh, pretty much what they do in London or Paris. They have lunch with each other. The difference is they're on the Croisette or on the beach instead of somewhere in Soho, and they go back home with a tan.'

'And they do talk,' Ernest said. 'Proper little gossips, all of them. I think that's a good idea.'

'I'll find out the dates and get Liz to send me a list of the delegates. We'll pick a few. I'm sure they'll come, just out of curiosity.'

They took their coffee outside and sat on the terrace. A half-moon hung over the Lubéron, and the bark of a distant dog carried up from the valley. By the side of the olive tree, the cherub urinated endlessly, and the soothing splash of the fountain mingled with the croak of frogs. The air was completely still, almost warm, hinting at summer. Simon glanced at Ernest, and thought he'd never seen such obvious contentment on a face.

'Still missing Wimbledon, Ern?'

Ernest smiled and stretched his legs and contemplated his gingham check espadrilles. 'Desperately.'

Now that the water in the pool had been heated up to a bearable twenty-four degrees, Nicole and Simon had started coming down to the hotel every morning before breakfast for a swim. Before long, as Nicole said, this would be guest territory, so they should take advantage of the chance to have it to themselves.

It was a novelty for Simon, starting the day with a swim, and he quickly became addicted to the first slight shock of water on his skin, his body coming awake, the stiffness of sleep wearing off and the cobwebs disappearing from his head and his lungs. Five laboured lengths gradually turned into ten, and then twenty. He realized that he was slowly and pleasantly getting fit.

He finished his lengths and hoisted himself out of the pool. Nicole was lying on the flagstones, her one-piece swimsuit rolled down to her waist, droplets of water drying on breasts that were already lightly tanned.

'Breakfast of champions,' he said as he bent over them, and then stopped. Something had caught the corner of his eye. He looked up just in time to see a bald head duck down behind the wall. 'Oh, shit.'

Nicole lifted a hand to shade her face against the glare of the sun. 'You know something, my darling? You get more romantic every day.'

'I'm not the only one.' He nodded towards the wall. 'You have a secret admirer. I just saw his head. I think we've got Peeping Tom for a neighbour.'

'Who?'

'A voyeur — he must be the husband of the Brassière Watch Committee.'

Nicole sat up, laughing as she looked at the wall. 'Monsieur Arnaud is an old goat, everyone in the village knows about him. Someone told me the other day that he hasn't seen his wife undressed since the honeymoon, forty years ago.'

Simon remembered the stern face and vice-like lips of Madame Arnaud. 'Probably just as well.'

'Don't worry. She may complain, but he won't. It's more fun for him than spraying his roses.' She smoothed Simon's wet hair from his forehead, and her hand slid down to the back of his neck. 'Now, what is this breakfast of champions?'

18

The opening had been fixed for the first Saturday in June. Not surprisingly, since the rooms were being given away, the hotel was going to be full for the weekend.

Nicole and Simon were having breakfast in the restaurant when Ernest emerged from the kitchen. He came over to the table clicking his tongue with disapproval and looking pointedly at his watch.

'Here we are, up at dawn and scurrying around like little woolly bears, and what do we find?' He pursed his lips and raised his eyebrows. 'The *patron* and Madame, lolling over their breakfast buns, and getting in the way of all these poor boys.' He fluttered a hand at the young waiters, spruce in black trousers and white shirts, who were setting up the tables for lunch. 'Now then. I think one final tour of inspection, don't you?'

Nicole and Simon gulped their coffee and allowed Ernest to chivvy them up the stairs. Françoise, in a demure cotton dress which was unsuccessful in disguising the effect of an aggressive new bra, was patrolling the reception area, checking her makeup each time she passed the handsome antique mirror that hung opposite the desk. Beneath it, on the dark, polished oak table, a massive vase of thick glass held fresh flowers, and their scent mingled with the faint smell of beeswax.

'*Bonjour*, Françoise. *Ça va?*'

Before she had a chance to answer, the phone rang. She clicked across to the desk, removed an earring and inserted the receiver carefully under her coiffure.

'Hotel Pastis, *bonjour*.' She frowned, as if the line was bad. 'Monsieur Shaw? *Oui. Et vous êtes Monsieur . . .?*' She looked across at Simon, and put her hand over the receiver. '*C'est un Monsieur Ziegler.*' She passed the phone to Simon and resumed her earring.

'Bob? Where are you?'

'LA, and it's the middle of the fucking night.'

'And you couldn't sleep, so you called to wish us luck.'

'Sure. Now listen. Hampton Parker called. His kid is taking a gap year from college, and he's leaving for France tomorrow. Do you know a place called Lacoste?'

'It's about twenty minutes from here.'

'Right. Well, that's where the kid is going. Some kind of art school. He'll be there for the summer, and Parker wants you to keep an eye on him.'

'What's he like?'

'Shit, for all I know he could have two heads and a crack habit. I've never met him. What do you want, a blood test? Jesus. It's only for the summer.'

Simon reached for a notepad. 'What's he called?'

'Boone, after his grandpa. Boone Hampton Parker. Weird goddamn names they have in Texas.'

'But nice big accounts, Bob.'

'Bet your ass.'

'How's it going?'

'It's going. Why? Getting bored?' Ziegler snorted, the closest he ever got to laughing. 'Listen, I'm going to get some sleep. Take care of the kid, OK?'

It had been one of the most congenial conversations Simon could remember having with Ziegler for years. Perhaps the little brute was becoming mellow, now that he had the world to himself.

Ernest stepped back from adjusting the flowers. 'For one ghastly moment, I thought we were going to have a surprise guest.'

Simon shook his head. 'Ziegler would never come down here. He's allergic to scenery.'

They spent the next hour going through the bedrooms, checking the bar, the pool area, the tables on the terrace, cool and inviting under the canvas umbrellas. The sun was high and hot, the early morning bustle was over, Madame Pons was having her first glass of the day. The hotel was ready for business.

Simon slipped his arm round Nicole's waist, and they

213

strolled over to the poolhouse bar, where Ernest was issuing instructions to one of the waiters about the aesthetically correct disposition of the bowls of olives and peanuts.

'What are the chances of a drink, Ern?'

They sat in the shade of the tiled roof, a bottle of white wine in the ice-bucket, the glasses chilled and opaque. 'Here's to you two,' Simon said. 'You've done a fantastic job.' They smiled back at him, teeth white against tanned faces.

'Here's to the guests,' said Ernest. 'God bless them, wherever they may be.' He looked up towards the terrace, and took a hurried sip of wine. 'Well, my dears, here they come.'

Françoise was standing on the terrace, a hand shading her eyes as she looked towards the poolhouse. Next to her were three figures in black, the sun glinting on dark glasses and bouncing off stark white complexions. The girls from the glossies had arrived.

They came down the steps, cooing over the view, and Françoise led them over to the poolhouse, where they identified themselves.

'*Interiors*. What a brilliant spot. Absolutely brilliant.'

'*Harpers & Queen*. Are we the first ones here?'

'*Elle* Decoration. You must tell me who did the façade. It's terribly clever.'

Simon was confused. The girls, all in their late twenties or early thirties, could have walked out of the same wardrobe, and were wearing almost identical uniforms – loose black tops, black trousers, black glasses with circular black steel frames, long and artfully disarranged hair, office skins and enormous shoulder-bags. They accepted wine and revealed their names, which added to Simon's confusion. They all seemed to be called Lucinda.

They sat back and congratulated each other on successfully having reached the end of the world. *Interiors* was the first to recover from the rigours of travel. 'Would it be possible,' she asked, as she nibbled at a colour co-ordinated black olive, 'to have a quick snoop round before the others arrive?'

Before Simon had a chance to answer, Ernest stood up. 'Allow me, my dears. Bring your drinks, and I'll give you the grand tour.' He shepherded them away, talking animatedly as he led them past the fountain – 'Discovered in a junkyard not far from here, actually, and luckily his bladder was in working order' – and back into the hotel.

Simon shook his head and grinned at Nicole. 'I think Ern likes all this.'

'I think so.' She looked at him appraisingly, one eyebrow raised. 'Don't you?'

'It's rather like showing clients round the agency. For the past few months, all I've thought about is getting the place finished, and now that it is ... I don't know, it's just a different job.' He reached over and touched Nicole's cheek. 'Stop frowning, or you'll frighten the customers. Let's go and see if anyone else has turned up.'

The small reception area was crowded and noisy, as half a dozen refugees from the advertising film festival, with girl-friends and wives, jostled for position in front of Françoise, talking to her cheerfully in loud English with the occasional French word tossed in. Jeans and running shoes, Panama hats and Ray-Bans, Rolexes on recently sunburned wrists, bags scattered everywhere, cries of *'Où est le bar?'* mingling with attempts to help Françoise locate their names on the guest list – and then ruddy faces, several with the two-day stubble that marks the free creative spirit, turning to look as Simon and Nicole arrived at the desk. Handshakes and claps on the back from acquaintances, hugs from friends and, after a few minutes, a semblance of order as two of the waiters started taking the bags and their owners up to their rooms.

Simon went behind the desk to help a flustered Françoise put names against room numbers, and reassured her that the English *en masse* were often boisterous, particularly when they were leading lights in the advertising business. He asked her if anyone else had arrived.

'Eh oui,' she said, pointing to the list, *'Monsieur Murat. Il est très charmant.'*

I bet he was, the old stoat, Simon thought as he rang Philippe's room.

'*Oui?*' Nobody else Simon knew could make a single syllable sound like an invitation to a dirty weekend. He probably thought Françoise wanted to come up and help him unpack.

'Sorry, Philippe, it's only me. Simon. Welcome to Brassière.'

'My friend, this is wonderful. I arrive, and already there are three girls here from room service.'

'Don't flatter yourself. They're from magazines. Didn't you bring anyone?'

'She was very surprised. She's in the bathroom.'

'Well, if you can fight your way through the women, come down and have a drink.'

Simon put the phone down and glanced at the guest list. Ten rooms filled, two to go. He looked at Françoise. '*Ça va?*'

'*Oui, j'aime bien.*' She smiled and half-shrugged, a twitch of one shoulder, and Simon wondered how long it would be before she'd start causing havoc among the waiters.

There was the sound of a car pulling up outside, and Simon went to the entrance. The tall, slender figure of Johnny Harris in his south of France outfit of pale yellow cotton suit unfolded itself from the little rented Peugeot. They shook hands over the open sun-roof and the blonde head of the passenger.

'You're looking well, for a middle-aged dropout.' Harris pointed into the car. 'This is Angela.' He managed not to wink. 'My research assistant.' A slim hand poked up through the sun-roof and waved its fingers at Simon.

'Pull in over there, and I'll give you a hand with the bags.'

Angela blinked in the sun as she got out, and rescued her dark glasses from their nest in her hair. She was a foot shorter than Harris, covered from throat to just below the pelvis in a suffocatingly tight layer of inevitable black, the only concession to colour on her feet, where scarlet peep-toe shoes revealed a hint of matching toenails. She looked like an eighteen-year-old with twenty years of experience behind her. She smiled sweetly at Simon. 'I'm bursting. Where's the Ladies?'

The hotel suddenly felt alive. There was the sound of splashing from the pool, and laughter from the bar. The advertising ladies were already greased and prone in the sun, spraying their faces from time to time with aerosols of Evian water. The girls from the glossies, careful not to get any sun at all, drifted from one patch of shade to the next, taking reference photographs and whispering confidential notes into their small black tape-recorders. Ernest darted solicitously from group to group, smiling and nodding and directing the bar waiter, and Madame Pons, in a vast white apron, was making a final stately tour of the tables to make sure that everything was as it should be for the start of lunch.

Simon found Nicole sitting on the terrace with Philippe Murat, who was showing her, with what Simon thought to be quite unnecessary intimacy, his miniature video camera, his arm round her shoulder as he helped her aim it towards the pool.

'You're breaking union rules,' Simon said. 'Don't fondle the camera operator.'

Philippe grinned and stood up to embrace Simon. '*Félicitations*. This is superb. How did you find it? And why have you kept Nicole a secret from me? I never meet lovely women like this.'

'You're a disgraceful old lecher, and you're far too brown for anyone with an honest job. Where have you been?'

Philippe pulled a face. 'We made a commercial in Bora-Bora. It was hell.'

'I can imagine.' Simon looked over to the pool. 'Where's your friend?'

'Éliane?' Philippe waved a hand towards the hotel. 'She's changing for lunch. After that, she'll change for the pool, then she'll change for dinner. She gets bored with her clothes every three hours.'

'*Elle*?'

'*Vogue*.'

'Ah.'

Nicole laughed. 'They say women are bitches.' She looked at her watch. '*Chéri*, we should get them in for lunch. Everybody's here, no?'

217

'I haven't seen Billy Chandler yet, but we can start without him.'

The guests, moving with the languor induced by sun and wine, were met on the restaurant terrace by Simon and Ernest and shown to their tables. Simon noticed Françoise, peering in fascination from an upstairs window at the assortment of outfits – the advertising ladies, glistening with tanning-cream, their swimsuits covered by long shirts or pareos, the girls from the glossies, looking wintry in their black, Angela in a body bandage of cerise lycra, Éliane (who had evidently been to Bora-Bora too), with cropped dark hair and in a shift of emerald green silk, slit to the hip. And then there were the men: apart from Philippe, in white trousers and shirt, the fashion of the day was long shorts and well-worn T-shirts. There was a kind of reverse snobbery, Simon thought, about what they wore; they looked like labourers down on their luck until you saw their women and their complicated watches and their cars.

He waited until they were seated, and tapped the side of a glass with his fork.

'I'd like to thank you all for dragging yourselves away from London and Paris and Cannes to help us open the hotel. I think you've met Nicole and Ernest, who did all the work. But you haven't met our chef, Madame Pons.' He stretched an arm towards the kitchen. Madame Pons, standing in the doorway, raised her glass. 'There is a woman whose cooking can make a man moan with pleasure.

'We're having a little party tonight, and you'll meet some of the natives. Meanwhile, if there's anything you want, ask one of us. And when you get back home, make sure you tell everybody about the hotel. We need the money.'

Simon sat down, the waiters moved in, and the drinking and gossiping continued. He looked around at the faces, glowing under the flattering light which filtered through the umbrellas, and smiled at Nicole. There was nothing quite like lunch outdoors in the early summer, overlooking a spectacular view. And they all seemed to love the hotel. He was at peace with the world as he took the first tiny mussel from its shell, dipped it in home-made mayonnaise, and lifted it to his mouth.

'*Monsieur Simon, excusez-moi.*' Françoise was standing at his shoulder, biting her lower lip. Simon put his fork down. '*Un monsieur vous demande. Il est très agité.*'

Simon followed her upstairs to the phone on the reception desk.

'Hello?'

'Simon? It's Billy. Listen, I've got a bit of a problem.'

Simon could hear him smoking. 'Where are you?'

'In Cavaillon. In the bloody nick.'

'What happened?'

'Well, I parked the car and went to get some cigarettes, and when I got back there was a bloke getting into it.'

'Did he get away?'

'No, he was only about four foot six, so I pulled him out and thumped him.'

'And they arrested you for stopping him stealing the car?'

'Not exactly. Wasn't my bloody car, was it? Mine was the next one down. They all look the same here, small and white. Anyway, he screamed like a stuck pig, and the law arrived. Rough buggers they are, too.'

'Jesus. I'll be right down. Don't say anything. Just stay there.'

'I think that's the general idea.'

The car was like an oven, and Simon's stomach was still getting over the disappointment of missing lunch. Another epic triumph for Billy Chandler, the most pugnacious photographer in London. Leave him alone for five minutes in a pub, and there'd be a brawl by the time you got back. The trouble was, the rest of him didn't match up to the size of his mouth, and Simon had lost count of the bunches of grapes he'd sent to various hospitals – broken jaw, broken nose, cracked ribs. He'd even been knocked out once by a model, one of those big girls he couldn't resist trying to jump on. Simon couldn't help liking him, but he was a definite social liability.

The *gendarmerie* at Cavaillon, up at the top end of town opposite a row of cafés, smelled of nervous people and black tobacco. Simon prepared himself for some apologetic grovelling and went up to the desk. The *gendarme* stared at him, stony-faced, silent, intimidating.

'*Bonjour*. You have my friend here, an Englishman. There was a misunderstanding.' The *gendarme* said nothing. Simon took a breath, and went on. 'He thought his car was being stolen. It was a mistake. He regrets it very much.'

The *gendarme* turned to call through the open door behind him, and finally spoke to Simon. 'The captain is dealing with it.'

The captain, whose moustache outranked the *gendarme*'s by several centimetres, came out, smoking and looking grim. Simon repeated what he'd said. The captain's expression became grimmer.

'It is a grave matter,' he said through a mouthful of smoke. 'The victim has been taken to the Clinique St Roch for X-rays. Bones may have been broken.'

Christ, Simon thought, the only decent punch he's landed in twenty years, and he has to do it here. 'Captain, I will of course undertake to pay any medical expenses.'

The captain took Simon through to his office. Forms were produced, a deposition was taken regarding the character of the attacker, the details of Simon's circumstances in France were noted, his passport demanded. Possible reparations to the injured party were discussed. The office grew thick with smoke. Simon's head ached. His stomach rumbled.

Finally, after two and a half hours, the captain judged that sufficient paperwork had been accumulated, and the prisoner was led out. He was wearing baggy black trousers and a white shirt buttoned at the neck. His thin, lined face under a bush of greying hair wore an expression of tentative relief.

'Hello, mate. Sorry about this. What a turn-up.'

The two of them nodded and bowed their way out of the *gendarmerie* and walked very fast down the street for a hundred yards before stopping. Billy let out his breath as though he'd been holding it all afternoon. 'I could murder a bloody drink.'

'Billy.' Simon put his hands on his friend's bony shoulders. 'If you think I'm taking you into one of those bars to go fifteen rounds against an Arab with a knife, and then spend what's left of the weekend in the police station, you're wrong. OK?'

Billy's face creased into a grin. 'Just asking.' He slapped Simon softly on the cheek. 'Good to see you again. It would have been nicer without the red alert, but I really thought the little sod was after my stuff. All right, what's the drill?'

By the time they got back to the hotel, the guests around the pool were beginning to stir from the stupor brought on by food and drink and sun. Simon was watching them from the terrace as Billy came out with a beer in his hand, apparently completely recovered from his ordeal.

'Well, my son,' he said to Simon, 'this is the life.' He looked down to the pool. 'Dear oh dear – it's enough to make your eyes water, all that. Be lucky if you could make six hankies out of what they're wearing.'

The ladies were obviously determined to get as close as possible to the total tan, naked except for brightly coloured triangles that in most cases were slightly smaller than their over-sized sunglasses. Simon glanced over to the wall, and nudged Billy. Just visible in the shade cast by a tall cypress tree was the top of a bald head.

'That's our neighbour. I think he's given up television for the summer.'

Simon took Billy down to the pool and introduced him, watching with amusement as the little photographer insisted on shaking hands with all the women, ducking and bobbing his head as low as he decently could over the array of oiled flesh. Simon left him as he was asking Angela if she'd ever done any modelling – how many times had he used that one? – and went to find Nicole and Ernest.

It was, everybody said, the most perfect evening, windless and warm, the sky flushed with the last of the sun, the mountains a hazy dark mauve. The terrace was filling up, locals and foreigners circling each other with polite interest as Ernest, resplendent in pink linen, encouraged them to mingle. Nicole and Simon, armed with bottles of champagne, moved slowly through the crowd, topping up glasses and eavesdropping on fragments of conversation. The French talked of politics, the Tour de France, and restaurants. The advertising group talked, as always, about advertising. The expatriates and owners of holiday homes compared plumbing disasters and, with a mixture of disbelief and secret satisfaction, shook their heads at the latest excessive leap in property prices.

Billy Chandler and his camera stalked pretty women; he always said they could never resist a fashion photographer. The girls from the glossies, black uniforms and sunglasses abandoned in favour of loose, pale tops, tight leggings and high-definition makeup, picked the brains of a decorator who specialized in making the interiors of old Provençal farmhouses look like apartments in Belgravia. Johnny Harris observed them all, and waited for the drink to take hold. Sober people watched their words too carefully.

Simon found him on the fringe of a group which included Philippe Murat, a French writer who was complaining about being famous, and a young heiress from Saint-Remy, wearing several kilos of gold jewellery and a permanent pout.

'Getting any scoops, Johnny?'

Harris smiled with relief. 'Can't understand a bloody word they're saying. What I need is an English-speaking gossip with an urge to confide in me.' He sipped his champagne. 'A nice, talkative expatriate with absolutely no sense of discretion would be perfect.'

Simon surveyed the mob of nodding, talking heads until he found the face he was looking for – chubby, tanned and animated, and framed by frizzy, shoulder-length light brown hair. 'That's your girl,' he said. 'She's a property agent, been here for fifteen years. If you want a rumour to get round here like a dose of flu, all you have to do is tell her in the strictest confidence. We call her Radio Lubéron.'

They picked their way through the crowd, and Simon put his arm round the woman's plump, bare shoulder. 'I'm going to steal you away to meet a gentleman of the press. You can tell him all about our charming neighbours. Johnny, this is Diana Prescott.'

'Johnny Harris.' They shook hands. 'I do a little column in the *News*. Simon tells me you might be able to give me some local colour.'

She looked at him through wide, prominent blue eyes,

and giggled. 'Is that what they call it nowadays? Well, where would you like to start? The top ten snobs? The actors who don't act? The decorators' Mafia? People think it's the back of beyond down here, but it's positively seething.'

'I can't wait to hear,' said Johnny. He appropriated the bottle that Simon was holding. 'This will be just between you and me and my countless millions of readers.'

She giggled again. 'As long as you keep my name out of it, darling.' She accepted more champagne, and Simon realized that she was already half-tipsy. 'Now, you see that tall man over there with the white hair and the stoop, looking terribly respectable? He has these parties . . .'

Simon excused himself, and left Harris to what would undoubtedly be a fruitful evening. He felt light-headed from drinking on an empty stomach, and was making for the buffet laid out in the restaurant when a hand took his arm. He turned to see Jean-Louis in *tenue de fête* – a salmon-pink shirt and a jacket the colour of vanilla ice-cream – and a man in a dark blue suit and tie.

'Permit me.' Jean-Louis smiled. 'I present my colleague, Enrico from Marseille.'

Enrico could have come straight from a meeting of senior management executives – conservatively tailored, carefully barbered – except for his curious stillness, the unblinking stare of his cold, dark eyes, and the scar slanting down his neck into his shirt collar. That didn't come from a flying paper clip in an office. He was, so Jean-Louis told Simon, in the personal insurance business. The bottom half of Enrico's face smiled. It would be a great pleasure to assist Monsieur, he said, if ever there was a problem at the hotel that was too pressing or delicate for the police. He lit a cigarette and looked at Simon thoughtfully through the smoke. Such a beautiful establishment, so close to Marseille, might be a temptation to some of the . . . elements on the coast. Jean-Louis shook his head and sucked his teeth. *Beh oui*. We live in dangerous times.

Simon suddenly felt that he had entered the hotel business a little impulsively. There was an air of menace about Enrico, despite his politeness and the fixed insincerity of his smile, that had nothing to do with conventional insurance. Thank God for advertising training, he thought. At least I know what to do in a situation like this.

'Let's have lunch, Enrico,' he said. 'When we can talk quietly.'

Mrs Gibbons moved carefully through the forest of legs, wary of stiletto heels and spilt champagne, her snout sweeping the flagstones in search of dropped canapés. She came to a stone bench at the edge of the terrace, and cocked her head. A large and interesting object lay under the bench. She sniffed it. It didn't move. She took a trial bite, and it was pleasantly squashy. She picked it up and looked for a place away from all the noise and feet where she could destroy it in peace.

Half an hour later, *Harpers & Queen* decided it was time to repair her makeup, and reached down for her bag. Her screech of alarm cut through the babble and brought Simon pushing through the guests, half-expecting to find Billy Chandler squaring up to an irate husband.

'My bag!' cried *Harpers & Queen*. 'Someone's taken my bag!'

Simon put aside thoughts of food once again, and joined the distraught girl in a hunt that started in the lavender bed and continued through the guests and down to the pool. As they searched, *Harpers & Queen* went through an increasingly hysterical inventory of the contents. Absolutely her entire life was in the bag, and the thought of her vanished Filofax brought on another wail of despair. Simon, stomach rumbling and another headache developing, was in no mood to listen to Jean-Louis' theory that the bag might be across the Italian border already, such was the speed of local robbers. *Beh oui.*

One of the advertising contingent hurried over to Simon, his sunglasses on their neck-loop bouncing against his chest.

'It's OK. We've found it.'

Simon's headache receded slightly. 'Thank God for that. Where is it?'

'Under that big table in the restaurant.'

Harpers & Queen almost swooned with relief, and then had a fresh attack of horror. Suppose someone had emptied it, stolen her life, maybe even her Filofax with all those private telephone numbers collected so carefully over the years? For a moment, social ruin stared her in the face.

'No, no, no,' said the advertising man. 'I don't think anything's gone. Not exactly.'

When they reached the long buffet table, they found a small group squatting on their haunches, apparently talking to the bottom of the tablecloth.

One of them looked up. 'We've tried her with salmon mousse and quiche, but she wasn't interested.'

Simon and *Harpers & Queen* got down on hands and knees and peered under the cloth. Mrs Gibbons stared back at them and curled her pink lips, which were flecked with fragments of a blue British passport cover. She growled briefly before resuming her attack on a Tampax.

'Oh, God!' said *Harpers & Queen*.

'Oh, shit,' said Simon. 'Where's Ernest?'

Françoise was doing her best to understand the little English photographer. He was, after all, very charming, and it was in no way disagreeable to be the object of such flattering attention, even if he had very few words of French.

'Now then, darling,' he said, 'let's do a few for *Vogue*. You know *Vogue*, yes? *Le top* magazine.' He stood back and tilted his head. 'Right. Let's have you on the couch here.' He patted the seat, and Françoise perched on the edge. 'No, I think lying would be better – *très relax*, OK? May I?' He adjusted Françoise until she was stretched out on the couch. 'There. That's better.' He knelt beside her. 'Now, I think this leg bent – there we go – and those top two buttons . . . here, let me . . . and the skirt, ah yes, magic . . .'

Ernest's pink and white striped espadrilles made no sound as he walked quickly through the reception area on his way down to the restaurant. He came to an abrupt halt, his eyebrows doing their best to meet his hairline, and coughed emphatically.

Billy Chandler looked back over his shoulder and grinned.

'Doing a few test shots here, Ern. You haven't seen my light meter, have you?'

'It wasn't secreted in the young lady's blouse, I take it? Or hadn't you finished looking?'

'We were working on a truly artistic pose, Ern, that's all.' He winked. 'Listen, you'd better go. I heard Simon calling you.'

Ernest sniffed. 'I'll send Monsieur Bonetto up, and then you can do an artistic portrait of father and daughter. Don't start without him, will you?'

The group around the table stood back and watched Ernest scold Mrs Gibbons into giving up what was left of her snack and then banish her, with her tail between her legs, to find sympathy with Madame Pons in the kitchen. *Harpers & Queen* was in despair as she gathered the remnants together and put them in a soggy, chewed pile on the table. Her Filofax had escaped major damage, but it was doubtful if her credit cards would pass through any machine that wasn't capable of accepting toothmarks, and she was going to need a new passport. She glared at Simon, her crimson mouth set in a tight, irritated line. Something must be done.

But what? The British Consulate in Marseille was closed for the weekend. Simon resigned himself to spending Sunday morning on the phone trying to track down the Consul. Ernest led *Harpers & Queen*, clutching the shreds of her bag, off to the nearest bottle of champagne, and the spectators drifted away towards the sound of music coming from the poolhouse.

It was nearly midnight by the time Simon sat down to lunch at a small table in the corner of the terrace, enjoying the floodlit view and the relief of being alone. Apart from the damned dog, everything was going well. Nobody seemed to be dangerously drunk, nobody was arguing, nobody had hit Billy Chandler. Someone was bound to fall in the pool sooner or later, but on the whole it had been a happy evening. Simon took a mouthful of salmon and allowed himself to relax.

'The *patron* resting from his labours.' Johnny Harris pulled up a chair and sat down. 'How's your face? Aching from all that smiling?'

Simon swallowed and nodded. 'How about you?'

'Feeling distinctly inferior.' Harris poured himself some wine. 'Angela never told me she had a First in modern languages. She's been babbling away to all the frogs while I've been standing there like a prat. They've been round her like flies. Quite a shock, really. She doesn't look the academic type.'

Simon remembered Angela's party outfit – a brief, backless dress and high heels that had attracted admiring glances from Madame Pons – and laughed. 'They do like intellectuals, the French, specially the blonde ones with long legs. Tell me, was Radio Lubéron interesting?'

Harris pulled a notebook from his pocket, and flicked through the pages. 'Amazing, but quite unprintable, most of it. Do you know there's an old boy in one of the villages round here who pays girls to climb up curtains while he watches and listens to Wagner and gets shitfaced on port? He's English.'

'He would be,' said Simon. 'A Frenchman wouldn't drink port.'

'Let's see.' Harris looked at his notes. 'Orgies in the ruins, backhanders in the property business – she knows a lot about that – the decorators' Mafia, fake antiques, genuine assholes like our friend Mr Crouch and his disciples . . .' Harris paused, and shook his head. 'And I thought the most exciting thing that happened down here was watching the grapes grow. Not a bit of it. Everything from adultery to Swiss bank accounts, take your pick. Not unlike Weybridge, really.'

'I'm finding out,' said Simon. He looked over Harris's shoulder to see Jean-Louis and Enrico from Marseille smiling at him.

'A wonderful evening,' said Jean-Louis. 'I am delighted that the affair of the handbag has resolved itself. A criminal with four legs, c'est drôle, non?'

'Very comical,' said Simon.

Enrico raised a hand to his ear, the thumb and little finger extended. 'Lunch?'

'I'll look forward to it, Enrico.'

'*Ciao*, Simon.'

Harris turned to watch the two men leave. 'Sinister-looking bugger, the one in the dark suit. What is he, a local politician?'

'Insurance.'

'I'd be inclined to pay the premium, if I were you.'

Harris looked down to the poolhouse, where Angela was demonstrating her abilities on the dance floor with Philippe Murat, and decided that his presence was required. Simon went back to his food. When Nicole found him, two hours later, he was asleep in his chair with a half-smoked cigar between his fingers.

19

It was four o'clock, the sun still a thud of heat on the head. Ernest was happy to come in from the terrace, where he had been discussing the dietary requirements of a vegetarian guest from Düsseldorf, and escape to the coolness of his office behind the reception desk. The hotel was taking a siesta; lunch had been cleared away, the tables set for dinner, a row of almost motionless bodies broiled themselves by the pool, turning occasionally like spit-roasted chickens. Nothing much would happen before six. Ernest sent Françoise off to get something to eat, and settled down to go through the day's correspondence, taking pleasure in the bundle of letters asking for reservations. The season was shaping up very nicely, he thought.

He heard the sigh of the main door opening, footsteps, and the sound of heavy breathing. He pushed the letters aside and got up.

'Yo!' called a voice. 'Anybody home?'

Ernest had never seen quite such a strapping young man. He was well over six foot, most of it muscle. He wore black cycling shorts and a sweat-darkened, sleeveless vest decorated with a legend that read: TEXAS U. FOUR OR FIVE OF THE HAPPIEST YEARS OF YOUR LIFE. Short fair hair, blue eyes and a wide white fluoride smile exposing the perfect and regular teeth that seem to be distributed only in America.

'Good afternoon,' said Ernest. 'Can I help you?'

'How you doing?' The young man stuck out a hand. 'Boone Parker? I'm looking for Simon Shaw?' He had, like many Americans, a way of talking with a lift at the end of each phrase, turning statements into questions.

'Boone, how nice to meet you. We've been expecting you. I'm Ernest.' The young man bobbed his head. 'Mr Shaw

229

should be here in a few minutes. I dare say you could do with something to drink.' He picked up the phone to call the bar downstairs. 'What would you like?'

'Two beers? That would be great.'

'Of course,' said Ernest, 'one for each hand.'

Boone killed the first beer with a single, seemingly continuous swallow, and sighed happily. 'Boy, I needed that. I came over by bike?' He grinned at Ernest. 'You got some mean little hills round here.'

As he dealt more slowly with the second beer, Boone gave Ernest his first impressions of France, which he thought was pretty neat, although he hadn't met too many girls. But it was great to be here in the cycling capital of the world, because that was one of his passions – or, as he described it, a major kick. That and cooking. He couldn't decide whether to be the next Greg Lemond or the next Paul Bocuse. It was wheels versus meals.

Ernest found it hard to imagine this amiable young monster bent over a stove or dicing shallots with those enormous hands, but Boone explained that it was hereditary.

'My daddy's in food, Ernie. Food's in my genes? I was cooking when I was nine – only eggs and refried beans and stuff like that – and now I'm into cuisine. I nearly went to one of those cookery schools in Paris, you know? The kind of place where they bust your ass if you can't make a tomato *coulis* with one hand tied behind your back. I love that serious French shit.'

'Well, young Boone,' said Ernest, 'I think you'll have to meet our chef. How's your French?'

Boone scratched his head and shrugged. 'Sort of rudimentary? My Spanish is good, but I guess that doesn't get you too far over here. I'm working on it.' He drank the last of his beer, and looked at the clock behind the desk. 'Shoot, I'd better go. I've got a class at five.'

'I'll tell Mr Shaw you popped in.'

'Sure. Nice talking to you, Ernie. Stay loose, you hear?'

Ernest stood at the door and watched him stand on his pedals as he rode away. What an engaging young man, he thought, and apparently quite unspoilt, not at all what you'd expect a billionaire's son to be. Some of his language was a little puzzling, though. Stay loose? Ernest shook his head and went back to his office.

Nicole and Simon, flushed and guilty from an afternoon in bed, arrived at the hotel to find Françoise and Ernest pinned against the wall by a small and irate woman. Simon recognized her as the voyeur's wife from next door. His smile was met by a frigid nod. Madame had reason to believe that one of the hotel guests had been exposing herself to the sun virtually naked. Simon's attempts to look horrified and persuade Madame that it was simply a flesh-coloured swimsuit were cut short by the appearance of a French guest, red-faced and indignant. He demanded that Ernest do something about the voyeur who had been staring at his wife over the wall, and who refused to budge. *Incroyable*!

There was a moment of silence when the protagonists realized they were standing side by outraged side, and then they turned away from each other to continue hissing their complaints at the assembled management.

'*Impudent voyeur*!'

'*Nudiste*!'

'*Insupportable*!'

'*Scandaleux*!'

Simon led Madame gently towards the door, nodding with all the solemnity he could muster, while Ernest did the same in the opposite direction with the husband. Nicole and Françoise melted away into the office, with faces kept resolutely straight. When Simon joined them some minutes later, he didn't look like a man who had achieved a convincing diplomatic victory.

'I don't know why you're laughing,' he said to them. 'This is a crisis of morality. Madame told me it was.'

'What can we do?'

'God knows. I offered to build a higher wall, but she said it would block their light.'

Françoise giggled. 'Buy her husband a shorter ladder.'

Simon tapped his forehead. 'Of course. How wonderful it is to have a logical French mind.'

231

He and Nicole went to join Ernest, who had mollified the husband with the hotelier's secret weapon, champagne for two, and was now humming happily as he made minuscule adjustments to the table settings in the restaurant. He told them about Boone Parker's visit – such a pleasant young man, and most impressively built – and then took a letter from his pocket. 'This came, just addressed to the hotel, but I think it's for you.' He passed it to Simon. 'Do you have an artistic uncle? You've been keeping him very quiet if you have.'

Simon looked at the large, manic handwriting on a sheet of paper headed Pensione San Marco:

Hello you young bugger,

News of your establishment has reached me here in Venice, where the muse and I are sharing the celestial views with 50,000 Japanese tourists. Painting is quite impossible. I long for light and space, the scent of thyme and lavender, a glimpse of honeyed skin, the rude vista of rock reaching eternally upwards to the unbearable blue of the sky. Ah, Provence!

I have sufficient funds for a railway ticket to Avignon, and will advise time of arrival so that suitable arrangements can be made. There is no need for me to return home to Norfolk immediately, and so we will have ample time to renew the precious relationship that I cherish above all others.

Until soon, as you say in France! Your affectionate uncle,

William

P.S. I am now called, by some of the more enlightened art critics, 'The Goya of Norfolk'. It would be false modesty on my part to quarrel with them. Bring on the reclining nudes, dear boy! My brushes bristle with anticipation.

'Shit.' Simon passed the letter to Nicole. 'I don't think I told you about him, did I?'

Nicole frowned over the letter. 'Is he a famous artist, this uncle?'

232

'Not as famous as he'd like. I see him about once every three or four years, and he's always broke, usually on the run from some widow he's promised to marry . . .' Simon paused, and looked at Ernest. 'We can't let him take up a room here for long. He'd think he'd died and gone to heaven. We'd never get rid of him.'

'In that case, dear,' Ernest said, 'we'd better find him a widow, hadn't we? Is he presentable, Uncle William?'

Simon thought back to the last time he'd seen his uncle, looking like an unmade bed in an ancient corduroy suit, an army surplus shirt and a threadbare MCC tie, smelling of whisky and turpentine. 'Not in a conventional way, Ern, no. But women seem to like him.'

'Ah. Then there may be hope. *Cherchez la veuve*, Nicole.' Ernest waved at a couple going up from the pool to change for dinner. 'I must fly. We're fully booked tonight – *le tout* Lubéron has heard about dear Madame Pons.' He gave a final tweak to the nearest tablecloth and went off towards the kitchen.

'There is a man,' said Nicole, 'who has found his *métier*. He's so happy. They all love him, you know.'

'It's strange. We've changed places. It's the complete opposite of how it was in London. I almost feel I have to make an appointment to see him. Do you know what he said to me? "We must have lunch one day, and a chat." Saucy old sod.' Simon laughed. 'That's exactly what I used to say to him.'

'Does that worry you?'

Simon looked down at her face. The half-smile didn't quite go with her serious eyes. 'Oh, I'll get used to it.'

Nicole reached up to straighten the rumpled collar of his shirt. How could a man become untidy just by walking around? 'If it worries you, you must talk about it. Don't be so English.'

'Right.' He leered at her, put his hands under her buttocks, and lifted her off the ground, burying his face in her neck. A waiter coming out of the kitchen stopped in his tracks, muttered '*Bon appétit*', and reversed back through the door.

*

It wasn't surprising, Simon thought later, that so many people had daydreams about owning a restaurant. He looked around the terrace. Every seat was taken, animated brown faces shone in the candlelight, laughter and conversation disappeared upwards into the sky, and Ernest, squatting on his haunches so that his clients wouldn't have to look up to talk to him, visited one contented table after another. It all looked so easy. Nobody, observing this panorama of relaxed enjoyment, could imagine the effort, the controlled panic in the kitchen, that had gone into producing it – sliced fingers, singed skin, split-second sauces, sweat, curses and spills, and always, before coming out of chaos into public view, the resumption of the calm expression, the steady hand and the solicitous, unhurried patience that is the hallmark of the good waiter.

Simon tried to put nationalities to faces, according to stereotype. The group of brawny, overtanned and over-jewelled men and women who had ordered Bordeaux rather than local wine should be German – prosperous, large and loud. Any table giving off a cloud of cigarette smoke should be French, just as a table of non-smokers, with more water than wine being drunk, should be Americans. The English loaded butter on to their bread and ordered the heaviest desserts. The Swiss ate neatly and kept their elbows off the table, alternating sips of wine and sips of water like clock-work. Simon smiled as he watched Ernest gliding between the tables, his eyes everywhere. He looked as if he'd been running a restaurant for years. There is a man who's found his *métier*, Nicole had said. And here's a man, thought Simon, who's still looking.

Now that the challenge of getting the hotel finished and open was over, he felt a sense of anti-climax. Ernest and Nicole were firmly in charge, the place was settling into a rhythm, and the only person without a steady job was the owner. Could he spend the next few years stroking guests and soothing his outraged neighbour? How different was that from stroking his clients and dealing with Ziegler and Jordan? The scale of the problems was different, certainly, but the technique of resolving them was familiar: tact, patience and bullshit.

Simon left the restaurant, nodding and smiling as he passed the tables, and went upstairs. Nicole and Françoise were in the office, sharing a bottle of wine and the evening pile of paperwork. Nothing much he could do there. Nicole waved him out of the office, blew him a kiss, and told him she'd see him back at the house. He stepped out into the night air, now beginning to turn cool, saw lights still on in the café, and went inside for a glass of *marc* and some company.

Ambrose Crouch, sitting at a table against the wall, looked up from last week's *Sunday Times*. The carafe in front of him was down to a half-glass of purplish dregs. He should have eaten something. He stared resentfully at Simon's back, and the wine he'd been drinking steadily all evening felt sour in his stomach.

'Escaping from your tourist friends?'

At the sound of Crouch's voice, Simon looked round from the bar, recognized the malignant face, and turned back to his drink.

'What's the matter? Do you only talk to rich Germans now, is that it? Kiss Fritz's ass and take his money?' Crouch finished his wine, and laughed. 'Of course, you've had plenty of practice. An adman knows all about that.'

Simon sighed, and walked over to the table. Crouch looked up at him. 'A visit from the *patron*. I'm honoured.'

'I think you're pissed. Why don't you go home?'

'You don't own the café.' Crouch fingered his empty glass, and leaned back in his chair. 'Or is that another of your plans? A nice tasteful renovation for the tourists?'

Simon hesitated for a moment and thought about leaving. Irritation got the better of him. He sat down. 'You're only a tourist yourself. You've just been here longer than the others. You're no more a native than I am, and on top of that you're a hypocrite – all that crap in your column about the horrors of progress; progress is fine when it suits you.'

'Is that so?'

'Of course it is. You've got a phone, you've got a fax, you've got electricity, I presume you've got a bathroom. That's progress, isn't it?'

'And what do you call the invasion of these villages by

people who tart up houses they only use for two months a year?'

'You'd rather they were left to rot, I suppose. You know as well as I do that the young people have been leaving for years, because they'd rather work in towns than on the land. Some of these villages would be dead without tourism.'

Crouch exercised his sneer. 'Where have I heard that before?'

'It happens to be true.'

'So we must resign ourselves to golf-courses and boutiques and nasty little villas and traffic jams – I presume that's what you mean by saving the villages from dying?'

'Tourism is a fact of life. It can either be handled well or badly, but you can't ignore it and hope it will go away.'

'I don't ignore it, Mr Shaw, as you know.'

Simon had run out of *marc* and patience. 'No, you don't. You make a living bitching about it instead, and sometimes you don't even have the guts to put your name to your own opinions.'

Crouch looked at him, a smile spreading across his sly, fuddled face. 'I don't know what you're talking about. There are others who share my view that tourism is a vulgar epidemic.'

Simon pushed back his chair and stood up. 'And where do they go on holiday, these others? Or do they stay at home and feel superior?'

It was an unsatisfactory draw, Simon thought as he left the café, an argument that he would have liked to continue with anyone less obnoxious than the drunken journalist. He stood for a moment looking up at the faded blue-black ink of the sky, and admitted to himself that he'd enjoyed it anyway. It had made a change from the perpetual pleasantries that were required from a professional host. And it had made him think. Tourism had turned most of the Mediterranean coastline into a crowded, polluted nightmare. Would that spread up through Provence? Or had some lessons been learned? Crouch undoubtedly had a point, even if he was a snob and a patronizing little prick. Simon smiled to himself in the darkness. He was in danger of becoming reasonable.

*

236

Boone Parker had fallen into the habit of cycling over to the hotel almost every afternoon, torn between his interest in watching Madame Pons at work in the kitchen and an increasing desire to overcome the language barrier that stood between him and getting to grips with Françoise. It amused Simon and Ernest to see the two of them circling each other like tentative young animals as they tried to find a bridge between Texan English and Provençal French. Boone could now ask for his beer ration in French, and Françoise had mastered the essentials of 'have a nice day' and 'how you doing'. They were moving on to higher academic ground one afternoon, identifying parts of the body, when studies were interrupted by a call from Avignon station. Uncle William had arrived from Venice.

Simon found him in the station bar, sitting over a glass of *pastis* and fanning himself with a tattered, yellowing Panama hat. He was wearing what looked like the same corduroy trousers that Simon had last seen him in, baggy and balding with age, and a creased linen jacket the colour of pale, soiled custard that is so often favoured by the elderly Englishman who ventures abroad into warm climates. His florid, perspiring face, under a wispy tangle of silver hair, lit up as Simon picked his way through the piles of baggage between the tables.

'Dear boy, how it does my heart good to see a familiar face in foreign parts – and so brown, too. You do look well. Provence must agree with you, and why not indeed?' He smoothed back his hair and put his hat on, tossed back the last of his *pastis*, shuddered, and began to pat his pockets. 'A small formality, and then we can be off.' He produced a handful of small change, and looked at it with dismay, as though he had been expecting to find a roll of banknotes. 'Ah. Do you think they take *lire*?'

Simon paid the bill, picked up the two cracked leather suitcases that Uncle William had indicated with a wave of his hand, and followed him out towards the car park. The old man stopped so abruptly that Simon nearly ran into him. 'Behold! Stern custodians of the papal city.' He stretched his arm in the direction of the ramparts on the other side of the

237

road. 'The whiff of history, the shock of the light! Ravishing, ravishing. Already I feel faint stirrings of the muse.'

'Let's get out of the way of the bus.'

Uncle William pounced on Simon's cigars in the car, and lit one with a huge sigh of satisfaction. Venice had not been a happy experience, he said. The crowds and the prices, those revolting pigeons everywhere, the misunderstanding over the bill at the *pensione* – no, there were no regrets at leaving. But what a joy to find succour and lodging in Provence, where an artist could bloom in the sun.

'I've got a bit of a problem with succour and lodging, Uncle Willy. The hotel's getting very booked up.'

'A detail, dear boy, a detail. You know me. My needs are few and simple.' He took a long draw at his Havana. 'A truckle-bed in a garret, soup and a crust, the noble purity of an ascetic life.'

Simon knew what that meant. 'Are you OK for money?'

Uncle William tapped ash from his cigar, and blew at the glowing tip. 'Alas, I am not immune from the recession.'

'You're broke.'

'I have a cash-flow problem.'

'You're broke.'

'I'm expecting a remittance.'

'Still? The same one?'

Uncle William, disdaining any further discussion of his finances, turned his attention to the beauties of the countryside. As they left the outskirts of Avignon and drove past the prostitute in the BMW, now in her summer ensemble of shorts and gold high heels, he raised his hat gallantly and muttered, 'Charming, charming.' Simon shook his head, and wondered where he was going to put Uncle William for what had all the signs of an extended visit. He could stay at the hotel for a week, no longer. After that, all the rooms were taken.

'A penny for your thoughts, dear boy.'

'I was trying to think of somewhere we could put you up. How long do you plan to stay?'

Uncle William murmured with delight as they passed a field of sunflowers, precise rows of bright heads all facing the same direction as if they had been individually arranged. 'Who knows? A month? A lifetime? Look at the years Cézanne spent painting Sainte-Victoire.' He waved his cigar at the view. 'This splendid scenery – the crag, the olive, the verdant vine – this must be sipped slowly, like fine wine, not gulped. The change of the seasons, I'm quite sure, will provide endless inspiration.' He leaned over and patted Simon's knee. 'And there is the added pleasure of being close to a loved one.'

'I was afraid of that,' Simon muttered, half under his breath.

Uncle William was, predictably, enchanted by the hotel, and since he was no fool, he recognized almost instantly that Ernest would make an invaluable ally. Within an hour of arriving, he had suggested a portrait – 'A head of classic proportions,' he said. 'I am reminded of certain Roman Emperors' – and when he insisted that Mrs Gibbons should be included, reclining at Ernest's feet, there was no doubt that he had established the beginnings of a rapport. The Goya of Norfolk was digging in for the summer.

20

The cyclists breathed easily, their legs pumping up and down with the smooth regularity of pistons. Watching them as they climbed the steep, curving road towards Gordes, it was difficult to imagine that first unsteady expedition, with its jelly muscles and cursing and coughing. The General was pleased. They looked like thousands of other serious club cyclists, good for a hundred kilometres on a sunny morning, with nothing worse to show for it than a heavy sweat.

They had ridden a long loop, over to Isle-sur-Sorgue, up to Pernes and across to Venasque and Murs before dropping down to the D2, and then one final hill, the back road into Gordes, to give them an appetite for the lunch that the General had laid on for them in the barn.

He had taken considerable trouble over lunch, setting up chairs and a trestle-table and a barbecue for the *gambas* and the thick slices of *gigot*. There were bags of ice for the *pastis* and *rosé*, and a dozen of the Châteauneuf that he'd been saving for their last Sunday of training, their last Sunday as poor men.

He'd driven on ahead to start the barbecue, and stood over it, watching the shimmer of heat rise into the air as the coals turned from black to grey. He poured a *pastis* and took pleasure, as he always did, at the sight of the liquid turning cloudy when he added ice and water. He raised his glass in a silent toast to the patron saint of bank robbers. There must be one, he thought; there was a saint for everything and everyone in France. Give us luck, whoever you are, and this time next week we'll be counting the loot.

He heard the sound of grunts and laughter from the road, and then they came down the track, wheeling their bikes to save the tyres from the stones, grinning and rubbing their backsides.

'*Bravo, mes enfants*! Who's for water and who's for *pastis*?'

They crowded round the trestle-table, mopping the sweat from their faces with their cotton caps and jostling for glasses and ice.

'Today,' said the General, 'we eat, we get drunk and we sleep in the shade. But first, ten minutes of business.'

He waited until they all had drinks and were sitting round the table. Seven dark faces turned towards him.

'*Bon.*' The General laid out on the table seven pairs of thin latex gloves and two keys. 'We all had our prints taken when we were in the *pissoir*, so on the night you wear gloves. Don't even take them off to scratch your ass. Now here' – he placed a packet of cigarettes on the table – 'is the back door, the way you get out.' He put his glass next to the cigarettes. 'Here, immediately on the left outside the door, I'll park the van – I'll have all day to get the spot, so you know it's going to be there. The bikes will be inside. During the night, I'll get them out and chain them to the railing right behind the van. One long chain, one padlock. Keep the gloves on for the chain, OK?' Seven heads nodded. The General picked up the keys. 'These open the padlock. If you lose one, there's a duplicate. If you lose both of them, you're *foutu*. Jojo, Bachir, you take one each, tie it round your neck, stick it up your nose, do what you like with it, but don't lose it.'

The General picked up his glass, took a drink, wiped his moustache. 'I've got trousers and sweatshirts for you to wear over your cycling kit. They're old and untraceable. Just dump them. You're going to get wet breaking in, but you'll have all night to dry off.' He looked around, and grinned. '*Voilà, c'est tout.* All we have to do then is count the money. Any questions?'

There was silence as the men stared at the pile of latex gloves and the padlock keys. All these months, and now it was nearly time to do it. The General knew what they were thinking: what if it didn't work? Another session in the dock, another *salaud* of a judge looking down his long nose, another stretch in that shithole.

'My friends,' he said, 'nothing's going to go wrong. Trust

me.' He slapped the nearest shoulder. 'What's the matter with you? Nobody's asked me what's for lunch.'

Uncle William, manoeuvring with the charm and cunning of the practised freeloader, had solved his accommodation problem, and was packing his suitcases for the move to Ernest's little rented house in the village, where he was going to occupy the spare bedroom as artist in residence. It was essential, so he had explained, to absorb Ernest's persona, the very essence of the man, before attempting to capture him on canvas. He could probably string that out for several pleasant weeks before getting down to work, and after that there was the statuesque Madame Pons. She had been by no means unreceptive to the idea of a portrait after Uncle William had softened her up with several flattering comparisons to the *Odalisque*. Why should the Louvre have all the treasures, he had said, and he had detected a definite twinkle in her eye as she looked at him over her glass of white wine. Yes, Provence was very much to Uncle William's liking, and he was in no hurry to go back to the draughty cottage and irate widow waiting for him in Norfolk. There was a slight problem of liquidity, of course, but Simon might be persuaded to offer him the facility of an advance against the mysteriously delayed remittance. Meanwhile, the living was free. Uncle William closed his suitcase, adjusted the ancient silk handkerchief that concealed two stolen cigars in his top pocket, and went downstairs to look for someone to buy him a drink.

Simon and his guest sat down at the quiet table in the corner. Enrico from Marseille removed his sunglasses and nodded with appreciation as he looked out towards the terrace.

'It pleases me to see how well your hotel goes,' he said. 'You must be a very busy man. I'm grateful that you could spare the time for our little lunch.'

Simon had been trying to duck it for days, but there had been increasingly ominous hints from Jean-Louis that it would be a mistake to disappoint Enrico, who had taken a personal interest in the hotel's success. 'I've been looking forward to it,' Simon said. 'What would you like to drink? A glass of champagne?'

Enrico folded his hands on the table, stubby fingers with nails that gleamed from a recent manicure. His thin gold watch, buried in the black hairs on his wrist, was half-covered by the cuff of his cream silk shirt. The suit, also of silk, was dark, businessman-blue. 'Oh, I'm just a boy from Marseille,' he said. 'I'll have a *pastaga*. Ricard.'

Simon ordered two *pastis*, and wondered what kind of small-talk would be suitable for the occasion of lunch with a gangster. New extortion techniques? The outrageous rise in the price of cocaine? The effects of inflation on the bribery market? 'Well,' he said, 'it's a beautiful day, isn't it?'

Enrico's mouth smiled. His eyes were busy, flickering from Simon to the tables on the terrace, which were filling up with casually dressed guests taking a break from the pool. 'Very profitable weather,' he said. 'The sun opens wallets.'

The drinks arrived, and Enrico toasted the future prosperity of the hotel. The scar on his neck rippled as he took his first swallow, and Simon had to make an effort not to stare at it, so close to the vein.

Enrico lit a cigarette, letting the smoke drift up from his mouth to disappear into his nostrils, and leaned forward. 'Monsieur Shaw, I come to you as a friend, as someone who wants to see your hard work rewarded, to see your investment grow.' He nodded, and took another slow sip of his drink. 'A large investment, I'm sure.'

Simon did his best to look relaxed, and shrugged. 'Nothing good is cheap these days.'

'Exactly. And as a businessman, you understand that investments have to be protected.'

Here we go, thought Simon, and looked away with relief from the smiling mouth and the hard, unblinking eyes as a waiter came with the menus. 'I can recommend the ravioli stuffed with cheese and spinach. Madame Pons makes her own pasta.'

Enrico studied the menu line by line, as though he were going over a contract. 'Yes,' he said, 'the ravioli, and then

243

the rabbit with olives. And you permit me to buy the wine, I hope? I have a weakness for Côte Rôtie.'

At 540 francs a bottle, Simon thought, I'm not going to argue. In fact, the thought of arguing with Enrico about anything was not pleasant. There was an air of brutality about the man, for all his manicured hands and quiet voice, and Simon wondered what form the proposition would take when it finally came. Bloody hell. You come looking for a peaceful life in the country, and end up having ravioli with a hit-man in a suit.

Enrico ate fastidiously, taking his time, dabbing his lips frequently with his napkin. While they were waiting for the main course, he returned to his thoughts on investment protection. Had Simon, by chance, heard about the affair not long ago at the Deux Garçons in Aix? Enough dynamite to blow the café and half the Cours Mirabeau to fragments had been discovered in the *toilettes*. It was complications such as this that made running a business in Provence so unpredictable. Imagine – all that work, all those millions of francs invested, and then . . . Enrico shook his head sadly at the depths to which human behaviour could sink, but brightened up to greet the arrival of his rabbit, bowing his head to inhale the steam rising from the plate. 'Ah yes,' he said, 'a correct sauce, a sauce thickened with blood.'

Simon found his appetite diminishing as Enrico continued to speak calmly of robbings and maimings and unsolved disappearances, interspersed with compliments about the cuisine and the wine, his voice not changing its emphasis from one subject to the other. Murder and the pleasures of the table were discussed in the same genial, confidential tone.

Eventually, Simon tried to steer the gruesome conversation round to the point where Enrico could be more explicit about the true purpose of lunch. It was no different from advertising, he thought. Nobody gets down to the real business before coffee.

'Enrico, these things you tell me – they happen in cities, not in villages like this, surely?'

'Times are changing, my friend. It's a very competitive market now, and too many amateurs are coming into it.' He

244

shook his head. 'Amateurs are impatient and greedy. They don't understand the most important principle of organized business.' The smoke curled up from his cigarette, and he sat very still.

Simon wondered what that might be in Enrico's line of work. Go easy on the dynamite and don't kill too many customers, probably. 'You mean . . .?'

'Everybody must profit.'

'Yes, of course. But I'm not sure where the hotel comes into this.'

'Ah.' Enrico stubbed out his cigarette, and his immaculate hands resumed the folded position. 'It arranges itself very simply. You use a laundry. You need supplies for your bar. Your rooms, from time to time, will need repainting. You buy meat and fish. Your splendid swimming pool must be maintained. You understand?'

Simon understood.

'I have colleagues,' Enrico continued, 'in all of these businesses, people of the highest quality. They will be delighted to assist you. I can promise it.' He smiled across the table, a man confident of his ability to get other men to do exactly what he told them. 'I personally guarantee that you will be satisfied. I use these people myself, at my home in Marseille. They are trained.'

And as a bonus, Simon thought, this month's special offer, I won't get blown up, kidnapped, kneecapped or robbed. Sounds like the opportunity of a lifetime. Simon felt as though he was being interviewed by a bank manager from Hell.

'I think I'm going to have a *digestif*, Enrico. How about you?'

'A *vieux marc*. The Réserve des Légats, if you have it, from Châteauneuf. You see? I am a local businessman. I support local business.' The smile on Enrico's face widened by two or three millimetres. 'And I will pay for lunch. I insist.'

'Everybody must profit, is that it?'

'Exactly, my friend. Everybody must profit.'

*

Jojo backed the van into the parking area opposite the hotel, next to a large black Mercedes. The chauffeur, also large and black, watched as Jojo opened the van door, careful not to touch the spotless bodywork of the Mercedes. It had been polished that morning, as it was polished every morning. The two men exchanged nods, and Jojo crossed the street, holding the envelope delicately between thumb and index finger so that it wouldn't get dirty. He stamped his boots on the pavement to shake off the dust, and went inside.

For personal reasons that he kept to himself, Jojo was always happy to come to the hotel, and so he'd volunteered when Fonzi wanted a bill delivered to Simon. He tapped the envelope against his palm as he looked round the deserted reception area. He could hear Françoise talking on the phone in the office, and walked out to the terrace in the hope of seeing Madame Pons, whose magnificent bulk occupied so many of his dreams.

He looked down at the tables. Perhaps she was taking a *digestif* with one of the clients, cooling off after the heat of the kitchen. He had visions of warm pillows of flesh, lightly coated with perspiration, and he shielded his eyes against the sun as he studied the figures sitting below him. There was the *patron*, the Englishman, with his jacket slung over the back of his chair, talking to . . . Jojo took a second, longer look at the face of the man in the suit, a face he'd seen in the newspapers.

'*Monsieur?*'

Jojo turned to see Françoise smiling at him. A pretty girl, he thought. Another twenty kilos on her, that's what she needed to turn her into a real woman.

He gave her the envelope and went out to his van. Now he knew who the Mercedes belonged to, he was extremely careful opening his door, and thoughtful as he drove back to the *chantier*. What was the Englishman doing with a man like that?

Nicole listened to Simon's account of the lunch with increasing disbelief. It was blackmail, it was intolerable, the police must be informed, this gangster must be locked up. She would immediately call the *gendarmerie*.

Simon took her hand as she was reaching for the phone. 'Don't get all French and hysterical. What are the police going to do – arrest him for buying me lunch? He didn't threaten me – well, not directly, anyway. He just told me some horror stories.'

Nicole paced up and down, smoking in short, agitated puffs. 'It's impossible. We must do something.'

'What? Set Mrs Gibbons on him? Tell him we're quite satisfied with the laundry service? Jesus, I don't know if he's dangerous or bluffing. He might be trying out a new sales pitch. Nicole?' She stopped pacing. 'Calm down. Your bosom is heaving.'

'I'm very mad.'

'Look, let's find out more about him, and then we can decide what to do.'

'Suppose he is what you think he is?'

Simon shrugged. 'I'll have him killed, or I'll change laundries.'

'You're not being serious about this.'

'I've given up being serious. I've got a lunatic uncle asking me for pocket-money, there's a hysterical woman next door whose husband lives on top of a ladder, and now my new friend Enrico wants to turn the hotel into a Mafia franchise. For all I know, Madame Pons is pregnant, and the German couple in Room 8 are cleaning their shoes on the curtains. How can I be serious?'

Nicole walked over to him and clasped her hands round his neck. 'You're not very happy, are you?'

He smiled, and shook his head. 'Do you realize we're hardly alone any more? You work late every night while I'm being the perfect host, we fall into bed and we're back here every morning by eight to start all over again.'

'*Chéri*, that's what a hotel is. It's full-time.'

They looked at each other in silence. Through the open door of the office, they heard Ernest's voice, polite but cool, and then murmurs and footsteps fading away in the direction of the terrace. Ernest came into the office, closing the door

247

behind him, and raised his eyes dramatically to the ceiling. 'Well, my dears, we're blessed with a visitation.'

'Who is it, Ern?'

'You will not be pleased, I'm afraid. The ex-Mrs Shaw has dragged herself away from Harrods to come and see us, and she's with her new friend.' Ernest sniffed. 'A rather ornamental young man. I sent them off to play in the garden.'

'This is turning into a perfect day.' Simon stood up, and sighed. 'Does he look like a lawyer?'

'Dear me, no. Far too well-dressed for a lawyer.'

Simon walked out to the terrace, squinting against the sun as he looked instinctively over to the wall. The bugger didn't even bother to duck any more, and Simon was tempted to invite him to climb over for a drink and a closer look at the bodies sprawled around the pool.

He saw Caroline's elaborate hair and the familiar profile, smiling as she turned towards the man at her side. She looked, as usual, expensive. When she noticed Simon coming across the terrace, she waved, the sun catching the heavy silver bangle on her wrist. He remembered buying it for her, and he remembered that she'd once thrown it at him.

'Simon, how are you?' She offered the small patch of cheek that wasn't covered by sunglasses to be kissed. 'You're so brown.'

'Hello, Caroline. You're looking well.'

'Simon, this is Jonathan. Jonathan Edwards.'

The two men shook hands. Jonathan was younger than Simon by several years, dark-haired and slim. In his double-breasted blazer and dove-grey flannels he looked impeccable and too hot. Be nice to him, Simon thought. This might be husband material.

'Why don't we go and sit in the shade?'

Simon noticed the care with which Jonathan pulled back Caroline's chair before sitting down himself, and the instant appearance of his lighter when she took out a cigarette. Promising behaviour, Simon thought, and composed his face into an expression of interest as Caroline prattled on about their drive down through France. They had stayed at the most divine hotel outside Paris the previous night, and now they were on their way to spend a few days on a friend's yacht near Antibes. It would do Jonathan so much good to take a break from the City, wouldn't it, darling? She called him darling every dozen words, it seemed to Simon, and touched his hand in a casual, possessive way to punctuate her sentences.

Jonathan himself said nothing, but had allowed himself to relax to the extent of undoing the crested brass buttons of his blazer so that the thick barathea lapels fell open. There was a small monogram on his blue striped shirt. He looked prosperous, and Simon wondered if he was capable of assuming the burden of Caroline's American Express bills.

'What do you do in the City, Jonathan?' Simon felt like a prospective father-in-law.

'Commercial property. I'm with Levenson's – we special-ize in vertically integrated developments. Work with a lot of the big fund managers.'

'Sounds fascinating,' Simon said. 'And where are you staying tonight?'

Caroline resumed her grip on Jonathan's hand. 'We thought here, didn't we, darling? It's too late to go on to the coast now.'

'I wish we could put you up.' Simon did his best to look disappointed, shaking his head as if he'd just heard bad news. 'But we're full. You could always try Gordes.'

'Oh.' Caroline's mouth tightened. 'What a bore. I rather wanted to have a little chat with you.'

Jonathan excused himself diplomatically, and went inside to call some other hotels. Simon braced himself. Caroline's little chats invariably began with sweetness and light and ended with threats, the old mixture of alimony and acrimony. But while she was lighting a cigarette and plotting the most direct route to the wallet, Nicole came across the terrace to join them. She winked at Simon before Caroline turned to look up at her.

'I'm so sorry. There's a call from America.'

'Oh, God.' Simon jumped to his feet. 'I'd better take it. Caroline, this is Nicole Bouvier.'

The two women inspected each other with a polite and

evident curiosity. Simon felt like a mouse between two cats. 'Well,' he said, 'can't keep America waiting.'

Simon came into the office and closed the door behind him with a sigh of relief. 'I don't know whose idea that was, but the timing was perfect.'

Ernest looked pleased. 'It was a team effort. When the young gentleman said that Her Highness wanted a chat with you, I assumed the worst, and Nicole volunteered to go to the rescue. Actually, I think she was dying to have a good look. You know what women are like.'

'Where's the boyfriend now?'

'He went down to collect her. We found them a room in Gordes, but they have to be there by five.'

Simon grinned. 'What a pity.'

'Don't start celebrating, dear. They're coming back for dinner.'

Jojo and Claude sat in the cool gloom of the Fin de Siècle café in Cavaillon. The first *pastis* had cut through the taste of the day's dust. That was quick and medicinal. The second was the one they both enjoyed.

Jojo lit a cigarette and felt the muscles in his back relax. 'You know I went up to the hotel in Brassière this afternoon? To drop off a bill.'

Claude grunted, and continued his study of the newspaper that someone had left on the bar.

'Guess who I saw there, having lunch? Mercedes the size of a house waiting for him outside, chauffeur in a uniform. *Cong*, what a way to live, eh?'

Claude looked up. 'Mitterand? They say he comes down here. Who's the other one? Jack Lang?'

Jojo shook his head. 'Remember a couple of years ago, the business with the ambulances in Marseille? The *flics* pulled him in, it was all over the papers, but they couldn't make anything stick. He walked away, clean as a bone, and then sued one paper for saying he was the king of the underworld. What balls, eh?' Jojo shook his head again, and took a drink. 'Anyway, it was him, all done up in a suit, tie, gold watch, everything, sitting there with the Englishman.'

'So? People have lunch.'

'But a guy like that, a *grosse légume* from Marseille, what was he doing in a little village? Tell me that.'

Claude rubbed his chin and went through the agonies of thought before giving up with a shrug. 'Maybe he likes the cooking. Maybe that's why he comes.'

'Sure. And maybe I'll go out tomorrow and hire a chauffeur.' Jojo sighed as he considered the evening ahead of him; a pizza, and a lonely early night. '*Putain*. What I could do with a few million francs.'

Claude grinned at him, and thumped him on the back. 'You could hire me. I'd be your chauffeur, and we could go to all the *bordels*. Or are you saving yourself for that chef?'

There was a lurid, angry tinge to the sunset that evening, and a faraway crump of thunder made the guests on the terrace look up from their food. The air was still, and thick with heat. If anyone had been listening, they would have noticed the dry, ratchety sound of the *cigales* come to a sudden halt.

Simon and Ernest were on duty by the bar. They had made the obligatory tour of the tables at the start of the meal and now, with the main course served and the second bottles of wine uncorked, the tempo of dinner had slowed down. The united nations were here again, with foreigners outnumbering French. That was a great advantage of doing business in the Lubéron, Simon thought. The sun attracted people from the north, whatever nationality they were, and if the Dutch were broke one year, the Swedes would be prosperous. Or the English, including his perennially prosperous ex-wife. Simon had been ambushed briefly by Caroline, but had escaped to attend to an imaginary crisis in the kitchen. She would try again.

Meanwhile, he was fascinated by a most unlikely couple sitting at a nearby table. Uncle William, his linen jacket surprisingly clean and pressed, was talking volubly, with frequent stops for wine, to Boone Parker.

Simon nodded towards them. 'What's going on there, Ern?'

'Dear Willy.' Ernest sighed. 'Such a scamp, but I do like

him. I happened to mention that young Boone's father was a person of considerable wealth. That may have encouraged Willy to take the boy under his wing, in an artistic sense.'

'I've no doubt. Who's paying for dinner?'

Ernest gave a small, embarrassed cough. 'Well, I did make Willy a modest advance. Against the portrait.'

'You're a soft touch, Ern.' Simon left the bar and went over to Uncle William's table. The old man looked up, his face the colour of a cherry, and beamed.

'My boy! Join us, join us. Cast aside the cares of office, and take wine with us.' He held up the bottle and gazed at it in dismay. 'Damn bottles get smaller every year. Have you noticed that?'

Simon ordered another bottle, another glass, and pulled up a chair. 'How's it going, Boone?'

'Real good. That Madame Pons is some cook, isn't she? I had the *pieds et paquets* – best thing I ever tasted. Swear to God.'

Uncle William used the arrival of the wine to nip this unpromising line of conversation in the bud.

'A toast,' he said, 'to art and friendship and hands across the water!'

Before Simon could ask him whose hands he had in mind, Uncle William leaned forward and extracted the leather cigar case from Simon's shirt pocket, talking excitedly as he did so. 'This delightful young man and I have been discussing the possibility of a major work, the definitive artistic study of Parker *père*, bestriding the state of Texas like a colossus, possibly on horseback, at home on the range.' He paused to light his cigar.

Boone grinned. 'Hate to tell you this, Willy, but my daddy lives on Park Avenue. Doesn't care too much for horses, either.'

A dismissive puff of smoke from Uncle William. 'Details, my boy, details. The great thing is to capture the spirit of the man, his vision, his very essence.' He took a gulp of wine. 'Of course, I'd need to spend some time with him, to absorb his persona, but fortunately I am not discouraged by the thought of travel. Did I understand that your dear father has an aeroplane?'

'A 707 and a few Lears.'

'Well then!' Uncle William slipped Simon's cigar case into his pocket and leaned back. 'What could be simpler?'

The storm, which had been growling its way in from the west, arrived in a gust of colder air. Lightning stabbed into the hills, and the sky exploded. For a moment, all conversation stopped.

'Magnificent!' said Uncle William. 'The brutal majesty of nature. Very inspirational. I think I'll have a cognac.'

There was a second crack of such closeness and violence that heads instinctively ducked, and all the lights in the hotel went out. The terrace was left in darkness except for the flickering pinpoints of candles, and an English voice could be heard commenting rather nervously on a jolly near miss. And then the rain came.

It came in sudden solid sheets that slapped on the canvas umbrellas and bounced knee-high off the flagstones, soaking the guests from below as well as above. There was a clumsy stampede into the darkness of the restaurant inside, the crunch of broken glass underfoot, a sodden jostling to get under cover, cries from the women, curses from the men, and a call for lifeboats from Uncle William, who had been the first to scuttle out of the downpour and install himself in a dry corner behind the bar, where he was searching for brandy by the light of a match.

Ernest was already organizing the waiters, distributing handfuls of candles. As their glow replaced the darkness, the effects of the ten-yard dash from the terrace could be seen. The guests stood in private puddles, their hair flattened, their clothes pasted to their bodies. Simon took a candle upstairs, and returned with Nicole and Françoise and armfuls of towels, which were passed among the dripping figures.

The response to adversity varied. Ernest, calm and resolutely cheerful, had joined Uncle William behind the bar and was administering alcohol to anyone who asked for it. Madame Pons, after one brief sortie from the kitchen, had gone back with a fresh bottle of wine and a candle. Caroline, her dress stained and her coiffure seriously rearranged by the rain, was in a bedraggled sulk. Boone, a beer in one hand and his French phrase-book in the other, was continuing his language studies with Françoise. The guests, for the most part, were behaving with the good humour that comes from surviving a minor catastrophe and being given free drinks.

Simon and Nicole were poring over a pile of bills at the end of the bar when Caroline appeared, in clinging wet silk, her face pinched with irritation.

'Simon, I've got to have a word with you.'

'Go ahead.'

'Jonathan's car is completely soaked. He left the top down.'

Simon sighed, and rubbed his eyes. It had been a long and difficult day, and it would be hours before he got to bed. 'I'll get someone to call you a taxi.'

Caroline was in no mood for taxis. 'I was hoping you'd offer to drive us back to Gordes, but I suppose that's too much to expect.' She pushed a strand of hair off her forehead, and her dress pulled taut over one damp and perfectly outlined breast.

'Magnificent!' Uncle William lurched along the bar, his eyes trying desperately to focus. 'If only I were twenty years younger!' He stopped in front of Caroline and leaned towards her, beaming. 'I speak to you, dear lady, as an artist, a student of beauty, and I can tell you that I have rarely seen a bosom to compare with your exquisitely arranged top deck. Are you available for a sitting, by any chance?'

Caroline went rigid with disdain.

'Nude for preference, of course,' Uncle William went on. 'I see you in a dappled bower, the play of light and shadow on every curve and cranny. How are your crannies, my dear? Have a drink.' He swayed slightly as he held out a large wine glass filled with cognac.

There was an involuntary snort of laughter from Simon. Caroline glared at him. 'You seem to think this disgusting old man is funny.' She turned and stalked away, calling angrily for Jonathan.

'Buttocks to match, I see,' Uncle William observed in a loud, admiring voice. 'What splendid little beauties they are, too. See how they . . .'

'Willy!' Simon took the glass from Uncle William's hand. 'I think it's time you went to bed.'

'Couldn't agree more, my boy. Which room is she in?'

Simon shook his head and turned to Nicole. 'Try to make sure he doesn't start biting people. I'd better go and sort something out for the happy couple.'

He picked up a torch and an umbrella from the reception office. Caroline was waiting by the entrance, peering out into the torrential blackness of the night. Simon shone the torch towards the parking area, and saw Jonathan wrestling with the half-raised top of a Porsche.

'The bloody thing's stuck,' Caroline said. 'Can't you do something?'

Ten minutes later, the top still obstinately jammed, the two drowned men gave up. Simon called a taxi. Caroline demanded towels to sit on, and asked Jonathan how he could have been stupid enough to have left the top down. The peevish monologue would continue all the way back to Gordes, Simon was sure. He remembered Caroline's stamina when it came to complaining, and watched the car's lights disappear down the hill with a profound sense of relief. Now all I need, he said to himself, is electricity, a hot shower and twelve hours' sleep, and then I'll be able to face the joys of hotel management for another day. He stood, alone and dripping, in the reception area and thought wistfully of Knightsbridge and Madison Avenue.

21

Jojo inspected the collection of items laid out on his narrow bed for the last time, checking them off against his list. He was naked, his legs and arms and face dark against the white skin of his torso. The plastic radio on his bedside table pumped out *les super-hits*, with short, ecstatic interruptions from the disc-jockey, who was pretending to have the time of his life in the Radio Vaucluse studio. It was, after all, July 14th, *Le Quatorze*, when every man, woman and child in France should be enjoying a *soirée de fête*.

Jojo lit a cigarette, and began to get dressed according to the list. He slipped the necklace of string over his head, and felt the chill of the padlock key against his chest. He pulled on the black shorts and the yellow, red and blue jersey, putting sunglasses, latex gloves and his folded cotton cap into the big pockets. An old pair of trousers and a worn sweatshirt, dark and loose, covered him from throat to ankle. The cycling shoes, thin-soled and black, looked out of place, but who noticed shoes on a *soirée de fête*?

Once more he went through the list. It wouldn't do to overlook anything, not when the General had put him in charge of the operation. *Bon.* He sat on his bed and smoked, waiting until it was time to meet the others just up the road in the Cavaillon station car park, and thought how it would be in Martinique as a gentleman of independent means. Rum on the beach and big native girls. *Cong*, that was the life.

Around Cavaillon, in hot, cramped apartments and in the concrete boxes that made up the town's suburbs, the others were looking at the crawl of time on their watches, checking their own lists, trying not to reach for the bottle to settle their nerves. Once it started, and the adrenalin kicked in, they'd be too busy to think about prison. But the waiting was bad. It always was.

Just before ten-thirty, the Borels' van pulled into the station car park. Jojo came out of the shadows.

'*Ça va?*'

Borel the elder, stolid and calm, nodded. Jojo climbed into the back of the van. It had been emptied of gardener's clutter, the mowers and rotavators and brushcutters, but it still smelled of two-stroke fuel and fertilizer. Jojo sat on one of the sacks of potting earth that the Borels had put along each side to provide cushions against the ridged steel floor. Looked at his watch. Lit another cigarette.

One by one the others arrived, Bachir, Jean, Claude, and finally, carrying a shopping bag in each hand, Fernand the *plastiqueur*. He passed the bags into the van, and laughed at the caution with which they were handled. 'Don't have a heart attack. It won't blow up until I tell it to.'

Borel started the engine, hoped to God there weren't any *gendarmes* out doing spot-checks on the roads, and turned right under the railway bridge. Nobody talked.

Chez Mathilde was having a good night, plenty of tourists, and several local families celebrating the 14th. Normally, Mathilde would have been content, watching the bills stack up on the spike next to the till, thinking that maybe this year they could take a proper holiday, somewhere abroad. Instead, she kept thinking about what her husband had told her that afternoon.

Madness. She'd said that to him. When everything was ticking over so well, a nice little business. They could sell it one day and retire, get away from cooking smells and dirty dishes. She'd been too shocked and furious to cry, and when he'd said that nothing could go wrong, she'd reminded him about the last time nothing could go wrong. Three years on her own, taking him pizza on visiting days. He'd promised never to get involved with that worthless bunch again. He'd promised. And now this.

The General went through the motions with the customers, pasting on the smile and opening the wine in between checking his watch and glancing surreptitiously at his wife. She hadn't taken it too well, poor old Mathilde, and she had that set look about her face now, an angry sadness not far from despair. He remembered that look from the last time. He'd tried to explain how he needed something like this, how he didn't want to be a glorified waiter until he was sixty, although he'd left out the other reason, the thrill of doing it. She wouldn't have understood that. With a sense of guilty excitement, he looked at his watch again. They should be there by now.

Isle-sur-Sorgue was always a nightmare for parking at weekends, and this was the worst night of the year. Borel had to go all the way through town before he found a space opposite the antique dealers' warehouse. The van would be safe there until they came back for it on Monday.

The men got out and stretched, yawning with nerves.

'Well,' Jojo said, 'here we go. Nice weather for a dip in the river, eh?' He touched the key hanging round his neck. 'We'll make sure the General got his spot. Fernand, let me take one of those bags.'

Fernand gave him the heavier of the two bags, the one with the torches and short crowbars and the sawn-off sledgehammer. He never let anybody else carry what he called his exploding toolkit.

They moved off, walking slowly, trying to look like any other group of friends in search of a good time on a hot, sticky night. As they approached the middle of town, a rhythmic thudding came from the middle of the human traffic jam that had taken over the small *place* just before the bank. Over the heads of the crowd, they could see lights – purple, green, red, orange, the official colours of every mobile discothèque in France – blinking on and off in time to the beat being thrashed out by a sweating drummer. Two girl singers, shimmering in skin-tight black sequins, strutted energetically on the tiny platform, scarlet lips wailing into their microphones, while the guitarists and keyboard player behind them went into spasms at their own musical virtuosity, heads and pelvises jerking as if they'd been electrocuted.

'*Putain*!' Bachir said. 'What a racket.'

'What do you want? Half an hour's silence so we can work in peace?' Fernand nudged Jojo, and almost had to shout to be heard over the electronic scream that was coming from a tortured guitar. 'Where have they set up the fireworks?'

They pushed their way to the other side of the *place* and on to the narrow bridge spanning the river. A dozen flat-bottomed punts, anchored at ten-yard intervals, stretched upstream, each punt with a framework of rockets and Catherine wheels, guarded by young men in their official festival T-shirts.

'That lot goes up at midnight,' Jojo said. He looked at his watch. 'Come on.'

The area behind the bank was unlit. As their eyes adjusted, they could make out a pattern of shapes – trees, with the humps of cars parked between them. A young couple, dancing in the dark to the sound of the music coming from the *place*, saw the seven men approaching them, and hurried off to the safety of light.

'*Voilà*,' said Jojo with relief. 'There it is, like he said.'

The General had backed the van up against the railing, just to the left of the plain rectangle of steel that was the bank's back door. Jojo looked around, took a torch from the bag he was carrying, shone it through the van's windscreen and clicked his tongue softly with satisfaction at the sight of the bikes stacked side by side in the back.

They stood in the deep shadow of a plane tree and looked at the stream ten yards away. On the far side, a stone wall. Beyond that the road, street lights and people.

Jojo took a deep breath. 'OK. I'm going to be up there on the road. Don't move unless you see the flame of my lighter. I'll signal each of you, one at a time. If you don't see the flame, it means somebody's coming, so wait. Got that?'

Jojo passed his bag to Bachir and went back across the bridge to take up his position opposite the entrance to the drain. He put a cigarette in his mouth, offered a silent vote of thanks to the rock band who seemed to be trying to break the decibel record, and looked up and down the road. Cars were no problem. It was only people on foot who might look over the wall.

Nobody. He turned, flicked the lighter, saw the first figure slip into the water and duck into the drain. That would be Fernand.

Two couples on the opposite side of the road. Better not risk it. He looked at his watch. They had plenty of time. He watched the couples cross the road and go towards the *place*. One of the men was patting his girlfriend's plump bottom in time to the music.

All clear. Another flick, another figure. And then another. Everything was going on wheels, Jojo thought, and then froze. A Renault 4 was coming towards him, slowing down. In the light of the street lamp, Jojo saw the dark faces of driver and passenger under their *gendarme*'s *képis*. The Renault stopped, and Jojo felt his heart suddenly get too big for his chest.

The *gendarme* stared at Jojo, that policeman's stare, up and down, cold and suspicious. Don't ask me for my papers, you bastard. Leave me alone. He nodded at the *gendarme*. '*Bonsoir*.'

The *gendarme* turned away and the Renault moved off. Jojo's heart returned to normal size as he let out his breath and felt his shoulders loosen up. He flicked his lighter. Two to go, and then it would be his turn.

Flick. Nearly there, plenty of time, try to relax. Jojo's cigarette was stuck to his lip when he tried to take it out of his mouth.

Somebody coming, a man on his own.

The man moved towards Jojo with the exaggerated care that drunkards adopt when the brain has given up and instinct takes over. He fumbled in his pockets, took out a cigarette, and stopped in front of Jojo, exhaling a whiff of stale *pastis*.

'Got a light?'

Jojo shook his head.

The drunk tried to tap his nose, and missed. 'Come on. You've got a cigarette. What are you going to do with it, eat it?'

It was reflex, and a desperation to get him out of the way, that made Jojo light the cigarette. The man looked over Jojo's shoulder, and his eyes widened and blinked. Two seconds too late, Jojo moved to block his view.

The drunk put a hand on Jojo's arm. 'Just between you and me, there's somebody down there in the river.' He nodded and grinned. 'Probably wants a drink.'

'No,' Jojo said. 'Nobody there.'

A puzzled expression came over the drunk's face. 'No?'

'No.'

'Well, it was a fucking big fish, then.'

Jojo steered the drunk away and left him on the bridge, staring at the water and shaking his head.

Back under the shadow of the plane tree, Jojo looked up at the road, crossed himself for luck and went out fast. A shock of cool water up between his legs, slippery, uneven stones beneath his feet, a plunge into the blackness of the drain.

'What a pity,' said Jean. 'You missed meeting the rats.'

They were crouched in single file up the length of the drain. Fernand, at the far end, passed down a sheet of black plastic and a fistful of mason's spikes. Jojo pulled on his gloves and blocked off the entrance, using the spikes to wedge the plastic into crevices in the stone, cutting off the faint glow of the street light. He tied one end of a long cord round a spike.

'Tell Fernand it's OK.'

A torch went on at the far end of the drain, shining on the slimy claustrophobia of brackish water and sweating walls, and the line of men moved further up. It was twenty metres, so the General said, from the mouth of the drain to the centre of the strong-room. The cord was passed from hand to hand until it was stretched to its full twenty metres. Fernand gave his torch to Jean, and started on the arched stone top of the drain with his sledgehammer and spike.

The mortar, old and soft with damp, came away easily, and in minutes Fernand had prised away two big stones. A shower of rubble and earth splashed into the water, and then his spike hit reinforced concrete, jarring his hand. He smiled at Jean. This was the part he liked best, the artistic part, using just enough to do the job without bringing down the building on top of them. He gave the hammer and spike to Jean, took the shopping bag that Borel had been nursing carefully above water level, and began placing his *plastique*.

Ten minutes to midnight, and the band in the *place* was going into its final paroxysm before taking half an hour off to watch the fireworks with everybody else. The *chef d'animation*, in his personal boat rowed by the Mayor's nephew, made a tour of the punts to make sure all the young men were ready to set off the fireworks in the correct sequence, which he himself would conduct from the bridge. The *gendarmes*, bored after an uneventful evening in their Renault, strolled through the crowds looking at the girls and killing time until the end of their shift. The men in the drain looked at their watches and waited.

'Two minutes,' said Jojo.

Fernand checked the detonators. 'All set. Everybody back to the entrance. A lot of the roof is going to come down.'

They waded back to the plastic curtain at the end of the tunnel and crouched in silence as Fernand shone the torch on his watch. Christ, Jojo thought, I hope he knows what he's doing.

'Sixty seconds.'

The *chef d'animation*, flanked by the two *gendarmes* who had cleared a space for him on the bridge, raised both arms to heaven. He liked to think of himself as the Von Karajan of the firework business, and had a pronounced sense of occasion. He looked with satisfaction at the banks on either side of the river, six-deep in people, all waiting for his arms to come down and start what he always referred to as a pyrotechnic symphony. He stood on tiptoe, hoping that the photographer from *Le Provençal* was paying attention, and as the church clock in the *place* chimed the arrival of midnight, he brought his arms down with a sweeping flourish, bowing his head at the same time towards the leading punt.

The explosion in the drain was surprisingly undramatic – a deep thump, much of its force absorbed by water, followed by the splash of falling rubble. Fernand crossed his fingers and waded up to look.

He shone his torch at the jagged opening, fringed with shreds of scorched carpet. The beam of light hit the smooth white surface of the strong-room ceiling, and Fernand turned back to the others with a grin. 'Did you all bring your cheque-books?'

One by one, they hoisted themselves up through the opening, and stood, dripping, elated and nervous, while Fernand began to doctor the strong-boxes with *plastique*, working his way methodically along the rows. 'Don't hold your breath,' he said. 'This is going to take some time.'

Jojo stripped off his wet trousers and wished he had a dry cigarette. 'Don't forget the fireworks stop at twelve-thirty.'

Fernand shrugged. 'World War Three could be going on in here and nobody outside would know, not with these walls. Listen. Can you hear anything?'

The sound of breathing, the creak of wet leather as one of them moved his foot, the faint plop as drops of water fell on the carpet, otherwise nothing. They were in a soundproof vacuum.

'Come on, then,' said Jean, 'blow the bastards open.'

The General knew that Mathilde was awake, lying with her back turned to him, but she didn't move when he swung his legs off the bed and got up. He was fully dressed except for his shoes. He grunted as he reached down for them. His neck was playing up again, stiff with tension.

'I'll be back soon.'

There was no response from the figure huddled in the dark. The General sighed and went downstairs.

Three in the morning, and Isle-sur-Sorgue was finally asleep. The General got out of his car and pulled on his gloves as he walked across to the van. There was a freshness to the air. He could smell the river, and hear the whisper of water turn into a rush as it tumbled down through the weir. He unlocked the back of the van and started taking out the bicycles, checking the tyres of each one as he stacked them against the railings. He looped the heavy chain through the crossbars and snapped the padlock shut, then stood for a moment in front of the steel door, wondering how they were getting on two metres away from him on the other side.

Fernand was laughing as he went through the contents of a large manila envelope. 'We'll leave these for the *flics*. Take their minds off parking tickets.' The others crowded round him, and passed the Polaroid photographs from hand to hand: a girl, naked except for boots and a mask and a bored expression; a stout, tumescent middle-aged man, displaying his erection with a satisfied smirk; other naked girls, brandishing whips and snarling at the camera.

'Friends of yours, Jojo?'

Jojo peered at a photograph of an older and very much larger woman strapped into complicated leather underwear. He had a brief but thrilling vision of Madame Pons in a similar outfit. 'I wish that one was,' he said. 'Look at the size of her.' He shuffled through the other photographs, then stopped as he came to the middle-aged man, frowning with concentration at the vaguely familiar face. 'I've seen him somewhere before, in that hotel we worked on. Eh, Claude – recognize him?'

The big man looked over Jojo's shoulder. 'Sure.' He nodded and laughed. 'That's the Englishman at the Christmas party, the one they said was a journalist.' He took the photograph from Jojo and looked at it more closely. 'Why has he still got his socks on?'

More than three hours had passed, marked by nothing more dramatic than a series of small explosions, and the men had relaxed. The boxes were all open, the pick of the contents piled on the table: some good pieces of jewellery, two linen sacks, bulging with gold Napoleons, and cash – mounds of banknotes, pinned together, stuffed into envelopes, rolled up and secured by thick elastic bands, French francs, Swiss francs, Deutschmarks, dollars – none of them had ever seen so much money, and they couldn't resist touching it each time they passed the table.

The floor was littered with discarded boxes and envelopes and documents. Property deeds and share certificates, last wills and testaments, love letters and Swiss bank statements. The police were going to have an interesting time sifting through the personal and sometimes illegal private affairs of the bank's clientele. The manager, neat and conscientious Monsieur Millet, would probably lose his job or be transferred to a branch in Gabon. The installers of the impregnable security system would undoubtedly be sued until they bled, and the insurance company, in the way of all correctly managed insurance companies, would find some clause in the fine print to absolve them of any financial responsibility. These thoughts, if they had occurred to the seven men in the strong-room, would only have added to their delight in sticking the finger up the Establishment's nose.

And now there was nothing to do but wait.

The men sprawled on the floor or prowled aimlessly round the room, wishing they could smoke. Bachir whistled tunelessly, and Claude cracked his knuckles. Jojo sensed that the early exhilaration had gone, and wondered what he could do to keep their spirits up. That's what leaders were supposed to do. Morale, that was the word. The General was always talking about morale.

'*Bon*,' Jojo said, 'now we've got it, what are we going to do with it?' The others looked at him, and the whistling and knuckle-cracking stopped. 'Me, I'm going to Martinique, get a nice little bar on the beach. Cheap rum, no more winters, girls in grass skirts with big . . .'

'Tahiti,' Fernand said, 'that's where they wear grass skirts. I've seen them on the PTT calendar.' He nodded at the Borel brothers. 'That's where those two ought to go, with their lawnmower. Eh, Borel, what about that?'

The elder Borel smiled and shook his head. 'Don't like islands. Too much sand, and if you have a little problem it's difficult to get out. No, we're thinking of looking at Senegal. Good earth in Senegal. You can grow truffles there, the white ones. Stain them dark, ship them out to Périgord, three thousand francs a kilo . . .'

'And five years in the dump.' Jean pulled a face. 'I'd stick to aubergines if I were you. What's the point of taking risks?'

Claude reached over and tapped Jean on the chest. 'What's this then, eh? Tell me that.'

'*Connard.* This is a career move.'

'Bachir?' Jojo turned to the dark man sitting quietly in the corner. 'How about you?'

A broad white smile. 'I'll go home and buy a young wife, very nice.' He nodded several times. 'A fat young wife.'

As the hours passed and talk of the future went back and forth, it became clear to Jojo that none of them, not even him, had any great ambitions. A little money under the mattress, an easier life, nothing too wild. The main thing – all of them said it, one way or another – was independence. No bosses, no more being told what to do, no more being treated like disposable people. Independence. And there it was, piled on the table in front of them.

The Sunday morning *brocanteurs* were out early, setting up their stalls as the sun gathered strength and began to burn the mist off the river. Yawning waiters, bleary after a late night and a short sleep, arranged tables and chairs outside the cafés, collected paper sacks of bread and croissants from the *boulangeries*, and hoped for record tips. The sellers of Loto tickets installed themselves in the cafés and ordered the first of half a dozen cups of lethally strong black coffee. Blunt-nosed vans, loaded with pizza, *charcuterie*, cheese and fish, butted their way through the narrow streets leading to the main *place*, and the gypsy girls with their lemons and pink garlic hissed at each other as they argued over prime corner pitches. Slowly, Isle-sur-Sorgue was preparing itself for another hot and profitable market day.

The first tourists, insomniacs and bargain-hunters, started to arrive just after eight, picking casually through the relics of other people's homes – old books and pictures, glasses cloudy with age, tables and chairs with mismatched legs and sagging cane seats, military medals from forgotten wars, mirrors and linen, vases and hats, the detritus from a thousand attics. The dealers on the other side of the street – the *antiquaires* with their Louis Quinze and Napoléon III, their Art Nouveau and their dark, important paintings – they were taking their time over breakfast. Their clients would come later, blocking the road with their large cars while they paid in the back room with 500-franc notes.

Jojo stretched, and looked at his watch. The General had said eleven-thirty, when the traffic would be like cement. Two more hours. He sat on the floor and leaned back against the wall. One or two of the others were dozing; the rest were staring into space. They had run out of jokes and conversation. The adrenalin had worn off, to be replaced by impatience and those worms of doubt that wouldn't go away. Would the door blow cleanly? Would the bikes be there? Waiting was a bastard.

The General gave up trying half-way through the morning. Mathilde wouldn't get out of bed, wouldn't go to see her sister in Orange as she always did, wouldn't even speak to him. He might as well go and sit it out in the barn, and get away from the accusing, silent presence. He patted her shoulder and felt it jerk away, and decided not to say good-bye.

He sat in the car for a few minutes, tugging at his moustache. She'd be listening for the sound of the engine and wondering if the next time she saw him would be in a prison visiting room. The sun bounced off the white gravel of the parking area and hurt his eyes, and he thought about a table in the shade and a very cold beer. Mathilde would be all right. She always had been before. He turned the key in the ignition and looked at his watch. Not long now.

The two gypsy boys had been having a thin time. Usually on a market day, there were handbags or cameras left for a few careless seconds on a café table or a *brocanteur*'s stall, to be swooped on and snatched up while the owner was looking the other way. But today the tourists had been very unhelpful, keeping their hands on their possessions. And a lot of them were now wearing those big pouches round their waists, which meant using a knife. It was getting harder and harder to earn a dishonest living.

The boys were strolling through the area behind the bank, trying the doors of parked cars, when they saw the bikes stacked neatly against the railings. Expensive bikes like that, in good condition, would be easy to sell. Even the old crook in Cavaillon who gave them next to nothing for the cameras they occasionally brought to him would be interested in a couple of racing bikes. The boys sidled closer to take a look at the heavy chain and the padlock. A big padlock, but not difficult. Their father had told them how to deal with padlocks. Feeling that their luck might have changed, they ran off to find him at the far end of the market, where he was selling the live chickens he'd stolen the night before. He had a little tool that he kept in his pocket. That opened padlocks.

'OK,' Jojo said, 'it's time.'

They made seven piles on the table. They packed the wide deep pockets of their jerseys until they bulged, and stuffed high-denomination banknotes down the front of their shorts, making their thighs look as though they had developed curious muscular growths. Fernand gave his hammer and the rest of his tools a final careful wipe before throwing them through the opening in the floor to splash into the drain below. The old clothes they had worn were taped over the charges fixed to the door, to be destroyed by the explosion.

The table was now empty except for the pile of Polaroid photographs, and Fernand insisted on arranging what he called an *exposition érotique*, using the last of his tape to stick them on the far wall, with Ambrose Crouch in his wrinkled black socks as the centrepiece. It would be a shame, Fernand said, if these photographs were damaged, as they were obviously souvenirs of great sentimental value. He stood back to admire the effect. '*Au revoir, mes belles.*'

Jojo looked round the room, and slipped the string with the key over his head. 'Caps on. Don't forget the sunglasses.' His watch said 11.25. Near enough.

They squeezed together in the corner, feeling the shiver of tension run through them like a cold breeze.

'Ten seconds,' said Fernand. 'Don't get lost on the way home.'

The gypsy boys, bent over the padlock, heard three muffled explosions so close together they almost blended into one, looked up in shock as the door sagged open, and were too busy running for their lives to find anything curious in the sight of a group of men in shorts and sunglasses and latex gloves emerging from the back door of a bank.

Jojo jammed the key into the padlock, wrenched it open, ripped the first bike out as the chain fell away. '*Allez, allez, allez!*' They ran, pushing the bikes through the cars, the screech of metal as a pedal scraped a door, a curse of pain as the end of a saddle, mounted in panic, caught one of them in the testicles, the frenzied fumble of feet into toe-clips, and then they were out in the road, going like sprinters through the central gap that separated two lines of jammed and motionless cars.

It had taken no longer than forty-five seconds, barely enough time for the desk *gendarme* to look up from his copy of *L'Équipe* and make the connection between the noise of the alarm and the flashing red light of the bank's security system.

He and his partner sat in the Renault, *klaxon* blaring, tightly wedged among cars that had no room to get out of the way. *Merde.* He jumped out and started running along the crowded pavement towards the Caisse d'Épargne building, clutching his *képi* to his head, his holster thudding against his hip. Why had he volunteered for the Sunday shift? *Merde* again.

The cyclists heard the wail of the *klaxon* in the distance, bent their heads lower over the handlebars, pushed their legs to pump faster, felt their hearts going like machine-guns, seven men in cocoons of fear and physical exertion. Just keep up with the man in front, watch for stones on the road, don't think about the car coming up behind you, don't look up, don't slow down, concentrate. For Christ's sake concentrate. They hurtled along the roads that cut through the fields of vines and lavender, their passing marked by the thrumming of tyres that hung in the hot air above the baked tarmac.

The General was waiting for them up on the road at the entrance to the track, sweating and chain-smoking, his eyes never leaving the bend 500 metres away. It should have worked. He'd done everything, planned for everything, anticipated everything. But as he knew, sometimes to his cost, accidents made nonsense of plans. A puncture, a dog in

269

the road, a swipe from a car – a hundred little things could happen. He didn't even know if they'd got out. Maybe they were still there, barricaded behind a half-blown door with an officious little *flic* waving his *pistolet* at them and thinking of promotion. He lit another cigarette.

He saw the first figure come round the bend, head almost touching the handlebars, then the others in a tight bunch. He let out a great bellow of relief and went into the middle of the road, jigging up and down with both hands clasped above his head in a triumphal salute. My boys! They did it!

They peeled off the road and skidded down the track, not bothering to dismount, and as the last of them went past him, the smile on the General's face froze, and then collapsed.

There should have been seven of them. He'd counted the figures going down the track. And he'd counted eight.

22

Boone Parker lay flat on his back on the grass, sucking in air and trying not to throw up.

As the dizziness began to wear off, he raised his head to look at the men sprawled around him, some lying face down, others sitting with their heads between their knees. He couldn't get over how fit they were for a bunch of old guys. When he'd seen them on the road going out of Isle-sur-Sorgue, he'd decided to tag along and break the boredom of his solitary training spin. He thought he'd show them that the French weren't the only ones who could push a bike around at high speed. But he hadn't even been able to overtake the last in the line; just keeping up had almost ruptured his lungs. These guys must have had steroids for breakfast. He decided that if he was going to take cycling seriously, he'd better knock off the beer. His head dropped back and he stared at the sky, waiting for the black spots in front of his eyes to go away.

The General, panting from his dash down the track, looked at the group of exhausted figures. Wads of banknotes had fallen from their pockets as they collapsed, and littered the ground around them. He counted the figures again. Eight. Jesus.

'Jojo!'

The little man looked up and grinned. 'We did it. *Cong*! We did it.'

'Who the hell is that?' The General nodded towards Boone, spreadeagled on the grass, his chest still heaving.

Slowly, the seven men, slack-mouthed and gasping, turned to look as the young Texan sat up and fanned his hand at them in a casual salute. '*Bonjour*, you guys.'

They stared at him in shocked silence. Boone looked around the ring of hard, suspicious faces, looked at the

271

money scattered on the ground, looked at the unusually bulky appearance of their jerseys. Shoot. This wasn't a normal group of Sunday riders. 'Guess I'll be getting along,' he said. He looked at his watch and gave them what he hoped was an unconcerned smile. '*J'ai un rendezvous*, OK? Thanks for the ride.'

He got to his feet. The others stood up in unison, looking at the General for orders.

Merde. The General tugged his moustache so violently he made his eyes water. Everything had gone so well, exactly according to plan, and now the whole thing was at risk because of this imbecile foreigner. What was he? English? American? And what were they going to do with him? He'd seen their faces, he'd seen the cash. News of the robbery would be in the papers tomorrow morning. They couldn't just let him go and hope he'd keep his mouth shut. *Merde*.

'Take him into the barn.' The General started to follow them, then stopped to pick up the banknotes that were being stirred by a light breeze. The cash in his hands, thick wads and rolls of it, made him feel a little better. He'd work something out. This was a setback, not a disaster. That was the way to look at it. Don't panic. He squared his shoulders, and went into the barn.

Boone was standing apart from the others, his eyes flicking apprehensively from one hostile face to the next. The General dropped the money on the table, next to the bottles and glasses he'd put out for the big celebration. He lit a cigarette, and noticed his hand was shaking. He walked across to Boone.

'*Anglais?*'

Boone shook his head. 'American.' He tried a smile. 'Texas. You know, the big state? *Très grand*. You all should come visit one day.' He looked round hopefully for some sign of comprehension, found none, and his smile gave up.

'American.' The General went to work on his moustache, thinking furiously. 'Jojo? We might as well have a drink.' The little *maçon* opened the *pastis* and started pouring.

'*Alors?*' said Jean. 'Now what?'

'Come outside,' said the General. 'All of you. I don't know how much he understands.'

They stood at the doorway of the barn, glasses in hand, heads turning towards Boone as they talked. He looked at their bulky silhouettes, and wished he'd gone to cookery school in Paris.

The General was quiet while the others cursed and shook their heads at their lousy luck. He was trying to arrange things in his mind. To profit from a crisis, he had always believed, was the hallmark of the great criminal. And this was certainly a crisis.

'We could lock him in here and piss off.' Fernand shrugged. 'Someone would find him in a couple of days.'

Jean cleared his throat and spat. 'And a couple of days later, the *flics* would find us. *Connard.*'

'All right, Einstein. What would you do with him? Take him to the PTT and airmail him back to America, to Texas?'

The General held up his hand. 'Listen. He's seen us. We can't let him go. Not yet.'

'Well, what are we going to do? Take him with us?'

'*Merde.* Shut up for five minutes and give me a chance to think.' Two words had set the General's mind off in an unexpected direction, certainly risky but possibly lucrative. It was well known that all Americans were rich. One saw them in the *feuilletons* on television. Even the children had large cars, and their parents lived in mansions, often with curiously impertinent servants. It was also well known that of all Americans, the richest were those men with high heels and oversized hats and properties where oil rigs grew like weeds. And where did they come from? A suburb of Dallas, the General thought, but certainly somewhere in Texas. This inconvenient young man said he came from Texas. Once they could understand each other, he and the young man, a solution to the problem might be found. All he needed was a little time. That, and a dictionary.

The General felt better. What it was to have a brain. '*Bon, mes enfants,*' he said. '*C'est pas grave.* Trust me. For the moment, he stays here, under guard.'

Jojo relaxed. You could always count on the General to come up with something, even if he didn't immediately tell

273

you what it was. He looked at the others. 'The boy stays here, *d'accord*?' His thigh was itching. He scratched it, and felt the bulge of forgotten banknotes in his shorts.

Monday morning's edition of *Le Provençal* was outraged at the daring and mystifying robbery that had taken place – *en plein jour*! – in Isle-sur-Sorgue. Where were the police? How did the robbers escape unseen? Was this the start of a crime wave that would engulf the Vaucluse and make honest citizens and tourists sleep with their wallets clenched between their teeth? Conjecture and comment filled the front page, pushing aside news of local lottery winners, *boules* tournaments and the birth of triplets to a young and temporarily unmarried woman in Pernes-les-Fontaines.

Françoise, having a quiet cup of coffee in the reception office, read the news with more than usual interest. She herself would have been in Isle-sur-Sorgue while the robbery was taking place if the hotel hadn't been so busy. Her father had offered to lend her the car, and she had planned to take Boone to see the market, in the new dress she'd bought specially. She was wearing the dress today. Boone would come in towards the end of the afternoon, as he always did. He'd see the dress then. She smoothed it down over her thighs and wondered if the colour would please him. But he never came, and when Ernest told her how pretty she looked, she just shrugged in disappointment.

The first official sign of anxiety at Boone's whereabouts came the following day, when the director of the school at Lacoste called Simon. Boone hadn't attended any of his classes, and when his room had been checked it was found that his bed hadn't been slept in. The director was worried. It was unlike Boone; he seemed such a steady young man. There was also, although the director didn't care to mention it, the possibility that Boone's father might change his mind about making a grant to the school if he thought it was the kind of place where students were allowed to vanish. All in all, it was a matter of considerable concern, not helped by Simon's irritation at being presented with another problem to add to his list. How the hell was he supposed to know where Boone was? Probably off in the bushes with some girl.

Simon put the phone down and looked through his messages. Two calls from Caroline in Antibes. A call from Enrico. A journalist wanting an interview, preferably over lunch in the hotel restaurant. A formidable bar bill, unpaid for several days, signed with a flourish by Uncle William. Simon pushed the scraps of paper away and went to look for Ernest and Françoise. They'd know, if anyone did, what Boone was up to.

The General was having a problem deciding on the exact figure. He'd started relatively low, at a million francs, and then reconsidered. A kidnap, even an involuntary one like this, was a serious crime with serious penalties. A big risk – and it should have a big reward, enough to set them all up for life. He opened the French–English dictionary that he'd bought before coming down to the barn, and looked across the trestle-table at Boone's unshaven, wary face.

'*Alors, jeune homme. Votre famille . . .*' he pointed to the word in the dictionary '. . . *est où?* Where?'

'America. New York City, but my daddy travels a lot.' Boone made one of his hands take off from the table. '*Beaucoup d'avions.*'

The General nodded, and licked his index finger, turning over the pages until he came to the word he was looking for. He was interested to find that it was almost the same.

'*Votre papa.* Rich?'

Boone had passed an uncomfortable and frightening night in the company of the big man called Claude and that mean little mother who kept playing with a knife. This guy seemed reasonable, unthreatening, almost friendly. Now that it looked as though they weren't going to slice him up, he felt an enormous flood of relief.

'Sure he's rich.' Boone nodded encouragingly. 'Loaded.'

The General frowned and turned to L.

Boone shifted his position on the hard chair. He ached from sleeping on the dirt floor. What were they going to do with him? Sounded like ransom, and his relief faded as he remembered stories he'd read in the papers of kidnappers sending fingers and ears through the mail to encourage prompt payment. Shoot. He'd better do all he could to keep this guy friendly. Maybe they'd let him call Simon. He could help, and he was close.

'*Monsieur? J'ai un ami, anglais.* Runs the Hotel Pastis in Brassière. *Je téléphone?*' Boone held his hand up to his ear. 'He's loaded too. *Pas de problème.*' He did his best to smile.

For another hour, the dictionary passed back and forth across the table as the General gradually discovered what he needed to know. It looked promising – promising but complicated. They'd need to get out of France very quickly, and they'd need false passports. That meant a trip to Marseille, and a bucket of cash. The General mentally added another million to the ransom, and wondered whether Boone's English friend was capable of raising that much in a short time.

'*Bon.*' The General closed the dictionary and lit a cigarette. The young man had been a piece of bad luck, but it might all work out very well. It was true what they showed on the *télé.* Texans were rich. He turned to the Borels and Jojo, who were on the day shift. 'I've got to go and make a few calls. I'll be back in an hour or so with some food.' He nodded towards Boone. 'I don't think he'll try anything.'

Jojo came closer to the General, so he could whisper, 'What are we going to do with him?'

'Sell him, my friend.' The General stroked his moustache with the back of his hand. 'Sell him back to his rich papa.'

Jojo shook his head in admiration. '*C'est pas con.*'

The General always saved telephone numbers. It was the habit of a methodical man, a man who thought ahead. One never knew when a contact from the past might come in useful. He placed the call to a bar in the Vieux Port in Marseille, and a voice he'd last heard in prison answered.

'I need a small service,' the General said. 'It's delicate, you know? I was wondering if that friend of yours could help.'

The voice sounded guarded. 'Which friend?'

'The *patron*. Enrico.'

'What kind of service?'

'Immigration. I need some passports in a hurry.'

'I'll have a word. Where can I reach you?'

The General gave him a number, and then added, 'Listen, I can call him myself.'

'Better if I talk to him.'

Better for who? the General thought. Greedy bastard. Everybody wants a cut these days. 'Thanks. I appreciate it.'

The voice laughed. 'What are friends for?'

Simon finished a hurried dinner and took a glass of Calvados up to the reception office to sustain him through the disagreeable conversation ahead of him. Caroline had left a third message, hinting at an urgent problem and leaving a number where she could be reached on Cap d'Antibes.

A woman's voice answered, and announced herself as Bacon, one of the best and most expensive restaurants on the coast. Caroline's urgent problem couldn't be starvation, Simon thought, as he waited for her to come to the phone. He heard the distant sounds of people enjoying themselves, and remembered taking her to Bacon years ago. He'd had the full *bouillabaisse*. She had picked at a salad and complained when they went to bed that he reeked of garlic. He probably still did and, knowing her, she'd probably smell it down the phone.

Simon made the mistake of asking her if she was enjoying herself. She wasn't. The boat was cramped and uncomfortable, she'd been seasick twice, and the boat's owner, Jonathan's friend, was behaving like Captain Bligh. Jonathan himself was turning out to be rather boring in such confined circumstances, and it was all too ghastly for words. No, she wasn't enjoying herself. Simon abandoned the hopes he'd had of Jonathan as husband material, took a mouthful of Calvados, and waited for the bell to go for round two.

It was all Jonathan's fault, Caroline said with the unshakeable conviction of the woman who is never wrong. An investment opportunity he'd recommended. A sure thing, he'd said, until yesterday, when he'd had a call saying that

277

the company had gone down the drain, taking Caroline's hard-earned alimony with it. And now she was destitute.

Simon propped his feet on the desk and studied the big toe that was showing through a hole in his espadrilles while he considered the thought of a destitute Caroline, with nothing in the world except a cottage in Belgravia, the contents of half the boutiques in London, and a new BMW. He made his second mistake, and asked if she'd thought of getting a job. There was a shocked silence as Caroline looked into the abyss of regular employment, and Simon held the phone away from his ear in anticipation of the tirade to come.

He endured it up to the point where the lawyers, never too far from Caroline's thoughts, were summoned as reinforcements, and then gently put the phone down.

It rang almost immediately. Simon finished his Calvados. The phone continued to ring. Shit.

'Caroline, we'll talk about this when you've calmed down.'

'Monsieur Shaw?' A man's voice, French.

'*Oui.*'

'Monsieur Shaw, I have a friend of yours.'

There was a pause, and then a strained voice came on the line. 'Simon? It's Boone.'

'Boone! Where the hell are you? We were worried about you.'

'I don't know, man. In some phone booth in the middle of nowhere. Simon, there are these guys . . .'

'Are you OK?'

'So far. Listen . . .'

The phone was taken away from Boone, Simon heard the mutter of other voices, and then the Frenchman came back on the line.

'Pay attention, Monsieur Shaw. The young man is not harmed. He can be released very quickly. You will make the organization.'

There was the clink of another coin being fed into the slot. 'Monsieur Shaw?'

'I'm listening.'

'*Bon*. You will arrange ten million French francs, in cash. You understand?'

'Ten million?'

'In cash. I will telephone tomorrow night at the same time with the instructions for delivery. And Monsieur Shaw?'

'Yes?'

'Don't talk to the police. That would be a mistake.'

The line went dead. Simon sat for a few moments, remembering Boone's voice, tight and scared. He looked at his watch. Late afternoon in New York, if Boone's father was in New York. And if he knew the number. He started to call international inquiries, and then changed his mind. Ziegler would have the number.

'Bob? Simon Shaw.'

'Is this important? I'm up to my ass over here.'

'It's Parker's son. He's been kidnapped.'

'Holy shit.' Ziegler switched off his squawk-box and picked up the phone. His voice sounded close and irritated. 'Are you sure?'

'He's been missing from school for a couple of days. I just had a call from the people who've got him. I spoke to Boone too. Yes, I'm sure.'

'Jesus. Have you told the police?'

'No police. Listen, I've got to talk to Parker. They want ten million francs to let him go, and they want it in twenty-four hours.'

'What's that in money?'

'Nearly two million dollars. Give me Parker's number in New York.'

'Forget it. He's on his way to Tokyo. Left this morning.'

'Shit.'

'You're goddamn right, shit.'

Simon could hear the laughter of some guests as they came up from the bar and wished each other goodnight. 'Bob, I don't have ten million francs in my back pocket. Can the agency put up the money?'

Ziegler's voice sounded reluctant. 'It's a lot of dough.'

Simon decided to appeal to Ziegler's humanitarian instincts. 'It's a big client, Bob.'

279

There was a pause while Ziegler considered the possible benefits that might come from providing an urgent personal service to Hampton Parker. If that didn't lock the account in for ten years, nothing would.

Ziegler made up his mind. 'The important thing is the kid, right? Human life is at stake here. Let it never be said that this agency doesn't have a fucking heart.' Ziegler was making notes as he spoke. This would make a terrific press release. 'OK. We'll wire the money over to your bank, and I'll get hold of Parker somehow and fill him in. Stay by the phone. He'll probably want to talk to you.'

Simon gave Ziegler the details of his bank in Cavaillon. 'It's got to be here by this time tomorrow, Bob. OK?'

'Sure, sure.' The tone of Ziegler's voice changed. 'There's just one detail.'

'What's that?'

'Security for the money. I'm CEO of this agency, responsible to the shareholders. If I start raiding the till for two million bucks, my ass could be in a sling.'

Simon could hardly believe what he heard. 'For Christ's sake, Bob. The boy could be killed while you're pissing around arranging a bloody mortgage.'

Ziegler continued as though he hadn't heard. 'Tell you what I'll do.' His voice became breezy, almost cheerful. 'I'll cut a corner here. I'll get Legal to fax you over a one-page agreement. Just sign it and fax it back. That'll cover me. Then we'll wire the money.'

'Sign what and fax it back?'

'Call it insurance, buddy. You pledge your shares in the agency, you get your money.'

Simon was speechless.

'I'll get on to it right now. You should have the fax in an hour, OK? Talk to you soon.'

Simon went down to the bar and made for the Calvados. Nicole and Ernest, sitting at a table going over the evening's bills, watched him as he took a glass and a bottle and came over to join them. He told them the news in a flat, matter-of-fact voice. And then they sat, asking each other unanswerable questions about the kidnappers and Boone, waiting.

The fax came through. Simon barely read it before signing it and sending it back. He'd heard somewhere that faxes weren't considered binding, but Ziegler probably had the whole legal department working on that at the moment. Little bastard.

Simon told Nicole and Ernest to go to bed, and sat in the office with a pot of coffee waiting for the phone to ring.

The call finally came at four in the morning, Hampton Parker's voice sounding thin with worry. Simon heard the intake of breath as he drew on a cigarette. He was at Tokyo airport, waiting for his plane to be refuelled and the flight plan to Paris approved. From there, he'd charter something smaller to get down to Avignon. He'd be bringing two men with him. They'd need somewhere to stay. He spoke in a controlled, mechanical way about details until the end of the conversation.

'You don't think they've hurt him?'

'No,' Simon said, with as much conviction as he could find. 'He said he was fine. He sounded a bit shaken, that's all.'

'He's my only boy, you know. The rest are girls. He's a good boy, too.'

'We all like him very much.'

'Those sons of bitches.'

'Try not to worry. We'll do everything they ask.'

'Appreciate it. I'll talk to you from Paris.'

There was nothing to do but go to bed and wait for tomorrow, but Simon was wide awake, agitated by tension and too much coffee. He went back to the house and upstairs to the bedroom. Nicole was breathing softly, one brown arm across his pillow. He bent down to kiss her shoulder, and she smiled in her sleep.

The bedroom was hot, despite the open windows. All through the first half of July, temperatures had been above a hundred, and even the thick stone walls of the house felt warm. Simon undressed, stood under a cool shower for five minutes, and went downstairs with a towel round his waist. He opened the door to the terrace and moved a chair so that he could sit facing the dawn, thinking evil thoughts about

281

the possibility of Caroline being kidnapped. She'd probably give the kidnappers one of her monologues and her lawyer's phone number, and they'd pay to get rid of her. Maybe they'd accept Ziegler in part-exchange. Simon yawned and rubbed at the grittiness in his eyes, and blinked as the first blinding sliver of sun appeared over the deep blue mass of the mountain. It was going to be another hot and beautiful day, wonderful weather for arranging a ten million franc ransom. He stretched, felt the rattan chair bite into his back, and heard someone down in the village greeting the morning with the prolonged, racking rasp of a forty-a-day cough.

The two detectives were waiting for Simon when he arrived at the hotel just before nine. The director of the school at Lacoste, knowing nothing of the kidnap but becoming increasingly worried about his missing student, had called in the police. Once the nationality and the financial eminence of the student's father had been disclosed, responsibility for the investigation had been passed upwards from the local *gendarmerie*. And now Avignon's finest, short and dark and longing for coffee, had arrived to deal with the case of the missing boy.

Simon showed them into the reception office, and was aware of eau-de-cologne and garlic. His offer of coffee was gratefully accepted, the sight of Françoise as she bent to put the tray on the desk noted and enjoyed, cigarettes were lit, and the notebooks came out.

'Before you ask any questions,' Simon said, 'I think I have to tell you what has happened.'

At first, the detectives were pleased. Only in a professional sense, of course, but now the case had assumed some real importance. A missing person, even a missing person from a rich American family, was one thing. A kidnapped person, however, was something altogether more exciting. They were no longer investigating a possible accident; they were in at the start of a certain crime. Glory and promotion, the gratitude of a billionaire father, even a brief, stern-faced appearance on national television – all these thoughts passed through the minds of the detectives as they listened carefully and made notes, stopping only to ask for more coffee and another sight of the quite admirable bottom and tanned legs of Françoise. What a stroke of luck, they thought, that they hadn't been given the bank job at Isle-sur-Sorgue instead.

They were less pleased to be told by Simon that any hint of police involvement might prejudice the safety of the hostage. The senior detective, his superior rank apparent from his habit of stealing his colleague's cigarettes and waiting for them to be lit, shook his head.

'Unfortunately, Monsieur Shaw, we have been informed. We have been involved, you understand? It is a *fait accompli*. How can I, a police officer, ignore a major crime?' He glanced down at his notebook and rubbed his chin thoughtfully. 'But I can promise you this.' He took another cigarette from the open packet on the desk, and cocked an eyebrow to indicate that it needed to be lit. 'I can promise you this,' he said again. 'We shall conduct this *affaire* with the maximum delicacy and discretion. *Le maximum*. We have much experience of matters like this. Why, I remember three years ago the abduction of a Swiss tourist during the festival of Avignon . . .'

Françoise put her head round the door. 'Monsieur Shaw? There are two men here for you.'

Simon went into the reception area and stopped short at the sight of a man with two cameras slung round his neck. His colleague was more modestly equipped, with a single tape-recorder hanging by a strap from his shoulder.

'*Bonjour*, Monsieur Shaw. *Le Provençal*. We've just come from the school at Lacoste. You have two minutes? We understand you know the young man who . . .'

Simon held up one hand. 'Don't go away.' He went back to the office, and shook his head at the two detectives. 'Maximum discretion, is that what you said?'

They nodded.

'Then tell me why there's a reporter and a photographer out there.'

The detectives shouldered their way past Simon and glared at the journalists.

'Out,' said the senior detective, jerking his thumb at the

door. 'There is no story. This is a confidential matter for the police.'

The journalists both started talking at once, their eyebrows, shoulders and hands jerking up and down in extravagant outrage. The press had a duty to report events – more, a constitutional right to report events.

'*Merde* to all that,' said the senior detective. 'You listen to me.'

Simon closed the office door and rested his head in his hands. A few noisy minutes later, the door opened.

'No problem,' said the senior detective, smiling at Simon as if he'd done him a personal favour.

'What do you mean, no problem? You can't stop them writing a story.'

The detective tapped the side of his nose. 'This is France, *monsieur*. Journalists know their place.'

Simon sighed. 'OK. Now what?'

'The kidnappers will be calling again, *non*? We will arrange for the call to be traced. Meanwhile, we wait.'

'Do you have to wait here? We're trying to run a hotel.'

With some reluctance, the detectives allowed themselves to be persuaded to leave the office and continue their duties with a cordless phone on the terrace overlooking the pool.

'Oh, there's one thing you could do while you're waiting,' Simon said. He pointed across the terrace. 'If you see a man looking over the top of that wall, arrest him.'

Simon called the bank to warn them to expect the money, and to have it ready for him to pick up at the end of the day. He did his best to soothe Françoise, who had just learned of Boone's disappearance. He thanked his lucky stars for Nicole and Ernest, who dealt with guests and staff as though nothing had happened. He deliberately woke Ziegler at 5 a.m. in New York to make sure that the money was being sent as soon as business opened. He was light-headed with fatigue, but incapable of sleep, and he knew that he was becoming increasingly short-tempered. The sight of the two detectives studying lunch menus on the terrace did nothing to improve his mood.

He returned to the office, and sat staring at the phone. There was nothing much the police could do until the kidnappers called again, nothing much anyone could do. And then he remembered Enrico. What was it he'd said? If ever there was a problem at the hotel, a problem the authorities might find difficult to deal with through official channels ... something like that. Simon pulled the phone towards him. It was probably all talk, but it was worth a try. Anything was better than sitting here feeling useless.

The guardian of Enrico's telephone growled. Simon identified himself, and lit a cigar while he waited to be put through.

Enrico sounded pleased to hear from him. There were certain unresolved matters to discuss before his people could start servicing the hotel. Perhaps another delightful lunch might be arranged? Simon cut him short. 'Enrico, listen. I don't know if you can help, but a friend of mine is in trouble. A young American. He's been kidnapped.'

'That's bad. In the tourist season, too. Amateurs. You must tell me everything you know.'

When the brief conversation was over, Enrico left his office for a stroll around the Vieux Port. He stopped twice, once to visit a bar, and a second time to go through the back door of a seafood restaurant. The men he spoke to got on the phone as soon as he'd left them. If this was a local job, somebody would know about it. And if somebody knew about it, Enrico would be told. He beckoned to the Mercedes that had been trailing him round the port. He would take a quiet early lunch, the *brochette* of *langoustines*, in the garden at Passédat, while he considered the business opportunities that this interesting piece of news might offer.

The bank called in the late afternoon to tell Simon that the money was ready, and he was half-way to the car before it occurred to him that walking round Cavaillon alone with ten million francs in cash might be a mistake. He went down to the terrace, where the detectives were keeping a watchful eye on the sunbathers.

'The money's arrived. It would be best if you came with me.'

285

The detectives adjusted their sunglasses, the mirror-lens models favoured by the motor-cycle cops for that added glint of menace, and followed Simon out to the parking area. They got into the unmarked police car, blistering hot and stale with yesterday's cigarettes, and the junior detective used the car phone for a laconic exchange of grunts and monosyllables with headquarters.

They double-parked outside the bank. The detectives looked up and down the street, saw nothing instantly suspicious in the sprinkling of slow-footed tourists and housewives shopping for the evening meal, and hurried Simon across the pavement. They pressed the buzzer next to the plate-glass door and waited. An aged bank clerk shuffled up to the door, shook his head and mouthed '*Fermé*', pointing at the opening hours printed on the glass. The senior detective slapped his identity card flat against the door. The clerk peered at it, shrugged, and let them in.

The manager of the bank greeted them outside his office, showed them in and closed the door. He let his breath out in a great sigh of relief. It had been a nightmare afternoon, money being delivered from the bigger branches in Avignon and Marseille, thoughts of a hold-up, visions of men with shotguns. But now, thank God, it was over. '*Voilà, messieurs.*' He pointed to his desk. 'If you'd like to count it.'

Simon looked at the stacks of 500-franc notes, banded together in *briques* of 10,000 francs. Somehow, he'd expected ten million francs to look more impressive, more bulky. He sat down and, as the others smoked and watched, arranged the *briques* in piles of 100,000 francs, counted the piles, packed them into a thick plastic sack, and hefted the sack in his hand. It was no heavier than the attaché case filled with work that he used to take home from the agency every weekend.

'*C'est bon?*' The manager put a form on the desk in front of Simon. '*Une petite signature, s'il vous plaît.*' He watched Simon sign the receipt, and relaxed. Now it was someone else's responsibility.

They shook hands, and went to the main door, Simon sandwiched between the two detectives, the sack bumping against his leg.

286

'*Merde*!' One of the detectives saw a traffic policeman slipping a ticket under the windscreen-wiper of their car. They ran down the steps as the policeman looked up at them, tapping his pen against his teeth. He enjoyed it when the owner of the car came back a few seconds too late. It relieved the boredom of the job.

The senior detective pointed at the ticket. 'You can take that off.' He opened the door to get into the car. 'We're from headquarters in Avignon.'

The traffic policeman smiled. 'I don't give a shit if you're from the Elysée Palace. You're double-parked.'

The detective went round the car so that he could glare at closer range. The two men stood out in the road, sunglasses almost clashing, blocking off the remaining clear lane. A truck pulled up with an angry hydraulic hiss, and the driver leaned out of the window, his arm raised in irritated frustration. The customers sitting outside the café opposite turned to get a better view of the argument. Horns started an impatient chorus behind the truck. The bank manager and his clerk stood watching from the steps.

Simon tossed the sack into the back of the car and got in. Maximum discretion. Jesus. They might as well have put it on the six o'clock news.

The duel of shrugs and gesticulations ended with the detective ripping the ticket from the windscreen and tearing it up. Two men from the café applauded. The detective got into the car as the traffic policeman shouted a parting obscenity over the blaring of the horns.

'And your mother!' said the detective to him out of the window. 'And your dog!' He snorted with the satisfaction of having had the last word. 'OK, let's go.'

The message waiting when they arrived back at the hotel said that Hampton Parker would be in Brassière in the early hours of next morning. Simon, like the bank manager before him, felt a sense of relief that both the money and the responsibility could soon be passed to different hands. He put through a call to Ziegler and waited, the sack between his feet.

'Any news of the kid?'

'They're calling tonight. Parker's arriving very early in the morning. I've got the money here, ready for him.'

Ziegler said nothing for a few seconds. When he spoke, it was in the crisp, decisive tone he used when he was making up a client's mind for him. 'Parker's not to be involved. No way.'

'But he is involved, for Christ's sake. He's the boy's father.'

'I don't want him anywhere near those goddamn dangerous goons.'

'So how are they going to get the money? Federal Express?'

'Jesus, Simon, we can't put Parker at risk like that. Suppose they decide to kidnap him as well? Suppose they ice him, for fuck's sake. No, you'll have to do it.'

Simon felt his stomach turn over. 'Thanks a lot. Suppose they ice me?'

Ziegler's voice changed, all warmth and reassurance, his new business presentation voice. 'Don't worry about it. You're not a billionaire, you're just the guy making the drop. Wear old clothes, look poor, you know? It's no big deal. You'll probably never see them. And hey, think what it'll do for our relationship.'

'Our relationship?'

'Parker will be in our pocket. The goddamn account will be set in concrete. It's a moral debt, buddy. We'll have him for life.'

Simon said nothing, but he knew that Ziegler wouldn't have listened anyway. As far as he was concerned, the decision was taken – probably the right decision, Simon had to admit. If the kidnappers thought they could get their hands on one of the richest men in America, who could tell what they might do?

Ziegler sounded impatient. 'So you're holding the ball, OK? Don't screw up.'

'You're a soft-hearted bastard, aren't you?'

'That's me. Sweetest guy in the business. I'll talk to you soon.'

Nicole found Simon in the office, smoking a cigar and staring out of the window, ignoring the detectives. He looked haggard, and bruised under the eyes. She stood behind him, and rubbed gently at the base of his neck.

'When this is over,' she said, 'I'm going to take you away.'

Simon closed his eyes and leaned his head back against her body.

'Promise?'

'Promise.'

The detectives sat and watched them impassively, wondering what they were going to be given for dinner.

Enrico looked at the pile of passports on his desk, and smiled. Contacts, greed and fear. They always worked when you were looking for information. Within hours of putting the word out, one of his men in Avignon had heard that the police were trying to keep the lid on a kidnapping. If these passports didn't have something to do with that, Enrico thought, he was losing his touch. He had decided to take a personal interest in the matter. One should never pass up the opportunity to meet people who might be useful. He put the passports in a large crocodile-skin attaché case, went downstairs to his car, settled himself comfortably in the back seat, and gave the chauffeur his instructions.

As the Mercedes headed out of Marseille towards the airport, the General thrashed his car along the *autoroute* from Cavaillon. Be in the underground car park at Marignane by eight, they had told him, and look for a black Mercedes 500 with Bouches-du-Rhône plates.

He found a space as far away as possible from the entrance to the terminal, cut the engine and lit a cigarette. He squeezed the plastic supermarket bag which held the cash. Five hundred thousand francs. He'd almost fainted when they'd told him the price, but what else could he do? Anyway, there was more where that came from, a lot more. As he looked at his watch, he saw the Mercedes nosing slowly through the lines of cars. He took a deep breath, picked up the bag and got out.

The tinted window of the Mercedes slid down, and the chauffeur and the General looked at each other in silence. With a start, the General remembered what he'd been told to say to identify himself.

'I'm a friend of Didier's. He sends you his best.'

The back door swung open. 'Come in, my friend,' said Enrico. 'It's cooler in here, with the air-conditioning.'

The General ducked inside, and perched on the edge of the deep leather seat. Enrico studied him through the smoke of his cigarette. 'You're a busy man, I'm sure,' he said, 'so I won't waste your time.' He stubbed out his cigarette, and flicked a speck of ash from the silk sleeve of his suit. 'Tell me, when are you picking up the ransom?'

The General felt sick, as if he'd been kicked in the stomach. How the hell did he know? He couldn't know. He was guessing.

Enrico reached over and patted the General on the knee. 'Come, my friend. Think of me as a professional colleague. We're already partners, after all. I have your passports, and I must say that considering the lack of time, they've turned out very well. Works of art. You won't have any problem there.' He smiled and nodded. 'Cigarette?'

The General's hand was shaking so violently that he almost lit his moustache.

'Relax, my friend, relax. Allow me to congratulate you. Americans are so scarce these days.' Enrico sighed. 'The recession, and the weak dollar. They don't travel as much as they used to.' His eyes never left the General's face. 'Well? When are you giving him back?'

How had he found out, this man who sat so still and never seemed to blink? The only sound in the car was the whisper of the air-conditioning as the General felt his shoulders slump. He wasn't going to get the passports unless he answered the question. He looked at the broad back and muscular neck of the chauffeur.

'Don't worry about Alphonse.' Enrico smiled. 'He's very discreet. We're all very discreet.'

The General let out his breath. 'We're making the exchange tonight.'

'And then?'

'Out of the country.'

'Ah, yes. Of course.' Enrico bent down and snapped open his attaché case. The General's eyes widened as he saw neat piles of banknotes, hundreds of thousands of francs. There was barely enough room in the case for the passports which Enrico took out and passed over. 'May I?' He took the plastic bag from the General's lap and started to count the money, tossing each *brique* of 10,000 francs into the case as it was counted.

'*C'est bon.*' With some difficulty, Enrico pressed the lid of the case shut, and leaned back as the General fumbled for the door handle. 'Now then,' he said. 'Your travel plans. I think I could be of some assistance.'

The General stopped, his hand still on the door.

'I have a little shipping business, cargo mainly, but we occasionally oblige passengers with special requirements. You understand?' Enrico didn't wait for a reply. 'An agreeable coincidence occurs to me. It happens that one of my vessels – not luxurious, but comfortable – leaves Genoa the day after tomorrow for Algiers. Very pleasant, the Mediterranean, at this time of year.'

The General let his hand drop from the door.

'You and your friends would be completely safe.' Enrico looked at his watch. 'As it happens, I'm driving to Italy now. Alphonse prefers the night, specially in July. The roads are impossible during the day.' He offered the General another cigarette. 'We could meet in Genoa. Just go to the docks and ask for my colleague, the captain of the *Principessa Azzura*. He'll know where to find me.'

The General did his best to look disappointed. '*Merde*, if only I'd known,' he said, 'but of course, I've made other plans.' He reached again for the door.

'My friend.' Enrico looked as friendly as death. 'I must insist that you take advantage of this unexpected blessing. It would be a great sadness if the police were to be looking for the names on those excellent new passports. Such a waste. I do hate waste.'

Bastard. The General nodded, and Enrico smiled back. 'You won't regret it. Sea air is so healthy.'

'But not cheap.'

'Nothing good in life is cheap.' Enrico shrugged in apology. 'But I will give you a *tarif de vacances*, since you are a group. Let's say 500,000 francs. You will eat well. They have a very good cook on board.'

It was the General's turn to shrug. 'I don't have 500,000 francs with me.'

'*Ouf.*' Enrico brushed the detail aside. 'We're businessmen, you and I. There is mutual trust and understanding. You can pay me in Genoa, and then we have lunch.' Enrico leaned across and opened the door. 'I'll pay for lunch. It will be my pleasure.'

The General stood and watched the big car pull away, and as the menace of Enrico disappeared, fear and shock gave way to anger. A million francs for eight lousy passports and a trip to Algiers on some rusty bucket, probably full of noisy *macaronis*. The General was a mild man, but this was taking unfair advantage, nothing less than daylight robbery. He turned to his car, and then stopped. He forced himself to think.

He had the passports. He didn't have to go to Genoa. He could stick to his original plan. Screw Enrico, he thought, and felt better. People like that, people with no business ethics, they didn't deserve to get away with it. He remembered Enrico tossing the passport money casually into his case, on top of the pile that was already there. And he wanted more, the bloodsucker. Well, this time he wasn't dealing with one of his tame dumb thugs. He was dealing with a man who used his head.

The General walked upstairs to the terminal, pushed his way through the Arabs at the bar, and ordered a Calvados. Courage returned as he felt the bite and warmth of the alcohol. He braced himself, went over to the bank of phones by the *tabac*, and made the call. He was sweating by the time he put down the phone. *Salopard*. Let's see how he gets out of that.

On his way back to the Lubéron, the General stopped for a coffee at the service station at Lançon and went over the possible effects of his call. Enrico wouldn't know for sure.

He might suspect, but he wouldn't talk too much – not because of honour among thieves, which all true thieves know to be crap, but because he would implicate himself in a crime that he hadn't even committed. There was something ironic in that, the General thought as he dropped the plastic coffee cup in the bin. Serve him right. Anyway, by the time he gets out of trouble I'll be a long way from Marseille, and he won't know where.

He drove carefully back to Cavaillon, observing the speed limit, and took the N100 up to Les Baumettes. He parked by the phone booth, feeling a pang of hunger at the sight of people eating on the terrace of the small restaurant on the other side of the road. Tomorrow, he thought, if all went well, he'd celebrate. He locked his car before going into the phone booth. It was only a few metres away, but there were so many crooks around these days you couldn't be too careful.

The phone was picked up after the first ring.

'Monsieur Shaw?'

'*Oui*.'

'You have the money?'

'It's here.'

'*Bon*. This is what you must do.'

Simon put the phone down and looked at the notes he'd made. The senior detective exchanged his toothpick for a cigarette and propped himself on the corner of the desk, pleased that there was finally going to be some action. '*Alors?*'

Simon recited from his notes. 'I go alone in the car up to the parking area at the edge of the Forêt des Cèdres, and leave it there. I take the forest road on foot. After four kilometres, I'll see a sign on the right marking the start of the Forêt Dominiale de Ménerbes. I leave the money under the sign. If everything is in order, the boy is released tomorrow morning.'

'We need a map,' said the senior detective, 'and a local man, someone who knows the forest.' He jerked his head at his colleague. 'Call Avignon, and tell them what's going on.

Tell them to cover both airports – but no uniforms, *d'accord*?'

Françoise was sent to fetch her father. Simon found a map, and was spreading it on the desk when Bonetto arrived, in singlet and shorts and slippers, his beetroot face serious. The men huddled over the map in a cloud of cigarette smoke.

Yes, Bonetto said, he knew the road well, from his hunting days. It ran along the spine of the Lubéron, from Bonnieux to just before Cavaillon, barred at each end by the forest service so that cars couldn't use it.

The detective asked him about escape routes. Bonetto scratched his head and bent lower over the map, jabbing it with a blunt finger as he spoke. 'On foot,' he said, 'one can go down the south face towards Lourmarin, down the north face to Ménerbes, west to Cavaillon, east on to the Claparèdes above Bonnieux, or anywhere here in this valley.' He shrugged. 'There are old mule tracks, dozens of them. The Resistance used them during the war. A man could hide in there for months.'

'But they won't want to hide.' The senior detective stared at the maze of contour lines and tracks on the map. 'They'll want to get out. They'll have a car somewhere. They'll have to get back to a road.'

'*Beh oui.*' Bonetto shook his head. 'But in the beginning, they'll go on foot. And on foot they can go in any direction.'

The junior detective, a young man with a liking for high technology and higher drama, proposed a helicopter with a searchlight and an assault force from the CRS. He himself would volunteer to go with them.

Simon held up both hands. 'Listen,' he said. 'No helicopters, no roadblocks, nothing. Nothing until we get him back. Then you can send in the bloody Foreign Legion and Mitterand's bodyguard, anything you want. But not until we get him back. They've worked it out. They're not going to bring him up with them. They've got him hidden somewhere, and if there's any sign of a trap . . .' His voice was hoarse. There was a strange taste in his mouth, dry and unpleasant, and he wondered if it was too many cigars or fear.

The Customs officer yawned, and wished it was time to leave his cramped cubicle and go home. Traffic was thin tonight; the usual procession of trucks, but not much else. If it came, this black Mercedes with the Bouches-du-Rhône plates, they wouldn't have any trouble spotting it. If it came. He yawned again, and turned to the man next to him, who had arrived an hour before.

'You don't think it's some *emmerdeur* with nothing else to do?'

The other man shrugged. He kept his eyes on the road, watching the traffic as it came into the glare of the floodlights that marked the end of France and the beginning of Italy. 'God knows,' he said. 'I don't. All I know is that Avignon took it seriously. They told Nice, and Nice took it seriously. It might be a grudge. The *mec* who tipped them off said it was tax evasion and currency smuggling. Some big sardine from Marseille. Apparently they've been after him for years.'

The Customs officer stretched. It made a change from checking load weights on trucks. 'We normally pass cars straight through,' he said, 'otherwise it would be solid from here to Menton.'

'That's probably what he's counting on. Or maybe he's just getting careless. Got a cigarette?'

'Given it up.'

'Me too.'

The two men stared at the headlights that streamed down the *autoroute* in straight lines before fanning out and slowing down to pass through the row of gates where they paid the toll. A truck from Torino, going home. A Volkswagen camper with windsurfing boards strapped to the roof. Two motor-bikes, travelling in convoy.

They saw it at the same time as it came smoothly into the floodlights, a black Mercedes 500, tinted windows, Bouches-du-Rhône plates.

'There's our boy.' The Customs officer got up. 'You tell the others. I'll go through the routine.'

He stepped out of the cubicle and walked across to where the Mercedes was waiting behind a German caravan. He tapped on the driver's window, and it slid down. Over the shoulder of the chauffeur, he could see a man asleep in the back, his hand resting on the attaché case by his side on the seat.

'*Bon soir, monsieur. Vous êtes francais?*'

The chauffeur nodded.

'Anything to declare?'

The chauffeur shook his head.

'Just pull in over there, would you?'

The whites of the chauffeur's eyes gleamed against his dark skin as he looked over to the side of the road. Four men in suits were waiting under the floodlights. One of them beckoned to the Mercedes. Enrico continued to snore softly.

Simon checked his watch, stood up, and dragged the sack from under the desk. 'I'd better go. I'm supposed to be there between midnight and one.' He picked up a torch and the car keys, and turned to the detectives. 'No games, all right?'

'Monsieur Shaw, if you should get a chance to see a face . . .'

Simon nodded. Sure, he thought. I'll do better than that. I'll ask them all to pop down for a drink after I've handed over the money, and we can have a party. He felt curiously calm, almost fatalistic, in between spasms of panic. What was he doing, taking a million pounds in a plastic sack into the middle of a bloody forest to meet a bunch of dangerous lunatics? This was madness. He picked up the sack, and went out of the office to find Nicole and Ernest talking quietly to a tearful Françoise. They went with him to the car, and as he drove off he saw them in the rear-view mirror, a forlorn trio in the middle of a shadowy street.

He stopped at the intersection below Ménerbes, where the D3 runs up the valley towards Bonnieux. Above the mutter of the idling engine, close enough to make the hairs rise on the nape of his neck, he heard a sound, half-sigh, half-groan.

He sat rigid, his hands suddenly sweaty on the wheel. It was one of them, going to jump him and take the money. His eyes flicked up to the mirror. Nobody. Nothing. But he could feel a presence behind him, he could hear breathing.

He gave in and spoke. 'Who's that?'

There was a loud, prolonged yawn. Very slowly, Simon turned his head and saw the squat, recumbent form on the back seat, all four legs in the air, tail moving lazily at the sound of a familiar voice. Mrs Gibbons was waking up.

Simon felt relief wash through his body. Bloody dog. He remembered now that she often took a nap in the back of the car until it was time to go home with Ernest.

Mrs Gibbons poked her head between the front seats and sniffed the sack of money. Simon put it on the floor, and she settled herself on the passenger seat, resting her heavy head on Simon's thigh, a comforting, warm weight. He fondled one of her ragged ears, and drove on.

He had the road to himself, the farms on either side shuttered and dark, the car's headlights forming a long, empty tunnel in front of him. It was just after the Lacoste turning that a gleam in the mirror caught his eye, a gleam that kept its distance as the road twisted through orchards of cherry trees, their leaves drooping in disconsolate swags after another arid day. He stopped at the foot of the hill below Bonnieux. The car behind him stopped. He looked down at Mrs Gibbons. 'The bastard's following us,' he said. The dog sat up and cocked her head, her tail thumping softly against the upholstery.

They drove through Bonnieux, past sleeping houses and startled cats, and followed the sign to the Forêt des Cèdres. Blackness on each side, blackness behind. Either he'd turned off his lights or he'd gone, now that he was sure Simon was alone.

The barrier blocking off the forest road, a straight, authoritative shape among the wizened scrub oaks and the clutter of rocks, appeared in the headlights. Simon turned them off and killed the engine, and felt the gallop of his heartbeat. Mrs Gibbons whined with excitement at the possibility of a walk. He rubbed her head. 'You stay here and look after the car.' She whined again, and scratched at the door. Simon sighed. 'Well, for Christ's sake don't bite anybody.' He let her out, picked up the sack and the torch, and stood for a moment by the car.

The silence was immense, broken only by the soft tick of the cooling engine and the sound of a miniature waterfall as Mrs Gibbons emptied her bladder. Moonshadows turned the shapes of bushes into crouching men. Simon switched on the torch, ducked under the barrier, licked his lips and tried unsuccessfully to whistle for the dog. The inside of his mouth felt as though it had been dry-cleaned.

The rope soles of his espadrilles made less noise than the leathery scuff of the dog's paws beside him. The road stretched straight ahead, running from east to west. On either side, towering dark cascades of cedar trees shut out the moon, and Simon saw that the beam of the torch was shaking. Shit. This was bloody lunacy. Nobody for miles, except – somewhere ahead of him, or behind him, or even watching him now from the deep still gloom of the forest – the kidnappers. They could kill him, and bury him up here. Maybe they'd already dug the hole. He shivered in the warm night air, and walked a little faster.

It was almost half an hour before he saw the wooden sign at the side of the road, faded letters in the torchlight: Forêt Dominiale de Ménerbes. Mrs Gibbons suddenly stopped, her great snout twitching, her tail stiff and horizontal, a long, gurgling growl coming from the depths of her throat. God, thought Simon, that's all I need, the bloody dog getting stuck into a kidnapper's leg. He dropped the sack, bent down and hooked his fingers through Mrs Gibbons's collar. His other hand held the wavering torch. He needed a third hand for the sack. Shit. Could he leave it in the middle of the road? They must be there, watching him, probably with knives and shotguns and deeply suspicious natures. Bloody dog.

The forest remained silent except for the faint breath of wind through the trees and the intermittent rumblings coming from Mrs Gibbons. Simon put the end of the torch between his teeth, took hold of the sack, tightened his grip on the dog's collar and moved in a crabwise, shuffling crouch across the road. This is ridiculous, he thought. I am a wealthy and successful man. What in God's name am I doing here? With a heave of his arm, he tossed the sack on to the grass at the foot of the sign. Mrs Gibbons strained against her collar. Simon cursed her through a mouthful of torch, picked up thirty kilos of bunched, aggressive muscle, and started to carry the dog back the way he had come.

Jojo and Bachir watched as the light from the torch became dim, and finally disappeared. They came out of the trees.

'I hate that dog,' Bachir said. 'It was always looking at me on the *chantier*. I don't think it likes Arabs. I tell you, I was shit-scared he'd let it go.'

Jojo clapped him on the back. 'Forget it.' He switched on his torch, and opened the sack. 'Look at that. Ten million *balles*. Let's go and be rich.' He picked up the sack. Martinique, here I come, he thought. The two men started down the overgrown track that would lead them to their rendezvous with the General by the quarry near Ménerbes.

Simon's pulse had calmed down to little more than twice its normal rate. He put the dog down and stretched his aching arms. Although he hated to admit it, Ziegler had been right; all the kidnappers were interested in was the money. And now, thank God, it was over. He quickened his pace, and began to feel optimistic. Boone would be back tomorrow, the detectives would be gone tomorrow, and he and Nicole . . .

Mrs Gibbons growled again, and Simon stopped dead. He heard movement, fast and clumsy, in the bushes. He swung the torch towards the sound, and his heart had another attack of hysterics as the beam picked up a massive head and a black, whiskery face.

Mrs Gibbons barked. The wild boar, head lowered, looked at them for a few long seconds and then lumbered back into the night, its tail flicking angrily from side to side. Simon felt limp, as if his bones had collapsed. His hands were still trembling when he reached the car, and he had to use both of them to fumble the key into the ignition.

The reception committee waiting for him at the hotel had increased by three. Hampton Parker, his face lined and sombre, was standing at the entrance, flanked by two large, watchful men. Nicole, Françoise and Ernest were grouped round the reception desk. The detectives had abandoned the office to pace up and down the lobby. As Simon pulled up, they swarmed round the car and peppered him with questions. He was giddy with nervous exhaustion and anticlimax, and desperate for a drink. Mrs Gibbons clambered over to the back seat and went to sleep.

The General heard them coming, hurried footsteps skidding on the loose stones of the track. He stamped on his cigarette and peered at his watch. Clockwork. The whole thing had gone like clockwork. The boy had eaten everything, and had passed out within twenty minutes from the double dose of Binoctal that they'd ground up in his spicy *pâté* sandwich. By the time he woke, they'd be well on their way to Barcelona, rich men. He wondered how Enrico was getting on with the *fiscs*. No beauty sleep for him tonight.

Jojo and Bachir came out of the darkness, and the General could almost feel them grinning.

'Here,' said Jojo. 'Catch.'

Ten million francs hit him in the chest, and he hugged the sack like a baby. They got into the van and went to pick up the others from the barn.

The hotel lobby was beginning to look like the waiting room at Avignon station – figures slumped on chairs, empty coffee-cups and glasses, full ashtrays. Stubble and fatigue darkened the men's faces. Nothing was happening, but nobody wanted to miss it.

When the bell went off, it was as if they'd all received a simultaneous electric shock. Simon ran to pick up the phone.

'So what's new?'

Simon shook his head at the faces turned towards him. It was only Ziegler.

'I delivered the money. Now we're waiting. There's nothing we can do.'

'Parker there?'

'Yes, he's here. Do you want to talk to him?'

Ziegler deliberated. 'Maybe it's not the moment.'

'What do you mean?'

'Well, two million bucks is two million bucks, buddy. I'm trying to run a business here.'

Simon dropped his voice. 'Bob, will you do me a favour?'

'Depends.'

'Go fuck yourself.'

Simon put down the phone and crossed the lobby to where Hampton Parker was sitting, his head between his hands. 'That was Bob Ziegler. He . . . well, he just wanted to know if Boone had got back.' Parker nodded. He looked numb. 'Do you want to try to get some sleep?'

The Texan loosened his tie and undid the collar of his shirt. Simon noticed the cords of tension in his neck. 'Guess I'll sit it out,' he said. 'Bourbon would help, if you have some.'

They went down to the bar. Simon took a bottle and two glasses out on to the terrace and they sat in silence, drinking and watching the long dark hump of the Lubéron gradually become more defined as night started to give way to dawn. Simon thought of a dozen unpleasant things he'd like to do to Ziegler. 'Two million bucks is two million bucks, buddy.' What a little bastard.

The long orange and brown coach, its diesel engine pumping fumes into the early morning air, was parked by the side of the Place de la Bouquerie in Apt. GONZALEZ VOYAGES, APT/BARCELONE, TOUT CONFORT/WC was ready to take on passengers. They stood in small groups in the sun, chattering and laughing, good-humoured at the thought of a holiday in Spain and all those cheap pesetas.

The General had told them not to wait all together in one big group, and not to sit together in the coach. He and Jojo stood off to one side as the others filed on board, each with a fully packed shoulder-bag, indistinguishable from the rest of the travellers in their nondescript blue denim. Only Jojo had dressed for the part, in a straw hat and a new T-shirt with *Vivent les Vacances!* printed on the front. He'd been rather pleased with that, a little touch, the kind of thing the General would appreciate.

He felt the strap of his bag, pleasantly heavy on his shoulder. Solid money. They were all, in French francs at least, millionaires. He looked around to make sure he couldn't be overheard.

'What made you choose a coach?'

The General smiled and stroked his moustache. 'What would you be looking for if you were a *flic*? A fast car, probably stolen, or a group of men buying last-minute tickets at the airport, something like that, *non*? Are they going to be looking for a clapped-out bus full of tourists? No baggage checks, either. And they probably won't even bother with the passports at the frontier.' The General tapped Jojo on the chest. 'Sometimes a slow getaway is best.'

Jojo adjusted his straw hat and nodded. '*C'est pas con.*'

They climbed into the coach and made their way down the aisle, not looking at the others, and settled themselves on worn plastic seats. They'd be in Barcelona this afternoon, then a train to Madrid. And from Madrid airport a man could go anywhere. The General felt tired. He closed his eyes, and thought of Mathilde. He'd give her a call from Madrid. She was a good old girl. It would be nice to see her with some money.

With a sigh from the hydraulic doors, the coach moved away from the kerb. The driver waved his thanks to the *gendarme* who had stopped the traffic to let him pull out.

Boone woke up and wished he hadn't. He had a mouthful of evil-tasting fur and a head as tender as a peeled egg, like the time he'd gone to Florida on a spring break and had all those upside-down margaritas. He didn't remember having anything to drink, either. Just that sandwich, and then a nose-dive. He felt the ground biting into his body, arched his back and opened one eye. Who was going to be on baby-sitting duty today? he wondered. He turned his head cautiously, and opened the other eye.

There was the trestle-table and some old crates. There, at the far end of the barn, was the closed door with daylight leaking through the cracks. He sat up and looked around. The place had been cleaned out – no bikes, no empty bottles, no trace that they'd ever been there except a scattering of cigarette butts in the earth. And no baby-sitters.

He got to his feet and walked stiffly to the door, gave it a tentative push, watched it swing open, and stood on the threshold, flinching as the glare penetrated his eyeballs and throbbed against the top of his skull. He stepped out of the barn. The clearing around it was empty, the grass flattened where cars had been parked. The track ahead was deserted. Nobody shouted at him as he went towards the road. He stood on the hot tarmac for a few moments, wondering where he was, and went off to look for a signpost.

Madame Arnaud, driving briskly along to her weekly rendezvous at the Sisters of Mercy Mission, where charitable ladies gathered to sip coffee and discuss good works, slowed down at the sight of the grimy figure waving at her in the middle of the road. She shook her head in disapproval. It was really scandalous, she thought, *marginaux* like him were everywhere these days – filthy, unshaven animals hoping to take advantage of respectable citizens like herself. He was quite young, too, she noticed, as she swerved to avoid him and accelerated hard. Scandalous.

23

Ernest and Françoise were distributing coffee and croissants to the creased and red-eyed inhabitants of the lobby. A group of guests, dressed for another day of blazing heat, looked with curiosity at Parker's bodyguards and the detectives, wondering why the hotel was suddenly full of men in city clothes.

With heads bent over their coffee, none of them noticed the figure that plodded past the window and stopped at the entrance.

'Yo, Ernie. Got a beer?'

Ernest spun round at the sound of Boone's voice, rushed across the lobby and hugged the grinning, malodorous young man, patting him as if to make sure he was all there. Françoise burst into tears, the bodyguards and detectives hastily put down their cups, and Nicole ran out to fetch Simon and Hampton Parker. Mrs Gibbons emerged from the office, examined one of Boone's bare and dirty legs, and rotated a welcoming tail.

'Well!' Ernest said. 'What a sight you are, young Boone. I think a shower and something to eat . . .'

The senior detective held up his hand in an official gesture, made somewhat less official by the half-eaten croissant he was holding. 'We have many questions to ask the young man.'

Ernest frowned at him. 'Yes, dear, I'm sure you have, but give the poor boy a chance. A shower first, and clues afterwards.'

The senior detective snapped his fingers at his partner. 'Call Avignon. Tell them we have him. They can get going.'

Hampton Parker ran up the stairs, followed by Nicole and Simon, and stood with his hands on Boone's shoulders, his face crinkled in a vast smile. 'Good to see you, boy.' He swallowed hard. 'Had us a little worried there for a while. You OK?'

Boone grinned and nodded. 'Good as new.'

'Now then, Mr P,' Ernest said. 'Why don't we get Boone tidied up and put some food inside him?'

'Sure.' Parker clapped his son on the back, and turned to Simon. 'Do you know, I never told the boy's mother. I was worrying enough for two. Guess I'll call her now, if you don't mind. Oh, and it might be an idea if I called Bob Ziegler. He was kind of concerned last night.'

Simon looked at his watch. Four a.m. in New York. He smiled. 'No,' he said, 'allow me.'

The next few hours passed in a blur of weariness as Simon interpreted between Boone and the detectives, who seemed to think that if they asked the same questions often enough, Boone would finally produce the kidnappers' names and addresses. The reporters from *Le Provençal* reappeared, convinced that they had a national scoop, and took photographs of anyone willing to stand still. Two puzzled American guests and the village postman posed obligingly for them in the lobby. Ziegler, whom Simon had found to be irritatingly wide awake, wanted to issue a press release describing his vital role in securing the safe return of the kidnap victim. Ernest insisted on arranging a celebration dinner. Uncle William, never one to miss the chance of ingratiating himself with a billionaire, volunteered to decorate the dinner menus. Simon craved sleep, and when Nicole came to rescue him from the detectives and take him home, he barely managed to crawl up the stairs before dropping, fully dressed, on the bed.

Six hours, a shower and a shave later, he felt surprisingly well, even exhilarated, as if a burden had been removed from him while he slept. He towelled his hair dry and watched Nicole as she put on a short black dress that he'd never seen before. He kissed the brown skin of her back as he fastened the zip.

'Does this mean I have to wear a tie?'

Nicole dabbed scent on her neck and the inside of her

305

wrists. 'Ernest would like us to look chic. He's such a sweet man. He wants to give Boone a special evening.'

'I'll wear a jacket. But no tie, and definitely no socks.'

'Slob.'

Simon grumbled without much conviction as Nicole chose a shirt and a lightweight cotton suit for him to wear, and dusted off a pair of shoes he'd last worn in London.

She stood back to look at him as he was putting on his jacket, her head tilted to one side, blonde hair falling away from her face, her bare, tanned legs and arms glowing against the dull silk of her dress. Simon had never seen a better-looking woman. I might be a slob, he thought, but at least I'm a lucky slob.

He smiled at her. 'You'll do,' he said. Arm in arm, they walked down to the hotel, talking quietly about tomorrow.

Madame Bonetto, watching them from the café window, called out to her husband. 'He's wearing a suit, the Englishman.' Bonetto grunted, and looked down with satisfaction at his faded blue shorts. '*Bieng*,' he said. 'I like to see a well turned-out man.'

A separate table for ten had been laid on the terrace, decorated with shallow bowls of Ernest's favourite pink-tinged white roses. Candlelight picked up the gleam of silver and glass and the long green necks of the champagne bottles that had been placed in ice-buckets between the flowers. The frogs who had taken up residence around the fountain creaked an intermittent chorus, and a scatter of stars hung in the warm sky above the Lubéron.

Nicole and Simon made their way down the steps towards the sound of laughter which drifted up from the poolhouse bar. Simon heard a loud, familiar voice rise above the conversation, and transferred his cigars to the inside pocket of his jacket. Uncle William was holding court.

'I see it now,' he was saying to a politely smiling Hampton Parker, 'the vast sweep of Texas, the towering canyons of New York, the rustic simplicity of our little corner of Provence – a triptych, something on the grand scale.' He paused to drain his glass, and held it out to the barman.

'The instant your dear son suggested it, I was intrigued, nay, fascinated. And now, having seen your head . . .'

'My head?' said Parker.

'Has nobody ever told you? Distinct resemblance to one of the Caesars. Augustus, if I'm not mistaken.'

Ernest, passing by, raised his eyebrows and rolled his eyes upwards. He was wearing his own version of traditional Provençal dress – white shirt, black trousers and waistcoat – with the added refinement of a wide pink and green striped cummerbund. He swept across to the bottom of the steps, a glass in each hand, and looked approvingly at Nicole.

'How nice it is,' he said, 'to see a proper frock. You look the picture of elegance, *madame*.'

Simon bent forward to look more closely at the cummerbund. 'I didn't know you were a member of the Garrick Club, Ern.'

'I'm not, dear, but I adore the colours. Now come along. Everyone's here.'

Parker's bodyguards, in suits and boots and with slightly bemused expressions, were listening to Uncle William's views on the Impressionists. Boone, scrubbed and cheerful, was gazing discreetly but with great interest down the front of the new dress that Françoise was at last able to demonstrate, a champagne flush beginning to colour her cheeks. Hampton Parker, in fluent, heavily accented French, was in deep conversation with Madame Pons, who had left the final arrangements to the sous-chef, and was wearing her smartest, most flowing tent of dark blue bombazine, and vertiginous high heels. Mrs Gibbons prospected for fallen peanuts and sleeping lizards, the red, white and blue ribbon that Ernest had threaded through her collar giving her the air of a disreputable regimental mascot.

Nicole tucked a hand under Simon's arm. 'Feeling better?'

He nodded. This was how he'd imagined it all those months ago: perfect weather, happy people, dinner under the stars, a dreamer's idea of running a hotel. He'd never anticipated that it took so much more than money – physical stamina, patience, tact, endless attention to detail, a passion for hospitality, all the qualities that Ernest had shown since the hotel opened.

307

'It's funny,' he said to Nicole. 'When I woke up this evening, I finally admitted something to myself. I'm one of life's guests. I'm a terrific guest. But I don't think I'll ever make much of a host.'

She squeezed his arm. 'I know. But you tried.'

There was the sound of a knife tapping against glass, and conversation stopped. Ernest looked round the group, and lifted his glass. 'Before we expire from pleasure at the dinner dear Madame Pons has prepared for us, I'd like to propose a toast to our guest of honour.'

Uncle William composed his expression into what he hoped was a suitably modest smile, and glanced down to make sure his fly was done up.

'Here's to young Boone. Welcome back, safe and sound. We missed you.'

Boone ducked his head and shuffled his feet as the toast was drunk, and raised his beer can in silent thanks. Hampton Parker offered Madame Pons his arm, and they led the way, bodyguards three paces behind, up the stairs to dinner.

It was, as they all told Madame Pons in French or English or Texan, a masterpiece. The *terrine* of fresh vegetables, worthy of Troisgros, with its technicolor mosaic of peas and carrots and artichokes and match-thin haricots bright against the pale *farce* of ham and egg white; the caviar of aubergines, wrapped in pink overcoats of smoked salmon and prickled with chives; a sorbet of rosemary to clear the palate for red wine and meat; the Sisteron lamb, rosy and aromatic with herbs and roast garlic, and Boone's weakness, potato tart, to mop up the juice; a dozen cheeses, from goat to cow to sheep and back to goat; chilled white peaches with raspberry sauce and basil; coffee, the *marc* from Châteauneuf that warms without burning, and the grey–blue smoke of cigars curling above the candlelight.

Even Uncle William was sufficiently tranquillized into silence by the pleasure of the moment, forgetting his artistic career as he puffed contentedly at the last of Simon's Havanas. The conversation, made lazy by full stomachs and good wine, was sporadic and quiet. The waiters came with more coffee, Boone and Françoise made their excuses and disappeared into the darkness, and Ernest and Madame Pons, her glass screwed firmly into her hand, went to close down the kitchen. Hampton Parker looked across the table at Uncle William, who had begun to snore, and smiled at Nicole and Simon.

'Think he'll be safe with my boys while we take a stroll?'

They left the bodyguards and the reclining artist, and walked through the garden to the poolhouse. Hampton Parker talked reflectively, with the confidence of a man who was used to being listened to. The shock of Boone's kidnapping had made him think about his own life – most of it spent on planes and in offices, doing deals, making more money than he knew what to do with. He was diversifying, he said, nothing too big – a tiny island in the Caribbean, an old and famous restaurant in Paris, a few miles of salmon fishing in Scotland – the kind of self-indulgent investments he could enjoy. If he ever had the time. He stopped to look over the valley towards the mountains.

'Boone's taken quite a shine to this place,' he said. 'We were talking this afternoon. Talked a lot. You know something? He doesn't want to come back to the States just yet. Says he'd like to work for Madame Pons and learn to be a real chef.'

'She likes him,' Simon said. 'That wouldn't be a problem.'

Parker gave a dry chuckle. 'I think that little girl has something to do with it. Where's she from?'

'Next door. She's the café owner's daughter.'

'Seems like a nice kid.' Parker sighed, and his tanned face looked serious. 'You'll have to forgive me. I'm getting too old to be patient. I have a little proposition for you.'

They came to the poolhouse, and sat in the deep rattan armchairs, looking out over the floodlit water. Parker was silent for a moment, and then smiled at Simon. 'You can always tell me to take a jump,' he said, 'but this is what I have in mind.' He lit a cigarette with a battered silver Zippo, and closed the cover with a snap. 'I need to find more time in my life, see more of the family, have a few more evenings like this.' He took a pull at his cigarette, and leaned forward. 'I've been spreading myself too thin. I guess most guys who build up a business from scratch are the same. We all think we're indispensable, and we all try to stay involved in everything. It's dumb, but it's human nature. You must have seen it a few times yourself.'

Simon thought of one or two of his old clients – brilliant, self-made men who couldn't resist interfering in details – and nodded. 'Dictators find it difficult to delegate,' he said.

'Right. That's where they screw up.' Parker grinned. 'Well, here's a dictator who's getting smart in his old age.' His voice became more businesslike. 'OK. One of my big problems is advertising. Like the guy said, half of the money I spend on advertising is probably wasted; trouble is, I don't know which half.'

'Lord Leverhulme,' said Simon.

Parker nodded. 'He hit it right on the button. Now, we're looking at a budget next year of close to half a billion dollars. That's a pretty big piece of change, and I just don't have the time to keep on top of it.'

'What about your marketing people?'

'Good, competent guys. But none of them has your background.' Parker ticked off the points on his fingers. 'One: you know the agency business inside out. Two: you've been damn successful at it. Three: you have enough personal money so you're not scared of being fired, and you can afford a truly independent opinion. And four ... well, I have a feeling we'd get along.' Parker smiled. 'Now you can tell me to take a jump.'

Simon looked across at Nicole, who was watching him with a half-smile on her face. He felt flattered and surprised and, he had to admit, intrigued. 'I don't know what to say, really. Just out of interest, where would I be based?'

'Wherever you tell the pilot to go. A plane comes with the job. And you'd report to me, nobody else.'

'How about hiring and firing? Agencies, I mean.'

'You call the shots.'

Simon looked out over the pool and scratched his head. It would almost be worth taking the job just to see Ziegler's face when he met his new client. Half a billion dollars, buddy, and you'd better behave yourself. That was certainly tempting, and so was the thought of what could be done with such an enormous budget. If he couldn't get some spectacular work out of the agencies with that . . .

A sudden sense of guilt made Simon look back at the lights of the hotel, where Ernest would be getting ready for another day. 'God, I don't know. I got Ernest to come out here. He loves it.'

'Good man, Ernest. I've been watching him work.' Parker studied the glowing tip of his cigarette. 'I've thought about him, too. Suppose I put together a deal, another little investment?'

'What do you mean?'

'Suppose I bought the hotel, and cut Ernest in? I'd take care of him. Be a fool not to.' Parker raised his eyebrows and grinned. 'How about that?'

'It's a very expensive way to hire someone.'

'I'm a very rich man, Simon.' Parker stood up, and looked at Nicole. 'You folks think it over. I hope we can work something out.'

They watched him walk away, and saw the bodyguards get up from the table and fall in step beside him, leaving Uncle William asleep in his chair with moths fluttering round his head.

Nicole left her chair and came to sit on Simon's lap. 'You're interested, aren't you? Something new and big like that?'

Simon stroked the smooth skin of her arm. 'How do you feel about it?'

She shook her head. 'Do you think I'd let you go off all by yourself with a suitcase full of dirty shirts?' She got up, and took his hand. 'Let's go and see Ernest.'

Half an hour later, the three of them were sitting in the kitchen, its floor still slick from being swabbed down, the steel and marble surfaces bare and gleaming, Madame Pons' notes for the menus of the next day pinned to a board by the door.

Simon had told Ernest about Parker's suggestion, and

had then found himself thinking out loud – admitting that the idea appealed to him, hedging his admission with protestations of concern about Ernest, about Nicole, about the hotel, about his own motives, finally ending up in a tangle that tailed off into silence.

'I think we should tidy up the last of the champagne,' Ernest said, getting up and going to the refrigerator. 'It's that sort of night.' He poured three glasses. 'It's a funny thing, but we always seem to be in kitchens when there's a decision to be made.' He looked at Nicole. 'This all started in a kitchen, you know, when I nagged him into taking a holiday.'

'*Santé*, Ern.' Simon raised his glass. 'You've been a good friend.'

'Let's hope there are a few more years to go, dear. Now, you'll have to forgive me for being honest – the kiss of death to many a friendship, I know, but there we are.' Ernest sipped his champagne, and frowned over his glass. 'The truth is, running a hotel is mostly maintenance work, and you're just not cut out for it. I know what a dreadful fidget you are. Once something's done, you want to move on, and if you can't, you get grumpy.' He looked at Simon beneath raised, accusing eyebrows. 'Don't think I haven't noticed.'

'That bad, is it?'

'Absolutely frightful. How poor Nicole puts up with you when you start sighing and tossing your curls, I don't know. And while we're on the subject of Nicole . . .' he turned to her and smiled '. . . you'll have to forgive my talking like this, but I've seen them come and go in my time, and he won't find another one like you.' Ernest stopped for another sip. 'And if he drives you away with his nonsense, he's a very silly man.' He sniffed. 'So if you ask me, dear, you should take Mr P's offer.'

'What about you?'

Ernest studied the bubbles racing up from the bottom of his glass. 'Well, this is everything I always wanted, I suppose. I'm just an old sergeant-major at heart. I love organizing people, and making things run properly. I'll carry on here.'

He poured some more champagne, and winked at Nicole. 'I can't tell you what a relief it will be not to have him under my feet all day long.'

Simon reached across the table and took Nicole's hand. 'I think he's kicking me out.'

She blinked and nodded and said nothing.

'And I very much hope,' said Ernest, 'that you'll take a few days off. You look like something the cat brought in.'

Simon rubbed his eyes. 'We've been talking about a holiday. No kidnappers, no detectives, somewhere nice and quiet like New York. Nicole's never been.'

Ernest nodded, smiled, and raised his glass. 'You'll be back, I dare say.'

'Yes, Ern. We'll be back.'

The plane swung out over the Mediterranean before picking up the flight path that would take them to Paris. Simon had made reservations at L'Ami Louis for dinner, and one of those rooms at the Raphael with a bath the size of a young swimming pool. They'd catch the morning flight to New York.

He felt in his pocket for the envelope that Ernest had given him when they said goodbye, and passed it to Nicole.

'He said you should open it.'

She took out a key with a brass tag. Hotel Pastis was engraved on one side, the figure 1 on the other, the top room with the best view of the Grand Lubéron. There was a card, and Ernest's handwriting.

Yours whenever you want it.

Love, The Management.